**Praise for Steven James
and *The Pawn***

"[A] riveting thriller. . . . A gripping plot and brisk pacing will win James some fans eager for his next offering."
—*Publishers Weekly*

"Tightly drawn and paced. . . . John Sandford might have to start looking over his shoulder." —*CrimeSpree Magazine*

"An exhilarating thriller that will keep readers up late into the night. *The Pawn* is, in a word, intense. As Bowers pushes toward checkmate, it's never clear to the reader which pieces will be left standing at the end of the game."
—*Mysterious Reviews*

"A captivating look at the fine line between good and evil. *The Pawn* is not to be missed."
—Ann Tatlock, author of *Every Secret Thing*

"Steven James combines twenty-first-century high-tech law enforcement techniques with eighteenth-century Sherlockian deduction to craft an exciting, suspense-filled story."
—Dr. Kim Rossmo, Center for Geospatial Intelligence and Investigation, Texas State University

THE
ROOK

STEVEN JAMES

AN ONYX BOOK

ONYX
Published by New American Library, a division of
Penguin Group (USA) Inc., 375 Hudson Street,
New York, New York 10014, USA
Penguin Group (Canada), 90 Eglinton Avenue East, Suite 700, Toronto,
Ontario M4P 2Y3, Canada (a division of Pearson Penguin Canada Inc.)
Penguin Books Ltd., 80 Strand, London WC2R 0RL, England
Penguin Ireland, 25 St. Stephen's Green, Dublin 2,
Ireland (a division of Penguin Books Ltd.)
Penguin Group (Australia), 250 Camberwell Road, Camberwell, Victoria 3124,
Australia (a division of Pearson Australia Group Pty. Ltd.)
Penguin Books India Pvt. Ltd., 11 Community Centre, Panchsheel Park,
New Delhi - 110 017, India
Penguin Group (NZ), 67 Apollo Drive, Rosedale, North Shore 0632,
New Zealand (a division of Pearson New Zealand Ltd.)
Penguin Books (South Africa) (Pty.) Ltd., 24 Sturdee Avenue,
Rosebank, Johannesburg 2196, South Africa

Penguin Books Ltd., Registered Offices:
80 Strand, London WC2R 0RL, England

Published by Onyx, an imprint of New American Library, a division of Penguin
Group (USA) Inc. Previously published in a Revell trade edition. For informa-
tion contact Revell, a division of Baker Publishing Group, PO Box 6287, Grand
Rapids, MI 49516-6287.

First Onyx Printing, December 2009
10 9 8 7 6 5 4 3 2 1

PUBLISHER'S NOTE
This is a work of fiction. Names, characters, places, and incidents either are the
product of the author's imagination or are used fictitiously, and any resemblance
to actual persons, living or dead, business establishments, events, or locales is
entirely coincidental.
    The publisher does not have any control over and does not assume any re-
sponsibility for author or third-party Web sites or their content.

For David and Kellie

The heart of the sons of men is full of evil, and madness is in their heart while they live, and after that they go to the dead.

—Ecclesiastes 9:3
King James Version

That motley drama—oh, be sure
   It shall not be forgot!
With its Phantom chased for evermore
   By a crowd that seize it not,
Through a circle that ever returneth in
   To the self-same spot,
And much of Madness, and more of Sin,
   And Horror the soul of the plot.

—"The Conqueror Worm"
Edgar Allan Poe

PROLOGUE

Thursday, November 5, 2008
Washington, DC
5:32 p.m.

The Chevy Tahoe sloshed to a stop in the soggy patch of unseasonably thick snow, and Creighton Melice stepped into the twilight.

He scanned the decrepit Washington, DC, neighborhood. Drug dealers on the corners. A few blank faces staring at him through the windows of dead buildings. Thick shadows spreading across the street. Creighton drew in a breath of the stale air. Ah yes. Being in the rotting core of the city as the day died around him made Creighton Melice feel right at home.

His lawyer, Jacob Weldon, whispered nervously out the window of the SUV. "So, do you want me to wait for you, then?"

Creighton glanced at him. Weldon. A timid little man with overripe eyes.

"No. I'll be all right."

"Be careful." Weldon sounded relieved.

"I always am."

Less than three hours ago Creighton had been in custody. Dank cell. Second-degree murder charges—and most likely a long prison sentence. But then, just as Creighton was rehearsing his story, Weldon showed up and announced he'd made bail. "You're a free man," he said.

"Don't screw with me."

"I'm serious."

"Who? Who paid it?"

Weldon shook his head. "I don't know. Someone. A friend."

Creighton scowled. "How could you not know? Didn't he have to sign for it?"

"Sent someone. A big guy. I've seen him before, sitting in on the preliminaries. But he was just a delivery boy. Someone else footed the bill."

"A friend, huh? Well, none of my friends has that kind of money."

"Maybe you made a new one. C'mon, let's get you out of this place. Whoever it was wants to see you."

So they left the jail, drove around long enough to make sure no cops were trying to keep an eye on him, and then ended up here at 1311 Donovan Street in front of this vacant gray building wearing a tilted sign that read "The Blue Lizard Lounge."

The place Creighton's new friend had chosen for the meeting.

After Weldon's Tahoe had disappeared around the corner, Creighton scoured the ground for a weapon, snagged a broken beer bottle, and leaned his hand against the dilapidated dance club's metal door. It clung to its latch for a moment and then creaked open.

A hallway stretched before him, lit only by a meager network of lightbulbs dangling at odd angles every six feet or so.

He didn't like any of this. The meeting. The confined space. Some guy he didn't even know paying his bail. Creighton tightened his grip on the neck of the bottle. He'd only used a broken bottle as a weapon once. That night had ended well for him, not so well for the guy who'd been hitting on the woman who was about to become his girlfriend. He figured he could do at least as much damage tonight if he needed to.

As Creighton approached the end of the hallway, he could see two doors, one on each side. A single word had been scrawled on each door. And, while it was hard to tell for sure in the dim light, the words looked like they might have been painted with blood. He reached out his hand. Felt the word *Pain*.

Still damp.

Tasted it.

Yes. Blood.

The word *Freedom* had been painted on the door across the hall.

Creighton glanced behind him. Only an empty hallway. Then he inspected the doors, checked for light seeping beneath them. Nothing. Looked around the hallway one more time.

Nothing. Just an empty hallway that terminated here. At these two doors.

Freedom or pain.

Creighton pressed his ear up to each door in turn. Listened. Not a sound.

He needed to make a choice.

The decision was easy.

Creighton chose pain.

With a soft click, the door mouthed open into a narrow entryway. Maybe fifteen feet ahead of him, a tightly focused light sliced through the center of an adjoining room, probably the abandoned club's dance floor. A spotlight?

Why a spotlight?

Creighton smelled cigarette smoke. Someone was waiting for him.

His new friend.

Creighton crossed the entryway, and as he stepped into the harsh light, a voice halted him. "That's far enough." The voice was electronically altered, but to Creighton, the speaker sounded male.

Creighton paused.

At the other end of the room, about twenty-five feet away, sat a figure with an industrial-strength halogen work lamp glowing behind his chair. Even though the person was starkly backlit, Creighton could clearly see that whoever it was had a gun.

"You chose the correct door, Creighton."

"Yeah, well, we'll see." He shielded his eyes, then gestured toward the gun. "So, did you set me free just so you could shoot me?"

Electronic laughter ricocheted around the room. The person motioned his gun toward the bottle Creighton was holding. "And did you come here just so you could slice me?"

"Maybe."

A pause. "I want to offer you something."

"I don't work for anyone, and you can't buy me off. So, if you're gonna shoot me, make it a good shot because if you just wound me, I'm coming for you." Creighton raised the cruelly tipped weapon. "I'm pretty quick, and if I make it across the room, I'm going to bury this in your belly. How's that for an offer?"

"Now, now. Don't I even get a thank-you? Your bail was no small sum, and we both know you won't show up for the trial. That's quite a little chunk of change I paid just to have you come here and threaten me."

Creighton tried to catch the tenor of the person's real voice, but whoever it was, he must have had a microphone up to his mouth that changed the pitch and tone of every word as he spoke.

"Well," said Creighton. "I never asked for your help."

A coarse voice coming through the mic. "Mr. Melice, I've been—how shall I say?—following your career."

"So, you're a fan. Well, that's just great."

"In a manner of speaking, yes. I am a fan. You have a great gift."

"Oh, is that what you call it." It wasn't really a question. Silence stained the room. Creighton waited for the guy to reply, and when he didn't, Creighton turned his head and tapped the broken bottle against the back of his neck. "The base of the neck, right there, or maybe the back of the head, would be your best choice. Although from that range you'd better know what you're doing. I'm turning to go now. Take your best shot." Creighton expected to hear the click as the guy snapped off the safety; it would tell him a lot if he did. None of the guys he'd worked with ever used a safety.

Creighton took two steps. Then heard the voice again.

"I know why you chose this door."

Creighton paused.

"I can get you what you want."

Creighton turned. "No one can get me what I want."

"My friend, you wouldn't be here unless I could. I never would have bothered with you. You're the one who posted the videos. I read your blog. I know what you want."

Creighton wanted to ask how he'd been able to link the

videos and blog to him, but obviously it had happened, and at this point that was all that mattered. "I'm listening."

"There's something I would like you to help me procure. Your background, skill set, and ... unique tastes ... make you eminently qualified for this job. When I have it in hand, I'll give you the one thing no one else on the planet can give you."

"What do you want me to 'procure'?"

A dismissive wave of the gun barrel. "More in due time, my friend. For now, I'd simply like to know if you're interested enough to continue this discussion. If not, you're free to go. I'll just consider the bail money an investment that didn't pay off."

"Free to go, huh? The next time I turn my back, you'll put a bullet in my brain."

"No," said the voice. "I choose the base of the neck instead."

A sudden chill. Miscalculation. "What?"

An instant later, Creighton heard the simultaneous crack of the gun and the bright explosion of glass beside him. He didn't feel the bullet's impact but quickly scanned his body for an entry wound, for a growing stain of blood. Found none.

It was only the bottle. The guy had shot the bottle out of Creighton's hand.

Right at the base of the neck.

"That," Creighton said, holding up what little remained of the bottle, "was an impressive shot."

"If I wanted you dead," the voice said, "you'd be dead. I want your help."

As Creighton threw the remains of the bottle to the ground, he noticed a spray of glass shards embedded in his thigh. Blood began to creep from a dozen wounds. He reached down and started wrenching the pieces of glass from his leg, thinking about how badly it should have hurt. "How do I know I can trust you?"

"You don't. And I can't trust you either. But that's the nature of these relationships, isn't it?"

Lately, Creighton had been working alone, but it hadn't always been that way. "Yeah," he said. "It is."

"So, are you in?"

Creighton didn't answer, just finished removing the glass from his leg and dropping it to the floor. But he didn't turn to go either.

"All right. Good. Then I have a surprise for you."

"And that is?"

"Your girlfriend. She's waiting for you out back, in the car."

Creighton straightened up. "My girlfriend?"

"Mmm-hmm."

He glanced around the room. "Where?"

The man waved the gun toward the far wall. "Door's over there. Keys are in the car. So is your plane ticket, driver's license, FBI identification badge, and a little spending money, Mr. Neville Lewis."

Creighton let out a harsh sigh. "Neville Lewis? That the best you could do?"

A crackle of electronic laughter. "Go on. We'll talk soon. I know you must be anxious to see her."

"Wait. You know my name. What am I supposed to call you?"

"You can call me Shade."

The light blinked off, and Creighton found that he couldn't see a thing except for the flashing residue of color swirling through his vision. The passageway he'd come from spit out a tiny pool of light, but other than that the room was pitch-black.

He heard a faint brush of movement beside the chair and realized that if he couldn't see the shooter, the shooter couldn't see him.

So.

One chance.

Take care of this guy now. Then you won't have to worry about trusting him, or working for him, or paying him back for any favors.

Creighton crouched low and skittered along the wall. Rushed toward the chair.

Groping through the dark, he knocked over the work lamp, and it clattered to the ground, the hot bulbs exploding on impact. Creighton's hands found the chair and he lifted it, swung it, hoping to find the person who'd shot the bottle from his hand, but he found only empty air instead.

He swung again. Shuffled around.

Nothing.

He prodded at the emptiness with the chair for a couple more minutes but found no sign of the man who'd invited him there. Finally, he decided the guy must have slipped away somehow, perhaps out another door.

Rather than waste any more time stumbling around in the dark trying to attack a phantom, he threw the chair to the ground and started for the far wall. The guy had promised that his girlfriend was waiting for him. He wasn't sure what to think about that, but he definitely wanted to find out.

Creighton found the door, eased it open. Stepped into the alley behind the club. A sedan with tinted windows sat beside a reeking Dumpster. Night had fallen, but a jaundiced street lamp at the end of the alley managed to give Creighton just enough light to see.

He made sure no one else was in the alley, then approached the car and tried to peer through the windows. Too dark.

He didn't trust the guy with the gun, and he wasn't sure what to expect when he opened the car door.

A car bomb?

But why? Why waste the bail money? Besides, the guy could have killed him inside the building.

Sounds, soft sounds from inside the car. He reached for the door handle. Clicked it open. "Hello?" he said.

No one in the front seat. He slipped into the car. "Hello?" Turned around.

And found her, lying in the backseat.

A woman he had never met.

Bound and tightly gagged.

He pulled the door shut. Her pleading eyes grew large with terror when she saw him, saw that he made no attempt to free her. They had never met, but he'd seen her face. He knew who she was. She squirmed. Couldn't get free. "So," he said, eyeing her, smiling at her, fondling her soft blond hair. "Maybe I can trust him after all."

Creighton swiveled around and started the engine. "C'mon, my dear. It's time we got to know each other. I'm going to be your new boyfriend."

As he pulled out of the alley, Creighton could hear desperate, muffled cries coming from the backseat. He didn't need to turn around to know what they were. He knew those sounds well. He'd heard them before.

She was trying to scream beneath her gag.

Yes, he knew those sounds well.

It looked like Weldon had been right after all.

Creighton Melice had made a new friend.

1

Three months later
Monday, February 16, 2009
San Diego, California
5:46 p.m.

I stared at the array of silverware surrounding my plate. "I can never remember which fork to use for the salad."

My stepdaughter, Tessa, pointed. "The outside one, Patrick. You start there and work your way in."

"You sure?"

She picked up my forks one at a time, a family of leather bracelets riding up and down her wrist, over the four rubber bands she wore beneath them. "Salad, main dish, then dessert."

As she set down my dessert fork, I realized how much we both stuck out at this restaurant. Everyone else wore a dinner jacket or an evening gown; we both had on T-shirts—mine, a faded athletic shirt from Marquette University, hers, a black, long-sleeve DeathNail 13 tee with the band's logo of an eyeball with a nail stuck through it. Beside the picture she wore a small pin: "Save Darfur. Now."

Tessa had chosen light pink lipstick tonight, but black fingernail polish and black eye shadow to match her raven black hair. I hadn't been too thrilled about the eyebrow ring and pierced nose she'd gotten last month without my permission, but I had to admit they were cute. And with her three-quarter-length black tights under a crinkly fabric skirt, she looked slightly Goth, a little edgy and dark, yet still girlish and innocent at seventeen.

"So, how do you know so much about table settings?" I asked.

"I worked at La Saritas, remember? Before Mom died."

Her comment blindsided me, took me back to Christie's funeral. I glanced out the window. The wind had been kicking up all afternoon, and now, just after dusk, the ocean looked ragged and gray. The remaining sunlight drained slowly into the sea as a few gulls meandered beneath the clouds, occasionally diving to retrieve a fish that had wandered too close to the water's rough, leathery surface. "Yeah, sorry," I said. "I guess I forgot. How long did you work there again?"

"Two days. The manager said I didn't have a 'team-oriented attitude.'" She took a sip of her ice water. "Jerk."

I'd chosen a table in the back of the restaurant, my back to the wall. Force of habit. For a moment I watched the servers maneuver through the maze of tables, observing the routes they took, the choices they made. Habit again.

A few minutes earlier, the girl who'd seated us had placed a platter of crusty bread in front of me. She'd set a bowl of some kind of oil next to it, and the people at the tables all around us were dipping their bread into the sour-yellow lubricant and then eating it. I decided to pass.

Our server, a slim-boned man with a beak for a nose, arrived to take our order. "Sir," he said. Then he faced Tessa. "Mademoiselle. Would you like to hear the specials? Tonight we are offering a lovely pork tenderloin finished off with a mango-and-pineapple reduction—"

Tessa gave him an iron stare. "Do you have any idea what kind of conditions those pigs are forced to live in before being shipped to the slaughterhouses? Wire cages. Tiny wire cages—"

"Tessa," I said.

"Where they're force-fed, drugged with growth hormones until they're too fat to stand—"

"Tessa Bernice Ellis."

"I'm just saying—"

I gave her my best be-quiet-right-now-or-we're-going-to-Burger-King look. Our eyes wrestled for a moment, and at last she gave in. "OK, OK. I want a house salad." She pointed to the menu. "And no apple-wood-smoked bacon."

"Yes, ma'am." He turned to me, tilted his head, offered a fabricated smile. He might have been a robot. "And you, sir?"

I noticed Tessa glaring at me. "I guess I'll have a salad too," I said. "But I'm hungry though. Make it a double."

"A double, sir? I'm afraid our dinner salad only comes in one size, but I assure you it's a most generous portion."

I'd seen some of those "generous portions" when Tessa and I had walked to our booth. "Well, I'll take two of those, then. Just dump them into one great big bowl. That'll work."

He scribbled something on his notepad, although I didn't think our order had been all that complex. Tessa cleared her throat. "Patrick, seriously, you can order the pork tenderloin if you want, and I promise I won't say anything about how the pigs are crammed into feces-ridden crates where they can't even turn around, taken to a slaughterhouse where they're hit with a stun gun that leaves them alive and squealing and bleeding to death while they're dropped alive into the scalding water that's supposed to remove their hair and soften up the meat so that restaurants like this can glaze them with mangoes and serve them to their patrons. I promise not to say a word."

The woman at the table beside us slowly lowered her main-dish fork to the table.

"How thoughtful of you, Tessa," I said. *Slaughterhouses. Great. Just the thing I need to be thinking about right now.*

I noticed that our server's face had turned pasty white. "Just bring me those two salads in one big bowl and a cup of coffee—wait. What kind of coffee do you have?"

He tried to compose himself. "We serve a variety of fine espressos and cappuccinos as well as both regular and decaffeinated—"

"No, no, no. I mean like a Ruiru 11 blend from Kenya, or Costa Rican La Magnolia, or something from the Cerrado region of Brazil. What kind of coffee? What country is it from?"

"I believe we buy it here in America—"

Oh boy. "When you get the coffee from the store, does it come in a great big metal can?"

He beamed. "Absolutely."

That was all I needed to hear. "Tea. A cup of tea."

"Thank you, sir."

I glanced at the bowl of oil. "And some butter too."

"Tea . . ." He mouthed the words as he wrote them on his pad. "And butter." Then he turned hesitantly toward Tessa. "And your drink, ma'am?"

"Root beer. And don't put any cheese in my salad, anything like that."

He gave her a small nod.

"Or ranch dressing. Ranch is disgusting."

"Yes, ma'am."

"Or eggs."

One more brisk nod, and then he disappeared.

"Well," I said. "Nothing like visiting a fancy restaurant. We should do this more often."

"Yup." She dipped a piece of bread into the oil and held it up to the light. Globs of vomit-colored oil plopped onto her plate. "Nothing like it."

I tried to relax and just enjoy the next few minutes. Tried to engage in a coherent conversation, tried to listen to her talk about a club she'd heard about that she wanted to visit but that I would never let her go to anyway, tried to think of clever things to say about the birdlike waiter.

Tried to, but couldn't. The image of a slaughterhouse had landed in my mind and refused to leave.

I could hear squealing coming from the inside. Sharp desperate cries. But neither this slaughterhouse nor the squealing had anything to do with pigs.

2

The last three months had been good ones for Creighton Melice, now known as Neville Lewis. He liked San Diego weather, and he especially liked living in a city with hundreds of thousands of undocumented, untraceable, easily misplaced people.

And so many of them women.

Lovely Hispanic women.

Potential girlfriends.

Creighton glanced around the warehouse office, and his eyes took in the dusty file cabinet in the corner piled high with a stack of manila folders, the swimsuit calendar that was still flipped to May 2007 pinned to the wall, and, of course, the large gray desk with his high-definition computer screen on top of it. Beside the keyboard was a stack of DVD cases.

He stepped onto a swivel chair and repositioned the right-hand camcorder, centering it in the hole in the wall so he could get a clearer view of his next girlfriend when it happened. Over the years he'd found that the videos were much more satisfying when he got the camera angles just right.

And, of course, a lot depended on the quality of your equipment. And whoever the guy was who'd shot the bottle from his hand that day in DC knew his stuff: the two professional-grade camcorders were the kind a news crew might use for a remote.

The warehouse had already been prepared for Creighton when he arrived in November. Everything was all set. Just waiting for him.

As he sat down at the desk, a large spider, ripe with babies, lowered itself onto his arm, but Creighton didn't mind, didn't brush it away. He'd always had an affinity for spiders.

He tapped at the keyboard to test the remote zoom capabilities. The spider skittered up his arm and across the back of his neck. A few more keystrokes.

Yes.

Excellent.

Now, for the second camera.

The server arrived with our order. He laid a large metal bowl beside me containing my two meagerly generous servings of salad. Then he placed Tessa's salad in front of her and quickly stepped back. "Anything else?"

"No," I said. "We're good. Thanks."

Tessa inspected her salad, probably looking for stray pieces of meat that might have fallen into it. "It looks OK."

As our server hurried off and we began to eat, I glanced at the routes of the two dozen servers again. Made note of which tables each person was serving, who yielded to whom as they approached the kitchen. Then, in between mouthfuls of lettuce, spinach, green peppers, and black olives, Tessa and I talked about how her junior year of high school was going, the colleges she was considering, the things we were both hoping to do in San Diego, and some bands I'd never heard of who were apparently amazingly sick—meaning good. But all the while, in the back of my mind, I was still thinking about the slaughterhouse.

Then, with a big bite of salad in her mouth, Tessa asked, "So, it feels good, doesn't it?"

A shiver squirmed through my gut.

I paused with my salad fork halfway to my mouth. "What did you just say?"

My tone must have been as harsh as the images climbing through my mind, because she blinked, and when she replied, she seemed almost intimidated. "I just mean, being in the middle of a case like this. Trying to catch this arsonist guy. It feels good. It's what you do. It's what you like, isn't it?"

"Yes, it is. It's what I do. It's what I like." My words were blunt. Unnecessary hammer blows. I didn't want to go where this conversation or my thoughts were taking me, so

I changed the subject. "But being here with you, I like this more." I set down my fork.

She gave me a tired you-can't-possibly-be-for-real teenager look, but I caught the hint of a smile. "Yeah. Whatever."

"I mean it."

"Thanks." She looked down at the table. Slightly embarrassed. It was nice to see.

Over the past couple years we'd both been through a lot. Tessa had been fifteen when her mother and I met, dated, and then married—sixteen when Christie died tragically of breast cancer.

Christie's parents had passed away years before, and Tessa didn't know who her real father was, so that left the two of us to try and work through Christie's death and form a family together. It hadn't gone too well. Nearly a year had passed since Christie's death, and it felt like Tessa and I were still at the starting line. But at least we were there together. And that was something.

I picked up my outside fork and aimed it at a miniature tomato in my salad. "So, four days in San Diego, huh?"

"Yeah. This is one time I'm actually glad Denver has year-round schools. All their screwy breaks."

"I thought maybe while we're here I could take you to the Sherrod Aquarium."

"An aquarium." She spoke with her mouth full. "Wow. How fun is that."

"It's supposed to be one of the best in the world."

She sighed with her eyeballs.

"They have sharks," I said. "Lots and lots of sharks."

She seemed to consider that for a moment. "Sharks are cool."

"Now," I said, "you know that I have—"

"A little work to do while we're here. I know, I know. The arsonist."

"Sometimes you may need to stay at the hotel by yourself—"

A slight pause. "I didn't come here to sit at some stupid hotel. I'm OK on my own, you know."

"It's just that we're not in Denver, this is a different city."

"In a few months I'll be old enough to live on my own."

"Eight months."

"Like I said."

I took a gulp of tea. "Anyway, I'll spend as much time with you as I can."

"We've been over all this already. It's no big deal." And then, "You don't have to babysit me."

Big issue. Deal with that later. "OK."

Tessa always begs to come along when I travel but likes her space too. Since I'm an FBI criminologist who tracks serial offenders, I can't usually bring her with me.

This time, though, Special Agent Lien-hua Jiang, one of my team members at the FBI's National Center for the Analysis of Violent Crime, as well as one of the Bureau's top profilers, had called me in. We were consulting with the San Diego Police Department on a series of fires that had been started in abandoned homes over the last ten months. No fatalities so far, just property damage.

The Bureau wants to encourage strong family relationships, and since this wasn't a case that would put Tessa in danger, and I wasn't the lead investigator, and I was willing to foot the bill for her trip, they had no problems with her coming along. So, all things taken into account, this seemed like a good chance for us to spend some time together, especially since she was on break from school.

"So," I said, changing the subject, "this is your first time visiting the Pacific Ocean, right?"

"I've seen the ocean before, Patrick. You know that. When we lived in New York."

"But that's the Atlantic."

"There's only one ocean."

I wondered if this was a joke and I was missing the punch line. "Last I checked there was the Atlantic, Pacific, Arctic, Indian—"

"Well, last *I* checked all the oceans were connected. One big body of water. One world, one ocean."

I peered out the window. Watched the black water lick at the shore in the rising moonlight. "I guess I never thought of it like that before."

"They do the same thing with land. Seven continents? Yeah, right. Only if you divide up Europe and Asia and split up North and South America and count the man-made Suez Canal."

I'd never thought of that either. "So why do you think we do that, divide things up like that?"

She shrugged. Took a bite of salad. "How should I know, I'm just a kid. Different cultures, maybe. Territorialism. Ethnocentrism. I don't know. It just seems dumb, though."

Ethnocentrism. That's just great.

Creighton pressed "record," swiveled the camera, took twenty seconds of footage.

Since visiting the Blue Lizard Lounge in November, he'd tried to uncover Shade's real identity, but so far none of his contacts had been able to dig up anything specific, and since Creighton had skipped town, his former lawyer Jacob Weldon wouldn't even return his calls. So Creighton hadn't discovered anything about his mysterious new friend, and, although he would never have admitted it to anyone, that troubled him somewhat.

All of their communications had been through voice-altered phone calls, text messages, and dead-letter message drops. All very cloak-and-dagger, which made Creighton think that he—or she or whoever—was probably a spy wannabe.

But maybe not a wannabe.

Maybe the real thing.

Anything was possible.

Creighton pressed "pause," then rewound the video. Played it through to the end. Adjusted the focus, then pressed "record" once again.

For the first few weeks, it had remained a complete mystery to him why Shade had chosen him for this specific job. But when Shade finally explained the grand scheme to him and then started naming names, he'd seen the beauty and irony of it all. Yes, he was the perfect person to do it.

Really, the only person.

He pressed "pause."

There.

That was it.

Yes, just a slight glint off the glass, but he could take care of that, just like he'd done in the previous videos.

The camera was set.

He put the ropes in the trunk of his car.

It was time to go find a woman interested in spending the evening with a handsome, slightly devilish male companion.

3

Victor Sherrod Drake, president and CEO of Drake Enterprises, sat at his desk on the top floor of Drake Enterprises' world headquarters on Aero Drive in San Diego. Most people didn't know that the biotech industry is the second largest economic force in San Diego, trailing just behind the military. But Victor knew. He'd helped make it a reality.

Most of his employees had gone home at five thirty p.m., but Victor preferred to stay a little later, especially at this time of year when the 2008 financial reports were rolling in. Of course, it meant keeping a skeleton work crew on-site after hours to make sure his time wasn't wasted, but that wasn't a problem. He could afford it.

Victor set his cell phone beside the papers on his desk so it would be available if his accountant called; then he perused the latest profit-margin reports and tapped his fingers to the rhythm of a tune he'd heard while driving to work earlier in the day.

Yes. Things were going well. Very, very well.

He glanced out the window at San Diego, the desert by the sea that humans had staked out as paradise. Victor liked looking down on this city. All the antlike inhabitants. Drones busily going about their petty suburban lives—

"Mr. Drake, sir." A sultry female voice interrupted his thoughts. He'd hired the woman behind the voice just for the way she sounded. He pressed the intercom. "Yes?"

"I have General Biscayne on the line."

Victor's fingers stopped tapping.

Biscayne.

Again.

Who cares if you work at the Pentagon? You do not go calling one of the world's richest men whenever you want to. No, you do not.

On the other hand ... the billions of dollars that the Pentagon's research and development arm, the Defense Advanced Research Projects Agency, or DARPA, was spending on this project could buy the general a few extra minutes of micromanaging.

"I'll take it on my private line," he told the voice he loved.

Victor swung the office door shut, snatched up his land-line phone, and tried to hide the irritation in his voice. "General. Good of you to call."

"I wondered if you might have gone home for the day."

"I like to work late." Victor calculated the time in the Eastern Time Zone. "You must like to as well."

"Hate it. Just got out of a marathon DARPA meeting, and we are, how shall I say, anxious to see the progress on Project Rukh."

"Well, I have good news, General: we've nearly completed the prototype. It'll be ready in only a couple of—"

"Actually, we want to see it now. ASAP. Give it a test run. See how well it performs."

Just the idea that they questioned whether it would work was insulting to Victor. Just the idea! You don't build the country's most profitable biotech firm by delivering faulty products—which was why Victor had arranged for his own internal tests. "When we deliver it to you, General, I guarantee it'll work."

"Well, if it does, I guarantee you that Drake Enterprises will be well-positioned when the bidding comes for DAR-PA's next project. But, if the device is not ready, we're pull-ing the plug on this thing. You've had two years to make it work, and so far we have nothing but a 2.5 billion dol-lar microwave—not exactly what you were contracted to build."

Victor could feel his grip tightening around the phone. He knew that if he lost the contract and word somehow leaked to the press—which the government would make certain happened—stocks would plummet and he would lose billions.

Not only that, but in the obligatory investigation that his board of directors would call for, it was possible, just possible, that some inconsistencies might be found in the third-quarter earnings statements from 2007. And after Enron and WorldCom, that might not fare so well for Drake Enterprises and its CEO.

Even worse, someone might uncover evidence of the tests.

"Drake," snapped the general, jarring him back to the conversation. "I'll be arriving on Thursday. I've scheduled a Project Rukh Oversight Committee meeting for 1400 hours sharp. I want you there."

"General, that won't be necessary. I can assure you that—"

"I want to see firsthand what our taxpayer money has gone toward producing. And I'm telling you now, the device had better work."

"But not in two and a half days. That's not possible. We have thousands of pages of research to evaluate before final delivery. It's not enough time—"

"You've had two years. That's plenty of time."

Victor had to try his hardest not to let on that he was speaking through gritted teeth. "Well, then. I look forward to your visit—" And before he could finish his sentence, the general hung up.

Drake slammed down the receiver. *No one hangs up on Victor Drake. No one!*

He yanked out a desk drawer, twisted open a bottle of pills, swallowed five of them, and then pocketed the bottle for later. Smacked the drawer shut.

So.

All right then.

They wanted to make sure it worked. Well, OK.

One more test.

One final test.

Tonight.

That would at least give Dr. Kurvetek Tuesday and Wednesday, two full days, to evaluate the results before the general arrived.

Victor called the team members and told them that he needed their services one last time and that they had better bring in some definitive results. He only used four men because he'd learned over the years that it's difficult to keep things confidential, so the fewer people who know your secrets, the better. He asked the fourth man, "Do you have the site picked out?"

"Have I ever let you down?"

"All right. You know the drill. Just don't get there early."

A pause. "The money better be transferred within twenty-four hours this time. I don't like to wait."

"It will be. Don't worry about that."

Victor ended the call and elevatored down to the parking garage, all the while trying not to think about the general's veiled threats concerning future contracts.

Just forget him. Forget Biscayne. Go home and relax. By morning, the test will be completed and you'll be able to give him exactly what he asked for.

Victor fired up his Jaguar, roared out of the garage, and aimed his car toward his estate on La Jolla Farms Road.

While his four team members prepared for the test.

4

As Tessa and I ate, I tried to steer the conversation away from my work, but when we were nearly done with our salads, Tessa steered us back. "So, Patrick. Is it true you have the highest clearance record for cases involving serial offenders in the history of the FBI?"

"Wow. That was random."

"You're not allowed to say that. You're over thirty."

I took a slim breath. "Tessa, where did you hear that statistic?"

"Fox News. A couple of weeks ago. After that whole thing with Ramirez."

Julio Ramirez had abducted young boys from playgrounds in Maine. He would take them to his home, do the things to them that parents have nightmares about, then lock them in a pit in his basement until they starved to death. Eight in all. My friend, Special Agent Ralph Hawkins, and I had caught him just after the first of the year.

"Well, I'm not sure if that stat is exactly accurate."

She punched her fork into her salad and stuffed an olive into her mouth. "They said it was."

"You can't always trust what you hear. Look, I don't really want to talk about all this right now. Let's plan our schedule for the next couple—"

"They only call you in when everyone else is, like, totally stumped—which is pretty cool, by the way, I have to say."

"Thank you. Now, let's talk about—"

"But don't get a big head or anything," she said. "Because, I don't really get it."

"You don't get what?"

"What you do."

I didn't like where this was going. "I thought you read the two books I wrote?"

"Well, I did. Sort of."

"Sort of?"

She dropped her gaze. Let it wander around the table. "I did read 'em, I mean . . . until I fell asleep."

A needle through my ego. Punctured. Drifting to the ground. "You fell asleep reading my books?"

"Look, I didn't mean to, OK? It's just . . . I couldn't help it." She stuffed some lettuce into her mouth. "No offense or anything, but don't quit your day job."

How nice.

"Anyway." Talking with her mouth full again. "What I mean is, maybe you can explain it better in person than on paper."

Boy, she really knew how to lay on the compliments.

I decided to go for it, though. I might not get another chance.

But make it quick. Then get back to planning the week.

"OK. Let's see, where to start . . . ? So, crimes only occur when five factors intersect."

"Time, location, offender, victim or object of desire, and lack of supervision or law enforcement presence. That was in the introduction to *Understanding Crime and Space*. I hadn't fallen asleep yet."

"Well, that's encouraging." I grabbed a salt shaker and slid it in front of me. It would be too complex to talk through all fourteen fires, but I could at least give her an idea of what I do by referencing four or five of them. "So then, with these arsons, let's say this is the site of the first fire . . ." I tapped the salt shaker, then moved the pepper to the far side of the table. "The next arson was down here, south of San Diego in Chula Vista . . ." I put the rental car keys behind my salad bowl. "And the third fire was here, in Clairemont . . ." I moved the coffee creamer and the teacup into position. "And these are fires four and five—what does that tell you?"

"Nothing. They're just spread out all over."

"Actually, it tells us several things." I crumpled up a napkin and set it in the middle of the table.

"Is that the next fire?"

"No, it's where I believe the arsonist might live. Think about this for a minute: if you started those fires, do you think you'd be familiar with the area?"

"I guess. So I'd know how to get away."

"Right. But if you committed the crimes too close to your home, you might draw too much attention to yourself." I dipped my finger in the bread oil and drew two concentric circles around the napkin, the outer one enclosing the salt and pepper fires. As I did so, our server approached, took one look at me finger-painting on the table, spun on his heels, and returned to the kitchen.

"So," I continued, "you end up with a range, the ideal range, a comfort zone, in between these circles. Far, but not too far. Close, but not too close."

She put my knife in the range, but on the other side of the table from the pepper. "Like the next fire might be here?"

"Right. Maybe. But I study what's been done, not what might happen."

"Does it change? This comfort zone thing? As you get more and more fires?"

"Yes. Because the arsonist isn't going to keep setting fires in an area where there would be heightened law enforcement activity. So I ask myself, 'What's the significance of these locations to our offender?' I look at the location, timing, and progression of the fires, compare that to the comfort zone, and then work backward to try and find the most likely location for the offender's home base—which might be where he lives or maybe where he works. We call it the hot zone."

"Sounds simple."

"In principle, yes. But you need to take into account *all* of the locations associated with the fires, as well as pathways to and from the scenes. There are a lot of mathematical formulas involved, algorithms based on travel theory, cognitive mapping, stuff like that."

"They call it a geographic profile, right?"

"Yes." I took a small bite of salad. "But it's not like a behavioral profile. Nothing like that."

"Yeah, you told me that before."

"Anyway, all the locations, right? So, where he bought the accelerants, where the fires occurred, which fire alarms were set off first, the location of the person calling nine-one-one, sight lines." As I said the words *sight lines*, I glanced at the table and noticed something. "Hang on." I moved my large salad bowl just to the left of the comfort zone. "Can you see the salad fork from there?"

She shook her head.

"What about the keys?"

She shook her head again. "The bowl is in the way."

Hmm. Yes.

"The bowl is in the way," I repeated softly.

"What's the bowl?" she asked.

I inspected the table, moved a few condiments around. "I think it might be Petco Park. Where the Padres play."

"Bark Park."

"Right." I looked at the relationship of the salad bowl to the teacup and coffee creamer.

Yes, yes. You'll need to look into that.

"What is it?" she asked.

Wait, Pat. Be here right now. Not somewhere else.

"Nothing." I shook the thought loose. I could come back to it later, after she was in bed. "Anyway, when I compare all those factors to the traffic patterns at the time of the crime, the layout of the roads, bridges, bodies of water, demographics, population distribution, I can begin to . . . well, you get the idea. Most investigators ask, 'Why did this happen?' or 'What was the offender thinking?' or 'How could anyone do such a thing?' But I ask, 'When was the offender here?' 'Where did he go?' and 'Where is he now?' That's environmental criminology in a nutshell."

She studied the table. Looked at the salt and pepper shakers, the keys, the salad bowl, the circle of oil, the coffee creamer. "And you got a doctorate in this?"

"Well, yes, I—"

"How many years of school was that again?"

"OK. So, the aquarium. Sharks. I heard the Sherrod Aquarium has more than a dozen different species—"

"So, you don't look for motive?"

If only more investigators were as persistent as she was. I tapped my finger against the table. "Not so much. No."

"Why not?"

"Trying to guess someone's motives always ends up

being nothing more than speculation, Tessa. It's based on inference rather than deduction, on intuition rather than evidence, and there's no way to confirm or to refute your guesswork. I'm an investigator, not a mind reader."

"What does Agent Jiang think of that? It's a sore spot, isn't it? Between the two of you?"

This conversation was going farther and farther astray. "We hold each other in high regard."

"So I've noticed," she said under her breath.

"What's that supposed to mean?"

"Nothing." She took one final gulp of her root beer. "So, can you tell where the next fire is gonna be?"

I shook my head. "No. Like I mentioned before, I work backward to try and find the home base of the offender. I don't do so well with predicting the future."

"But try. I mean, if you were going to."

"I can't predict the future, Tessa."

"OK." She flew her eyes to the other side of the room. "Whatever."

"You can pout all you like, it's not going to help me predict the future."

"Fine. Whatever. I'm not pouting."

Still no eye contact.

Then she added quiet, nonchalant humming.

Wonderful.

OK. Fine. I studied the table, moved a few more objects around to represent the different fires so far. *If I were going to predict the next fire, where would it be?* I leaned over the empty salad bowl and checked the sight lines, then used my dessert fork to verify the distances between the fire sites represented on the table.

A few ideas. Nothing solid.

She watched me playing with the silverware and seasonings. "A doctorate, huh?"

"Listen." I took the napkin and wiped the oil off the table. "Do you want any dessert?"

She seemed to be considering it when one of the servers paused beside her and lowered a platter of the pork tenderloin with mango-and-pineapple sauce onto the table next to us.

Tessa grimaced. "Ew, that is so disgusting." I noticed that she pulled back one of the rubber bands she wore around her wrist and snapped it against her skin. "The poor pig. You can still see the blood."

Slaughterhouses.

Yes, you can. You can still see the blood.

"I think I'm gonna be sick." She stood. "Let's go."

"I need to pay," I said.

"I'll wait for you outside." She grabbed the khaki canvas satchel that she uses as a purse and hurried for the door.

5

After taking care of our bill, I stepped outside and found Tessa waiting beneath one of the orange-yellow vapor streetlights nearby. She was writing something in the small notebook she often carries with her. When she saw me, she surreptitiously slipped the pen and notebook back into her satchel.

I decided not to pry.

The wind had picked up even more since we'd entered the restaurant, and it whipped her shoulder-length black hair around her head in a small frenzy. "So," she said. "How many people were in there when we left?"

"Tessa, I don't want to do this."

"Sure you do, c'mon."

"Let's go, OK?"

She folded her arms. Leaned against the streetlight. I knew she wouldn't budge until I answered her.

"All right. Sixty-two."

"When we entered?"

"Forty-nine. How did you know I'd keep track?"

"It's what you do. Which one of the servers worked there the longest?"

"Tessa—"

"You don't know, do you? That's why you're avoiding the question."

"Allison Reynolds. She was the one with six piercings in her left ear, three in her right. Based on her route proficiency, I'd say she's been working at Geraldo's for over two years. I heard a few snatches of dialogue. She's from the Midwest, most likely southwestern Michigan or northern Indiana."

After a quiet moment. "You can't turn it off, can you?"

I drummed an anxious finger against my leg. "You ready to go?"

"I don't really want to go back to the hotel yet."

I thought for a moment. I don't remember exactly when, but at some point in the last couple months, I'd first started calling Tessa "Raven." She'd always reminded me of a raven, and sometimes the nickname just slipped out, as it did now, "Well, then, Raven, how about a walk beside the world's only ocean?"

She shrugged. "I guess so."

We grabbed our Windbreakers from the car and found a stretch of sand that was damp enough to walk on easily but not so close to the water that we would have to be constantly avoiding the incoming waves. We walked for a while, side by side, but also oceans apart. Every once in a while, a rogue wave would slap farther up the shore than the others and we'd scurry up the beach to stay out of its path.

Mists carried by the steady surf began curling around us.

After one of the bolder waves had chased us up the beach, Tessa said softly, "So do you ever wonder what it would be like? Being one of them? You know. On the other side? An arsonist, a killer, something like that? The people you help the cops find?"

Everyone is on the side of being human, of being fallible, but I knew what she meant. "Sometimes I do. Sometimes I wonder those kind of things. But I try not to get caught up dwelling on them."

"It's scary to think about, isn't it?"

"Yes."

"Well," she said. "I'm glad you're not like them."

"Thank you." A dim silence spread between us.

"Right?" She stopped walking and waited until I'd stopped as well. She stared at me through the moonlight. "You're not like them, are you?"

"No, of course not." I couldn't tell her what was really bothering me. It was something I'd never told anyone. "Of course I'm not like them."

It feels good, doesn't it?
Yes, it does.

She stood there, a raven in the moonlight. "Something's bothering you, isn't it? Tonight, I mean?"

Sometimes I wish she wasn't quite so astute. "I'm sorry, Tessa. He's been there, in the back of my mind. It doesn't mean you're not important—"

"The arsonist?"

"That's right."

And it was true, I was thinking about the arsonist. But it wasn't the whole truth.

I was also thinking about someone else.

Richard Devin Basque.

We walked for half an hour, talking some, but mostly keeping our thoughts to ourselves. The moon inched its way higher into the sky, and eventually we sat down on some dry sand next to a clump of sea grass that the waves had deposited on the shore earlier in the day.

And as we sat together on the sand, I let my thoughts take me back thirteen years to my early days as a detective in Milwaukee; to the night I arrested Richard Devin Basque in that abandoned slaughterhouse on the outskirts of Milwaukee.

6

Even though I was on the beach, I could see the slaughterhouse all around me. Dusky sunlight slanting through the windows. Huge, rusted meat hooks hanging from the ceiling. The image of a man holding a scalpel, standing over the bleeding woman. She was still alive, choking on her own blood. That was the most disturbing part of all to remember.

The doctors never could explain how she survived as long as she had.

Then, the moment outside of time when I ordered him to drop the knife, to back away, and how he just stood there instead, holding the red glistening blade, staring at the barrel of my gun.

I yelled again, followed procedure after procedure, warning after warning, until at last he spun, took three steps, then pivoted with a Smith & Wesson Sigma in his hand and fired. Missed.

I pulled the trigger of my .357 SIG P229, but for the first time in my career my gun malfunctioned, refused to fire. I lunged to the side as he took another shot, pegging my left shoulder, sending a bright splinter of pain riding up my neck, across my chest. I rolled to my feet, rushed him, and swung one of the meat hooks at his face. When he ducked out of the way, I threw my arms back and tackled him.

As we crashed to the concrete floor, I could hear the moist sounds of the woman struggling for breath only a few feet away, gasping, coughing.

Dying.

Basque drove the scalpel into my right thigh, but I

knocked his gun away, and as he crawled for it, I snagged his arm and twisted it behind his back, my shoulder and leg screaming at me the whole time.

Pinned him to the ground.

Cuffed him.

Then, I shoved him aside, and as I bent to help the woman, I heard him say softly, "I think we may need an ambulance, don't you, Detective?" I could hear a smirk in his voice.

I tried to help her, tried to save her, but the bleeding was coming from so many places it was impossible to stop. There was nothing I could do, nothing anyone could have done.

The scalpel was still in my leg, but if I removed it, the wound would bleed badly. It throbbed as I awkwardly dragged Basque to his feet to read him his rights.

I couldn't help but take note of his face. Hollywood handsome, and yet possessed with pure evil. He was staring at the motionless, blood-soaked body of the woman. "I guess we won't be needing that ambulance after all."

And that's when it happened.

Something inside of me snapped.

Rage and fear cascading through me. Rage, because of what he'd done to her. Fear, because if humans were capable of doing that, and I was human . . .

Well.

I lost it.

I punched him as hard as I could in the jaw. The force of the blow sent him spinning to the ground. I dropped to my knees beside him and raised my fist. Punched him again. Drew my fist back, ready to unload a third time.

When I was training for law enforcement, my instructors taught me to control myself. To avoid getting emotionally involved. But sometimes you can't help it. The violence and suffering get to you. And in that moment, I was ready to hit him again and again and again until I'd made him suffer as much as the woman he'd just killed. Part of me wanted to take the scalpel and cut him. Cut him just like he'd cut her.

He gazed at me and licked at the hot blood on his lips. "It feels good, doesn't it, Detective? It feels really good."

It feels good, doesn't it?

And the thing I've never told anybody, never mentioned

in any of my reports, was that it did. It did feel good when I hit him. A rush of fire and anger and power. And, to a certain part of me, it would have felt good to grab the scalpel and keep going, to give in to the primal drift in my soul. Part of me would have enjoyed the savagery.

I didn't answer him that day, but I think my silence spoke my thoughts.

Later, Basque told the interrogating officers that he'd broken his jaw when the meat hook hit him in the face. And that's what went in the case files and I didn't correct them. So for the last thirteen years, by his silence and mine, we've shared a secret that has frightened me more than any killer I've ever faced. The secret that it felt good to take a step in the direction of evil. Yes, it did.

I found out later that the woman's name was Sylvia Padilla. She was his sixteenth victim.

At least, that's how many we know about.

And that day, as she died beside me and I saw the extent of the horrors one human being could do to another, a cold shiver burrowed its way deep into my soul and has wormed around inside of me ever since.

A dark reminder of how close I came to becoming what I hunt.

Tessa's comments in the restaurant and on the beach had struck a nerve, because this month, after more than a dozen years on death row, Richard Devin Basque was being retried as the result of some DNA test discrepancies. And since I'd only caught him at the scene, not in the act of murder, the case wasn't going to be a slam dunk. My buddy Agent Ralph Hawkins would be testifying tomorrow. The trial would probably go on for months, and eventually I would be called in to testify too. But that's not what was bothering me as I sat beside my stepdaughter. I was thinking of the secret I shared with Basque.

That, yes, it felt good.

"You're not like them, are you?" she'd asked me.

And I'd told her no.

But maybe I am.

7

Sitting beneath the pale moonlight, Tessa and I watched the hungry waves lap at the shore. And for a few moments it seemed like we had always known each other, that she really was my daughter, that I really was her father, and that we had a lifetime of shared memories stored up someplace, ready to take us through whatever rough times might lie ahead.

But the feeling lasted only a moment. Then it was gone. Sea mist entwined us and the cold spaces between the distant stars landed on the beach all around us. I felt a chill. Maybe it was the wind. Maybe it was the deep night creeping slowly up the shore.

"I'm getting cold," Tessa said.

"Me too," I said. "Let's go. It's still a long walk back to the car."

As we stood, she gazed at the world's only ocean one last time. "Being here, right now, with the wind and the night and everything. It reminds me of something I read once."

"What's that?"

She gave the moonlit waves a steady, thoughtful stare. "'It was, indeed, a tempestuous yet sternly beautiful night, and one wildly singular in its terror and its beauty.'" And then, looking toward me, she added, "Poe. 'The Fall of the House of Usher.'"

"That's eerie," I said. "And beautiful too."

"You're right," she said. "It is. It's both."

I thought for a moment about reaching over and putting my hand on her shoulder, but I decided not to. The wind blew salty gusts in from the ocean, and somewhere above us a gull screeched its way through the night. For a moment, the gull's cry sounded like a human scream stretched out across the water.

Like a woman's scream echoing off the concrete floor of a slaughterhouse.

I reached into my pocket, and as I pulled out the car keys, I remembered where I'd placed them on the table, behind the salad bowl. "Come on," I said. "There's something I want to show you."

"What's that?"

"The future."

8

Creighton Melice parked his car in front of one of the bottom-feeder bars in a gang-infested neighborhood of southern San Diego. He figured that at least half of the people in the place would be carrying, so he made sure he'd chambered a round in his Glock before stepping out of the car.

A few women who'd ignored the cool weather and were wearing skintight wisps of clothing propositioned Creighton on his way into the bar, but he just brushed them off. He wasn't interested in their kind.

He wanted a girlfriend with a little more class.

Some of the gangbangers lurking around the tables stared at Creighton as he entered. A few of them eyed his face and hands, focusing on the array of scars and burn marks he carried, but most of the bangers were probably just wondering if he was a cop. The attention didn't bother Creighton. He knew how to act around bangers. After all, he'd been one himself back in the day.

In a gang, it's all about respect. So instead of staring down or provoking the little punks, he just gave them each a casual nod as he walked past.

They seemed to accept that and, one by one, drifted back to their murmured conversations, keeping one cautious eye on him as he took his seat at the bar.

Creighton ordered two beers and let his eyes browse the room. The woman sitting by herself beneath the Bud Light sign looked a little too drunk. Pass.

The African-American woman who was checking him out from the booth by the end of the bar appeared a little too eager. Never a good sign.

He took a long, slow drink and found his attention drawn to an attractive, dark-skinned brunette sitting alone at a table beside the window. She didn't look like an untraceable, undocumented immigrant, but she was appealing to Melice for other reasons. She looked bored and was apparently confident enough not to feel the need to dress like a ten-dollar whore to find a guy.

Hmm. Interesting.

He grabbed the two beers and maneuvered through the crowd to her table.

Being confident. That's the key. It's all about confidence. If you're confident enough, people will go wherever you lead them, believe whatever you say. That's how Jeffrey Dahmer did it. Complete confidence. He once convinced two cops that the drugged, naked guy in handcuffs wandering around the streets was his drunk lover. So the officers dropped the guy off at Dahmer's apartment, where he promptly killed and then ate him. Another time some cops came to his place to investigate the smell seeping through the walls of his apartment, and Dahmer convinced them that it was just the aquarium he hadn't gotten around to cleaning. They didn't bother to check his bedroom, or they would have found the rotting corpse on his bed.

So.

Confidence.

Creighton set both beers on the brunette's table. "I need some advice."

She looked at the bottles of beer and then gave Creighton a slight grin. "Oh yeah? What kind of advice?"

Over the years Creighton had discovered that people are more suspicious of you if you offer them something for nothing. The kinder you are, the more they think you want something from them. People trust need, not charity.

He leaned his hand against the chair beside her. "I'm new around here. I need someone to show me around the city."

A raised eyebrow. A little sarcasm. "Do I look like a tour guide?"

"You look like someone who's tired of all the scumbags in this hellhole leering at you. You look like someone who knows you could do better for tonight, if only the right guy wandered into your life."

So.

Now.

Wait.

Just wait.

She'll respond somehow, she has to respond somehow.

Confidence. That's the key.

Creighton took a swig of his beer.

She might just blow him off. Yes, she might.

But maybe.

"Well," she said at last. "You're right about this place. And I do know the city pretty well . . ." She stood and slipped her arm around his elbow. "All right. Tonight, I'll be your guide."

"I can't wait," he said, and led her to the door.

9

Since I'm six-foot-three, I was thankful yesterday when Avis upgraded us to a full-size car. At least this way I could steer with my hands and not my knees.

I turned off a street peppered with tattoo studios, car dealerships, and small ethnic restaurants and then cruised past a group of homeless immigrants who stared blankly at our car from the curb. "Patrick," said Tessa. "We can go back to the hotel now if you want to. I mean, I don't mind. Just so you know. It's OK with me."

"Don't worry. It's all right. The neighborhood we're going to isn't so bad."

"How do you know?"

"This is what I do."

We drove for another ten minutes and then I said, "So earlier you asked if I could tell where the next fire would be, right?"

"Yeah."

"Well." I let the car roll to a stop beside a series of brown stucco homes lining one of San Diego's many sagebrush-covered hills. "This is it."

"Here?" She sounded excited, like I'd just suggested we move back to New York City.

"Yes. If I were going to predict the future, I'd say the next fire is going to be somewhere right around here."

We stepped out of the car, and she looked around the desolate neighborhood. Not much to see. A small tobacco store stood on the corner at the end of the block. The hills were fringed by palm trees and dotted with quiet homes now fast asleep. The traffic on the Five murmured to us through the night. A commuter train, which they call trolleys here, roared down the tracks in the distance. It wasn't the worst neighborhood in the city, but I didn't want to keep Tessa here too long, either.

"Do you really think there's going to be a fire here?" she asked.

"Of course not. I already told you I can't predict the future. It's just that if I were going to ... that is—based on the arsonist's pattern, if I were him, this is where I'd choose."

She looked around expectantly. "So, when is it supposed to happen?"

I looked at my watch. "All right, let's see ... three ... two ... one."

She turned slowly, eyes wide. "Are you sure?" she asked.

I noticed a transient Hispanic man lurching across the street at the end of the block. He wore a tangle of scraggly clothes, and when he arrived at the curb he began to walk in odd circles around one of the murky streetlights. "Tessa, I already told you I can't do this. What, do I look like Nostradamus?"

She nodded, still scanning the neighborhood. "That's a good line. I'd hang on to that one."

"Thanks."

"I don't see a fire."

"Of course you don't." The homeless man was about thirty meters away. He appeared to be mumbling to himself. He looked our direction and then began to stumble toward us.

"I think it's time to go," I said.

Nearby, I could hear the rattle and hum of the trolley coming closer.

Tessa slid into the passenger seat. "So, how much did you say graduate school cost you?"

"Apparently, way too much."

As I pulled away from the curb, the vagrant began staggering down the center of the road toward us. He stopped directly in front of the car. I couldn't safely pass him so I let the car idle. He stood only a few meters from us, frozen, staring into the headlights.

"What's he doing?" Tessa asked.

"Probably just wants some money."

I was about to get out of the car and tell him to kindly step out of the way, when he let out a wild screech and rushed screaming toward our car, clambered up the hood to the windshield, and stared at us through the glass. I threw open my door. "Tessa, stay in the car. Lock the door."

She did.

He looked at me menacingly, eyes wild in the night. "Brraynn," he screamed. Before I could stop him, he slammed his face against the glass.

Tessa scrambled back as far as she could. "Patrick!"

Drugs. He's probably on drugs.

I grabbed his arm. "Sir, you need to settle down. Come on. Let's get you off this car." He pulled away, shook his head violently, and smacked his forehead against the windshield, sending an array of cracks flying across the glass. Then he looked at me with a crazed, twisted expression, his nose now bloodied and broken. His teeth were rotten nubs, his breath a putrid cloud.

He was incoherent. High. Maybe drunk, although his breath didn't smell of booze.

"Sssllllleee," he screeched. "Mergh. Whikl!"

Restraining people high on crack is never fun. Inhuman strength. Combative. Out of control.

But I needed to protect him from himself.

I pulled him off the hood, but as I did, he let out a shriek, swung his head toward me, and buried his rotten teeth through my Windbreaker and into the meat of my forearm. I jerked my arm away, and one of the stained teeth peeled out of his mouth and stayed lodged in my arm. He toppled off the car and sprinted with surprising speed toward the tobacco store, where a man in his early twenties had just exited.

I rapped at the window, made sure Tessa was OK, and then I ran toward the tobacco store and called for the college kid to get away!

The transient, who was either mentally ill or high—or both—was now holding a rusted tire iron. Whether he'd had it hidden nearby or just found it, I didn't know.

"Hey!" I had to yell loudly to be heard over the clatter of the approaching trolley. The guy was fast, frantic. I ran toward him. "Stop!"

"Preehl!" he screamed.

Rumbling from the tracks nearby, the trolley was accelerating.

I sprinted toward the transient. "Put it down." I reached for the plastic restraints I carry in my back pocket. "Do it now!"

This was spinning off bad, bad.

The vagrant turned in a circle, delirious. Disoriented. "Rrrrhhhhkkk."

Finally, the customer who'd been standing outside the tobacco store backed away and slipped into the thick shadows beside it.

Good, that's good.

But you still need to restrain this guy so he doesn't attack someone else.

I closed the distance to the homeless man, and he threw the tire iron at me, then bolted toward the trolley tracks. His impromptu weapon clanged to the sidewalk beside me as I ran toward him.

Only a few more meters.

The rushing thunder of the trolley became more pronounced here, because just past us, the track descended into a tightly cut trench through the city. A stiff black metal fence two meters high lined the sides of the rift to keep people from falling in.

Or jumping.

Oh no.

The transient grabbed the railing and began to climb. I sprang forward to clutch his leg. Almost had it. Almost.

There. I had his ankle.

But then he screamed one last unintelligible word, fiercely kicked my hand away, and threw himself over the top of the railing directly into the path of the oncoming trolley.

10

Even above the sound of the trolley rattling over the tracks, I could hear the wet, grisly sound of the trolley's impact.

No, no, no.

I ran to the railing.

The engineer was braking the trolley, but it wouldn't matter anymore to the man who'd jumped. I wondered if the people aboard had felt anything, if they had any idea what had just happened. I noticed something wobbling to a stop beside the tracks. Then I realized what it was.

The man's shoe.

And it looked like it might still have his foot inside it.

A sour, churning flood of nausea swept through me. Some people grow numb to it all. To the death and blood and violence. You'd think in my job I would have, but it still bothers me. It still breaks my heart and turns my stomach.

I took a deep breath to calm myself and then remembered Tessa. I swiveled around and ran to our car, part of my mind cataloging the scene.

Entrance and exit routes—K Street and 16th. No mobile traffic.

Check.

License plate numbers—five parked cars, memorize the plates.

Check.

Potential witnesses—trolley riders? Unlikely. In the channel, they couldn't see out. . . . College kid, store owner? Possibly. Tessa, me.

Check.

Surveillance—no visible cameras.

Check.

Tessa was sitting in the passenger seat, rocking back and forth, both hands covering her face. My phone was still in the car beside her. I knocked on the window and called for her to unlock the door.

When she didn't move, I flagged down a man in a maroon Ford Mustang who'd just turned onto our street. At first I didn't think he'd stop, but when he saw me glance at his plates, he pulled to a stop beside the curb.

"What's going on?" he asked. His eyes landed on the blood seeping out of my arm.

"Do you have a phone?"

"Sure. Yeah."

"Call nine-one-one. Tell them a man jumped in front of the trolley."

He kept gazing at my arm.

"Do it."

He dialed.

I had to shout to Tessa four or five times before she finally unlocked the door and I was able to climb in beside her. "Are you OK?"

She was shaking.

I pulled her close. Held her tight.

"Did he do it?" Her voice fragile, broken. "Did he jump?"

Good. She didn't see. Thank goodness she didn't see.

"Don't worry about that—"

"Did he jump!"

"Yes." I had to be straight with her. "He did."

She began hitting me with small, rigid fists. "He shouldn't have done it, Patrick. He shouldn't have."

"I know."

"Why did he do it?"

We always want a reason, an explanation, but sometimes there aren't any. "He was confused," I said. "He made a terrible mistake." I hugged her, tried to calm her. "Now, are you OK?"

"I wish we hadn't come here."

"Me too. I'm sorry."

"Can we go?" She was wiping a tear away. "Please. Let's go. OK?"

A man had just died, just killed himself, and since Tessa

had covered her eyes and the college kid had bolted, it looked like I was the only one who'd seen what happened. I knew the police would need my statement, so, as badly as I wanted to, I couldn't leave the scene quite yet. On the other hand, I didn't want Tessa anywhere near here. I definitely needed to get her back to the hotel.

Just relax and think for a minute, Pat. Think.

I looked up and saw that the windshield was spider-webbed with cracks and spotted with crimson. Beyond John Doe's blood spatter, I could see that a crowd was already forming along the edge of the tracks, staring down. Pointing. On the other side of the tracks two men trudged past the onlookers. I couldn't see their faces, but one walked with the measured steps of an older man, and the bigger, younger guy was carrying a large black duffel bag. The man in the Mustang had swiveled around the block and was picking them up.

"Well?" Tessa said.

"I won't be able to leave for a little while," I said. "Let me see if I can find someone who can take you back to the hotel."

11

Special Agent Lien-hua Jiang leaned against the pillows of her hotel bed with her notebook computer on her lap. Fighting the bleariness in her eyes, she scrolled through the case information about the serial arsonist.

For the umpteenth time.

With San Diego's dry climate and dense population, the city officials were nervous about any fires—especially with the memory of the Santa Ana winds that caused the devastating fires of 2007 still fresh in their minds.

Lien-hua had first worked on this arsonist's profile last fall, but since then there'd been six more fires and the police still didn't have any solid leads, and lately he'd been progressing, waiting less time in between fires. So, Lieutenant Aina Mendez, the head of San Diego's Metro Arson Strike Team, or MAST, had called Lien-hua back to update the profile. And this time Lien-hua had asked Special Agent Patrick Bowers to help analyze the timing and sites of the crimes.

She told herself that she'd asked him to come because of his expertise at finding serial offenders, and not because of any kind of personal interest she might have in him.

That's what she told herself.

He'd agreed to the assignment immediately, just as she knew he would.

Even though Lien-hua had six solid years of experience as a behavioral profiler, she'd never seen anything quite like this before.

By its very nature, arson is one of the toughest crimes

to solve. The fire destroys evidence, and the suppression and rescue efforts leave the crime scene contaminated. Because of that, arson is a great way to hide one crime inside another.

So, when she'd started on the case last fall, she began by looking for motive. What other crime might the fires be masking?

Insurance fraud wasn't the issue; she'd checked on that right away. The property value on the buildings was comparatively low by San Diego standards, and the owners had no apparent ties to each other. No fatalities so far, thankfully, so he didn't seem to be setting the fires to cover up a crime—well, not murder at least.

But what, then? If not for profit or to cover up evidence, why start the fires?

Maybe for the sheer thrill of watching things burn?

Possibly, except Lieutenant Mendez and the Metro Arson Strike Team had interviewed and followed up on everyone in the crowds at each of the fires—even the responding officers and firefighters. A few leads so far, but nothing substantial.

From everything Lien-hua had seen, this guy didn't stay to watch.

So then . . . what was his motive? Why did he do it?

During her career Lien-hua had mostly worked homicides rather than arsons, but Lieutenant Mendez told her that the efficiency of the fires pointed to someone who understood the flow patterns of buoyant gases and could locate the most ideal point of origin so that the building would come down fast.

In other words, a professional.

But if he was a professional, who was hiring him?

And why?

Even now, after fourteen fires, the police still didn't have a single suspect . . .

They had thousands.

Lien-hua sighed and massaged her forehead with a tired hand.

She left her laptop on the bed and walked to the vase sitting beside her purse on the desk. She'd brought the vase with her, as she always did, and bought the flowers when she arrived in town. Traveling as much as she did, she'd found that she needed something in addition to yoga and kickboxing to calm her mind and recenter her spirit when she was in the middle of a case.

The simple act of creating beauty and symmetry out of chaos brought her a sense of calm and a welcome escape from the pressures that come with being an FBI profiler—not to mention the grace that the flowers brought to the nondescript hotel rooms she stayed in so often.

Ten years ago, in the months following the "accident" that no one in her family ever dared to talk about—and that Lien-hua still didn't believe was an accident—her mother had started flower arranging. And over the next seven years, before the car wreck that took her life, Mei Xing had become somewhat of an expert.

After her mother's death, Lien-hua had decided to take up flower arranging in her place. Maybe in honor of her mother, maybe to work through her grief, she wasn't sure. After all, the hardest person to know, the hardest person to profile, is yourself.

Flower arranging is supposed to be peaceful and relaxing, but at first Lien-hua found it to be just the opposite.

Frustrating, exasperating, time-consuming? Yes.

Calming and soothing? Not quite.

And yet, in time Lien-hua had learned to distinguish the different moods that a slight change in the arrangement of a single petal could produce. Tranquillity. Excitement. Wonder.

Allure.

She angled the two cyclamen to face the white irises and tilted one of the star-of-Bethlehem petals so that it would gather more light. Using all white flowers in a white vase gave the room an elegant feeling. Pure and innocent.

Lien-hua stepped back.

There. Much better.

She plopped onto the bed again and pulled up the computer files, but just as she was about to look over the list of possible accelerants, her cell rang. She answered. "Yes?"

"Lien-hua, I need your help."

"Pat?" He sounded upset. "What is it? Are you OK?"

"There was an accident. I'm with Tessa—"

A cold chill. "You're not hurt—"

"No. We're fine, but listen, can you come get Tessa, take

her back to the hotel? I need to stay here, give my statement to the police. If you can just hang out with her for an hour or two until I get back, it would really help out. I think she'll be all right, I just don't want her to be alone."

"Of course. Where are you?"

He gave her the address and they ended the call.

Lien-hua grabbed her purse, but in her rush she bumped her elbow against the vase and it toppled off the desk, scattering her flowers across the carpet.

She took a moment to evaluate the mess and then quickly slipped the flowers back into the vase. She could refill the water later when she had more time.

As she set the vase onto the desk, she noticed that some of the petals had been bruised by the fall.

Wounded petals.

Bruised innocence.

She thought back to the incident that had brought all the flowers into her family's life. An awkward drop of guilt splattered inside of her.

The arrangement will never be the same again.

Never the same.

As she left the room, she shut the door harder than she needed to, then hurried down the hallway to pick up Tessa from the site of the accident.

12

While I waited for Lien-hua and the police, I took some digital pictures of the scene with my cell phone and e-mailed them to the dispatcher to forward to the responding officers. It used to be that we had to wait for a photographer to show up at the scene of an accident or a crime.

Not anymore.

Welcome to the twenty-first century.

I noticed that the transient's tooth was still embedded in my arm. Without letting Tessa see, I pried it loose. It hurt more than I thought it would, and my fingers were quivering a little as I dropped it into my pocket and snugged up the elastic cuff of my Windbreaker to stop the bleeding.

A few minutes later, three police cars and an ambulance pulled to the curb, and as if on cue, Lien-hua arrived and parked just behind them.

I noticed the eyes of all the male—and female—officers following Lien-hua as she crossed the street. I wasn't surprised. After all, she carries herself with Oriental poise, has an elegantly beautiful face with a slight nose and high cheekbones, and is, to put it mildly, very, very fit. Of course, she's also brilliant, cool under pressure, single, and, at thirty-two, just four years younger than me.

Overall, she's one of the most stunning women I've ever met. But as she approached, I tried not to think about all that, and instead, after a quick greeting, I focused on explaining to her what had happened. One of the EMTs gave me a tube of antibiotics for my arm, and I pulled back my sleeve as we approached Tessa, who was sitting on the curb halfheartedly snapping a rubber band against her wrist and occasionally writing something in her notebook.

After a moment, Lien-hua sat beside her. "Hello, Tessa."

Without looking up. "Agent Jiang."

"Are you doing OK?"

Snap. "Don't psychoanalyze me or anything. I just want to go to bed."

Lien-hua dragged a slender finger across the sidewalk. "Fair enough." Then she stood and offered her hand to Tessa.

I finished smearing some of the antibiotics on my arm and twisted the cap back onto the tube. "Tessa, I asked Lien-hua to stay with you for a little bit while I finish up here."

Snap. Snap. "I don't need anyone to stay with me."

When Lien-hua saw that Tessa wasn't going to take her hand, she lowered it.

"Please."

She set her jaw, got up, and huffed over to Lien-hua's car.

Snap. Snap. Snap.

I need to talk to her about that rubber band thing.

Once Tessa was out of earshot, I told Lien-hua, "It's been a rough night, but I think she'll be OK. I'll see you at the hotel, all right?"

"Sure."

I touched her elbow softly. "Hey, thanks for coming."

"You're welcome," she said. "I'm glad I could be here for you."

Her words tumbled through my head, meaning more to me than she could have possibly meant them to. "Yeah, me too."

Then she climbed into the car beside Tessa, and a police officer whose face looked like a block of meat with thick stubble glued to its base called out, "Where do you think you're going?" An old scar crawled across his cheek and dragged one of his lips down into a sneer. His arms were two tattooed pythons hanging out of his shirtsleeves. He wore a detective's badge.

"They didn't see what happened," I said.

He looked at me suspiciously. "And you are?"

"Patrick Bowers. I'm a federal agent. FBI."

As I pulled out my ID, he studied my outfit, apparently taking note of my jeans, running shoes, and T-shirt. "Fed, huh? If you're an FBI agent, where's your wingtips and dorky little tie?"

I almost asked him where his doughnut and dinky little mustache were, but I wasn't sure that would be the best way to jump-start our friendship. Instead, I just showed him my federal ID.

Lien-hua had waited, but now I nodded for her to take off. The detective didn't seem interested in the two women anymore. He looked over my ID, working his jaw back and forth. "So, now the Feds are involved in this too?"

"Involved in what?"

He handed me the ID. "Look, if you're gonna come in here and start some kind of turf war—"

I read the name off his badge. "Detective Dunn, I wasn't sent in to investigate anything. I'm only here because I was the witness to John Doe's suicide. Is there something going on I should know about?"

He stepped close enough for me to smell his garlicky breath. "This is my city. The next time you and your pencil-pushing lawyer buddies from Quantico decide to stick your nose into an ongoing investigation, at least have the courtesy to go through the proper channels."

"I'd suggest you back away," I said. "Now."

He backed up slowly.

"What ongoing investigation are you talking about, Detective?"

"Don't insult me. You know or you wouldn't be here." He rubbed at the sandpapery stubble on his cheek. "So, you the photographer too? Little snapshots of the trolley you're e-mailing to everyone."

This guy was something else. "Your badge says you're a homicide detective. I was a detective in Milwaukee for six years and I know that dispatch wouldn't send you here to work an eyewitness corroborated suicide, at least not until foul play was suspected. What's going on here?"

He grinned. "Oh. I see. You want to play it like that. Well, you're the hotshot federal agent. Why don't you work that out for yourself?"

"Well, you know, Detective, that sounds like a good idea. I believe I will."

His voice stiffened. "So, the guy who called this in, you didn't happen to get a good look at him, did you?"

"Mid- to late thirties, blond hair, no sideburns, slight goatee. He was seated the whole time, but his head was near the ceiling of the maroon 2003 Ford Mustang he was driving, so height was maybe six-three or six-four. He used a Nextel phone, had a bald eagle tattoo on his left forearm but no other visible body markings or jewelry. The Mustang has a scratch approximately twenty centimeters long on the front panel, driver's side. Arizona plates number B73—" Dunn just stood staring at me. "Are you writing this down?" I asked.

"Are you making this up?"

"No," I said, looking past him to the profile of Petco Park against the skyline. "This is what I do."

During the last two hours, Creighton Melice and the brunette, who'd told him her name was Randi—with an "i"—had shared drinks at a downtown wine bistro and visited two nightclubs. Now, he was aiming the car toward the shipyards while she fussed with her hair in the car's flip-down mirror. "So, where are you staying, Neville?"

"I have a place down in Chula Vista."

Creighton loved how she'd gotten into the car by her own choice. He hadn't been sure that she would, but it ended up being just that easy. Open the door. Let her climb in. Close the door. It was so much better when it happened that way. So much more satisfying.

Creighton kept an eye out for cops. You could never be too careful. He stopped at a light.

"You said you're new to Diego," she said, flipping the mirror up. "What brought you here?"

"A film project I'm working on. I tend to move around a lot."

"How long are you planning to stay this time?"

"Depends."

"On what?"

"On how long it takes to tie things up here."

The light clicked green, and he turned onto the street that led to the warehouse with the cameras.

*   *   *

In my job, you don't often have the luxury of working only one case at a time. As you move forward solving one crime, another one creeps up on you from behind. So, even with the arson case at the center of my radar screen, I couldn't ignore the fact that the odd circumstances revolving around John Doe's suicide were tapping me on the shoulder.

So, I made room in my mind for both cases.

I didn't think it was likely the man with the black duffel and his buddy were just passing by and yet didn't bother to look at what happened. Most people naturally rubberneck, unless, of course, they want to appear disinterested—and usually it's only people who have something to hide who want that. Besides, I had a growing feeling that something more was going on here, especially after hearing the words of my new jurisdictionally paranoid detective friend.

So, after I finished giving my statement to Detective Dunn and letting a paramedic bandage my arm, I took a few minutes to ask the people who'd been on the trolley if any of them had seen a man with a black duffel bag aboard the trolley before it stopped.

None of them had.

I could check video surveillance from the trolley depots later to see if the two men had boarded.

Before leaving the scene, I walked to the metal fence again and looked down into the rift.

A couple city workers were scrubbing off the front of the trolley. One of them was complaining about missing Leno, the other guy was trying to get his buddy interested in discussing the Lakers' starting lineup.

Just past them, a somber-looking police officer retrieved the shoe.

And just like I thought.

It wasn't empty.

I took one more look around, then hopped into my car. Since human bites nearly always result in infections, I stopped by the hospital for some more antibiotics. The emergency room doctors also did a hepatitis C and HIV test because of the bite, and told me to check back with them in a week and then get retested in six months. Nothing more to do about all that right now, so I put it out of my mind.

Before leaving the hospital, I took a moment to picture what the Avis representative's face would look like on Saturday when I explained what had happened to the windshield.

That would be interesting.

I didn't want Tessa to see the streaks and splatters of John Doe's blood on the glass come morning so I went searching for a twenty-four-hour car wash.

My mind cycling back and forth between the two cases the whole time.

13

Creighton and Randi arrived at the warehouse's expansive parking lot. He saw Randi sending a text message.

"Who's that to?"

"My roommate. I'm telling her not to wait up for me."

"That's a good idea."

She closed up the phone and set it down, then peered out the window. "Where are we? I thought we were going to your place."

"I need to take care of something here first. Come on. I don't want to leave you out here alone."

"What are you talking about? What do you need to do here?"

He didn't answer her, just opened his door. But as he did so, the cell phone in his pocket vibrated to life. He knew who it was right away. Only one person had this number. He retrieved the cell. "Yeah?"

"It's time," the electronically altered voice said. "We do it tonight."

"What?" Creighton's eyes danced over to Randi. "You can't be serious."

A pause. "You're ready, aren't you?"

"Of course I'm ready. But we were set up to do it during the day. I need at least a few hours to find her and—"

Randi folded her arms. "To find who?"

"Shh," he said.

"Who's there?" asked Shade.

"It's nothing," Creighton said. "Listen, I'm telling you, tonight's no good. I don't like being rushed. The plan was to pick her up on her way home from work—"

Randi put away her makeup, then zippered her purse shut and set it on her lap. "Pick up who, Neville?"

Creighton turned the phone away from his mouth and glared at her. "Just a minute," he hissed.

"Things have changed," Shade said. "We do it now. Hunter's on the run. Don't let me down."

The phone went dead and Creighton realized it was too tough to jam it into his pocket while he was sitting down. He set it beside him, between the seats.

"What's going on?" asked Randi.

Creighton rubbed his rough fingers together. It seemed he needed to make a decision. "Let me think."

"It's another girl, isn't it?"

"Quiet."

Creighton weighed his options. Randi ... Cassandra ... Randi ... Cassandra ... who should he give this night to?

"Who is she?" Randi asked.

Then Creighton made his decision and started the car. "We're not going to my place. Something's come up."

"Oh?"

"Get out."

Randi looked at the weary warehouse district stretching to the ocean. "I'm supposed to get out here? You're not dumping me out here in the middle of nowhere!"

Creighton let his voice become a two-by-four. "Get out of the car." He reached across her, cranked open the passenger side door.

She cussed loudly as she scrambled to grab her things, and then swung her legs outside. "I could have given you a good time." He put a hand on her back, pushed her out the door. She staggered to her feet. "You don't know what you're missing!"

"Neither do you." Before she could close her door, he stamped on the gas, jerking the car forward, using the momentum to slam the door shut.

In the rearview mirror he saw her kick at the tire of the car as he sped past her. She was shaking her arm at him, yelling.

For a moment he was tempted to go back for her, to see just how good a time Randi with an "i" might have provided him. But no. He had a job to do for Shade, and if he stuck to the plan, then he would soon die happily ever after.

But before that, an FBI agent would die too.

But not quite so happily.

Creighton needed to pick up a few things. He wanted to break the speed limit but was careful to keep all the traffic laws on his way to his condo to pick up the darts and the dart gun Shade had given him to use.

After all, you can never be too careful.

14

Victor Drake was irritated. And when he got irritated, he couldn't sleep.

And when he couldn't sleep, it only made him more irritated.

So, after lying wide-awake in his bed for nearly two hours, he climbed out and plopped into the Jacuzzi in the glass-enclosed sunroom overlooking the ocean. He shut off the whirlpool's jets so he could hear the high-def TV screen mounted on the wall beside his Monet, but then got annoyed at the sound and turned it down and simply watched the numbers of the Nikkei Stock Index scroll across the screen.

Just as he was beginning to relax, the guard at the front gate buzzed him.

Victor ignored the buzzer. All he wanted to do was unwind enough to go to sleep.

Another buzz.

Victor didn't move.

Another.

He slammed his finger against the remote control, and the television screen split into two images, with the mute stock index on the right side and the live video feed of the guard station at the driveway's entrance on the left.

"What!" yelled Victor.

"Señor, I have two men here who—"

"Do you have any idea what time it is?" Victor shot back.

"I know, señor. They are very insist—"

"You don't bother me unless—"

Another voice cut him off, and a face appeared on the

screen next to the guard. "It's Octal. I've got Geoff with me. We're coming up."

Victor's fingers shook slightly and he dropped the remote control into the whirlpool. He cursed and fished it out, but by the time he'd retrieved it, he saw on the screen that Dr. Octal Kurvetek's BMW had cruised past the confused-looking guard and was on its way to the house. Victor decided to fire that useless rent-a-cop tomorrow, but for right now, he needed to deal with Geoff and the doctor. They were never supposed to come here.

Never.

He'd made that very clear.

Victor switched off the television, stepped out of the tub, and dried himself off. A few moments later, before he had time to finish getting dressed, he heard the footsteps of the two men on the stairs. He knew he'd locked the front door earlier, but that hadn't seemed to slow Geoff down one bit. Victor cinched his bathrobe around his waist and stalked out of the master bedroom.

The two men were waiting for him in the hall.

"What are you doing here?" His voice was seething. "I told you never to—"

"I know what you said." Geoff was an immobile mountain of a man with a broad nose that looked right at home mounted on his bulky face. "But this is important."

The other man stood beside him quietly. A gray-bearded man in his sixties with cool, piercing eyes, Dr. Octal Kurvetek had worked for twenty years for the Texas Department of Criminal Justice as the supervising physician for the executions by lethal injection. He'd always made Victor nervous, but his skills had made him the perfect man for the job Victor had hired him to do.

Victor tore his eyes off Dr. Kurvetek and glared at Geoff. "Well, what is it? And this better be good."

"There was a slight problem." Geoff's face registered no emotion.

"What kind of problem?"

"Hunter never showed up," Dr. Kurvetek added.

"What?" gasped Victor. "He didn't show up? How could he not show up?"

"The subject reacted unexpectedly," Dr. Kurvetek said. "And the police were called in."

"And?" Victor demanded.

"Obvious suicide," said Geoff. "Hunter probably bolted."

"We kept an eye on the scene, but even after everyone left, he didn't come," Dr. Kurvetek said. "We went to his apartment but he wasn't there either. His drawers are a mess. It looks like he left in a hurry. I thought that instead of calling you on the phone we should discuss this in person."

Victor tried to connect the dots. It was hard to tell how much Hunter knew. He hadn't been told much, but it was almost certainly enough to hurt them if he decided to talk to the authorities.

Plus, General Biscayne would be arriving on Thursday.

No, no, this couldn't be happening. Not now.

"Where's Suricata?"

"At Hunter's," said Geoff. "Case he comes back."

Victor let all this sink in for a moment. If anything happened to the device and the Project Rukh Oversight Committee found out about it, Drake Enterprises would lose its defense department contract. And then the investigations would begin. "And, you took care of the—"

"Don't worry," Dr. Kurvetek said. "It's safely tucked away at the base. We did that first."

This was one time Victor was glad he'd put Octal on the books so that he could receive unlimited access to Building B-14, but still he didn't want to think about any of this. His head was beginning to hurt. It was all too much. But at least the device was secure. He needed a drink. "Take care of the house, and find Hunter. Call me when you know more. Let's rein this in. No more loose ends."

The two men left the house and Victor went searching for his bottle of pills.

It only took Creighton five minutes to gather the necessary items from his condo. Even though he didn't like the idea of having to move on this so quickly—and he was more than a little ticked off at having to say good-bye to Randi—now that everything was in play his adrenaline was jacked up and that was something he liked very much.

After loading the darts in the hydraulic-powered dart gun, he left to find Cassandra Lillo, the woman he'd already started to think of as his next girlfriend.

15

I rose before dawn for a jog. Tessa would be asleep for another three or four hours, so it gave me a chance to be alone, think through the events of the previous night and not feel guilty about splitting my attention between her and my work.

The wind had calmed down but left the morning cool enough to warrant sweatpants. Despite all that had happened the night before, after twenty-five minutes of running I felt my mind clearing.

Last night, when I'd returned to the hotel and tapped on Tessa's door, Lien-hua had stepped into the hall and told me that Tessa was asleep.

"Is she doing all right?" I'd asked Lien-hua.

"I believe so. Yes. But I thought it would be best to stay with her, anyway, until you arrived."

It seemed like there might be something else on her mind. "Are you OK?"

"Just processing some things. Maybe we can talk about it tomorrow. I need some sleep. I'll see you in the morning, OK?"

There was more to be said, but it wasn't going to happen that late at night. After I'd thanked her again and she'd left for her room, I began to wonder if maybe Tessa had said something to her. Maybe John Doe's suicide had been harder on Tessa than I thought. If so, my plans for the week might have to take a dramatic detour.

* * *

As dawn arrived, a streak of high cirrus clouds drifted above me, and early-morning sunlight squeezed out the night. But with the day came the heat. In contrast to last night, it seemed like God had dialed the thermostat for Southern California up all the way the moment he sent the sun to awaken the city.

I came to an intersection, saw a sign for Bryson Heights High School, and wondered if they might have a track or a fitness trail. I jogged toward the school, found that they didn't have a track, but they did have a football field. And that was good news because football goals meant I could crank out some pull-ups.

I found the goalposts, jumped up, grabbed the horizontal bar, and it felt good to get into the rhythm. Up. Down.

Up.

Down.

When I was nineteen I worked for a year as a wilderness guide and I fell in love with rock climbing; and the best way to stay in shape for the crags is doing pull-ups. At first a couple hundred pull-ups a day was impossible—I could barely do ten. But over the years, I've worked my way up, and, after more than four thousand days of doing them, pull-ups come almost as natural as walking.

Up.

Down.

I squeezed out a set of forty, took a breather, and then tried flying solo with my left arm. The homeless guy's bite didn't affect my arm as much as I thought it might, but with every pull-up I could still feel it sting.

Up.

I thought of him. Bewildered. Raving. Losing his life. All so meaningless. So tragic.

Down.

Most of the time I try to focus on the positive impact that my work at the NCAVC has, but sometimes I wonder what the point of it all is.

Up. The majority of people who've ever lived on our planet have led short, difficult, brutal lives and then died before their dreams could come true.

Down. People like Sylvia Padilla and that man last night and Christie, my wife who passed away last year, taking all of our plans for the future with her.

Up. It's tragic and pointless, but it's the way the world is.

Down. We live in a country where television newscasters are allowed to get excited about the score of a baseball game but aren't allowed to show emotion or remorse while reporting a homicide, a suicide bombing, or a rape.

Up.

Down. That's our world.

Enough with the left. Only managed nine. Time for the right.

Sweating, sweating. Today would be a scorcher.

Every time I pulled my chin toward the goalpost, I was able to glimpse the stoic ships in the harbor and catch the glisten of sunlight on the ocean. Without last night's anxious wind, the sea was early morning still.

Up.

Coronado Island stared at me from the bay. The island was a study in contrasts, with thousands of naval personnel living in anonymous-looking barracks right across the street from some of the most expensive real estate in the world; and of course one of America's most lush hotels, the Hotel del Coronado, lay only a quarter mile from the Spartan living conditions of the Navy SEAL Amphibious Training Base.

Down.

I snagged eleven with my right arm. It's my stronger arm, anyway. I could feel the burn. I did as many sets as I could until my arms were blown out, and the bandage on my left forearm began to get soaked with something other than sweat. So I started my jog again. This time I chose a path that took me along the beach.

The water beside me seemed so still, so tame in the dawning day, so different from last night. A few timid waves tiptoed across the surface, just enough to keep the ocean from becoming an endless sheet of glass.

And if I didn't know what went on deep beneath those ripples, I probably would have felt a sense of calm. But I'd been scuba diving enough to know the truth: deep beneath the surface, in the places where the sun's light will never reach, lies a whole different world. Even on days like this, when the surface looked peaceful and serene, dark currents, swift and strong, were snaking endlessly through the depths. Never tiring. Never resting. Always, always on the move.

As I ran beside the paradoxical ocean, I couldn't help but think of my walk with Tessa last night.

Both eerie and beautiful.

And then I thought of John Doe's suicide.

It was only another mile or so to the trolley tracks where he died. I decided to cruise past the scene, see if I noticed anything different in the daylight.

As I crossed Kettner Boulevard, I could hear the Orange Line approaching, so I knew that the trolleys were running again.

Life moving on.

Soon, the people of San Diego would be listening to their MP3 players, sipping their lattes, and deciding what movie to see this weekend, as they rode the trolleys to work, oblivious to the dark stain on the tracks beneath them.

Just six more blocks. Sunlight blazing. The day had come in at full force. It would probably hit eighty-five degrees Fahrenheit today. Maybe more.

Life is a puzzle to me with its moments of inexpressible joy and its seasons of heart-wrenching pain—sunlight dancing on the surface while the deadly currents roam below.

Suffering comes crashing into our lives and then washes away and we find a way to go on.

Or we don't. Some people don't.

I rounded the block.

It's a balancing act. You want tragedy to hurt, you need it to hurt, because once it stops hurting, the part of you that matters most becomes hollow and numb. Part of being human is letting life hurt.

But on the other hand, if it hurts too much, if you get caught dwelling on the meaninglessness and suffering, you can drown in it. I've seen people get jaded and I've seen them pull apart at the seams. Either extreme, you lose. I haven't figured out how to strike the balance in my own life yet, but I know this much—every time the dark currents rise to the surface, they take a little of my optimism back with them into the abyss.

Only three more blocks.

At two blocks I began to catch the scent of scorched wood.

At one block I saw a hazy layer of smoke hovering above the pavement.

It couldn't be.

I came to the corner of K Street and 15th and I froze. My skin felt clammy and cool, even as the day blazed to life around me.

Gray smoke smudged the morning, curling up from the blackened shell of a charred but still structurally intact two-story home.

The house lay directly across the street from where the homeless man had appeared last night—less than one city block from where I'd parked and tried to predict the future.

I stood staring at the smoldering ruins, trying to catch my breath, trying to process what this might mean.

If a crowd had been there earlier, it had dispersed, and instead a few tired-looking firefighters lingered by their truck. Beside them, I noticed Lien-hua and Lieutenant Aina Mendez walking toward the cooling remains of the home.

After allowing myself a brief glance at a certain section of freshly scrubbed track, I jogged over to join them.

16

Based on the amount of water soaking the home's foundation, I guessed the building had cooled sufficiently, which meant the fire had been suppressed several hours ago. And based on the limited degree of structural damage, I figured that the firefighters must have made it here almost immediately. Maybe they received a tip.

Lieutenant Mendez waved to me. "*Buenos días*, Dr. Bowers. I didn't think you would come. I couldn't get in touch with you."

I gestured to my outfit. "Went for a little jog. Left my cell at the hotel. And Lieutenant Mendez, I keep telling you my friends call me Pat."

She gave me a polite nod. "*Sí*, Dr. Bowers."

I'd first met Aina three weeks earlier when I came to San Diego for a day to do an initial assessment of the case. I liked her right away. She struck me as savvy, street smart, and, most impressive of all, open-minded. Too often detectives only look for evidence that confirms their suspicions or fits their "gut instincts." Not Aina; she trusted facts above feelings. And that makes all the difference in the world.

Though it was still early in the day, Lien-hua wore dark sunglasses. She tipped them up and eyed my soaked T-shirt. "How many did you get in?"

"A hundred forty-eight, total."

"Slipping in your old age, huh?"

"You don't know the half of it."

I asked Aina for a pair of latex gloves and snapped them on. After all, evidence is evidence, even if it's covered with soot. Then she signaled for two of the firefighters resting on the curb to lend Lien-hua and me their boots. They grudgingly obliged, and we pulled them on and followed Aina into the blackened mouth of what used to be someone's front door.

17

"Whoever started this fire," Aina said, "did so after the officers finished processing the scene of John Doe's suicide. We're guessing two a.m. as the time the first fuel was ignited."

Detective Dunn and his team must have finished up as quickly as they could to keep the trolleys on schedule. It didn't surprise me, though. It all seemed simple enough: a drug-crazed homeless guy throws himself in front of a trolley. Period. Except that the timing and location of the fire told me that things weren't as simple and clear cut as they seemed.

"Any chance the fire was accidental?" I asked Aina.

"Unlikely. You'll see when we get to the point of origin."

"Witnesses?" Lien-hua asked.

Aina led the way through the soot-stained kitchen. "No one who's talking, but that's no surprise. People in this neighborhood don't generally like talking to the police. Oh, but we did find the young man who was at the tobacco store."

"Anything?" I asked.

"He's a foreign exchange student from Korea. We spoke with him early this morning. He didn't witness the suicide and was at his apartment when the fire began. I can't see any connection. The store owner didn't see anything, either."

I nodded. "Lien-hua," I said. "Talk me through your profile. Just the highlights."

"It pains you to say that, doesn't it? To ask me for the profile?"

"More than you know."

Aina must have given her a questioning look because Lien-hua tightened her voice and explained, "Pat thinks profiling is a complete waste of time."

"Not a complete waste of time," I said. "It keeps a lot of novelists off welfare."

Lien-hua stepped on one of the boards underfoot hard enough to crack it, and I wondered if the board represented anything specific to her. Probably best not to ask.

"Well," she said. "We have no eyewitnesses, no footprints, or other incriminating physical evidence of any kind, so he's forensically aware. He's experienced, older than most arsonists. Probably midthirties. He's precise and exacting, takes pride in his work. Possibly admires news reports about the fires to his friends: 'See that fire? That guy really knows what he's doing.' Things like that. He works alone on the fires. Lives alone. Has military experience."

"Military experience?" asked Aina.

"A significant percentage of arsonists have military experience. Until I can show otherwise, I'm starting with the hypothesis that ours does too. He doesn't seem to start the fires for profit or to mask another crime. And since he doesn't stick around to watch the buildings burn, I doubt he's doing it for the thrill. He has another motive, though I'm not sure yet what it is."

"Let's not forget timing," I said. "Each of the fires, except for this fire last night, was set when the wind was less than ten miles per hour. That's rare in San Diego."

"So what changed his pattern?" Lien-hua asked.

"Well, Agent Jiang." I cracked my knuckles. "That's what I'm here to figure out."

She shook her head. "You've been watching too many cop movies."

I was trying to think of a witty reply when Aina paused at the threshold of the living room and asked, "So, how many fires have you worked?" She directed the question to both of us.

"Enough," I said.

"Not so many," replied Lien-hua. "My specialty is serial homicides."

"Well," said Aina, "a few basics. If we can identify the direction and spread of the fire, we can narrow down the most likely location of its origin." She pointed at the wall. "Heat transfers from the flame to the surface of the walls or the ceiling. The farther the flames move from the fuel package, the less heat they'll have, and the less damage they'll cause."

Lien-hua's eyes scanned the room like careful lasers. Beautifully dark, mysteriously inviting lasers. Then she pointed. "So, here, the wallpaper is scorched and peeling ..." She stepped into the room beside us, looked over the walls again. "But here, the wallpaper at that same height is gone, and the fire ate into the drywall. So, this room is probably closer to the place the fire started."

I love watching her work.

Actually, I don't mind watching her, whatever she's doing.

"*Sí,*" Aina said. "Of course, other factors can affect heat flow—the building materials, room layout, airflow, and so on, but the extent of surface damage is one of the first things we look for."

As we picked our way through the corpse of a home, it struck me how similar Aina's job is to mine. Both of us evaluate the evidence, study the way something moves through space and time, and then use what we know about patterns to pinpoint the point of origin. She studies the flow and movement of smoke and flames; I study the flow and movement of people. But the principle is still the same. The secret to solving a case boils down to timing and location.

I heard a ring tone. Aina glanced down, tugged her phone off her belt. "Excuse me. I need to take this. You two look around. I'll be back in a minute."

Lien-hua and I stepped carefully past some blackened boards. Nearly all of the structural supports and door-frames were still in place, but most of them were at least partially charred by the blaze. I directed Lien-hua's attention to the ceiling on both sides of a doorframe. "See how only one side is covered with soot?"

She walked back and forth beneath the doorjamb, examining the ceiling on each side. "Yes."

"Buoyant gases move though the air similar to the way water flows down a river," I said. "When water meets a rock, it passes around the rock, and then some of the water curls back toward the rock."

"You sound like an ex–raft guide."

"Guilty as charged."

"It's called an eddy, right?"

I nodded. "Sometimes the eddies are so strong the water actually flows back upstream. That's what happens when hot gases pass through a building. As the gas passes through a doorway, some of it curls back toward the ceiling, creating an eddy of air that doesn't consume the wood but leaves a sooty residue. By identifying these eddies, we can work backward through a structure—"

"To find the source of the fire."

"Right."

We passed through several more rooms, Lien-hua carefully observing the eddies above the doorjambs, working with surprising acuity to lead us to a room at the back of the house. From the evidence I'd seen so far, I agreed that this room was probably the source of the blaze. "Not bad for a profiler," I said.

"Yeah, well, this environmental stuff isn't that complex. Maybe I should write a novel about it."

"Touché."

The electricity in the house was off, but enough sunlight cut through the window for us to see around the room. I noted that the glass in the window frames was still intact.

With an exacting gaze, Lien-hua traced a line up the wall toward the ceiling. "These marks, here—what do they mean?"

"The fire plume made those. Usually, when you find them, they indicate proximity to the point of origin."

I heard Aina's footsteps by the doorway. "Very good, Dr. Bowers," she said. "When a fire is started against a wall, the wall does two things: it reflects heat and doesn't allow the cooler air to escape the blaze. This creates a taller flame than a similar fire with the same heat release rate located in the middle of a room. In corners, the effect is increased, creating an even higher fire plume. And see how the floor directly beneath the plume is consumed? That's where he put the accelerant."

I examined the room. "But this room isn't extensively damaged, never reached full involvement. Not like the point of origin for the other fires."

"That's because he used a different accelerant this time, probably gasoline."

Lien-hua looked confused. "How can you tell?"

"Gasoline flares up, burns very rapidly," Aina said. "It devours all the oxygen in the room before the rest of the materials in the room become hot enough to ignite. It's a sloppy, beginner's way to start a fire. In the movies, arsonists slosh gasoline around, toss in a cigarette, and *voom*! But that's not how the professionals do it. To start an effective fire, you need a fuel package that'll burn longer."

"Lien-hua," I said, "are you sure our arsonist is working alone?"

"Not certain," she said. "But up until now, that's where everything has pointed."

"Do we know anything about the accelerants for the other fires yet?" I asked Aina.

She shook her head. "Not yet. Chromatograms were inconclusive. We're tracking purchases of acetone and methylated spirits in the days prior to each fire, but so far, nothing solid."

I scanned the room. Out the window, I had a direct sight line to the street corner that John Doe had rounded before he jumped onto the hood of my rental car. I gazed at the fire's point of origin again. "The fire's placement in the room isn't right either," I said. "On the flight from Denver, I looked over the building diagrams that you sent me, Aina—the ones from the other fires—and our arsonist likes to use vents, stairwells, windows, the natural airflow through a building, to keep feeding his fires oxygen. But the guy last night, he started the fire along an exterior wall, with no consideration of airflow." I pointed. "He didn't even open the window. Taking into account the change in accelerant and inefficient point of origin—"

"It's not the same guy," Lien-hua said.

"That's what I've been thinking too," said Aina.

The evidence at this scene certainly seemed to point to a different offender, but I wasn't convinced. "And yet this home's location makes perfect sense in relationship to the other fires. That's what's got me. If it wasn't him, how did the guy last night know to start the fire on this street?"

"Coincidence?" Aina said.

"I don't believe in coincidences," I said.

She tapped at her phone. "I really have to go. We found the person who called in the fire. I'd like to speak to her. I'll get back in touch with you."

Lien-hua and I nodded, Aina left, and for a few minutes Lien-hua and I looked around the room. Finally, I said, "I'm really stumped here. We have the right kind of crime, the right location, and timing that fits the escalating progression of the series, fourteen fires by the same guy, and now, suddenly, a different arsonist shows up?"

"It doesn't fit, does it?"

"No. Either that, or I'm missing a big piece of the puzzle."

"OK. Let's walk through it," she suggested. "Reconstruct what happened."

"Good," I said. "Based on what we know, there're two arsonists, so for now let's just say it's the two of us."

"OK," she said. "It's just the two of us."

The way she said those words gave me pause. I wanted to ask her something, wasn't sure how to phrase it. "Wait," I said. "Before we start. There was something you wanted to tell me last night. Outside Tessa's door."

"Now's not the time, Pat," she said.

"Is it Tessa? Is something wrong?"

"No, no, no. Nothing like that. I just need to sort some things through. I shouldn't have said anything. Let's just forget it, OK?"

I wanted to press her, get her to tell me more, but knew it would only make her less willing to open up. "OK," I said. "Fair enough."

Then it was back to business. "Now," she said. "Let's reconstruct this crime."

18

Lien-hua mimed splashing gasoline across the floor, then lighting it. "So we're inexperienced, we don't know what we're doing. We start the fire, then what? Maybe wait a few minutes to make sure it's burning?"

"Yes, I think so."

"Then where do we go? How do we get out?"

I studied the room. "Well, we don't want to get caught . . . You can see the front door too easily from the intersection and from the tobacco store across the street. The front would be too risky."

"So, we head for the back door." Lien-hua led the way through the house. Really, the home was small enough so that only one route made sense. As I followed her, I carefully examined the blackened floor to see if the offender had left any shoe prints or impressions in the soot, but there were at least six different tread mark patterns visible, in addition to the ones that matched the boots I'd borrowed. The prints must have been left by the firefighters or the MAST officers who'd processed the scene. It would take a lot of checking to figure out if one of the shoe prints didn't really belong. I gazed at them carefully.

"What about the gas can?" I said. "Would we leave it here or take it with us?"

"We're new to arson, so we might not have thought about that before starting the fire . . . Or maybe we're careless and we tossed it outside . . . Of course, we might have used a plastic canister and then tossed it onto the fire . . . Or we might have—"

"I guess we're not ready for that question yet," I said. "Too many mights. We need more evidence—"

"And less conjecture," she said, finishing my thought.

"Oh. Have I said that before?"

"Once or twice."

With my gloved hand, I eased the back door open and noticed the yellow crime scene tape hanging limp in the breezeless morning, encircling the house's property at about a four-meter perimeter.

Lien-hua must have seen me staring at the location of the yellow tape, because she said, "Aina told me her criminalists already processed the scene, everything inside the tape. Didn't find anything."

Most law enforcement agencies use the terms "crime scene investigative unit," or "forensic science technician," but some places, and especially overseas, the term "criminalist" is more common. Either way, I'm usually amazed not by how much evidence the teams notice but by how much they miss.

"Did they check outside the tape?" I asked.

"Outside it?"

I pointed at the yellow police tape. "Don't you find it a little too convenient that the crime scene just happens to be exactly the same size as the area encompassed by these telephone poles?"

"They were handy."

"Yes, they were. But a crime scene is defined by the evidentiary nature of the crime and the physical characteristics of the site itself, not the location of the nearest telephone poles." Oops. I'd started lecturing. I needed to watch that.

"Good point."

I peered beyond the caution tape to see if our inexperienced arsonist might have dropped the gas can on the hill. "You'd be amazed how many times I've found a murder weapon only a few meters outside of the police tape. But people rarely think to look there because it's not part of 'the crime scene.'"

She joined me beyond the tape, on the dusty hill that climbed at a slow slope away from the house. "So the tape actually hinders the investigation," she said thoughtfully.

"We don't see the evidence because we're looking in the wrong place. It's a blind spot."

A blind spot.

Yes.

"Lien-hua, if we were the arsonists, where did we park?"

She pointed. "Other side of that hill?"

I jogged to the top. My mind was spinning. "Poor access. Too many streetlights, too much traffic. And we didn't park to the west of the house over there, since that home is too close—the porch is only ten or twelve meters away. So, maybe we parked in the alley off to the east."

"Or maybe not." Her words caught my attention, and I saw that she was pointing to a pair of black leather gloves strewn about fifteen meters away, beside a worn footpath that led over another small hill.

I joined her beside the gloves. I didn't have an evidence bag with me, but I leaned close to the gloves. Sniffed. "Gasoline," I said.

"Take off your gloves," she said.

"Why?"

"Humor me. Take them off, toss them to the ground."

As I removed the latex gloves, Lien-hua watched me thoughtfully. When both gloves were on the ground, she said, "So he pulls one glove off, then the other one, just like you did. And see how one of your gloves landed on each side of you? It's natural. So he was on the trail here, between the leather gloves, heading north."

"Good work," I said. Then I thought through the way I'd taken the gloves off. "And it also means he touched the outside of the second glove with the fingertip and thumb of an ungloved hand as he pulled it off. If his hands were sweaty enough from wearing gloves or from the heat of the fire—"

"We might have some prints."

"Call it in," I said. "Let's have Aina get the criminalists back out here."

Lien-hua pulled out her cell, and while she spoke with Aina, I followed the footpath over the hill and found that it ended in a long, scraggly, brush-covered ravine. I was gazing across the ravine when Lien-hua rejoined me. "I hope," she said apprehensively, "that you're not thinking about searching all of that."

I shook my head. "We'd need more eyes. We'll let Aina's team work the ravine."

I froze.

More eyes. A blind spot.

We're looking in the wrong place.

I was starting to feel the juices flow. "Lien-hua, what's different about this crime?"

"The offender. The accelerant."

"Yes, but not the location. It fits. So our serial arsonist didn't start the fire last night."

She seemed surprised I was repeating what we'd already hypothesized. "That's our working theory, yes."

Facts, facts locking together. "Because someone else did."

"What are you thinking, Pat? Where are you going with this?"

"Somehow the crimes are connected. If we can find the guy from last night, he might be able to lead us to the arsonist from the other fires. It's like you said, we're looking in the wrong place . . . What are some of the reasons crimes that are started aren't completed?"

"Well, victim resistance, law enforcement activity, natural interruptions. I don't see where you're—"

"Right." I turned toward the house. "Natural interruptions."

She hurried to catch up to me. She was smart and I knew she'd catch on. "So," she said, "you think maybe the serial arsonist was interrupted by John Doe's suicide?"

"Yes. And then someone else came to finish the job." I was jogging down the hill by then. "I need to check on something."

Yes, yes, yes.

Exits and entrances.

"Pat?" She was following me. "Is everything OK?"

"No, it's not," I said. "The bowl is in the way."

"What are you talking about?"

I ran around to the front of the house. "Do you have your computer with you?"

"No. It's at the hotel. What's gotten into—"

"We need to go." My mind was clicking, pieces falling

into place. I threw off the borrowed boots, grabbed my shoes. "Now."

"Pat, what did you see?" She caught up to me. Put her shoes on. "Did the guy leave something else behind?"

"Yes."

She unlocked her car and we jumped inside. "What's that?"

"A map."

19

As gentle and soft-spoken as Lien-hua is, when she's in a hurry she drives like Jackie Chan on caffeine.

But I have to say, I like it.

As long as the car has air bags.

We flew around a corner, and I put my hand on the dash to avoid slamming into the door.

"You need to explain yourself," she said. "What do you mean he left a map? And why do we need to hurry?"

"Do you have a notepad?"

"There should be one on the backseat."

I snagged her legal pad and started calculating as many of the geographic profiling algorithms as I could freehand, but algebraic equations never were my specialty. I really needed my computer.

"So, why the big hurry?"

"Because I'm not as smart as I pretend to be. I need my computer before I lose my train of thought. I think I might be able to get us a picture of the original arsonist."

"How? What's going on?"

"The bowl is in the way."

"Why do you keep saying that? What does it mean?"

"You're familiar with cognitive mapping, right?"

"Sure. It's how people envision their environment. Everyone creates mental pictures of the roads they take, the routes they travel, estimated distances between points on the map. Things like that."

"Right, but the mental maps are distorted by—"

"Barriers and familiarity. Yes, I know. Attitudes, past experience, and comfort with different locations all skew our perceptions of distance and space. And we overestimate the distance between two points when natural and man-made barriers appear—things like rivers, mountains, bridges, malls."

"Wow. I couldn't have said it better myself."

"I know. I was paraphrasing from your book. Your word choice was a little too stilted. I had to change it."

I cleared my throat slightly. "My point is that we all create cognitive maps without even being aware of it, even those of us who are serial arsonists. And sports stadiums are large mental barriers. So, because of the proximity to the fires, Petco Park would change the way the arsonist views the city in his mind and change the dynamics of the geo profile."

"So is that the bowl?"

"The big salad bowl, yes. You see, they were serving pork tenderloin with mangoes and pineapple and I had to order two salads—never mind, it's a long story. Can we go any faster?"

"Not without filing a flight plan. How are you going to get us a picture of the arsonist?"

"I'll get to that. Listen, as soon as you drop me off, I need you to call Aina, see if she can meet us. If not, ask her for the access codes for the videos taken at the depots for all of the city's mass transit stations." We were pulling into the hotel parking lot. "Got it?"

"Yes."

"I'll need to search their databases, not just view the live footage."

Lien-hua braked at the entrance to the hotel. "OK, but I'm not sure I understand—"

"I'll meet you in my room as soon as you're done parking." I jumped out of the car.

Then, carrying her legal pad, I hurried to the elevators, hoping I'd be able to decipher my scribbled notes and formulas when I finally got my computer in front of me.

Acquiring Cassandra had been easier than Creighton expected. She'd barely struggled at all. And, once they arrived at the warehouse and she'd regained consciousness, she'd been a model subject.

Yes. The last couple hours had been very productive.

Creighton almost had enough footage to finish the video.

Then all he had to do was wrap up the editing and make the phone call that would put everything into play.

He could hardly wait.

The anticipation of her coming death, and his own, made his fingers quiver with excitement.

20

In my hotel room, I pulled up the computer files I'd been working on yesterday morning when I'd started comparing the geographical and demographic data with the timing and progression of the fires.

I'd been on the right track, just on the wrong, well . . . track.

I was typing in my scribbles when Lien-hua tapped at the door.

"It's open," I called.

"Aina can't come." Lien-hua had her computer with her. She sat on the edge of the bed and flipped her laptop open. "The nine-one-one caller was a dead end, but she's busy evaluating potential ignition systems from the previous fires. She gave me the codes."

"Good. Give me a minute. Then I'll need them." I clicked on one of the icons on my screen, and a map appeared with each of the arson sites marked by a small flickering flame. "See the placement of the fires?" I punched a couple of keys, and a series of red lines laced the city, highlighting the streets and highways of San Diego. I traced one with my finger. "Roads."

"Oh. Is that what they are?"

"Sorry. I'll try to stop stating the obvious." I tipped the screen so she could see it. "Now, if you look at the distribution of the fires, what do you notice?"

She studied the map carefully but shook her head. "Nothing."

"Neither did I, until . . ." I uploaded the trolley routes and overlaid them against the map of the fire locations. A couple more keystrokes, and my computer-mapping pro-gram calculated the distances between the fires and the nearest trolley depots and flashed the totals in the lower left-hand corner of the screen. "See? The fires all occur within two hundred meters of a trolley stop, usually the Orange Line or the Blue Line."

She gave a soft gasp of acknowledgment. "He's starting the fires and then boarding the trolleys to get away."

"I think so. Let's check the timing. Look up the trol-ley schedule for me, and I'll compare it to the times of the fires."

She surfed to the San Diego mass transit site and read off the trolley arrival and departure times, and I punched them in. Hit enter.

A crisscross of lines appeared along with a detailed tim-ing chart on the right-hand side of the screen.

"It fits," I said.

She gave a long, soft whistle. "So, except for last night's fire, each of the other fires was reported between five min-utes prior to a scheduled trolley departure or eight minutes after the trolley left. How long would it take to walk two hundred meters?" she asked.

"I don't know. Maybe three to five minutes. We also need to factor in the time it takes for the fire to grow, get noticed, and be reported. We can have some officers walk the distances to confirm the timing. But it looks like he didn't park. He rode."

"So, if that's how he's getting away . . ." Then it struck her. "Access codes."

"Right," I said. "Every trolley depot is monitored by video surveillance. Let's see how photogenic our arson-ist is."

21

I surfed to the city's mass transit DVA, the Digital Video Archives, and logged in with the access codes Lien-hua had gotten from Aina. I was annoyed to find that the older footage had been deleted, so only the last six months were available. That left us with only eight fires, and I wasn't sure if it would be enough, but I downloaded the footage from the trolley depots that correlated to the time and location of those eight fires to give it a try. "This gives me a good chance to try one of the new toys Terry's designing," I said. "You know him, right? Terry Manoji? My buddy from the NSA?"

"We've met," she said coolly.

"You don't like him?"

"He hit on me at a conference once. Told me I reminded him of someone, striking resemblance. Not something you tell a girl."

"At least he has good taste."

She didn't smile.

"Don't worry. He told me he's seeing someone. I haven't met her yet, a woman from the West Coast. Anyway, he sent me this new program he's designing. Watch this. It's called CIFER."

"What does that stand for?"

"Characteristic Inventory for Focused Evaluative Recognition."

She shook her head. "The government could save millions each year by not spending so much time coming up with acronyms."

I opened the program and pulled up the file menu. Lien-hua didn't seem too impressed. "It looks like a facial recognition program."

"More like identity recognition." I was getting juiced. It felt good to be cranking forward on a case. All I wanted to do was find this guy and then I could spend some quality time with Tessa.

And maybe a little with Lien-hua.

Who knows.

"This program combines facial structure and characteristics, just like traditional facial recognition software, but also evaluates height, weight, pace, posture, nonverbal communication, and spatial movement patterns. Even voice recognition, if we have audio. Plus it amplifies Sagnac interference to block GPS tracking of the user's location. It's for field ops, just in the testing stages right now. This is the only other copy, but from what I've seen so far—"

My computer beeped and displayed seven faces in separate panels across the screen.

However, none of them looked anything like each other.

One man appeared to be a transient, another a business executive, the third, a jeans-clad man with a prominent beer gut, and the four other men all looked unique as well. Beard, no beard. Wavy flaxen hair, then black. All were similar height, but that was about it.

"Strike one," Lien-hua said. "It's a different person each time."

"I . . . I don't understand," I mumbled.

"Maybe the program isn't all it's cracked up to be."

Or maybe I'd improperly weighted the importance of some of the signifying trait values. "Wait, let me try something." I tapped at the keyboard and brought up the similarity index, altered the values.

The same men appeared.

I glanced at the legal pad, then typed in a few default changes to CIFER's index, and punched enter.

Still the same men.

I was ready to scrap the whole idea, but then I noticed something. "Hang on, Lien-hua." I punched a button, and the videos began to play in slow motion, the time counter flashing at the bottom of each image. "There."

She studied the screen. "What?"

I hit "pause," then "play" again. "Look."

"What is it?"

"Just a sec." I adjusted the sharpness and saturation of the pictures to make them less grainy, rewound to the beginning, and hit "play" again. She still looked confused.

"Do you want me to play it in—"

"Wait." She studied the videos carefully. "I got it. Disguises, right?"

"Yes."

"And pedal supination with his left foot?" she said.

"I think that's what it's called . . . when he rolls his foot outward after each step?"

"Yes," she replied. "That's supination. When your foot rolls inward, it's called pronation." And then she added, "I pronate."

"I won't tell anyone. I promise."

"How kind." She reached across my lap and hit "enter" to play the videos again. "Yes," she said. "His is very pronounced. Maybe from an old injury. A broken ankle, something like that."

"Wait. Hang on." I pointed to one of the videos on the bottom of the screen. "This guy is limping on his left, this guy isn't."

"You can fake a limp," she said, "but you can't fake the way your foot turns when you lift it after taking a step, or maybe you could, but almost no one would think of doing it." Lien-hua shook her head. "Whew. It may surprise you, but I'm actually tracking with all this. But I have to say, you're telling me your computer thinks it's the same guy because of the way his foot turns when he walks?"

"The way he walks, the spatial relationships with the other people at the depots, arrival times compared to the distance of the depots from the fires, facial similarities, arm length, bone structure—"

"OK, I get it."

"So," I said. "We need to find a guy who broke his left ankle, likes to wear disguises, and lives"—I pointed to the hot zone—"within this ten-block radius."

"I'm not sure that narrows it down much, Pat. That's got to be at least eight thousand—"

"Military experience," I mumbled. "You said he's got military experience, right?"

"Yes. But this is San Diego, half the people in the city are employed by the navy or work as subcontractors for the Department of Defense."

"But how many of them are professionals at burning down buildings?"

Suddenly, she saw where I was going. "Explosive ordnance training," she said.

"Yes. Coronado Island. Home of the Navy SEAL Amphibious Training Base, the only place on the West Coast where the government actually trains people to blow stuff up and burn things down and then get away undetected. I'm wondering if our guy might be a Navy SEAL."

Video editing always takes longer than you expect, and with the sunlight piercing through the windows, it created more glare than usual.

Plus, Creighton's computer had crashed once before he'd saved some of his changes. All of that had set him behind, but he was pretty sure he could still get the video edited in time.

Just a few more minor tweaks and it would be ready to send to Austin Hunter, former arsonist, future terrorist.

22

Lien-hua called the Amphib Base, and, after they'd verified her clearance codes, they transferred her to Leslie Helprin, a Petty Officer 2nd Class who worked with the medical records division. It turned out Petty Officer Helprin was good at her job. It only took her a few minutes to locate the records of all Navy SEALs who'd been trained in incendiary diversionary tactics and had been treated for an ankle or leg injury on the left leg over the past five years.

I typed while Lien-hua relayed information to me from the phone. "We have twelve names, Pat. Ten men, two women. Plus a SEAL who left the service last year, honorable discharge."

"Well, our arsonist isn't a woman," I said.

"How do you know?"

"Posture. Frame. Weight distribution in his stride. So that gives us ten, eleven if you count the guy who left last year. Have Petty Officer Helprin e-mail me the photos from their personnel files. Let's see if they match any of the faces on our videos."

Lien-hua spoke into the phone again and then shook her head. "No good. They don't have photos on file."

"How could they not have photos?"

Lien-hua relayed the question, then gave me Petty Officer Helprin's answer. "Not in the medical files, just the personnel files. But that's a whole different division."

Of course it was. Typical military bureaucracy.

Our guy was into disguises anyhow. "OK, forget that for now. We can follow up on that later. See if she can get us the— Wait a minute. One of them left the service last year?"

"Yes."

"When?"

Lien-hua passed the question along and then said, "February."

"The fires started in April. Do they have an address? Maybe somewhere they're sending his commission checks?"

Lien-hua scribbled down a street address and showed it to me. I zoomed the computer in on the street.

The man lived only two blocks outside of the hot zone.

And his name was Austin Hunter.

Creighton Melice attached the video of Cassandra Lillo to the e-mail message he'd prepared for Austin Hunter and pressed "send."

Overall, Creighton thought he did an amazing job on the piece, but he doubted Hunter would appreciate the time he'd spent to get it right. Creighton opened the door that led to the main section of the warehouse to check on Cassandra. No change. She was secure.

She wasn't going anywhere.

Then he went back to wait for confirmation that the e-mail had gone through. While he waited, he sharpened the narrow six-inch-long metal shiv. It would need to be sharp—very sharp—in case Shade told him to switch to Plan B.

23

I needed to confirm some of my suspicions before calling Aina.

We tracked down the navy's human services division and they e-mailed both Lien-hua and me a copy of Austin Hunter's personnel files and military service records. We each pulled them up on our own computers so we could examine them at the same time.

"So," I said. "Served for fourteen years—missions in Ecuador, South Africa, Afghanistan, even two excursions into North Korea. Diversionary tactics. Covert surveillance. Spent two years as a SERE instructor: survival, evasion, rescue, and escape. This guy is the real deal. But then, on a training exercise, he fractures his left fibula and—"

"Look at this." Lien-hua pointed to the screen. "Paragraph 3-ba. The navy covered the cost of his surgery and physical therapy, but after he recovered, they pulled him out of SEAL Team 3 and gave him administrative duty."

I shook my head. "The guy was one of the most highly trained, elite fighters in the world, and they stick him in a cubicle to send faxes and transfer phone calls. They must have known he would resign as soon as his commission was up."

"Which he did." She was reading right along with me. "I guess the navy doesn't want to worry about a SEAL's old leg injury slowing him down on a covert op somewhere. And, of course, after his honorable discharge, he was no longer their problem. Since he didn't complete twenty years of service—no retirement."

"And since his leg injury wasn't a permanent disability—

no medical coverage, either," I said. "So after spending his entire adult life as a SEAL, he leaves the special forces with nothing except for a set of nontransferable skills. I mean, what kind of job do you get after that? Night watchman? Maybe a bodyguard? Private investigator maybe?"

Lien-hua had set her computer to the side and stared introspectively out the sliding glass doors of the hotel room. "Not a guy with his service record."

"Mercenary?" I said. "Or maybe work for a private security firm in the Middle East? At least then you can still blow up buildings and shoot wicked-cool guns without anyone asking a whole lot of irritating questions."

"Did you just say wicked-cool?"

"I heard Tessa say it one time." Then I remembered what Tessa had said to me the night before: *It feels good. It's what you do. It's what you like.* "Or maybe," I said to Lien-hua, "you just start burning down civilian buildings, because it's who you are and you can't turn it off."

We called Aina and gave her an update on everything we'd discovered. All the evidence so far was circumstantial, but at least it was a place to start. "We'll send a car over to Hunter's place," Aina said. "Have a talk with him. Good work."

"Great," I said. "Let us know what you find out."

After we ended the call, I took a deep breath. "Well, it looks like we can take a little break."

"Good," she said. "Because you need a shower. And I need to get out of these smoky clothes."

"All right. I'm supposed to meet Tessa at ten o'clock downstairs for brunch. Why don't you join us? Maybe we'll have heard something about Hunter by then."

She accepted the invitation, left to change clothes, and I headed to the shower.

But instead of relaxing, I kept wondering what Hunter's connection might be to the guy who started the fire last night—or if it was really a different arsonist after all.

Creighton checked his watch again.

Nine a.m.

OK, that should be enough time.

He picked up his phone and dialed Austin Hunter's mobile number. Shade had found a way to route the call so it would appear to Hunter that it was coming from Cassandra's cell, so he was confident Hunter would answer.

A man picked up. "Cassandra? Where are you? You were supposed to meet—"

"It's not Cassandra." Creighton didn't bother masking his voice. It wouldn't matter in the end.

"Who the—?"

"Listen to me carefully—"

"Where's Cassandra? Tell me—"

"Interrupt me again and I guarantee you'll be sorry."

"You work for Drake, don't you? That's what this is about?"

"We're getting to that." Creighton made note of the name—Drake. *Could that be Shade?* Maybe. He could look into all that later, but for now, he needed to stick to the script. "Listen to me, Austin. You were supposed to meet Cassandra Lillo for breakfast three hours ago, but she didn't show up. You waited thirty-five minutes before leaving Cabrillo's—"

"Where is she? I swear to God—"

"Don't blaspheme. I get impatient when people blaspheme. And when I get impatient, bad things happen. Check your e-mail. I'm guessing you have your computer with you?"

Creighton waited as Austin Hunter fumbled around with his laptop. He heard the corny little tune as it booted up, and then the chime announcing that the e-mail had arrived. "Play the video, Austin."

Creighton waited. The video was one minute and fifty-two seconds long. He watched the time tick by on his watch. At about forty seconds he heard a gasp. At one minute, Hunter exclaimed, "Oh, my God—"

"I warned you about blasphemy once. I won't warn you again." Creighton waited until he was sure the video was over, especially the last ten seconds. "Now, listen to me very carefully—"

"You're messing with the wrong man. As soon as I find you—"

"I said *listen*. All this interrupting is making me impatient."

Another pause. "Let me talk to her. I want to know she's alive."

Creighton had expected that request. He passed through the door, walked to where he was keeping Cassandra, and held the phone up to the glass. "Austin wants to talk to you," he called.

"Austin?" Her voice was muffled but audible. She was sobbing.

"Cassandra, where are you?"

"Please." She struggled to spit out the words. "Please, Austin. He's going to kill me—"

"Cassandra!"

Creighton retraced his steps to the manager's office of the warehouse while Cassandra continued to cry out; then he closed the door and cut her off. "Actually, I said I was going to kill her *slowly*. She forgot that last part."

"Where is she? Tell me where she is, you freakin'—" This time Austin cut himself off in midcurse. He must have realized he was making the man on the other side of the phone upset.

Good. That meant he was finally ready to hear the conditions.

"Austin, do you know the etymology of the word *deadline*? It's very fascinating. Before it came to mean 'the time before which something must be completed,' it meant 'the line over which you must not pass.'" Creighton would never have phrased things like this. He would have been a lot more blunt. But for now he wanted to stay on Shade's good side, and since he figured somehow he'd be listening, Creighton recited Shade's script word for word. "In a Civil War prison, the 'dead line' was a boundary line that you were not allowed to cross, and if you did, you'd be shot on the spot. No one who passed the dead line would survive. Are you following where this is going?"

"What do you want from me? Why are you doing this? Is it because of last night?" The change in tone told Creighton that Mr. Hunter was becoming a much better listener.

"If you do what I ask of you by eight o'clock this evening, you'll see Cassandra again. Now, take a good look at that video. If you go to the cops, the FBI, anyone, you can guess what's going to happen to her. So, eight o'clock is your deadline as well as Cassandra's. And do you understand how, in our case, we'll be drawing from both the original and the contemporary meanings of the word?"

Silence.

"We'll be watching you. We'll know if you try anything. Got it?"

"Yes." No fear in his voice. Just resolve. "What do you want me to do?"

And then, Creighton told him everything Shade had written down. Since the directions were specific and included rendezvous times and locations, it took a few minutes. Hunter listened quietly the whole time and finally, when Creighton was finished, Hunter said, "OK, I'll do it. But it can't be done by eight o'clock. Not enough time. I need to do recon, surveillance, I may need explosives ... That's on a secure military—"

"It's enough time. You'll find a way."

"I'm telling you—"

"OK, then," Creighton said sternly, "she dies right now." He threw the door open. "I'll hold the phone up nice and close so you can hear her screams."

"No!" cried Cassandra.

Creighton approached her. "And I'll make it last a long time—"

"No, please!" she yelled.

"OK—" said Austin.

"And I'll send you the video when it's over—"

"OK! OK. Listen. I'll do it, all right? Just leave her alone. Promise me you'll leave her alone."

"Here's my promise—you do what you're told by eight o'clock tonight or I kill Cassandra Lillo and record every second of her suffering and then post it on the Internet for the whole world to see." Then Creighton slapped the phone shut and returned to the warehouse manager's office.

He would still make the video of her death either way, of course, but Hunter didn't need to know that.

Yes. Things were going to work out.

He set down the phone and stared at the door. Cassandra was just on the other side. He couldn't think of any good reason to leave her in there all alone.

No good reason at all.

And so Creighton Melice went to spend some quality time with Austin Hunter's girlfriend while the countdown to her death officially began.

24

Tessa rolled over in the hotel's supposedly comfortable bed.

Yeah, right.

She'd hardly slept at all since Agent Jiang left last night. And that was a whole-nother-story—the whole deal with Patrick and Special Agent Lien-hua Jiang. Tessa didn't know exactly what was going on between them, but she was pretty sure she didn't like it.

Sunlight blazed through the slit between the curtains. Tessa groaned and wrapped a pillow around her face, rolled over, tried to go back to sleep.

Failed.

She tried for a few more minutes, but it was no use.

Finally, she sighed, flopped out of bed, rubbed a hand across her face, and shuffled to the bathroom. A complete zombie.

Open the shower curtain.

Water on.

Crank the dial.

Tessa liked her showers hot. Very hot. Ever since she was a kid and she and her mom lived in Minnesota for two years. Maybe that's what did it—the cold winters and the frozen lakes that her mom was always warning her against walking across. That, or the long, bitterly cold nights when the wind sliced through the cracks beneath her bedroom window. Who knows?

While Tessa waited for the water to warm up, she took off the necklace Patrick had given her for her birthday and shed her clothes. As she did, it struck her once again that nearly every one of her friends had at least one tattoo, but that she didn't have any. It was kind of weird, really, that she hadn't gotten inked yet.

Maybe on this trip. It might be kind of cool to return to Denver with a tattoo from Southern California.

She splashed her hand under the faucet. Ouch.

OK, not that hot.

Tessa dimmed the scalding water back a few degrees and stepped into the shower. For a few minutes she just stood there without moving, letting the water wake her up gently. It felt really good. She took a few deep breaths, relaxed, and smoothed some shower gel across her shoulders and then down her arm and over the series of straight ridges on the inside of her right forearm.

She'd given these scars to herself with an X-Acto knife and a razor blade during the last year, trying to find a way to let out some of the pain and sadness after her mom died. The blood always grossed her out, but the cutting seemed to help. At least a little.

But ever since October when this psycho serial killer guy who called himself the Illusionist had tried to kill her, all the other stuff in her life hadn't seemed quite as bad. So, lately, over the last couple of months, she'd stopped cutting—mostly. She guessed that Patrick knew she still self-inflicted sometimes, but he didn't make a huge deal out of it—which was cool because if he had, she probably would have done it more.

And of course, on the inside of her left arm, she had the scar the Illusionist gave her. That scar bothered her because it brought back memories of that day.

She'd rubbed tons of lotion on it every day, just like the physical therapist had told her to. It was supposed to help the scar go away, but it didn't work. The scar was still there, and so were the memories.

Warm water poured over Tessa's head. She lathered shampoo through her hair and let the water rinse out, leaving her hair dripping in straight, black tendrils along the back of her neck.

Memories. Memories.

Of the killer pressing the cloth against her mouth before she could even scream . . .

Of lying tied up as he drove her toward whatever kind of twisted psycho lair he'd built in the mountains . . .

She ran her fingers through her hair. Time for the conditioner.

Memories.

It all came back to her, then, in a rush. The quiver of hope when she was finally able to cut herself free, and then the satisfaction of jabbing the scissors into the guy's thigh, and then the confusion as the world outside the windshield started spinning, skidding, and everything was turning at the wrong speed in a smooth wide circle as he lost control and they headed for the cliff.

Snow.

It was snowing that day.

Death and ice and space reaching for her.

Now she was in the shower, a spray of hot water cascading over her head.

Now she was spinning toward the edge of the world, a twirl of snow falling all around her.

In the bathroom.

The front seat.

Standing. Falling. Waking. Dreaming.

Back in the shower, a blanket of steam enfolding her.

Back at the cliff, feeling the impact as they punched through the guardrail. And then she was dropping, plunging into the bottomless day, the snow swallowing everything in the world.

Falling.

And then.

An abrupt smack. Slamming into that tree halfway down the gorge. A strange moment when time stopped to catch its breath, to feel out what it would be like to inch forward again.

Groans next to her. The Illusionist smiling a dark smile, yanking the scissors out of his leg. And then.

Then.

Patrick's voice floating down to her.

That's when the killer cut her, sliced her arm. And she was bleeding. Bleeding. Fading, watching the melting snow slide down the cracked windshield. The day was crying for her. And she was wrapped in a nightmare, slipping away. Falling again, but in a different way. Falling toward forever.

But Patrick came for her.

He came for her and he saved her. Like a father would, like a hero would, he risked his life to rescue her. Rappelling down, reaching out, catching her just in time.

She'd never thought of him in those terms before that day. As a father. As a hero. But it was true. He cared about her and she cared about him and they were a family. Kind of weird. Kind of screwed up, but still a family.

But it was confusing.

Sometimes she felt like a little girl who wanted to hold his hand, to call him Daddy; sometimes she felt like a young woman getting ready to move out and live on her own.

Caught between two worlds. Drifting. Falling.

Tessa turned off the water and stood still in the warm steam, letting the water drip off her body, her memories, her scars. After a moment she stepped out of the shower stall and wrapped a thick towel around herself.

And then there was that whole bizarre thing last night. That crazy homeless guy had actually killed himself right there, just like that, and if she hadn't covered her eyes, she would have seen him die.

Falling headlong.

Falling and dying.

Tessa caught sight of her outline in the mirror, a faint reflection, distant and blurred, surrounded by steam and dreams. For a moment it hardly looked real. Just the vague shape of a girl with dripping black hair, faceless, emotionless, obscure around the edges. In a fog. Her reflection reminded her of looking at a phantom.

An Eidolon, she thought, remembering the phrase from Edgar Allan Poe's poem "Dream-Land": *Where an Eidolon, named* NIGHT, *On a black throne reigns upright . . .*

Poe really seemed to understand the landscape of pain, and she'd walked through it with him since her mom died, reading his poems and stories over and over, letting their stark images soak into her—the raven and the pit and the cask and the thumping heart. Usually after reading something once or twice, she could remember it pretty well, but she remembered some stanzas of "Dream-Land," word for word.

There the traveller meets, aghast,
Sheeted Memories of the Past—
Shrouded forms that start and sigh
As they pass the wanderer by—
White-robed forms of friends long given,
In agony, to the Earth—and Heaven.

Her reflection.

A ghost in the slim shape of her mother.

Sheeted memories of the past.

A phantom lurking in the land of dreams.

Tessa spread her fingers against the mirror. It felt warm against her fingertips, but cool too. She slid her hand across the glass, and her eyes and forehead became visible. But just that much. The rest of her still remained a ghost, wrapped in white, lost somewhere in the misty curls of thick, warm steam.

Caught between two worlds. Drifting. Falling.

A raven unable to fly.

And then Tessa snapped the rubber band against her wrist and did it again and again until the skin was red and raw.

But it didn't help her feel better at all.

And the drops of water began to trickle down the mirror, as if her reflection were weeping to see her standing so sad and alone on the other side of the glass.

25

As I sat in the hotel lobby and waited for Tessa, I thought about the man's death the night before. I'd told Detective Dunn I was going to untangle the circumstances surrounding John Doe's death. I intended to keep my promise.

Using my cell phone's Internet browser, I logged onto the city's digital video archives and reviewed the videos of the trolley's departure, but found no images of men with black duffel bags boarding the trolley. *So, the two men who climbed into the Ford Mustang were already at the scene when John Doe committed suicide.*

I put a call in to the Bureau to run the plates on the Mustang. I also left a text message for the San Diego County medical examiner's office to see if he'd been able to identify our John Doe from last night, and then I set up a meeting with Lieutenant Graysmith, the head of the SDPD homicide division. I wanted to find out more about Detective Dunn and his interest in John Doe's death.

I looked around the hotel lobby again.

Still no Tessa.

I grabbed an apple from the bowl at the hotel's registration counter.

She likes to sleep late, but since we only had a couple of days here in San Diego, she'd agreed to get up by nine, and that was over an hour ago.

After I finished the apple, I checked the time and realized I'd been awake for over five hours. No wonder I was so hungry. I pushed myself out of the leather lounge chair and was halfway to the elevator when I heard heavy footsteps behind me and a harsh, growling voice that I recognized right away. "Morning, Pat."

"Ralph?" I turned. Special Agent Ralph Hawkins came lumbering toward me. I greeted him with a slap on the shoulder, and it felt like I was hitting a bag of concrete. Ralph had started lifting weights again, and I could tell. "What are you doing here? I didn't expect to see you until next week. I thought you'd still be testifying at Basque's retrial in Chicago."

"It's a mess up there." Ralph's voice sounds just like what you'd expect from a man who can twist a frying pan around a burrito with his bare hands. "A real circus." Ralph worked his shoulders back and forth, probably trying to make them comfortable in the shirt that he'd obviously bought before he started pumping iron again last year. He's not quite in the shape he was as an Army Ranger twenty years ago, before he joined the FBI, but he's close. "Defense found out one of the state's DNA experts, guy named Hoyt, lied on his resume. Never attended Ohio State at all. Messed up our case even worse. Pushed things back at least a month."

I felt an echo of the chill I'd known in the slaughter-house. Even without this kind of delay, trials as complicated as Basque's typically last several months. This would drag things out even longer, and all the while Richard Basque would be out of maximum-security prison. Not something I wanted to think about.

Ralph tried to hold back a yawn. Failed.

"Long night?"

"Got in late, plus they lost my bags. Can you believe those—" Then Ralph filled the air between us with a string of inventive and somewhat profound curses, and I was glad Tessa hadn't arrived yet after all.

"Well, anyway, it's good to see you. Brineesha doing OK?"

"I'm a happily married man; she's a very patient woman. We're good, Tony too—just turned eleven. Tessa?"

"Witty. Sarcastic. Endearing."

"Good to hear."

My stomach grumbled, reminding me once again how hungry I was. I looked past Ralph to the bank of elevators.

Then it struck me. "Wait a minute. You never answered my question. Why are you in San Diego, anyhow?"

"Margaret has a couple meetings out here on the Coast. She's—"

"Margaret Wellington is coming to San Diego?" At least for the moment, I'd lost my appetite. Margaret and I get along about as well as two piranhas in the same tank.

"Probably in L.A. right now," Ralph said, "but she'll be flying here sometime this afternoon. She's on some kind of defense committee or something. Guess it goes with the territory of being an executive assistant director, and since I'm heading up the NCAVC for now, she wants to brief me on some policy changes."

Ralph, Lien-hua, and I all work for the FBI's National Center for the Analysis of Violent Crime, and Ralph was currently serving as the division's interim director while human resources looked for a replacement for Louis Chenault, who'd retired on the first of the year.

"You know how Margaret is," he continued. "She didn't want to wait until next week, and since my testimony's been put off indefinitely. She decided to fly me in." He picked at his travel-weary, crumpled shirt. "Last night Delta told me my bags were in Minneapolis. Do I look like I'm standing in Minneapolis, Minnesota?"

I sensed that he was winding up for a fresh round of curses, so I said, "I still can't believe they gave Margaret the position."

He finished brushing off his shirt. The elevator behind him dinged. "Most power-hungry woman I ever met. But don't worry; she's not here to see you. I doubt your paths will even cross." As the elevator doors began to open, he let a sly smile play across his face. "Besides, being here in California gives me the chance to keep an eye on you and Lien-hua." A wink. "Keep you two kids in check. Know what I mean?"

"No," said one voice from the elevator.

"Why don't you tell us?" said the other.

First voice: Lien-hua.

Second voice: Tessa.

"Oh." Ralph's voice shrank to the size of a mouse. "Good morning, Lien-hua. Hi, Tessa."

Lien-hua's arms were folded. "Hello, Ralph. What a surprise."

An unreadable expression crossed Tessa's face. "Nice to see you, Uncle Ralph."

Ralph patted Lien-hua's shoulder and gave Tessa a quick shoulder hug. "I'd better go track down those suitcases," he muttered. "You boys and girls have fun now." Then he ambled through the uncomfortable silence and left me alone with the two women and their four raised eyebrows.

I looked from Lien-hua to Tessa. "OK," I said, "so, who's hungry? I know I am. Famished. Let's get in line before they run out of quiche." Then I hurried off to the hotel's restaurant, wondering how I'd ever come to the point in my life where I would've actually been willing to eat quiche if necessary.

While Creighton watched Cassandra through the video cameras, he thought of spiders crawling across his face and of the videos he'd taken of the women over the years, and he thought of Shade.

Creighton had met some elusive characters over the last ten years, but this guy, Shade, was like a ghost. Every time Creighton thought he might be able to catch a glimpse of him—nothing. Even though Creighton had no idea what it was like to feel fear, he suspected that the growing discomfort he felt whenever he talked to Shade was close to what other humans felt when they were afraid.

A few times over the last two months, Creighton had thought about taking off, just slipping away into the shadows. But two things kept him here: he knew Shade would find him, and Project Rukh really did exist. All the Department of Defense documents that Shade had sent him regarding the project checked out. The device was real. And from everything Creighton had been able to uncover, the prototype really did what Shade said it would.

Building B-14. That was the key to everything.

Freedom or pain?

Pain.

And as Creighton thought of that word, he imagined the meeting he would have with the FBI agent later in the week, and he thought once again of the closure Shade offered.

Everything coming full circle. Yes. Creighton was the perfect one for the job after all.

Shade wanted to keep their communications to a minimum, and Creighton wasn't expecting to hear from him until three o'clock, so after leaving Cassandra alone again, Creighton pulled out a pair of handcuffs and practiced escaping from them just in case he needed to do so in the next couple days.

Yes. He was the perfect one for the job after all.

26

In line for the brunch buffet, I tried to guide the conversation away from Ralph's comments as quickly as I could. "So what took you two so long to get downstairs?"

"Shower," said Tessa.

"I was on the phone with Aina," said Lien-hua. Then she lowered her voice to a whisper. "She told me Austin Hunter wasn't home, but MAST managed to get a warrant. Aina wants to talk to you. She said to give her a call as soon as you can. They found gasoline and a professional makeup kit in his spare bedroom."

I began ticking through the possibilities. *Gasoline? I thought we'd eliminated that as the accelerant for the earlier fires. Unless* . . . My mind flashed back to previous arson cases I'd worked over the years . . .

Unless . . .

I saw Tessa grab her plate and I remembered that even though I'd already had a full morning, the last thing she probably remembered was the bloody pork tenderloin and John Doe's suicide last night.

The arsonist could have mixed it with something to make it burn longer. That would do it.

I was torn; the biggest parts of who I am were wrestling with each other again: the FBI agent part and the dad part. I knew the dad part was supposed to win, and I wanted it to, but I didn't know exactly what that was supposed to look like in real life.

Tessa was busy lifting the metal lids off the chafing dishes to see what was for breakfast.

Sausage links. "Ew." Then bacon. "You have got to be kidding me." And finally breakfast patties. "I am so done with this." She clomped to a nearby spread of fruit and pastries.

Well, she seemed to be acting normal enough. I decided it would be OK to return Aina's call. I loaded a bowl with oatmeal, and dialed her number.

"Dr. Bowers. *Gracias*."

"What do you have, Aina?"

I piled a plate with hash browns and followed my nose to the coffee carafes.

"No sign of Hunter," she said. "But, it looks like someone broke into his apartment. His dresser drawers were disturbed, but his checkbook is sitting in plain sight on the kitchen counter, so I don't think it was a robbery. And, even though his cell phone and laptop are gone, he left the cords here."

"Car keys?"

"Gone."

"So, Hunter left in a hurry."

"*Sí*. And you were right about the gloves. We lifted a partial. It's not Hunter. But—"

He would have pulled off the first glove with his dominant hand, and then left the print with his non-dominant one. "Which glove had the print?"

"The left. But I need to tell you—" *So, the arsonist from last night is most likely left-handed.* Then she finished her sentence by saying, "It's the print of one of our officers."

"What? He contaminated the evidence?"

"*Sí*."

Why didn't that surprise me?

"Just a minute." Exasperated, I balanced the phone on my plate. One of the restaurant staff was standing beside the coffee carafes. "We proudly serve Starbucks coffee," she told me with a smile.

I didn't say the words aloud, only thought them: *Starbucks is to coffee what McDonald's is to steak.*

The woman was still smiling at me. "Oh," I told her as cordially as I could. "Actually, I'm just looking for the juice bar."

"Right over there, sir."

"Thank you." I headed over to get a glass of OJ. Maybe later in the morning I could track down a cup of coffee that had actually been roasted within the last two months.

Wait a minute.

Juice.

Yes.

Orange juice.

I grabbed the phone. "Aina. Check Hunter's freezer."

"His freezer?"

"Give it a shot."

By the time I'd found my seat she'd finished her search. "Mr. Hunter must be a juice lover."

"So, he's got the juice," I said softly. "Have one of your officers check the nearest Dumpster to his apartment. Look for empty boxes of laundry detergent."

"Concentrated orange juice and powdered laundry detergent," she said. I could hear agitation in her voice. "*Claro.* I should have thought of that earlier. Mix them together with low-octane gasoline, make a paste. Burns hot enough to create full-room involvement—"

"But slow enough to sustain sufficient oxygen in the room for the fire to spread."

"So, you have worked arson cases before," she said.

"A few."

"Between the two of us we should have thought of it earlier."

"Well, without any suspects I'm not sure it would have done us any good." I downed some of my juice. "So, if he's got his laptop and his cell phone, what does that leave us? Any snail mail there? Return addresses, postcards we can check on?"

I heard her shuffling through some letters. "All bills. That would have been too easy anyway."

"OK, GPS. Track his cell phone or his car."

"We tried. Nothing. Older models."

"Ex-wife, fiancée, girlfriend? Someone he might have gone to stay with?"

"We're working on it. He has a photo on the wall of him on the beach with an attractive young woman, late twenties, scuba gear beside them. Her hand is resting on his thigh so I think they're more than just friends. We checked his phone records, found his favorite number to call, and sent some cars to her place. She's a shark researcher. Works for the Sherrod Aquarium. Cassandra Lillo."

"Cassandra Lillo," I mumbled. "The aquarium, huh?

OK. E-mail me whatever you pull up on her, and call me back if you find the detergent boxes." As I hung up, I noticed that Tessa, who had been watching me carefully, let her eyes wander past me toward a couple of cute guys laughing in a booth nearby.

During the next few minutes, I ate in hungry silence but then I noticed Tessa's long-sleeve T-shirt slide back from her wrist, exposing a red, inflamed streak beneath her bracelets.

"What happened to your wrist, Tessa?"

She pulled the sleeve back in place. "Nothing."

Over the last year Tessa had struggled with cutting, and I wondered if maybe the rubber band snapping was her way of trying to break the habit, kind of like smokers who start to chew gum instead of lighting up. But it was still a bad habit, and obviously, since her wrist was raw, she was taking it too far. "You need to stop snapping that rubber band so much. You're hurting yourself."

"I'm all right."

"I'm just saying—"

"I'm all right!"

Lien-hua, who had been eating quietly beside us, cleared her throat softly. "Anyone else want some coffee? I'm going for a refill."

Tessa and I both shook our heads.

Lien-hua rose and I decided that now was as good a time as any to tell Tessa what I'd started considering while I was waiting in the lobby. "Hey, listen. I was wondering if maybe we should head back to Denver."

"What? Why?"

"Well, I just thought that after last night, after that guy, well . . ."

"Killed himself? Ew. Yeah. That was totally disturbing."

"Well, I thought if we went back to Denver, we could maybe, you know, deal with it together. Talk it through."

"He's dead. What is there to talk about?"

"I know. But it happened so close to us."

"As if people don't die in Denver. Besides, I want to stay."

"You're right. People do die everywhere, but . . ." I let my words trail off as I noticed Lien-hua pause beside one of the tables. A woman who appeared to be deaf was anxiously trying to communicate with one of the restaurant managers. Lien-hua stood between them, interpreting. She watched the deaf woman's quick gestures, then spoke softly to the manager, listened to his reply, and let her own fingers fly nimbly through a series of words to the deaf woman. A sandy-haired boy, maybe eight or nine years old, sat beside the worried-looking woman. Lien-hua had mentioned to me a few weeks ago that one of her brothers had been born deaf, just like her paternal grandfather, so I wasn't surprised she knew sign language, but this was the first time I'd seen her use it.

"Patrick, *hello!*" Tessa was waving her hand in front of my face. She didn't look happy that Lien-hua had grabbed my attention.

"I'm sorry. What were you saying?"

Tessa's eyes flickered toward Lien-hua, then back to me. "I was saying that they need you here. And besides, we only have a couple days, and what am I supposed to do at home? I'm fine. Really."

The two guys in the neighboring booth had finished their meal and were now busy checking out Tessa. That is, until they saw me glaring at them. They looked at least three or four years older than she was. I leaned close to her. "You're sure you don't want to stay just so you can scope out those cute surfer guys at the booth over there?"

She purposely avoided looking at them. "What? I was not."

"Yeah, right. They were checking you out too."

Her eyes brightened and skipped toward the boys. "They were?"

"Watch out for those older guys. They're nothing but trouble." *You're getting off track here, Pat. Decide if you're staying here or going to Denver.*

"So, seriously, Raven." My cell phone started to ring. "You want to stay?"

"Yeah," she said. My phone rang again. "I want to stay here, see the beach, the aquarium. The sharks. All that stuff." Phone still ringing. She stared at my pocket. "Are you gonna answer that already?"

I flipped out my phone.

"Dr. Bowers, it's Aina. We found the boxes but no girlfriend. We contacted the aquarium. Ms. Lillo never showed up for work today."

Hunter's keys were gone from his apartment. Maybe they took off together.

"Aina," I said. "That's great. But I'm in the middle of something."

"Her car's still in the parking lot of the aquarium, though. Dispatch sent a team of criminalists to look through it."

She told me that last part on purpose. I know she did.

"Thanks, Aina." I hung up.

"OK," I told Tessa. "I don't want to argue with you here. If you're good to stay, we stay."

"I'm good to stay."

"OK."

"Good."

Lien-hua returned with her coffee, and I asked her, "Was everything all right over there?"

She nodded. "The boy is allergic to peanuts. His mother saw him eating one of the cinnamon rolls with walnuts and pecans and was afraid it might contain peanuts as well. But the manager assured her that there weren't any."

"That's good to hear."

"Yeah, no kidding," Tessa said, staring at the boy. She's allergic to peanuts too, so I knew she could relate.

"Good." I really wanted to inspect Cassandra's car and work space before the criminalists got to them. If Hunter was the arsonist, it was possible she was working with him, and we could wrap this whole thing up if we could locate her. I stood. "Tessa, I think Agent Jiang and I are going to go check—"

"Can I come to the aquarium with you?" Tessa asked.

I blinked. "I never said we were going to the aquarium."

"But you are, and I want to come too, and don't tell me it's not safe or anything, because if Austin Hunter really is the arsonist and he was taking off with Cassandra, they wouldn't hang out at the place she works; they'd get out of town. Right? Besides, it sounds like you should be looking for him at a Keva Juice or a Laundromat, not an aquarium."

Lien-hua and I just stared at her. Before I could say a word, Lien-hua said, "Tessa, how do you know all that?"

"I was listening to you guys. He talks loud on the phone, and you oughta know that when you whisper something it just makes people nearby listen more closely." She pushed back from the table. "It's a good thing you two aren't spies."

"But you only heard my side of the phone conversation," I said.

"I filled in the rest."

Forget college. I should send her to the FBI Academy.

"Sharks are cool, right?" she said. "Remember? So, can I come?"

Something didn't quite jibe. "Hang on, Tessa, you're always asking to go off by yourself, to do things by yourself, to be left on your own. But whenever I'm working a case, you want to tag along. It doesn't make sense. It's not consistent."

"I'm a teenage girl. I'm exempt from being consistent."

I looked at Lien-hua, who shrugged. "She's right about one thing, they wouldn't hang out at the aquarium."

Well, that was helpful.

"So," said Tessa. "Can I come? We were gonna go to the aquarium anyway."

"OK. Look. You stay in the public section while we check out Cassandra's office. You stay by a crowd of people. No sneaking around. You're never alone. Got it?"

"Got it," she said. "No problem."

27

As Tessa went back to her room to get her satchel, she thought about the conversation she'd just had with Patrick. On the one hand he was right, it didn't seem to make sense—she wanted to live her own life, but she also wanted to be part of his: to need him but also be free of him. It was kind of weird, or maybe it was normal, she didn't know. She was still trying to get used to the whole idea of having a dad around.

Besides, Patrick wanted two things just like she did. He wanted to work on his cases but also spend time with her. Both were important to him, she knew they were. So what was the difference? Maybe she and Patrick weren't all that different after all.

She grabbed her satchel, as well as the lotion to rub on her scar, and walked back to the elevators.

On my way to the car, the medical examiner returned my call but scoffed when I asked about an autopsy. "We already know how John Doe died—death by trolley. Besides, there wasn't enough left of him to put in a Ziploc bag, let alone enough for an autopsy."

You have to hand it to these MEs. They really know how to humanize a tragedy. "I was hoping we could look into this a little more," I said. "There's something here that doesn't add up. Have there been any other suicides like this recently?"

"Bowers, this is the sixth-largest city in the country. What do you think? The guy had no driver's license, no social security number, no passport, and thus, no identity. As far as the system's concerned, he doesn't exist."

"What about relatives?"

"No one showed up to claim the body, and no one will. This is a city of 1.3 million legal residents, plus nearly three hundred thousand illegal ones. What do you want me to do, interview each one of them, see if I can find someone who's related?" He paused to catch his breath. "I need to get back to work."

I thought maybe I could speak to one of John Doe's relatives at the funeral, but when I asked the ME about the time of the interment, he said, "Unless someone claims the . . ." I could tell he was searching for the right word and *body* wasn't it. "Unless someone claims the remains, there'll be a public burial on Thursday. That's all I know." And then, in a tone bordering on compassion, he added, "So, why does this guy matter so much to you, anyhow?"

"Because he deserves to matter to someone." I reached into my pocket and felt John Doe's tooth; then the ME ended the call and Tessa arrived.

Trying to put the tragedy of his suicide out of my mind, I slid into the car next to Tessa and we headed to the aquarium, where Lien-hua had agreed to meet us.

At exactly eleven fifty-six a.m. Creighton Melice discovered Randi's cell phone in his car.

He'd decided to move the car eight blocks away from the warehouse so there would be no way of connecting him to it, or it to him. But when he opened the car door and saw a phone on the dashboard, he realized it was hers. A tight knot formed in his gut.

Where was the phone Shade had provided him? Creighton searched between the seats and then beneath them and then behind them, but the phone was not in the car.

Creighton remembered Randi grabbing a phone as he shoved her out of the car.

She took the wrong one.

Randi now had the phone Shade was going to call.

And in that moment, despite how strongly he felt about not blaspheming, Creighton Melice did exactly that.

28

Last year after Victor Drake had hired Geoff and Suricata and was considering the final two people for his team, he'd carefully researched Dr. Octal Kurvetek's job responsibilities at the Texas Department of Criminal Justice. During the vetting process, Victor had found out that the doctor oversaw the proper administration of the three-drug cocktail used for lethal injections at the time: sodium thiopental, to induce unconsciousness; pancuronium bromide, to induce paralysis; and potassium chloride to bring about cardiac arrest.

From 1986 through 2006, Dr. Kurvetek had been the on-site medical supervisor for 219 of the 369 executions by lethal injection that took place in the state of Texas. His experience at the TDCJ and his background in neurophysiology all seemed to make him ideal for the job that Victor Drake was trying to fill. So he'd hired him.

It was only after Dr. Kurvetek had been on the team for six months that he told Victor his secret. "It was always more satisfying to let the convicts remain conscious while the pancuronium bromide and potassium chloride were administered. I didn't do it all the time, of course. Just when the mood struck." He seemed proud of what he'd done. "It's prohibited by the Eighth Amendment, of course, which states that executions may not include 'the unnecessary and wanton infliction of pain.' But I don't necessarily agree with that provision."

"And?" Victor had said, anticipating the answer.

"Let's just say that administering those two drugs to a conscious person would cause"—Dr. Kurvetek's lips curled into a wormlike grin—"an unconstitutional amount of pain."

In a nutshell, Dr. Kurvetek's specialty was death.

Death by pain.

And now, Victor had to rely on this man not only to pull the Project Rukh research findings together but also help take care of the problematic Austin Hunter. Victor didn't want to, but finally he dialed Kurvetek's number. "Have you found Hunter?" he asked as soon as the doctor answered the phone.

"No," Octal replied evenly. "Geoff even checked GPS for his phone as well as his credit card use. Nothing. It's as if he disappeared."

Of course it is. That's his specialty! That's one of the reasons he was hired, because he can disappear without a trace.

"All right," Victor said. "I need you to focus on the test results, give me everything you can. I have a meeting on Thursday afternoon with the general and I need to make sure he's convinced the device is operational. Have Geoff and Suricata find Hunter."

And then he ended the call before Dr. Kurvetek could reply. After all, the doctor wasn't calling the shots; Victor was.

That's what he told himself as he went back to work managing his vast biotech empire.

29

As I drove to the aquarium, I asked Tessa to read me the Sherrod Aquarium brochure that she'd picked up from the hotel lobby.

"You're kidding, right?"

"No. Go ahead. I want to find out as much as I can before we get there."

She complained for another minute or two, but at last she obliged me. "'When it was completed in November 2008, the Sherrod Aquarium was the largest and most ambitious aquarium complex in the world. Boasting more than five hundred thrilling exhibits, this world-class vacation destination promises fun, educational, and memorable experiences for the entire family. Also respected around the world as a cutting-edge shark research facility . . .'" She stopped and mumbled, "Do I have to do this?"

"I know it's not Pulitzer Prize–winning material. Just humor me."

A sigh. Then, "'When you arrive, plan to visit Poseidon's Odyssey, an interactive 4-D adventure that will leave you stunned, and amazed!'" She paused. "There's an extra comma in there that they don't need, by the way." Then she continued. "'And don't miss the world's largest indoor aquarium attraction. The Seven Deadly Seas exhibit holds more than seven million gallons of water, as well as the world's largest bull shark in captivity. Prepare to be awestruck and overwhelmed. But be wary! Sixteen vicious species of sharks roam its deadly waters—' Patrick, puh-*lease*?"

"Just finish it up," I said. "We're almost there."

Another impatient sigh. "I'm skipping to the end. 'Spear-headed by entrepreneur and philanthropist Victor Sherrod Drake, the Sherrod Aquarium stands as a monument to his generosity to the people of' blah, blah, blah. It just goes on like that for a while."

"OK," I said. "That's good. We're here."

She set down the brochure, looked up, and uttered one word: "Whoa."

The Sherrod Aquarium spread before us. The architects had made brilliant use of mirrored glass and expansive sweeping canopies, creating a breezy, windswept feel that made the three interconnected wings of the world's largest aquarium look like giant glass sails billowing toward the sea. Sunlight and sky danced across the glass sides of the buildings, merging the aquarium seamlessly with the ocean that lay just beyond it.

A landscaped grove of towering palm trees and exotic flowers wove euphorically between the three buildings. Even the parking lot had been well planned, with shaded walkways, jogging trails, and small playgrounds containing interactive learning centers for children.

I fished out my ID, and the guard at the main entrance waved us through to the staff parking lot, where we found Lien-hua already waiting for us.

"How did she beat us here?" asked Tessa.

"Ride with her next time," I said. "You'll find out."

"I rode with her last night."

"She must have been holding back. C'mon, it's time to see the sharks. Just give me a couple minutes first."

Tessa and Lien-hua went to pick up some passes from the front desk while I pulled on a pair of latex gloves and approached Cassandra's car. She'd parked at a hurried angle between a pair of the parking lot's light posts, and the two criminalists who were pawing through the trunk had used the light posts, as well as the back bumper of the Cassandra's car, to define the crime scene.

Why not? After all, they were handy.

One of the criminalists was shaped like a pear, the other reminded me of a giraffe. I found out that the squat, round man was named Ryman, the gangly, long-necked guy, Collins. After identifying myself, I flipped open the sheath on my belt, pulled out my Mini Maglite flashlight, and leaned into the car.

"What are you looking for?" Ryman asked me.

"Clues," I said.

Silence.

I stood back, scanned the parking lot, taking note of the location of the employee's entrance about twenty meters away, the surveillance camera pointed directly at the door, and the service road that wound around the back side of the building. Based on the angle of her car, I guessed that Cassandra had entered via the service road rather than the main entrance.

I knelt and looked under the car, then beneath the seats. Cassandra had kept the interior of her vehicle meticulously clean, no trash, no scattered papers. I didn't even see any sand on the carpet, which was especially surprising considering we were in the beach city of San Diego. "So. Have you moved anything?"

"No," Ryman replied.

Cassandra's purse sat upright on the front passenger's seat. A suitcase lay in the backseat. I looked through her purse and then opened the suitcase. A pile of clothes was strewn inside. "Did you go through these clothes, or is this how you found them?"

"I told you we didn't move anything." Ryman seemed to be the spokesperson.

"Was the car locked or unlocked?"

"Locked. We had to break in."

"Engine?"

"Off."

"Headlights?"

"Off."

I inspected the glove box, then asked, "What station is the radio set to?"

After a blunt silence, "What?"

"The radio station?"

"I don't know."

I checked. The radio button wasn't depressed. I pressed eject, no CD in the player, no mp3 player input. So, she'd had the radio off when she arrived. No music playing.

They just looked at each other. "What does that matter?" asked Collins.

"Everything matters."

I took note of the climate control settings, the predominant genre of music of the CDs stacked between the seats, and the position of the driver's seat and steering wheel. Based on the seat position, I figured Cassandra was tall for a woman. Not much shorter than me: five-eleven or perhaps six feet tall.

I took one final look around, thanked the criminalists for their cooperation, and turned to go.

"You're done?" I heard Ryman say.

"Yeah."

I'd made it six steps when I heard Collins whisper, "Idiot Fed."

All righty then.

As anxious as I was to get inside, I figured I could spare one more minute. I turned and faced them. "Gentlemen. What's your take on this? What do you think happened here?"

"She was arriving for work," Ryman said. "Got out of her car. Maybe someone snatched her. Maybe she went for a walk. Who knows? Probably took off with her boyfriend."

"If Cassandra had been heading to work for the day," I said, "would she have parked crookedly, taking up two parking spots instead of one, and left the purse containing her makeup, cell phone, wallet, lunch pass, and name badge in the car?"

He hesitated. "Probably not."

"She parked with the intention of quickly retrieving something or delivering something, and never made it back to the vehicle," I said.

"Maybe she was grabbed as she got out of the car."

"Then the car doors would have been unlocked. If you abduct a woman as she's leaving a car, you don't take the time to lock the doors behind you." I pointed. "Also, we have these light posts close by, no other cars in the vicinity. She would have seen her abductor approaching, even though it was dark when she arrived."

Collins stuck his hands on his hips. "How do you know she got here in the dark?"

"Heater settings. This morning was cool early, but the temperature rose quickly right around dawn. Her heater is set on high. If she arrived anytime after sunrise she would have had her air-conditioning on, or she would have at least turned off the heat."

Both men stared at me blankly.

OK. Enough. This lesson could go on all day. Time to get inside. My guess was that whoever met her—or abducted her—waited until after she entered the aquarium, to avoid being captured on the surveillance camera aimed at the employees' door.

"Thanks for your good work, gentlemen. I especially like how you used those lampposts to mark off your crime scene. Very clever."

"Yeah," Ryman said. "That was my idea."

"I'm not surprised."

So.

I knew something I hadn't known before: Cassandra's jumbled suitcase in the back of her impeccably neat car told me that she'd rushed to pack and then left in a hurry—just as it appeared Hunter had done. It seemed likely they were planning to meet, maybe flee together. But why now, after all these fires? And what was the hurry? Was Detective Dunn's presence last night related to Cassandra's disappearance? And what was so important to her that she had to stop by here early this morning?

Too many questions.

I retrieved my computer bag from my car and stepped into the lobby of the aquarium.

Time to get some answers.

30

I found Lien-hua and Tessa admiring an expansive tank of tropical fish that created the backdrop for the main ticketing area. "OK, Tessa, this is where you're on your own."

She didn't look away from the fish. "OK."

To our left, a labyrinthine passage wove past a series of small exhibits featuring squid, octopuses, and sea horses. A walkway on the right disappeared into a dark cove emitting eerie music and guarded by a large tank of grim-looking barracuda. Three more paths led to additional attractions and interactive oceanographic and marine biology exhibits in different arms of the aquarium. I assumed that eventually all the walkways would converge at the huge Seven Deadly Seas exhibit at the far end of the facility.

I pointed to a concession stand nearby, at the center of the hub for all the different wings. "Tessa, meet me over there by that snack area in one hour, OK?"

"One hour."

"Look at your watch, OK?"

She did. Then, without another word, she set off on her own.

When Tessa was out of earshot, Lien-hua read my mind and said, "Cassandra was taken, wasn't she?"

"Yes. She arrived in the dark, deep in thought, planning her day, left her car with the intention of returning, and never made it back."

"How do you know she was deep in thought?"

"Working theory. Her radio and CD player were both off. Typically, people drive without music only when (a) they're on the phone, but it was probably too early for that;

(b) when they're talking to someone in the car, but as far as we know she was alone; or (c) when they need to concentrate on something. My money's on C."

"Hmm. I do believe you've started profiling, Dr. Bowers."

"No, no, no. It's called induction. Very different. Completely different."

"Uh-huh," she said as we went to find the aquarium director.

An hour ago Creighton had pulled some of Randi's personal information off her cell phone and then ground the phone to pieces beneath his heel.

Since then he'd been in the manager's office considering his options.

It was possible that Randi would come back looking for her phone. He doubted she'd be able to find the warehouse, but it was possible. So maybe he should just wait and take care of her then.

But then again, since it was the middle of the day, she might not come alone or she might tell a friend where she was going. In either case, it was likely she'd be missed and then others would come looking for her. Not good. Too many bad scenarios.

Before he destroyed her phone, he'd gotten enough information from it to find her, so he could go after her. Maybe he should pay her a little visit.

That's what his gut told him to do.

Find her.

Get the phone back.

Teach her a lesson or two.

Yes, that's what his gut told him, but his mind told him not to rock the boat any more than necessary. He really shouldn't leave Cassandra alone, and besides, he knew that if Shade tried calling the phone Randi had grabbed, Shade would immediately discover the mix-up and find another way to contact him, but only if Creighton stayed put.

So. Stay or go looking?

Really, the best choice was to stay. Trust that Shade would be in touch, but still keep an eye out for Randi and only deal with her if she somehow did find her way back to the warehouse.

Creighton watched Cassandra for a moment through the video monitor. Then he had a thought. Now that he'd completed the video for Hunter, he only needed one camera trained on her.

Which meant he could use the other camera for something else.

Yes. If he moved one camera outside, he could keep one eye on Cassandra and the other on the road to see if Randi came back.

As he began to unhook the output cords of the camera on the left, Creighton admitted to himself that he hoped Randi would come back looking for her phone. Then he could kill two birds with one stone. So to speak.

A lanky man in his midforties led Lien-hua and me through a door marked "Restricted Area! Aquarium Staff Only!"

"This is where our aquarists work," he informed us proudly. Like the rest of the staff, he wore shorts, a Sherrod Aquarium polo shirt, and sport sandals. Stenciled on the pocket of his shirt was the name Warren Leant and his title: Managing Director, Animal Husbandry. He had a weary face and made me think of someone who takes the elevator up to his condo in order to work out on his stair-stepper. "Please." He motioned for us to follow him. "The animal husbandry wing is right through here."

"So, Pat," Lien-hua said as we followed Warren Leant past the backstage entrance to the Poseidon's Odyssey 4-D attraction. "Back at the elevators earlier this morning, what were you and Ralph talking about?"

"Mostly Margaret. She's on the West Coast."

"But didn't I overhear Ralph say he wanted to check on you and me? What was that all about?"

"Maybe he thinks there's something going on." I said the words before I realized I'd done more than just think them.

Oops.

"Well?" she said softly. "Is there?"

Thankfully, Mr. Leant interrupted our conversation. "Animal necropsy rooms." He gestured toward a hallway that led to a row of six rooms. "You know what necropsies are?"

Lien-hua and I answered almost in unison: "Autopsies on animals."

"Oh." He looked deflated. "Yes. That's right. All right then. It's just a bit farther."

He led us down the hallway, and I felt the pressure of Lien-hua's question leaning against me.

"Well?" she repeated. "Is there?"

Once on a stakeout we'd almost kissed, but at the last moment we both hesitated and retreated back into ourselves. Since then we'd never spoken to each other of that night, but it brought both an understated intimacy and a careful distance to our friendship. But now, with the question laid so prominently on the table, I said, "I'd like it if there was."

Lien-hua was quiet, and I wasn't sure how to take her silence, but then we arrived at the animal husbandry facility and I knew we'd have to finish this conversation another time.

The stark scent of antiseptics mixed with the wet smell of dead fish greeted us as we entered a brightly lit anteroom to the main work area. Leant gestured toward the far end. "Ms. Lillo's office is just past the shark acclimation pool. You don't think anything might have happened to her? I mean, it would be bad for the aquarium if it did—not that I'm unconcerned about her or anything, it's just that I want to be prepared for the worst. For the media. You understand. So, if there's anything I should tell our board of directors . . ."

"Right now," I said, "our main concern is just finding and speaking with Ms. Lillo, wherever she is. I need access to your security camera footage for last night and early this morning. Let's start with nine p.m. through seven a.m." I figured I could convince Ralph to assign a team of agents from the San Diego FBI field office to review the videos, to see if we could catch a glimpse of either Cassandra or the offender. "And I'd like you to clear your staff out of this wing but keep them here at the aquarium. I don't want them to leave, but I want them out of the way."

"Well, you see, that might be difficult. We're already behind schedule with our shark feeding, and eight of our sharks haven't been fed since last night."

"Mr. Leant, with all due respect, I'm more concerned about finding Cassandra than about when your fish have lunch," I said.

"Yes, well, I really don't see the need for—"

"I'm not asking."

"This is highly unusual."

I glanced at Lien-hua. "If we can't process this area properly, we might need to shut down the aquarium for how long? Two, three days? Does that sound right to you?"

"At least three days."

Warren opened his mouth as if he were going to respond, then closed it soundlessly, stepped to the side, and dug out his walkie-talkie.

I knew that the animal husbandry area for an aquarium this size would need to be large, but I didn't expect it to be fifteen meters wide by forty meters long. The wall on our left held four offices and then opened on the second story to include access to the water filtration towers that rose from a lower level, passed up the offices, and nearly touched the ceiling. They looked like giant cones with horizontal ribs.

The wall on our right held a series of inset view ports to the neighboring Seven Deadly Seas exhibit. A glass door led to a pathway that I could see allowed surface access. The shark acclimation pool Warren had mentioned lay beside one of the view ports halfway to the far wall.

The ceiling of the husbandry area climbed nearly four stories above our heads to accommodate a suspended track that ran through the center of the room. One end of the track terminated above the shark acclimation pool's sliding metal door that separated it from the Seven Deadly Seas attraction. The other end of the track stopped abruptly beside a double-sized garage door that I assumed led to the outside of the aquarium.

"Must be for transferring sharks into and out of the exhibit," said Lien-hua.

I set down my computer bag, approached the acclimation pool, and peered inside. Dimensions: four meters deep, five meters wide, five long. Sides made of thick, reinforced glass that appeared strong enough to stop even a frenzied half-ton shark. I guessed that the sturdy steel drain located on the pool's bottom allowed the aquarists to empty and then replace the water, maybe after transferring a shark into or out of the exhibit, or quarantining a sick shark. Since the pool was empty, I assumed they were currently in the process of doing that.

When I looked up, I saw that Lien-hua had approached the doors to the food preparation area on my left. Two aquarists wielding slender knives were skinning fish for the next shark feeding. Buckets of white meat smeared pink with blood lay on the floor beside the sink. Lien-hua caught my eye and spoke softly enough so that only I could hear her. "You don't think . . ."

It was a gruesome possibility. "We'll need to check. See if there's any evidence of an unscheduled feeding this morning. We'll also need to have an officer interview those two."

"I'll make the call."

She stood beside a row of scuba tanks to call dispatch and the aquarium's water quality control center, and Warren strode over to me with a young Hispanic woman in tow. He raised his nose as if he were sniffing me. "The staff will be waiting in the employees' break room. And I certainly trust you'll do all you can to make this . . . inspection go as quickly as possible."

"You have my word."

"Yes, well." Nose still in the air. "I hope you'll forgive me, but I have to go and change the text on the television displays *again* so our paying customers won't be disappointed when the feedings they were planning on viewing don't occur." He gestured toward the nervous-looking woman beside him. "Maria works with Cassandra. She'll show you around. And if you need anything else, don't hesitate to contact me. Obviously, I would like to help wrap up this whole matter as quickly as possible."

"Obviously."

He went to summon the aquarists from the food prep area; I greeted Maria, and my guided tour began.

31

Grace and death.

Those were the two things Tessa thought of as she watched the sharks patrol the Seven Deadly Seas. She'd seen sharks on TV and in movies and in books and everything, but that was nothing compared to watching them glide only a few feet away from her face, just on the other side of the glass.

Tessa quickly identified the distinctively shaped hammerheads and the sand tiger sharks with their ferocious-looking, snaggly teeth. She also recognized the shortfin makos, nurse, lemon, bull, and tiger sharks. She saw a number of other species, too, that she couldn't identify. And that kind of bugged her.

From inside the glass-enclosed pathway that wandered along the floor of the twenty-foot-deep exhibit, the sharks looked like a flock of great, dark, six-hundred-pound birds—who just happened to have rows and rows of razor-sharp teeth.

Tessa leaned closer, close enough to see her breath flutter across the glass. And being that close, it almost seemed like she was in the water with the sharks as they soared silently around her, with perfectly honed power rippling through their supple, deadly bodies.

Silent beauty.

Primordial hunger.

Grace and death.

Tessa glanced at her watch. She wasn't too concerned about the one-hour deadline Patrick had given her, but she didn't want to be in the glass observation tunnel during the next shark feeding, which was scheduled to start any minute, especially if they were going to use live fish.

Ew. Disgusting.

She stepped onto the conveyor-belt-people-mover-thing on the right side of the passageway and was halfway to the next exhibit when she saw the message appear on one of the plasma TV monitors mounted on the ceiling that the shark feeding had been postponed.

Hmm. Good.

More time with the sharks.

She stepped off the conveyor belt and returned to the world's largest shark exhibit. This time, she raised both hands against the glass, her arms extended like wings, and imagined that she was flying with the sharks through a vast, water-filled sky.

A sky with no boundaries and no restraints.

But of course, the whole time her feet remained planted reluctantly on the floor of the aquarium.

32

Maria quickly pointed out the water quality testing stations, the quarantine tanks for ill or injured animals, and the stairwell beside the shark acclimation pool that led down to a small observation room on a lower level. Although I couldn't be sure what the animal husbandry area usually looked like, nothing appeared out of the ordinary.

I gestured to a two-meter-long metal basket on the deck near the acclimation pool. "Is that for transferring the sharks?"

Maria nodded. "We call it the Cradle. Some of the sharks weigh over a thousand pounds. Without that we wouldn't be able to get them into or out of the acclimation pool." She aimed her finger at the three-inch-long hook that hung from the cable above the Cradle, and then guided my eyes up the cable, past the place it coiled around a large drum, to the control panel on the wall. "It's hydraulic," she said.

I noted that a lifeguard's backboard and a highly advanced automated external defibrillator were hanging on the wall beside the controls, readily available in case any of the divers needed to be rescued. Next to them was a phone.

Maria's eyes jumped restlessly across the room toward the door. "Cassandra's OK, right? I mean, nothing bad happened to her or anything? Right?"

"As far as we know, Cassandra's fine," Lien-hua said.

"But why would her car be here if she was OK, though?"

"Maria," Lien-hua said gently, "can you tell me a little more about Cassandra's work? What exactly does she do here? Is she an educator?" I noticed that Lien-hua had unobtrusively positioned her digital voice recorder in her pocket. I assumed she had also pressed "record."

"No, that's more what I do. I coordinate the tour guides' schedules. Cassandra's a researcher. She's always diving with the sharks." Maria tapped the first two fingers of each hand rapidly against her thumbs. "Mostly, she's studying the ampullae of Lorenzini. Government work. A grant, I think. It's kind of a big deal to the aquarium, being one of the leaders in the world in understanding the ability of sharks to—"

"Wait," I said. "I'm sorry. You're going to have to back up for a minute. The ampullae of what?"

"Lorenzini. They're these little organs on a shark's head and snout that can sense electromagnetic fields."

Lien-hua and I exchanged glances. "Sharks can sense magnetic fields?" I asked.

Maria nodded. "The ampullae are filled with a jellylike substance that acts like a semiconductor."

She seemed to be relaxing somewhat now that she was in her element as a shark educator. She walked to a life-sized anatomical diagram of a lemon shark that hung from the wall, and pointed to a series of large pores on the shark's head and snout. "Electric fields are produced whenever fish swim through the earth's magnetic field, and naturally when muscles contract. Sharks can locate fish by sensing these minute charges. In fact, sharks can even find a flounder buried beneath the sand, just by its electronic impulses."

"They can actually sense these impulses through matter, through sand?" Lien-hua said.

"Yes," said Maria. "Other cartilaginous animals have the sensory organs too, but the ones on sharks are by far the most advanced. Sharks can even use these organs to swim thousands of miles and return to their exact starting position in the ocean by using the earth's magnetic field to track their navigation."

Geomagnetic orientation. Electroreceptors. I was amazed. I'd never heard any of this before. "So, sharks can really do this? Really identify a fish's location just by the electric or magnetic impulses created by muscle twitches?"

"Actually their sensory system is so precise they can

even locate paralyzed prey. So really, she's OK then? Cassandra is?"

Lien-hua is much more tactful than I am so I decided to let her address Maria's question.

I noticed a door with Cassandra's name on it, and with the words *paralyzed prey* ringing in my head, I entered her office.

33

As Tessa watched the sharks, an enthusiastic aquarium-educator girl led a group of little kids around the corner. All the kids were wearing orange T-shirts that read "Third graders rock the world!!!" Tessa tried to sneak past them before they filled the corridor but didn't quite make it.

Great.

With a practiced flourish, the aquarium girl gestured for the children to stop.

"How many of you know how to smell?" Her voice was high and chattery and to Tessa it seemed to echo way more than the acoustics of the corridor should have allowed. All the children raised their hands. "And taste things like pizza or hot dogs ... or broccoli?" At the words *pizza* and *hot dogs* the children smiled, at the word *broccoli* they grimaced but faithfully raised their hands. "And touch and hear and see?" More hands.

"Well," she continued, "those things are called our *senses*. Most of us have five, although some people may lack one or two. Well, sharks belong to a group of fish that have *no bones in their whole bodies* and are the *only animals on the planet* who have a scientifically proven *sixth sense*! Sharks can hunt fish even when they can't see or smell them! The man who discovered this unique ability was named Stephano Lorenzini. Let's say that together: Stephano Lorenzini. Isn't that a *nice name*?"

Tessa drew in a thin, aggravated breath. Aquarium Girl was doubly annoying. Not only was she way too chipper, but she didn't even have her facts straight. Lorenzini didn't discover the receptors; Marcello Malpighi did—fifteen years before Lorenzini ever started taking credit for it. Tessa felt like correcting her but decided against it. Years ago at school in Minnesota, she'd learned the hard way that it's best to keep your mouth shut when you know more than the teacher does.

Aquarium Girl went on. "When sharks move their heads back and forth, they're not looking through the water, they're *sensing* where other fish are. Kind of like using a *metal detector*. Let's all do it together!" The girl began wavering her head back and forth like a shark using his electrosensory organs to search for food, and the class of children imitated her.

Tessa most definitely did not.

Above and around them, the sharks circled in their three-dimensional patterns. Endlessly swimming. Endlessly moving, watching, sensing.

Grace and death.

Both eerie and beautiful.

The girl who didn't know who Marcello Malpighi was coughed up something that had been caught in her throat, swallowed it again, and then launched into her closing speech. "Sharks, the sea's magnificent prowlers of the deep, have roamed the earth's oceans for millions and millions of years. And so," she concluded, "untouched by nature and time, sharks remain one of nature's most magnificent and enduring miracles."

That was it. Tessa couldn't put up with Aquarium Girl anymore. First, she taught historical inaccuracies, and now logical inconsistencies. After all, if sharks were miracles, they couldn't be from nature, and if they were from nature, they couldn't be miracles. You can't have it both ways.

Time to go.

But as Tessa was easing past the children toward the next exhibit, she saw a bull shark turn suddenly and swim directly toward the glass. It pivoted at the last moment, curled toward a shiny fish the size of a large cat, and bit it in half.

All around her, the children began shrieking and pointing. Some of the third-grade boys were yelling, "Cool! That shark just ate that fish!" Some of the third-grade girls were wailing about how gross it was.

Tessa heard Aquarium Girl stutter something about

how sharks don't normally attack *that* kind of fish and that it might have been a *mistake* that someone put that fish in there, and that really there was *nothing to worry about* since sharks are *basically good creatures* just like all animals because only *humans are truly dangerous*, but Tessa noticed that her voice didn't sound quite as chipper as before.

The remaining portion of the fish twitched awkwardly as it sank, until a tiger shark swooped forward, gulped it down, and then circled once again, stony-eyed, through the water. And all the while, a thin trail of blood rotated slowly toward the surface of the water, like autumn mist curling up in a breeze.

Grace.

And death.

Blood seemed to be following Tessa everywhere. She hurried past the children to find a bathroom where she could throw up.

34

I scanned Cassandra Lillo's office.

File cabinets. Overstuffed bookshelves. Scuba gear on the floor. Low-lying desk covered with papers and research findings. Nothing seemed out of place.

A dog-eared medical journal lay on the file cabinet. I flipped through some of the highlighted pages. Cassandra seemed to be very interested in a new technology that I wasn't familiar with called magnetoencephalography. I skimmed the article and found that magnetoencephalography, often known as MEG, is a way to measure the magnetic fields that are caused by the electric impulses of the neurons firing in your brain.

Hmm. Just like sharks.

The article contained a picture of an MEG machine. The eight-ton beast looked like an MRI or a CAT scan machine but was designed for someone sitting up. It was located inside a chamber with thick protective glass walls. Apparently, there are only a few dozen of the nine-million-dollar machines in the world. And according to the article, four of them were located here in San Diego. That might be something to look into.

I memorized the issue number, set the magazine down, and touched the spacebar on Cassandra's keyboard to wake up her computer screen. A small window hovered in the corner: "Welcome, Cassandra Lillo. You are logged on to the Drake Foundation Network. Log-in time: five oh three a.m."

So, the Drake Foundation Network . . . that would explain why Victor Drake received such glowing praise in the aquarium's brochure.

Unless someone else knew Cassandra's password, she must have arrived before dawn and logged into her computer at approximately the same time I went jogging. It also confirmed my theory that she hadn't been abducted by her car, but had most likely been attacked while inside the aquarium.

I checked the CD drive to see if she'd been transferring files.

Empty.

I started searching through her file registry to see which documents she might have accessed this morning, and that's when I overheard Lien-hua talking with Maria just outside the office door. "Maria, do you know anything about Cassandra's family?"

"Her parents are divorced. Her mom died around Thanksgiving. Murdered, I think. Her dad lives out East somewhere, but I think he got remarried a couple more times. Cassandra told me once she'd kept her mom's last name. She never mentioned any brothers or sisters."

"What about her boyfriend?"

"Which one?"

"She has more than one?"

"There's this one guy from New England she used to see, but lately it's this guy named Hunter—I don't know if that's his first name or his last name. It's just what she called him. They met at a beach party a few months ago. Both of them are into triathlons."

Just as I came across a folder of encrypted files, I heard Lien-hua ask, "Maria, do you know anything else about Cassandra's work? Anything at all? Maybe someone who was envious of her grant? Someone at the aquarium who was angry with her?"

Maria was silent for a moment and then said, "There was one thing she said to me once, but it's probably nothing."

OK. That kind of comment always gets my attention.

"Anything you can tell us would be helpful," Lien-hua said.

"I really don't want to get into trouble."

And that one's even better.

I could check these files later. I didn't want to miss what Maria said right now. I stepped to the doorway in time to hear Lien-hua encourage her, "Please, Maria. We just want

to talk to her. If she's in any kind of danger you'd want to
help her, wouldn't you?"

Maria bit her lip. "OK, but I didn't tell you this."

And that's the most enticing comment of all.

"OK," said Lien-hua. "You didn't tell us anything."

Maria took a deep breath and lowered her voice, even
though we were the only people in the animal husbandry
area. "Cassandra comes over to my apartment sometimes.
We party together, you know? And when she has too much
to drink, she . . . well . . . one night she told me she was helping make some kind of top secret weapon for the government with her shark research."

I'd been hoping for something a little more helpful.
Cassandra's comment sounded exactly like something a
drunken aquarist might say. "A top secret weapon with
sharks?" I said.

"Yeah. Some kind of killer ray gun or something like
that. I don't know."

I tried to retain my professional objectivity, to keep an
open mind. "A ray gun," I said.

"A killer ray gun."

"Sorry. And she was making this for the government?"

"That's what she said."

Fact. Fiction.

Fiction. Fact.

Sometimes it's hard to hold them apart. But in this case,
whatever Cassandra was involved in, I was pretty sure it
did not involve helping the government create a shark-
based killer ray gun. I impatiently scanned the animal husbandry center again as Lien-hua asked Maria a few polite
follow-up questions about the comments Cassandra had
made while she was drunk. I rubbed my forehead.

Stay on track here, Pat. Get back to the basics. Timing.
Location. Sight lines. Entrances and exits.

OK.

So.

If Cassandra really had been abducted, why here? Why
this morning? How did her assailants approach her? Did
they lure her, surprise her, trap her? How did they control
her? Through threats, force, restraints?

And if she was abducted while she was in the animal
husbandry area, how did the offender get her out of the

aquarium? The front door and the staff entrance were both monitored by video cameras.

I glanced past Maria to the acclimation pool and the stairwell beside it.

The stairwell.

Oh.

I hurried past the two women, jogged down the steps, and found a tight room encircling the acclimation pool. An open doorway stood on my left. Half a dozen wet suits, weight belts, and regulators hung from hooks behind the stairs.

"What is it, Pat?" called Lien-hua.

"Just a minute."

I pulled out my flashlight and shone it into the dim region beyond the doorway. The sterile smell of disinfectants and the vibrating sound of the aquarium's huge filtration motors filled the air. This was apparently the walkway past the foam fractionators to the aquarium's water quality control center. Nearby, I saw the two filtration towers that rose toward the ceiling of the husbandry area.

My light revealed a network of dimly lit pathways that ran beneath the floor of the animal husbandry area to more filtration units and what appeared to be a vast water storage facility in the neighboring wing of the aquarium.

If I were going to try and get someone out of the animal husbandry area without being seen, this would be the place to do it. "Maria," I called up the stairs. "Do any of these walkways lead to an exit?"

Her voice floated down the steps. "You can get to an emergency exit back by the Dumpsters. But no one ever goes that way. It's kind of creepy being down there by the filtration tanks. Everyone avoids it."

Creepy is good. Creepy is very good. They always go for creepy.

This is it. He came through here.

I shone the flashlight against the walls, looking for fingernail scratch marks, scuff marks from shoes, other impressions, any sign at all of a struggle.

Nothing.

Next, I looked for fibers, clothing, or hair that might have gotten caught on the crisscrossed metal steps, but found none.

Finally, I scanned the floor and found that a fine, sandy grit covered the tiling. Probably some kind of residue kicked into the air by the sand-based filtration system.

At first I didn't notice anything unusual, but when I knelt to inspect the floor more carefully, I found two streaks leading through the thin layer of dust beginning at the base of the stairs. I knew right away what those two tracks meant. I'd seen them before on a beach in South Carolina. When you hold an unconscious person's armpits and drag her from the water, her feet leave impressions in the sand.

Or, when you drag her backward down a set of stairs and into a water filtration center.

"Lien-hua," I called. "Come here. Maria, stay where you are." I studied the smeared footprints beside the drag marks and realized they were unusable.

I slid my .357 SIG P229 from its holster and heard Lien-hua's quick, light footfalls on the stairs. "What is it, Pat?"

"Look." I aimed the flashlight at the two streaks that disappeared away from us into the catacombs of the filtration facility. "He dragged her through here."

She removed her weapon as well. "Do you think they might still be here?"

"It's possible," I said. "Let's find out."

With my arm flexed and my weapon ready, I led Lien-hua into the dark network of walkways before us.

When Victor Drake's cell phone rang and he saw Warren Leant's number come up, he cursed.

Warren Leant, that idiot aquarium manager. Just the fact that he was calling could not be good. Definitely not.

Victor answered, "What?"

"Mr. Drake, sir, it's Cassandra Lillo. She didn't show up for work this morning, and at first I didn't think anything of it, but then the police started going through her car and two FBI agents showed up and wanted to look around. You told me to let you know if—"

"I know what I told you," Victor barked.

FBI agents?

Normally, someone in Warren Leant's position wouldn't even have this number, but Victor had flagged two dozen researchers in his various companies and told their supervisors to call him if there were any disciplinary or supervisory problems with those personnel. After all, Victor needed to keep close tabs on everyone involved in Project Rukh.

"So, what do you want me to do?" asked Leant.

"Stall. Whatever you do, don't let them look around her files."

A long pause. "Um. It's a little too late for that, sir. I already showed them to her office."

Victor's head felt like it was ready to explode. *No, no, no, no.*

Enough of Leant's ineptitude.

Victor hung up the phone. Decisively.

Cassandra Lillo. The shark woman, the one researching the mucopolysaccharides. The cute one. Yes. He'd interviewed her himself. But what was it about her? There was something else, something else . . .

Hunter?

Yes.

He'd heard Austin Hunter mention her name once. That he was going diving with her and that he'd be unavailable for any assignments over the next two weeks. Yes, they'd dated each other.

So, they were in this together. Terrific.

Oh, this day was just getting better and better.

Victor thought for a moment about sending Geoff and Suricata to teach Leant a lesson, but then decided the time had come to pay a personal visit to the aquarium and see firsthand what was going on.

35

Lien-hua and I crept through the walkway and entered the filtration facility. The series of pathways that meandered around and between the filtration towers and foam fractionators were lit only by the dim operating lights high above us and a few amber bulbs attached sporadically to the walls. The air hummed with the low murmur of the motors pumping, filtering, cleansing the millions of gallons of water needed for this aquarium.

A few scattered signs pointed to the animal husbandry area, the Seven Deadly Seas purification station, the water management center, and a number of other behind-the-scene locations. But other than that, the paths fingered out all around us into a gloomy maze.

The area really was creepy, just like Maria had said.

As we rounded the third tower, I heard movement behind one of the water storage tanks about eight meters ahead of us.

Maria said no one ever goes down here.

"Stop," I said. "Put your hands in the air."

Footsteps.

I raised my gun.

"I said stop right there."

Then someone rounded the corner; I raised my weapon and eyed down the barrel.

At Tessa.

"Don't shoot!" she screamed. "What are you doing aiming a gun at my head?"

I swung the gun to my side. My heart slamming, my hand shaking. "Tessa? What are you doing down here?"

"I got turned around."

I reholstered my gun. "How could you get turned around? This area is off limits."

Her voice was jittery, I assumed because of the gun. "I was just looking for the little girls' room."

As if I believed that.

"This place sure is spooky, huh?" she said.

To my left, Lien-hua pushed an exit door open. Blinding sunlight swept through the chamber. "Pat. C'mere."

I glared at Tessa and corralled her over toward Lien-hua.

Outside the door, a road ran past a pair of rusty Dumpsters on the way to the food service's main delivery platform another forty meters or so farther down the building. "The delivery road," Lien-hua said. "If he dragged her down the steps, he could have had a car waiting back here and never would have had to drive past the guard station."

I saw something small on the floor beside the exit.

A dart.

I bent to inspect it and heard Tessa shuffle up to me. "Step back, Raven."

"Is she dead? Is Cassandra dead?" I glanced at Tessa and saw that her face was flushed. I heard her snap the rubber band against her wrist.

"See?" I could feel my anger rising. "This is why I don't want you to come along on these things. And would you stop it already with the rubber band thing?"

Snap. "She's dead, isn't she?"

"We don't know where she is," I said sternly. "We don't know what happened to her. I almost shot you—do you hear me?"

"That would have really sucked."

"Yes. It would have." I handed Lien-hua my cell phone. "I'm taking Tessa upstairs; can you take some photos? The dart. The exit. The pathways." Lien-hua accepted the phone, and I took Tessa's arm and led her through the palely lit passageway and back up the stairs.

I could feel my gun, uncomfortably weighty in my holster.

I was furious at Tessa.

Furious, because I loved her.

But mostly I was terrified, because I'd just seen my stepdaughter's face at the end of a gun barrel and I was about ready to squeeze the trigger.

Maria greeted us at the top of the stairs with an anxious, perplexed expression. "Where did she come from?"

"I got turned around," said Tessa innocently.

"Maria," I said, "can you please lead this young lady to the front counter?"

Tessa stared at me with fierce independence, but I also saw a shade of fear. "Stop yelling at me. OK? I didn't know where I was."

"I told you not to wander off." Tessa shouldn't have been down there, but I still hated myself for yelling, for making her afraid. That was the last thing I wanted to do. Images of the slaughterhouse flashed past me. That tangle of anger and fury. Rising, rolling, coursing through me.

I noticed Lien-hua ascending the stairs but addressed Tessa, "I'll deal with you in a minute." She just shook her head and walked off with Maria.

Resting a gentle hand on my shoulder, Lien-hua spoke softly, just loud enough for me to hear. "Are you OK, Pat?"

"Yes. I'm fine." I took a slow breath. "I'm OK."

She let it be at that. "So, good news. While I was downstairs taking the pictures, I got a call from the water control center. All the water tests are clear, no human blood. Nothing on video either. Cassandra wasn't fed to any of the sharks."

"The drag marks support that conclusion too," I said.

"I'll let the police know about the drag marks, have them search the filtration area. Make absolutely certain no one is down there. Maybe they'll be able to get some prints off the exit door."

"I need to check on a couple things in Cassandra's office. Then I'll meet you by the entrance."

Without another word, she left, and I picked up my computer bag and returned to Cassandra's office. I'd had an idea earlier, while searching through her files.

This morning I'd suggested that Aina look for a return address on Hunter's envelopes. Well, maybe we didn't have a return address on an envelope, but we might have one on an e-mail.

36

I quickly scrolled through Cassandra's most recent e-mail, but none of the messages shed any light on who might have abducted her or what she was doing at the aquarium earlier in the day.

However, I did find a Gmail address for "SEAL-Hunter1," which I assumed was Hunter's account.

Follow up on that later. Finish up here and go talk to Tessa.

Before I left, I connected my computer to Cassandra's to copy the encrypted files I'd come across earlier. Maybe I could have someone from the FBI cybercrime division, or Terry, take a look at them, pull something useful. As I hit "enter," my cell phone rang. Ralph.

Before I could say a word, he shouted, "Did you call Dunn's supervisor in the homicide division? Some guy named Lieutenant Graysmith?"

"You don't sound happy."

"Well, guess who's golfing buddies with FBI director P. T. Rodale."

"You're kidding me."

"An hour ago Graysmith called Rodale to complain about an FBI agent who was refusing to follow protocol and was interfering with an ongoing investigation in San Diego. Twenty minutes ago, Rodale called Margaret. And five minutes ago, guess who called me."

"Sorry, Ralph."

"What's going on here, Pat?"

"That's what I'm trying to figure out." My computer told me it would be done copying the files in one minute.

"Just call Lieutenant Aina Mendez with MAST, have her straighten things out with Lieutenant Graysmith. She requested our help for this arson investigation, and everything we've been following up on so far is related to the fires. I don't know why Homicide is involved in any of this, since, as far as we know, nobody has been killed." I finished with the files and closed up my computer.

"Well, listen. I'm supposed to call Director Rodale back before three o'clock, so I need you to bring me up to speed on this thing. I'm at the FBI field office on Aero Drive. Room 311. Come by and—"

"Ralph, I need to take care of something with Tessa first. It's important."

Ralph's a dad. He understood. "All right. But remember, I gotta call him by three."

"By the way, did they ever find your bags?"

A storm of anger clouded his one-word answer. "No."

"I'd offer you some of my shirts, but I think they might be a little too big in the biceps area for you."

"Oh. You're very funny. I'm tempted to tell you how I feel about the airlines, but you know what my mom always says."

"What's that?"

"If you can't think of anything nice to say, shoot something and then get back to work."

I blinked. I'd met Ralph's mom. I couldn't be sure if he was joking. "No, she didn't."

"Well, she should have. Get your butt over here as soon as you can."

We ended the call. Then I took one more look around Cassandra's office and returned to the main lobby to talk with my stepdaughter, the advice of Ralph's mother disturbingly reminiscent of what had just happened in the filtration chamber.

I found Tessa waiting for me beside the barracuda tank. She drew back when she saw me approaching.

"Hey, listen." I spoke as gently as I could. "I'm sorry I got so mad. You know that, right?"

Silence.

"It's just that I care about you so much. You're the most important person in the world to me. I love you. I don't want anything to happen to you." I thought she might argue with me, might make a snide comment, like, "Oh. Do you typically shoot the people you love?" but she didn't.

"I was gonna do what you said." I detected no trace of anger in her voice, just a thread of loneliness. "About not wandering off by myself, or whatever. But then these two sharks totally ate this fish, like, right in front of me, and I kind of freaked out. I went looking for you."

She came looking for me.

She came looking.

"Listen," I said. "There's a lot going on with this case right now—"

"That's all good. I understand. I know you're probably mad and everything, but I was hoping to have some time by myself today. Just to chill. If it's OK."

She wanders around the back rooms of the aquarium and now she wants me to give her more freedom? Not going to happen.

"I don't think so, Tessa."

She threw a question at me out of nowhere. "Did you see the jawfish?"

"The what?"

"The jawfish." She pointed to a nearby exhibit just past the barracuda tank. "Male jawfish carry the developing eggs of their young in their mouths. Did you know that?"

"No, but I'm glad I'm not a jawfish." She'd cut me off, switched subjects. I wondered if she'd been listening to me at all. I started to get even more annoyed.

"Other fish do it too," she said. "Like arwana. Even after their fish hatch, the male continues to carry the young fish in his mouth, to protect them while they grow."

Oh.

So this wasn't a conversation about fish.

"How does he know when to let the young fish go?" I asked.

She stared at the barracudas, then at the jawfish. "When they're big enough to make it on their own, then he lets them swim away. I think sometimes they probably go where they're not supposed to, but he trusts them, even though they're not perfect."

I felt my throat squeeze. "Do the young fish come back?"

"Maybe," she said. "If the dad makes them feel safe."

I sighed. "You're good, you know that? You're really good." Earlier in the day she'd convinced me to bring her with me, now she'd nearly convinced me to let her go off by herself.

She gave me a soft smile.

"So," I said, "you want to leave my mouth and go swimming around on your own for a while."

"I'll come back."

"Where will you go?"

"I don't know. Maybe hang out downtown a little. I mean, I need to stop by the hotel first—but, is that OK?"

"Hold on. Let me think about this." I tried to sort out my frustrations from my feelings, my trust from my hesitation, my—

"Well?"

"Quiet, I'm thinking."

She waited maybe four seconds. "So?"

"I'm still thinking."

"You think slow."

"Insulting me will not help your case."

"Sorry. Didn't mean to. How about this: you think a lot faster than most men your age."

"That counts as an insult."

Make her feel safe. That's your job. So she'll always feel safe swimming back. "OK, Tessa. Take the afternoon. We'll both get some space. But if I call to check up on you, don't give me a hard time about it."

"As long as you don't do it, like, every five minutes."

"I want you to know, you're more important to me than my work. You know that, right?"

She was quiet for a moment and then, without any sarcasm or scorn, she said, "Yeah. I know that."

"I'd do anything for you."

"OK, I know you love me, but let's not overdo the caring-dad bit here, all right?"

Well, back to normal.

"And we'll have supper together," I said. "We'll figure out a time and a place later."

She nodded. "That'll work."

We headed for the door. "So, you have to tell me. Did you have that jawfish speech prepared, or did you just make it up on the spot?"

"I'm pretty good thinking on my feet," she said. "So, can I ride back to the hotel with Agent Jiang?"

"Agent Jiang?"

"Yeah. You told me to before. Remember? That I should ride with her to see how she drives."

"OK. And then tonight I'll see you for supper." We passed the front ticket counter with its tropical fish. "By the way, " I said, "have you heard of the ampullae of Lorenzini before?"

"No. What are those?"

"They're these electrosensory organs on a shark's head. A researcher named Lorenzini discovered them."

"Huh," she said. "How about that."

As we were exiting, a man wearing a suit that cost more than I make in a week brushed past us, almost knocking into me. "Watch where you're going," he grunted.

Then Lien-hua met Tessa and me outside by the steps, and as they were walking away, I saw a patrol car grind to a stop in the middle of the No Parking zone.

Detective Dunn clomped out and tossed a cigarette to the pavement.

It's never a good sign to see a homicide detective show up during a missing person investigation. I hoped that didn't mean Cassandra's body had been found.

I decided that before going to see Ralph, I needed to talk with Detective Dunn.

37

On their way back to the hotel, Lien-hua tried to ease up on the gas. After all, teaching Tessa bad habits would not be the best way to cultivate Pat's friendship.

Tessa sat quietly, staring out the window. Lien-hua decided it would be polite to start a conversation, but she didn't want Patrick's stepdaughter to feel like she was being profiled, psychoanalyzed.

Start with something safe.

"So, Tessa, what did you think of the aquarium? Not the spooky backroom stuff, I mean the fish. The sharks."

Tessa shrugged. "Yeah, I liked it, but I saw a couple sharks eat this fish. That was way disgusting. I don't like watching things die."

Oh. Great conversation starter that was.

"Well, we have that in common then. I don't like watching things die, either." *Change the subject, change the subject.* "I heard Pat call you Raven. Is that your nickname?"

"Just for him. No one else."

"You don't like it?"

"No. I do. But don't tell him. I never had a nickname before. I like Raven." Tessa paused. Stared out the window, at the clouds. "Sometimes I wish I could fly like they do. Today, I pretended I was flying with the sharks."

"While they were swimming over your head?"

"Yeah. I thought it'd be cool to swim with 'em. I used to swim a lot, when I was a kid. For a while I even wanted to be a lifeguard." She swung her gaze to Lien-hua. "Do you swim?"

"No. I never learned how. Just between you and me, I've always been kind of scared of the water."

"Afraid you might drown?"

Lien-hua drummed her fingers against the steering wheel. "Are you hungry, Tessa? Need to grab a bite to eat?"

"I'm OK."

Lien-hua noted the mileage. Nine more minutes to the hotel.

"So, Agent Jiang. Your first name, Lien-hua, what does that mean, anyway?"

Good. Safe ground again.

"It means lotus. My mother was Buddhist—"

"Was? What, did she switch to something else?"

"I'm afraid she was killed, Tessa. In a car accident. Three years ago."

Death again. Why does this conversation have to keep coming back to death?

"Oh. Sorry, I didn't mean to . . ."

"It's OK."

A taut silence. They'd both lost their mothers prematurely. *Unrelated by blood,* thought Lien-hua, *but sisters in sorrow.*

After a few moments, when the time finally felt right to continue her explanation, Lien-hua said, "Many Buddhists consider the lotus the most beautiful flower in the world. It grows in the mud, but blooms pure and white, untainted by the soil. The *Lotus Sutra* is one of the most sacred Buddhist texts."

"A sutra. That's a discourse, right?"

"Yes. A teaching of Buddha. In the *Lotus Sutra*, the lotus represents how humans live in a corrupt world but can reach enlightenment and live uncorrupted lives, with absolute happiness and beauty, free from life's illusions." Lien-hua paused for a moment. The next sentence reminded her too much of the incident no one in her family spoke of. It was hard to say the words. "So, when I was born, naming me after the lotus seemed like a good way to honor my mother's faith."

"So, do you believe that too?" asked Tessa. "The stuff about enlightenment and happiness and everything?"

Lien-hua nearly missed her turn, whipped the car to the right, snaked between an SUV and a minivan—both with babies in the backseat, both driven by women talking on cell phones—and jumped onto the Five.

"Sorry about that," Lien-hua said.

"No, it wasn't bad," said Tessa. "Patrick was right."

"Anyway, to answer your question, well ... I used to believe in those things, but in this job ... well ... I guess I've seen too much corruption in people to believe them anymore. I think we can live beautiful lives, Tessa, wonderful lives, but we're not just rooted to this world, we're also a part of it. I don't think we can ever be perfectly free or pure. We can't rise above who we are."

After a long pause that stretched into awkwardness, Tessa asked softly, "Can someone else lift us?"

The girl's question caught her unaware. Lien-hua searched for the right words. The right answer. Found none. "I don't know, Tessa. I guess I never thought of it quite like that."

When Lien-hua was talking about how people are corrupted, but also beautiful, Tessa thought that, for just a flicker of a moment, she sounded like her mom.

When Tessa's mom had found out she was dying of breast cancer and that the chemo wasn't working, she told Tessa one day that everyone has a form of cancer. Tessa hadn't understood what she meant, but then her mother, who was a faithful churchgoer, explained, "Even Jesus knew that. It says in the Bible that he didn't trust people because he understood human nature. He knew what mankind was really like."

"That's in the Bible?"

"Not an exact quote," her mother had said. "But it's in there. Second chapter of John, the last couple verses. We have cancer of the heart, Tessa. Evil doesn't crawl into us— Jesus said that too. It's already there, in our hearts; always looking for a way to climb out."

Corrupted.

Rooted to this world.

Just like Agent Jiang said.

And just like Agent Jiang, Tessa's mom didn't believe people could become pure; however, her mom did believe people could become purified—lifted from the soil when they found God finding them. Like her mom used to say, "Nobody reaches the Light on their own, but the Light can reach us." The last time Tessa saw her before she died, she'd asked her, "So, what was God doing when you found him?"

And her mom's answer had totally floored her: "Shaking me with both hands, trying to wake me up."

But now as Tessa thought about her mom again—her mother's words, her mother's death—the feeling that Agent Jiang was like her mother passed quickly.

Agent Jiang was not like her mother. No she wasn't. Not at all.

Tessa pulled the lotion out of her satchel and tugged up her shirtsleeve. "So," she said. "Is that why you got into law enforcement, then? To fight the corruption in the world?" She started massaging the lotion onto the scar the killer had given her. "Or was it just to meet guys?"

Lien-hua was silent for a moment. "Someone I knew was killed, Tessa. Someone very close to me."

"So, revenge?"

"Maybe. A little. Maybe to try and make a difference. Motives aren't always that easy to pin down."

"Yeah. That's what Patrick says."

"I'm sure he does."

Tessa spread some more lotion onto her hand and pressed it against the scar.

Rubbed.

Well there you have it. This scar right here proves how corrupted people really are. Evil coming out of someone's heart and scarring me forever.

They pulled into the hotel parking lot, and Agent Jiang said, "It hurts to lose those we love, Tessa. We don't always know what to do about it. So we do what we have to do. We all find different ways to deal with our pain and loss."

Tessa stopped rubbing the scar. Pain and loss. Yeah, she knew all about those. The loss of her mother. The painful memory of how she got this scar.

Tessa could deal with the scars she'd given to herself while she was trying to deal with the loss of her mother. Those were her problem. Those didn't bother her so much.

But the scar that guy gave her last fall, that one was different. That one she didn't want anything to do with, ever again. And no matter how hard she rubbed it or put the stupid lotion on it, it was never going to go away. She should have realized that weeks ago.

If only she could get rid of it. Cover it up. Never see it again.

We all find different ways to deal with our pain and loss.

Tessa pulled down her sleeve, then closed the bottle of lotion and slipped it into her satchel.

Trying to heal her scar hadn't worked.

Maybe it was time to try another way of dealing with it.

A way of never having to see it again.

As she stepped out of the car and Agent Jiang said good-bye, Tessa drew out her cell phone, brought up her Internet browser's search engine, and typed in the keywords "Tattoo Studios, San Diego, CA."

38

My conversation with Detective Dunn concerning Cassandra Lillo was brief and to the point. He told me that Cassandra's body had not been found, but that if a body *were* found—hers or anyone else's—it would be his jurisdiction, not mine. Period.

His words left me both relieved and annoyed. I still didn't have a clue as to why Homicide was involved in any of this, and, unless Lieutenant Graysmith changed his mind or Detective Dunn got a personality transplant in the next day or two, I couldn't count on their help to find out. Also, we still had no solid leads as to Cassandra Lillo's or Austin Hunter's whereabouts. We didn't even know for certain that either of them had committed, or been the victim of, a crime.

After my chat with Dunn, I checked my voice mail. Two messages.

First, the plates on the Ford Mustang came back belonging to an ex-con named Suricata Horan. History of assault, a manslaughter conviction, served some time in New Mexico. Typical hired thug. I figured I could bring him in, have a little talk, but at this point it would probably be a waste of time. Guys with his kind of rap sheet almost never open up unless you have something specific on them. But I made a note of his name to keep in mind as the case unfolded.

When I listened to my second message, I was surprised to hear an old, familiar voice: "Patrick, my boy, I'm giving a lecture at UCLA today and I hear you're just down the road. If you can make it up here, perhaps we can meet for dinner. Please, do give me a ring."

The man didn't have to tell me who he was, I would have recognized his voice anywhere—Dr. Calvin Werjonic, PhD, JD. My mentor.

Calvin had pioneered the field of environmental criminology more than forty years ago. But computing and correlating all the factors that affect the spatial and temporal aspects of crimes is so complex that only advanced computer operating systems can handle the algorithms within a manageable and useful time frame, so only in the last two decades had technology advanced to the point where his theories about geographic profiling and geospatial investigation could actually be implemented. Calvin is a brilliant man, a kind man, a legend in the field of criminal investigation, and a longtime friend. I'd seen him the previous week on CNN, and even though he's over seventy years old, he appeared as lucid and incisive as ever.

I lead seminars on criminology all over the world, but in the presence of Dr. Calvin Werjonic I still feel like an elementary school student.

I knew I couldn't make it to L.A., not with this case heating up, but as I drove to the FBI field office, I returned Calvin's call and asked if he could swing through San Diego before heading back to his office in Chicago. "Calvin, it would be great to see you. Besides, I wouldn't mind talking over this case with you and . . . well, talking over this case."

"I see," he said thoughtfully. "So you have a personal matter you'd like to discuss and it's so sensitive you don't wish to mention it over the phone. You were hoping to bring it up offhandedly in the course of our conversation, no doubt."

Sometimes having friends who are professional investigators can be really annoying. "Something like that," I said. "So do you think you could meet me down here?"

And, to my surprise, he agreed. "Yes, well, I believe I can, my boy. I'll change my flight connections and swing through before leaving for Munich tomorrow evening. We'll meet in the morning, then—ten thirty a.m., in the parking lot beside the Alcazar Garden in Balboa Park. Bring your walking shoes and some of that good coffee you so enjoy. I'm six-two with speckled gray hair. I'll be wearing a tan—"

"Calvin, that's enough specifics. I'm sure I'll recognize you."

"Yes, of course. All right, my boy, I'll see you then."

A few minutes after our conversation ended, I arrived for my meeting with Ralph at the San Diego FBI field office.

You wouldn't know that the imposing green and brown building on Aero Drive was a federal building just by looking at it. There's no sign, just a street number, and the dark-mirrored windows, prominent video cameras, and security fence make it look like any one of a dozen other office complexes in San Diego's biotech corridor.

No, you'd never know that 9797 Aero Drive was an FBI field office unless someone told you so.

There's nothing as effective as hiding in plain sight.

As I entered the facility, I gave Terry a call. If anyone could get us into Austin Hunter's Gmail account, Terry could. "Hey, Terry. It's Pat."

"Oh no."

"What?"

"Whenever you call, it means I'm about to do something illegal."

"Yeah, but you can cover your tracks so well, you'll never get caught."

I could hear him tapping at his keyboard. He was probably at the NSA headquarters in Fort Meade, Maryland, although it was hard to tell. He often worked from one of their remote, undisclosed sites. "Listen," I said. "I'm wondering if you can hack into someone's Gmail account. I've got the address right here."

"That's it? My thirteen-year-old niece could do that for you."

"This is an important case, Terry. I think it might help us track down a missing woman."

Without a moment's hesitation. "Give it to me."

I gave him Austin Hunter's Gmail address. "The password might be encrypted," I explained. "He was a Navy SEAL. He might have taken extra precautions."

"Passwords were made to be cracked. The Chinese have a whole division of military hackers. Back in June of 2007 they were able to get into the Department of Defense database and download submarine navigation schedules before the DOD was able to shut down that part of the system."

"I never heard that before," I said.

"That's because, according to both the Chinese and U.S. governments, it never happened." More tapping at the keyboard. "I'm at least as good as the Chinese. Stay on the line," he said, "this'll only take a minute."

"I'm stepping on the elevator," I said. I looked at my watch. Terry was fast—let's see how fast. "Call me back in three."

Victor Drake slammed the door to his office.

He'd just left a useless—completely useless—meeting at the aquarium with that imbecile Warren Leant. The man was clueless, and he would soon be jobless.

Cops were all over that stupid aquarium. All over it.

From the very beginning of the project, Victor had demanded that the Project Rukh researchers keep only hard copies of their files and leave nothing sensitive on their computers. After all, anyone with half a brain knew how to hack into someone else's system these days, and on a project like this, you couldn't take those kinds of chances.

Thankfully, it looked like Ms. Lillo had followed protocol and only kept printed notes and then sent them by courier to Building B-14. However, while the idiot cops were dinking around on the lower level, through his own ingenuity, Victor had managed to sneak in and erase Ms. Lillo's hard drive, just in case.

Victor assessed his situation. He still didn't have the information pulled together for the general, who would be arriving in less than forty-eight hours, and he still had no idea where Austin Hunter was—or where that little wench Cassandra Lillo had run off to.

Not good. Not good. Not good.

He needed to get a handle on this whole situation. Maybe meet with Dr. Kurvetek and those two gorillas, Geoff and Suricata. Figure out what to do if Austin Hunter or Cassandra Lillo decided to go to the authorities.

Victor picked up the phone, and, as much as it annoyed him to have to rely on other people to help solve his problems, he punched in Geoff's number.

*   *   *

Less than a minute and a half later the elevator doors opened and my phone rang. Terry. "The last e-mail Hunter received has a video attachment," he said intensely. "And . . . you need to see this one, Pat."

"Tell me."

"You're going to have to watch it."

I stepped into room 311, and I signaled with my finger to Ralph that I'd be off the phone in a moment.

"Terry—"

"I'm sending it to you right now."

I was getting exasperated, but I didn't want to waste time arguing. "All right. Thanks—"

"And, listen. There's a lot of chatter out there right now. I figured if you haven't heard yet you will soon enough. I wanted to be the one to tell you. He's back."

"Who is?"

"Sebastian Taylor. He was sighted last week in DC."

Terry's comment almost made me forget about the video. Taylor had been the governor of North Carolina until a few months ago. Before that, he'd officially worked as an overseas diplomat for the state department. However, in October, Terry had helped me uncover Sebastian Taylor's other, not-quite-so-official job with the CIA. As a result, I'd outed Taylor as an assassin and he ended up murdering a man in cold blood, and almost succeeded in killing me too. He'd been on the run ever since.

"Any leads?" I asked.

"No. But believe me, they're looking." He paused and then he continued. "Watch the video, Pat. Find this woman. Do it fast. You only have till eight o'clock."

His tone of voice chilled me. "Terry, when I hang up, call me back for a video chat. I might have some questions for you after watching this thing."

I ended the call and turned on my computer's video chat camera. Then I positioned myself next to Ralph and gave him a quick update on the arsonist case and Cassandra's disappearance. He nodded. Listened. Took a few quick notes. Then I told him that Sebastian Taylor had been sighted.

"I had a feeling he'd be popping up again," Ralph grumbled. "I just hope he shows up here somewhere near me." Ralph took a moment to redirect his thoughts. "By the way, I called Lien-hua. She's on her way over."

I nodded and then connected my computer to the large high-def screen on the wall so that both Ralph and I could watch the video.

Then Terry's face appeared on my laptop screen. "Be prepared," he said. "It's intense."

I opened his e-mail's video attachment and pressed "play."

39

The video began with a close-up of a human eye. Dark brown. Bloodshot. A tear poised on the tip of the eyelash. The smeared mascara told me it was a woman's eye, and it looked like she'd been crying for a while.

The image lingered there until the tear dropped sadly from her eyelash. Then the video slowly panned backward to reveal the rest of her face. I recognized her immediately from the photo I'd seen on her name badge in her purse. "It's Cassandra Lillo," I whispered to Ralph. "Our missing woman."

After a moment, Cassandra stared up, then down, then from side to side as if she were looking for something.

Another tear fell.

The only audio was the sound of a man's slow, heavy breathing.

The cameraman.

My heart began to hammer. I didn't like this. I knew already that this video was not going to have a pleasant ending.

The image continued to widen until Cassandra's shoulders came into view. I could see that she was standing facing the camera, but where, I couldn't tell. The background was blurry. She shuddered, and a thin shiver ran through her. There were two dress straps draped across her shoulders.

I felt my heart churning in my chest.

The cameraman's breathing continued to grow faster. The image widened, and I could see that Cassandra was wearing a crimson evening gown. Maybe silk. It looked expensive. She was terrifyingly beautiful.

And very, very afraid.

Another shiver caught her, held her. Shook her.

The center of the picture reflected a fine glint, and now I saw why. She was standing behind a pane of glass.

I leaned closer. The image widened.

No, not just a pane of glass. Cassandra was in a large tank. If she was five-eleven, the tank was about three meters wide, deep, and tall. Eight pipes, inserted through holes in the glass, formed the top of the tank, the spaces between them providing air for her to breath.

The camera tilted, and the video traveled down her body, down her legs, to show us that she was standing barefoot in a pool of water that reached her knees. Something was around her ankle.

The camera drew in for a close-up, and I saw that her abductor had clamped a shackle around her left ankle. A chain led from the manacle to a rusty ring at the bottom of the tank.

My beating, beating heart.

Cassandra kicked her foot uselessly against the chain. Her ankle was raw from previous kicks, but she didn't seem to care. Still, only the sound of the cameraman breathing; now faster, though. She kicked again, harder. His breathing quickened. He was getting excited by what he saw. No sound of Cassandra's cries. No sound of the splashing water or the chain.

Then, the camera swept up to the top corner of the tank where a gray pipe was spitting out a narrow, but steady, stream of water.

No, no, no.

He's going to drown her. He's going to film her as she dies.

I felt a rush of the same cold, terrifying anger that I'd felt thirteen years earlier when I saw what Richard Basque had done to Sylvia Padilla in the slaughterhouse. Anguish and terror flooding through me.

What humans are capable of . . .

What humans do . . .

Suddenly, Cassandra closed her hands into tight, desperate fists, squeezed her eyes shut, threw her head back, and screamed—but to us, her bloodcurdling terror remained silent, muted, then overlaid with the cameraman's breath-

ing. Seeing Cassandra standing there screaming at the top
of her lungs, and yet making no sound, sent chills down my
back. It was more disturbing, more heartbreaking, than if I
could have heard her.

My heart slammed against my chest.

She screamed until she was out of air, and then she
shrieked soundlessly again as the camera panned to the
side to reveal dark red words, the color of blood, scrawled
on the gray plaster of a nearby wall:

Freedom or Pain?
You decide.
8:00 p.m.

Finally, the camera returned to Cassandra, one last time.
She'd crumpled to the floor of the tank and was now sitting
tragically in the water. Her hands covered her face. Her
shoulders shook as she wept. The water rippled and washed
against the glass.

Then, the video dissolved into black, and all we could
hear was the sound of the cameraman's breathing. Until
that, too, faded.

And then all was dark and still and silent.

Except for the deafening roar of blood, rushing, pumping, screaming through my heart.

40

2:49 p.m.
5 hours 11 minutes until Cassandra's deadline

Ralph and I sat in silence after watching the video. Terry stared at me quietly from my computer screen. A long moment and then another passed. The stillness in the room seemed like sacred ground, and none of us wanted to be the first to trespass across it.

Ralph was clenching and then unclenching his fists. "Terry, make sure this isn't posted anywhere on the Web. You know Angela Knight in our cybercrime division?"

"Yeah. She's good."

"The best." Ralph looked at his watch, no doubt factoring in Quantico's three hour time difference. I knew Angela works nights, comes in at five. "Give her a call," he said to Terry, "and get her a copy of this. Have her sweep the Web, look for any postings. If this is on the Internet we need it taken down. Now."

"OK." Terry began clicking his keyboard. "If it's on there, we'll get it off. We'll also analyze the video, the digital resonance, the content. Everything."

"Good," I said. "When was the e-mail sent?"

"At eight fifty-one a.m."

"Can you tell where it's from?"

I saw Terry referring to some handwritten notes beside his computer. "Whoever sent it knows how to hide his tracks. He positioned it as a piece of junk mail and sent it through a spam router in the Ukraine. Ever since I opened the file I've had my computer tracking it." He glanced at his notes. "So far we're up to seventeen transfers in four countries. It could take ten or twelve hours to find the original source."

I shook my head. "We don't have—"

"I know," he said. "I know."

"All right," said Ralph. "Keep on it."

"Terry," I said, "I have some encrypted files for you from Cassandra's computer. I'll send them to you. See what you can decipher."

"Done."

After we'd ended the chat and I'd sent him the files, I asked Ralph, "Can you tell what kind of building that tank is in?"

He shook his head. "Hard to say. Concrete floor . . . hardly any basements in California, so maybe a garage. Could be a deserted factory, a boiler room somewhere. Any of a hundred warehouses down by the shipyards."

"OK," I said. "So unless Austin Hunter sent this video to himself, he's no longer our primary suspect in Cassandra's disappearance."

"Exactly," he said.

"Let's watch it again. But this time, look at everything except Cassandra. Whoever filmed this video was concentrating on her, distracted by her. You could hear it in the way his breathing changed. He might have been careless, let something slip into the frame that can help us find her." I clicked "play" again.

We were halfway through the second viewing when Lien-hua arrived. I saw her stand frozen beside the door. When the video ended, her lips parted as if she was about to say something, but it never came. She shook her head, her eyes intense. Frighteningly intense. I don't think Ralph noticed. But I did.

"Is that Cassandra?" she asked.

I nodded.

She took a seat beside me. "Play it again."

I did. And when it was finished, a moment of silence washed over the room once again.

Lien-hua pulled out her notepad. "All right. At least we've got time on our side."

"How do you figure?" asked Ralph.

"After all the work of constructing that tank, abducting

Cassandra, then chaining her inside, it's unlikely he'll move her. If we can find where she was when he shot the video, we'll find where she is now."

Her words rang true to me. "OK." I looked at my watch. "It's three oh one. Assuming eight p.m. is really our deadline, that gives us less than five hours to find Cassandra." I set the timer on my watch to go off in four and a half.

"Lien-hua, what's your take on this?" asked Ralph. "What struck you when you saw the video?"

"Everything is specific: the camera angles, the timing of the shots, the tank. It all plays into his fantasy. The camera doesn't shake. There's no hesitation. He's done this before. Cassandra isn't his first." This was her turf. Profiling. And even though I didn't want to admit it, her observations seemed to be right on target.

"All right," said Ralph. "Before we go any further, I'll call the police department, see what kind of help they can give us. Maybe Lieutenant Graysmith's attitude will change when he sees this video. Also, I need to call FBI director Rodale back and brief him. We meet back here in five minutes." I was glad Ralph was here to take the reins, that way I could focus more on the case than coordinating a team.

While he made his calls, I stepped out of the room to grab a drink from the water fountain at the end of the hall, the words *paralyzed prey* ringing in my head once again.

Shade phoned Melice and had started to give him instructions when a woman's voice said, "Who is this?"

End call.

It was Shade's first mistake.

And Shade vowed it would be the last.

So Melice had given the phone away, or lost it. That did not make Shade happy. No, everything lay in too delicate a balance to be making foolish mistakes.

Perhaps track down and then eliminate the woman? Yes. That could be done easily enough.

But on the other hand, it would be better to stick to the plan for the time being. Only move on her if necessary.

No, Shade hadn't said enough to her to cause suspicion. Not nearly enough.

Shade tapped a cell phone key, and a photo, sent from a friend, filled the screen. Shade stared at the twenty-two-year-old woman standing at a funeral, her grief captured in digital clarity.

Dark glasses. Black hair.

Lien-hua Jiang.

Long before she became a special agent. Even before she was a detective. The tears on her cheeks, frozen in time.

This was the key, the reason for everything that was about to happen.

Shade would find another way to be in touch with Melice. Until then, it was just a matter of watching and waiting and staying focused.

Without making any more careless mistakes.

After Ralph had made the calls and we were all back in the room he said, "All right. This has officially shifted from a missing person investigation to a kidnapping. It's related to the arson investigation, though. I explained to Rodale that you two know more about what's going on here than anyone, and that we need your help to find Ms. Lillo. He gave you the green light to stay involved. So, let's do this and let's do it right."

"Good," I said, glad to be officially on the case.

"OK. Let's watch it again," said Lien-hua.

"This time," I said, "let's be specific. Ralph, watch for images on the glass. Earlier when we watched it, I saw a glint. Maybe you can see something in the foreground, a reflection of the cameraman."

He nodded, his jaw set.

"Lien-hua, concentrate on Cassandra: the way she's blinking, could it be Morse code? Is she mouthing anything? Her hands—is she signaling in some way? Look for any indication that she's trying to get us a message."

She nodded, positioned her legal pad in front of her, and slid a pen into her hand.

"I'll focus on the chain and the pipe and the message on the wall," I said.

Then, I began to play the video once again.

Inside the office of the warehouse, Creighton Melice checked his watch. Shade was supposed to have contacted him fifteen minutes ago, at three p.m., but he hadn't heard from him at all since the call last night directing him to pick up Cassandra. Of course Creighton didn't have his phone, but he did have e-mail and Shade had often used that before. Creighton didn't like it when things did not go according to schedule.

He glanced at the live video feed of the tank.

The water was up to Cassandra's waist now. She couldn't sit down to rest any longer. So it looked like it would be a long afternoon for her. He would have preferred filming all of this in real-time Web streaming, but Shade had insisted that it would be too easy to track the location if they posted it on the Web.

Possibly.

Probably.

As annoying as he was, Shade did tend to be right.

But still, it would have made for a satisfying day.

He watched her press her hands uselessly against the glass. Yes. He would use the tank one last time with the woman Shade had promised him, and then everything would come to a glorious finish.

She took a breath, bent into the water, and tugged at the chain with both hands.

Let her tug.

The others had tried that as well. That chain was not going to break.

41

After twenty-five minutes of reviewing the video, we'd come up with only four observations that seemed potentially helpful.

Ralph noticed that the video had been edited in several places—right after the close-up of the shackle around Cassandra's ankle, and then ten seconds from the end when the handwritten words appeared, just before panning back to the final image of her sitting in the water. "This creep took his time to shoot it, edit it, splice it," he said.

"He's patient," Lien-hua said, echoing my thoughts. "Self-controlled. Back when I was a detective in DC, I worked a similar case of a man who filmed his murders. The care that killers like this take in making their videos speaks to the seriousness of their intentions. Our man doesn't just want to blackmail Hunter, he also wants to kill Cassandra. And he's going to do it."

During our third viewing, I saw that Cassandra's body cast a faint shadow across the water to her right. The shadow's size shifted after each of the videos edits, which led me to surmise that the light source was natural rather than artificial, and the change in the length of the shadow marked a change in time as the sun rose higher in the sky. "Terry told me the video was sent to Austin Hunter at eight fifty-one a.m.," I said. "Taking into account Cassandra's height and her shadows in relationship to the sun's position in the sky—"

"We're not looking at a garage," said Ralph.

"No," I said. "The light source at the filming site would need to be higher. Windows on the second or third story. So, she's probably in a warehouse." Ralph called the SDPD to have them start canvassing the warehouse districts of the city, but I knew there wouldn't be enough time to check them all.

Beyond that, we didn't have much to go on.

FBI director Rodale notified Ralph that he was personally reassigning seven agents from the field office to help us find Cassandra, as long as we kept Lieutenant Graysmith in the loop.

Ralph agreed and we adjourned for fifteen minutes so he could coordinate the efforts of the FBI with the San Diego Police Department. Lien-hua went to a quiet room to work on developing her profile of the abductor, and I headed for the door to get some fresh air and call Tessa to see how she was doing.

42

Tessa was in one of San Diego's downtown Internet cafés, surfing the Web and thinking about the kind of tattoo she wanted to get, when Patrick called. "Hey, Tessa, how are you?"

"Good." She shifted the phone to her shoulder so she could keep typing and clicking through Web sites.

"What're you doing?"

"Just checking my e-mail."

"Are you at the hotel?"

"Naw. I'm at this Internet place nearby. You'd like it. They have all this weird-sounding coffee from Central America." Tessa was glad to see that the café also had printers. That way she could print out exactly what she wanted.

"I'll have to check it out," Patrick said.

"How's the case?"

A pause. "Honestly, the farther we move into this thing, the more tangled up it gets."

"Well, at least it's interesting, though." Tessa thought she knew which image she liked best, but she scrolled through one more Edgar Allan Poe site just to make sure.

"That's not exactly the word I would use. People's lives are in danger."

"No, that part's horrible. It's just, I mean, pain—that's what's interesting."

"What are you talking about, Tessa?"

How to put this without sounding unfeeling? . . . "I mean, think of a good story. It's only interesting if something goes wrong. No one wants to read a story about someone who always does what she should and gets what she wants. So like, Poe's stories are interesting because all sorts of bad things happen. In 'The Pit and the Pendulum,' things just get worse and worse all the way through right up till the end, so it's great."

"I could deal with things not always getting worse and worse."

"It's not that I mean I want people to get hurt..." She scrolled past Poe's short stories to his poems. She knew what she was looking for, but the setup of the Web site was lame. Very twentieth century. Hard to find stuff. "It's just when you read a story you want to worry about the main character. You want to wonder if he'll catch the bad guys, if he'll get the girl, if he'll survive at the end of the book. It doesn't always happen, you know. The more danger, the more interesting the story. We want things to keep getting worse." She thought about that for a second. "Maybe we like stories so much because there's something in us that just wants to see other people suffer."

Patrick was slow in responding. "That's a very troubling thought. Let's hope you're not right." He took a breath. "I'm sorry I have to change the subject, but I don't have a lot of time here. I'm wondering, when do you want to meet for supper?"

She paused the cursor in the middle of the page. "Um ... yeah ... Could we, like, make it late? I wanna go for a walk, maybe visit Balboa Park or something." It wasn't exactly a lie. She did want to go on a walk and she did want to visit Balboa Park before leaving San Diego; it just wasn't all she wanted to do.

"Balboa Park, huh? That's where I'm meeting Dr. Werjonic tomorrow morning."

"Dr. Calvin Werjonic?"

"Yes. How did you know?"

"You wrote about him in your books. In the parts where I..."

"Didn't fall asleep."

"Right. Maybe I could meet him too. If it's OK."

"Well, we'll be talking about..." Patrick paused and then must have decided to change what he was going to say because he actually agreed to her request. "Yeah. That would be good. I'm sure he'd like to meet you too. So you're going to go on a walk this afternoon, then?"

She decided on the tattoo she wanted. There. Yes. It was

perfect, really, for a bunch of reasons. Tessa sent the picture to print and started gathering her things. "Yeah, or maybe check out some stuff downtown. Then we'll have supper."

Silence. A bit too long. "OK. That'll work. I'll call you later to figure out a time."

"OK."

"Have fun. And be careful."

Tessa's friends had told her that in the last couple years tattoo studios were getting all uptight about making kids get their parents' permission before letting them get inked. Someone's mom must have freaked out and sued a tattoo parlor somewhere because her kid came home all tatted up. Because of that, and since Tessa wasn't eighteen yet, she'd need to go to a certain kind of tattoo studio—the kind that wouldn't require a parent's signature; the kind of tattoo place that definitely wouldn't take checks or credit cards. So, the first thing she needed was cash. A couple hundred dollars probably.

She stopped by the counter. Waited for the printout.

She'd saved up almost two hundred dollars from helping edit other kids' term papers back home—three dollars per page to clean up the manuscripts. Not cheating or anything, just helping them make their writing sound halfway intelligent. It was amazing how bad most of the kids in her class were at writing—and how willing they were to pay someone to fix it. Anyway, if she worked at it, she could probably make back the money in two or three weeks.

OK, so visit an ATM.

She paid for the printout, the coffee, and the computer time and stepped outside.

An hour ago when she'd entered the café, she'd seen a bank halfway down the block. They should have an ATM machine. She started for the bank and peered up between two towering buildings at the narrow strip of Southern California sky above her. Then she pulled out her notebook and wrote, *"Strands of future rain scratch at the sky as the concrete rises up to meet my feet."*

Yes. She could tinker with the wording later, but it wasn't bad for a first draft.

Tessa found the ATM machine, slipped her card in, punched a few numbers, and retrieved her cash.

OK. Time to cover up some corrupted soil.

43

3:51 p.m.
4 hours 9 minutes until Cassandra's deadline

After calling Tessa, I returned to the conference room. As I waited for the team to gather, I couldn't help but think about the video.

I hated to admit it, but this video wasn't as unique as I wished it was. Videos of torture and abuse have become disturbingly popular among people who think it's cool to see others getting mutilated, raped, or killed, and who just can't get enough of it from the torture porn Web sites and the new torrent of shock-and-awe splatter movies.

But these days, special effects aren't enough. Now, viewers want to see the real thing.

And finally, technology has advanced enough to let them.

With the click of a mouse you can watch footage of terrorists beheading American hostages, of young children getting sodomized in a pedophile's basement, of women in northern India being gang-raped by *dacoit* bandits, of Burmese political prisoners being tortured and then assassinated. Any time of day you can watch the most horrifying things humans do to each other from the comfort of your living room. Just boot up a computer, surf to your favorite video sharing site, and watch other human beings suffer and die.

I could only hope that the video of Cassandra hadn't been posted yet.

In 2006, after the death of the "Crocodile Hunter," Steve

Irwin, the footage of him being killed by the stingray was stolen from the police storage facility in Queensland, Australia, and posted on the Web. Within hours, it shot to the top of all the major video viewing sites and stayed there for months. Even now, years later, it still receives thousands of views every day.

I remember Ralph talking to me about all this a few months ago. "Twenty-first-century rubbernecking," he said with a profound sadness. "Everyone wants to peek over the yellow crime scene tape, see if there's a body in the wreck on the other side of the road. It used to be just from your car. Now, it's from your laptop computer, your cubicle, your cell phone."

I shook my head. "Isn't there enough pain in the world already? Enough death to satisfy people?"

"I guess not," he said softly.

Nope.

I guess there isn't.

Maybe Tessa was right. Maybe humans do find pain interesting. Maybe there is something in us that wants to see other people suffer. I hoped not, but the evidence from real life made me think she might be right.

Creighton Melice caught sight of movement in the video monitor of the camera he'd set up outside the warehouse's south side entrance.

A police car.

He grabbed his gun and watched as the car pulled to a stop in the warehouse's parking lot.

An officer stepped out of the car, and then, so did someone else.

Randi.

The warehouse only had a few doors and most of them were chained shut from the inside.

But one of the doors was not chained.

That's the door Creighton headed toward. If Randi and the cop decided they wanted to visit him, he would give them a little welcoming present.

A team of seven agents followed Ralph into the conference room, and we all watched the video together.

Then Ralph rose and began to pace. "As of right now,

this is a joint investigation with the San Diego police. Blair, I want you to work with 'em. Look into Cassandra's background. Family, ex-boyfriends, colleagues, the whole deal." One of the agents acknowledged Ralph with a nod. "Hernandez, find out which companies nationwide could manufacture a tank like that, and if any have been shipped to this region." I wasn't surprised Ralph had learned the agents' names when they joined us during the break. He was cut out for leadership. A natural.

He threw me a glance. "What do you think, Pat, start with the last six months and work backward? Look for companies in Southern California first, then spread out?" Even though he was officially in charge, we'd worked together on so many cases that it felt routine for him to consult with me.

"Yes," I said. "Good call."

Blair and Hernandez nodded. Rose. Left.

Lien-hua walked to the whiteboard. "Let's not miss the big picture here. When I was a girl, my parents once took my family to Yosemite. I sat behind my father, who was driving. When cars or trucks would pass us, they'd go right past my window."

The newly assigned agents listened intently. I didn't know where Lien-hua was going with this, and it didn't look like they did either.

"Whenever a semi would pass our car and I'd look out my window, since all I could see was the truck, it didn't look like our car was traveling at fifty-five or sixty miles per hour, but rather it looked like the truck was standing still—"

"And your car was going backward," exclaimed Ralph.

"Right."

"So," I said, finally tracking with her. "Point of reference. Things are not always what they appear."

"Right. The perspective you use to address a problem. It affects how you view the situation."

"OK." Ralph rapped his knuckles against the table. "Maybe we need to step out of the car and look at this from the side of the road."

"Yes," Lien-hua said. "Or climb into the cab of the truck." She picked up a dry-erase marker. "Let's imagine we abducted Cassandra." She looked around the room. "Why? What possible motive could we have?"

One of the agents to my right called out, "Ransom."

Lien-hua nodded, wrote it on the board. Ralph had let her take control of the meeting without any objection. He's not the kind of guy to feel intimidated by someone else's competence.

"What else?" Lien-hua asked.

"To kill her," a female agent said grimly. "Or to abuse, or torture, or rape her."

Lien-hua wrote the word *harm* on the board. "I think you're right," she said. "So. Two categories so far: to harm the victim or benefit from the abduction."

"Or both," I added. "In this case, it appears Cassandra's abductor wants to torture her, but he also gave a time and a choice: 'Freedom or pain? You decide.' It seems that if something happens before the deadline, it could buy Cassandra's freedom."

Lien-hua wrote *both* on the board. "Any other thoughts?"

I didn't want to stand on my soapbox, but I did want to make sure we stayed focused. "People want lots of things out of life," I said. "Money, love, power, sex, respect, fame, whatever. The list goes on. We want to be happy, comfortable. We want meaning and adventure, as well as some sense of security or safety. Sometimes we want all of them at the same time. Trying to decipher someone's motives is like trying to follow the roots of a tree. They all intermingle beneath the surface. You can't pull one up without uprooting many others as well."

Lien-hua set down the dry-erase marker. "But, Pat, everyone has something that matters to him more than anything else. That one thing that he would die for, or risk everything for."

Ralph leaned both of his mighty arms on the table. "It's one way to control people," he said. "If you can find the thing that matters most to someone and either promise to help him get it or threaten to take it away, he'll do almost anything for you—go against his values, his morals, his religion. Find that one thing and you own him." He rapped the table with his fist. "Army Ranger Interrogation Techniques 101."

Lien-hua gave us a decisive nod. "So. The e-mail was sent to Hunter. Someone is trying to control him. So what does Austin Hunter want?"

"Cassandra," I said. Nods from the people in the room. We were on the same page. "But," I added, "if Hunter is our arsonist, what did he want when he started the other fires?"

Lien-hua looked at me with a light grin. "It sounds like you're trying to decipher motives, Dr. Bowers."

"Just trying to be cooperative."

Ralph was taking notes on a scrap of paper, figuring out all the threads of the investigation we needed to pursue. He nodded to one of the men in the room. "Peterson, check Hunter's bank accounts, see if our guy made any sizable deposits around the time of the fires. Graham, Castillo, have Lieutenant Mendez take you back through Hunter's apartment, see if there's anything there that might lead us to him. Solomon, you're all over that dart. Find us a brand name, manufacturer, distributor. And Mueller, go through Hunter's personnel records and start following up with the other guys on his SEAL team. Maybe there's a connection we missed. I'll work with Lieutenant Graysmith, have him send a team to Cassandra's place." I could feel a growing urgency in every word he spoke.

"But," Lien-hua said, "the big question we still need to answer is: if eight o'clock really is the deadline, what determines whether or not Cassandra gets set free? What does Hunter bring to the table?"

"He specializes in starting fires," I said.

"What do you think?" Ralph was addressing the whole team. "'Burn down a building and you get Cassandra back.' Sounds like ransom to me."

"Yes," said Lien-hua thoughtfully. "But if he started other fires before, why not just *ask* him to start this one . . ." Once again she was doing what she did best: diving into people's motives, thinking like they think. Reasoning like they reason. "Wait. Maybe this is a building he wouldn't normally agree to burn down. He's always been careful to set the fires so that they burn out quickly. No fatalities. No injuries."

Uh-oh.

"You think maybe a building filled with people?" asked one of the agents nervously, mirroring my thoughts.

"We can't rule it out," Lien-hua said. "Like Ralph said before, if you threaten to take away the one thing that matters most, a person will abandon his values, everything he holds dear."

In the icy silence that followed her statement, I decided what angle I had to pursue. I stood up. "I'll follow up on the videos from the aquarium, see if we got any footage of the abductor. Also, Cassandra was working on some kind of grant from the government. I want to know exactly what it involved. I'll fly through some of her files, see if I can figure out why she went to the aquarium this morning. Maybe that'll tell us what the people who took her are after."

"I'm going to watch the video of her again," said Lienhua. "Try to climb into our kidnapper's head."

"All right," said Ralph. "And the SDPD is sending a dozen cops to comb the warehouses by the shipyard."

"A dozen?" Lien-hua said. "That's it?"

"All they could spare." And then he said, "Everyone's got a job to do. Let's do it."

Without another word we stood and went our separate ways.

I looked at my watch. We had less than four hours to find Cassandra Lillo before she died in the tank.

44

Creighton stared calmly down the gun barrel at the head of the cop standing beside Randi. The door was cracked open just enough for him to watch them, and to kill them if necessary. All he needed was a good reason to pull the trigger.

Both Randi and the cop were about sixty feet away, easily within range, and Creighton could hear them talking.

"I don't know," Randi said. "I think this looks familiar. But it's hard to tell for sure. It was dark."

"This is the sixth warehouse we've been to." The cop sounded exasperated. "Look. I gotta go. They need us to sweep through this area for another case and I'm already late. I'll drop you off at the station."

"No, I think this might be the one. I'm pretty sure."

"You think *it might be*; you're *pretty sure*. That's what you said about the last one. Look, there's no car here. No phone. Go to the mall, buy yourself a new phone, and just be thankful nothing worse happened to you last night."

Randi protested one more time, but the cop had already started walking back to his car. She took one final look around the parking lot and then followed him.

Well, it was probably better this way.

But not nearly as much fun.

Just before they climbed into the squad car, Creighton heard the cop say into his radio, "Yeah, this is Officer Brandeiss here. There's nothing at the old Lardner Manufacturing place. It checks out. We're good to go."

Creighton waited by the door until the two of them had driven away.

So, for whatever reason, the cops were looking into the warehouse district. A tip? Who knows. But now it didn't matter. Officer Brandeiss had just reported the area clear.

Thanks, Randi, thought Creighton as he went back to see how high the water had risen in the tank. *Now no one else will disturb Cassandra and me for the rest of the day.*

45

The grammatically incorrect and utterly moronic sign outside Dragon's Tail Tattooing read, "Tattoo's! Done while
you wait." Tessa just shook her head. She stood for a moment trying to decide if she really wanted to go through
with this. Especially here.

Tangy smoke met her at the door. She recognized the
smell, and it didn't come from a cigarette. Harsh, driving
music pulsed toward her from inside the studio. One of her
favorite bands. DeathNail 13. At least that was cool.

Lien-hua's words from earlier in the day came back to
her: *We do what we have to do.*

She stepped inside, and a looming greasy-haired guy behind the counter turned down the music and snuffed out
what he'd been smoking. He wore a T-shirt that read: "Drunk
chicks dig me." Tessa could hardly believe she was going to
trust her arm to someone like this, especially when she saw
his eyes crawl across her body, lingering in all the places she
would've expected a guy wearing his T-shirt to stare.

"Should I buy you a camera?" she asked.

"Huh?"

"To take a picture. That what you want?" She gave him
the finger. "Take a picture of this, jerk."

Someone shrouded in a pool of shadows in the left-hand
corner of the room laughed. She couldn't make out his face
but saw that he was wearing shorts and flip-flops. He lit up
a cigarette.

She surveyed the place. Stenciled pictures of tattoo art-
work covered every spare inch of the walls. On the right,
two open doorways led to the tattoo rooms. Inside each of

them, she could see a sink, countertop, needles, and a tattoo machine waiting in the corner.

"So, then," grumbled the guy behind the counter. "What can I do for you?"

"This is a tattoo parlor, isn't it?"

"I'm afraid you're going to need your parents' permission. Did you bring your mommy with you?"

"My mom is dead."

A flat silence. "Oh. Sorry."

"Yeah, right."

Enough with this guy.

She looked around the dingy, smoky room and saw that the guy in the corner had leaned forward. He looked like he was in his early twenties. Curly, blond, surfer hair. A little soul patch. Glistening blue eyes.

"The music from before," she said. "When I came in. Is that what you like? DeathNail 13?"

"Yeah. Their last CD rocked." He had a cool, breezy, memorable voice.

"Which track did you like best: 'Terrible Plight' or 'Don't Open Your Eyes'?"

He took a drag from his cigarette. " 'Terrible Plight.' "

"Me too," she said, then continued by quoting the song's lyrics, " 'Currents of pain beneath the golden sky. Just can't seem to find solid ground.' "

" 'I'm always looking for a place to stand,' " he said. " 'Never finding the promised land.' Yeah. That song rocks."

She tore her eyes off him. It wasn't easy. "So," she said to the greasy-haired guy who looked good to drunk girls. "Can you give me a tattoo, or do I have to go somewhere else. I have money."

"Let's see it."

She laid the stack of twenties on the table. He plucked them up, flipped through them.

"Satisfied?"

"Lachlan," said the surfer guy. "Give the girl a tattoo."

"I don't know if it's enough money. Depends on what she wants."

"It's enough." He took another slow drag. "Give her whatever she wants. You work for me, and I'm tired of paying you to just stand around there doing nothing."

Lachlan mumbled something in Spanish, reached below the counter, and pulled out a beat-up clipboard with a blank form on it. "So," he said. "You're eighteen or older, right? Just say 'right.'"

"Right."

"Good."

"Sign this. It says that if you die from infection you can't sue us."

"Oh," said Tessa. "And does that happen often, then? Dead people suing you?"

The guy in the corner laughed his easy free laugh, and Tessa tossed him a smile. He tipped his cigarette to her, sending a curl of smoke in her direction.

"Just sign it," said Lachlan.

She jotted down the day's date, her contact info, and then scribbled an indecipherable name across the bottom of the form. Slid it back to him. Without even looking at it, Lachlan yanked the paper off the clipboard, pulled open a file drawer, and stuffed it inside.

She glanced at the blond guy in the corner. "Thanks."

"For what?"

"Letting me have whatever I want."

He seemed to consider her words for a moment. "Don't mention it. I'm Riker."

"That your first name or your last name?"

"It's what people call me. What do they call you?"

She thought fast. She didn't want to give him her real name. "Raven." It felt like a slight betrayal to say it, but she covered her discomfort with a smile. "I like Edgar Allan Poe."

"Cool. Well, pleasure to meet you, Raven."

Oh, he was so cute. And twenty at least. And he was flirting with her. She felt a flutter of excitement ride through her and tried to keep it out of her reply. "Pleasure to meet you too, Riker."

Then he leaned his chair against the wall again.

Lachlan stepped into the first tattoo room and twisted the chair beside the tattoo machine so that it faced Tessa. "So, where do you want it? Let me guess, your ankle? Back? Lotta girls are doing feet these days—"

"My arm." She rolled up her sleeve.

He stepped to her and pinched her biceps loosely, gazing at it like a farmer might look into the mouth of a horse. "Here, on the bottom of the arm," he said, "it's one of the most painful places to get one. One of the most sensitive places on your body."

"Don't worry about it."

His eyes paused on her scar. "That looks pretty recent."

"Couple months ago."

"Still hurt?"

"Naw. It's OK. That's where I want it." He was still feeling the skin on her arm. It was starting to creep her out.

"Around the scar?"

"No. Over it." She pulled her arm away.

"Scars don't hold color so good."

She turned to Riker. "Is this guy any good?"

Riker let out a swirl of smoke and leaned forward, bringing his face out of the shadows once again. He really did have gorgeous eyes. "Gotta go to L.A. to find anyone better. Trust me. He's the real deal. Just ignore the smell, you'll be fine."

"Very funny," said Lachlan. Then he looked at Tessa. "So, OK. You wanna cover up your scar."

"How many different ways do I have to say the same thing?"

He walked over to the sets of needles spread across the countertop beside the sink. "All right, whatever. So what do you want? Lotus? Butterfly? Heart? Tribal—"

"I want a raven." She didn't just want a raven because of the poem by Poe, but mainly because of Patrick, because he called her his little Raven sometimes and it made her feel special and loved and accepted in a quiet, private way. Since they were trying to draw closer to each other, she thought it might be cool to get a raven. She wasn't sure he'd be happy about her getting a tattoo, but she was sure a raven would mean a lot to him.

"You want a raven?" said Lachlan.

She called over to Riker and let sarcasm color her words. "Is he always this good at listening?" It was a way of flirting with him, and it felt good.

"He's on his A-game today."

She rolled her eyes lightly. "Oh. Great."

"Would you two knock it off?" said Lachlan. "I gotta get a visual of what she wants."

"OK. Here's what I want." She pulled out the picture she'd printed at the Internet café and handed it to him.

He studied it. "Looks like a crow."

"It's a raven, OK? And I want it on the front of my arm with its tail feathers curling around the back to cover the scar that the serial killer gave me after I stabbed him with a pair of scissors—kind of like those lying right over there on the counter. That's what I want. Can you do the tat or do I need to go somewhere else?"

"I can do it. I'll do it. Just chill." Lachlan's eyes traveled back and forth from Tessa to the scissors. "But a tat that big, wrapped around your arm like that, it's gonna take me, I don't know, maybe four or five hours if you want it done right."

"I'm cool with that. I want it done right."

"You want it filled in, like this picture? Some bluish highlights, maybe a little sliver of sunlight reflecting off the feathers, gray talons?"

"Exactly."

Lachlan shrugged, pulled out a razor and some shaving cream, and started shaving the light, feathery hair from the area surrounding Tessa's scar. "So be straight with me," he said, somewhat hesitantly. "You stabbed a serial killer?"

"Yes, I did."

"For what?"

"Asking me too many stupid questions."

Riker's laughter cut through the room and landed in her lap, and she returned it with a smile. After a few moments, Lachlan started sketching out the raven that was about to land on her arm. And, as Tessa began anticipating the first prick of the first needle, she promised herself that she wasn't going to cringe, no matter how much it hurt. Not with Riker watching her.

46

I was striking out. The only image of Cassandra on the Sherrod Aquarium's surveillance video was the one of her entering through the employee's door at five oh three a.m. No footage of her abductor.

Solomon swung by my workspace to tell me he'd found a match on the dart. "It's a Sabre 11, military issue. He could have gotten it at any of a dozen places in town. No prints."

"What about the drug?"

"Tox screening is backed up. It could take a couple days."

"We need it now. Get on their backs, and if they won't put a rush on it, sic Ralph on them."

He nodded and was about to leave when he added, "Oh, and by the way. We still don't have anything solid on Cassandra's family. We confirmed her mom's death, found strangled in an alley, but can't find any record of her dad. He might be dead too. No way to tell."

That was par for the course. "Thanks."

Solomon left and I returned to my research on Cassandra's grant, but that didn't seem to lead anywhere helpful either. All I found were a few references to something called Project Rukh and some PDF files with additional information about magnetoencephalography technology and mucopolysaccharides, the jellylike substance that acts as a semiconductor in the shark's electrosensory organs. But how was it related to the case? *A way to improve an*

*MEG's efficiency for a new generation of machines? Maybe
trying to figure out how sharks can sense and locate fish so
you can find a way to do it synthetically?*

Possibly. But how that might be connected to her abduction I couldn't even begin to guess. To use Lien-hua's
analogy, I needed to step out of the car. Or maybe look out
a different window.

Since the aquarium was owned by Drake Enterprises,
I thought maybe I could find out more about the grant by
following the money backward.

Their Web site featured a prominent picture of the CEO,
Victor Drake, and I recognized him as the man who'd almost knocked me down when I was leaving the aquarium
earlier in the day. Even though I hadn't heard of his company before this week, he'd apparently managed to build
one of the leading biotech firms in the country.

But how is that relevant? How is it connected?

Biotech?

Shark research?

Magnetoencephalography?

They all seemed to have something to do with the fires
and with finding Cassandra, but what?

It seemed like every step I took toward gathering more
clues led me farther away from the heart of the case. I
looked at the clock: five thirty-four p.m. With each passing moment, the chances of finding Cassandra alive were
shrinking and I was tense, so when the phone rang it jarred
me. I grabbed it. "Pat here."

"Dr. Bowers, it's Aina Mendez. Agent Hawkins told us
that Hunter might go after an inhabited building."

"It's possible."

"Well, because of that, we brought the bomb squad to
his apartment. They found traces of radioactive isotopes on
Hunter's clothing."

"What?" I gasped.

"Cesium-137. It's nasty stuff. Faint, but definitely present. It might have come from something as innocent as visiting a chemo lab at a hospital, or from someone working
on a dirty bomb. The team is doing a more extensive sweep
now, but I thought you should know."

The case cycled through my head, facts tumbling over
each other. "Aina, have your team check the fire sites,

see if they find any traces of the cesium there. Start with last night. I'm wondering if Hunter might have added something else that we didn't think of to the paste he used as an accelerant. And hurry. We don't have much time."

"But we've already done that."

"You have?"

"*Sí.* San Diego is one of the world's most important seaports and military hubs, so MAST regularly does sweeps through the city to look for radioactive isotopes, for any evidence of terrorist activity. In the past we've identified traces of cesium-137, but mostly that's from the medical research facilities here."

"Cross-check the records."

I knew I was getting tense, and I think she could hear it in my voice because it was a long moment before she said, "All right. I'll let you know what we find."

We ended the call. I looked at the clock.

Five thirty-seven p.m.

Lien-hua Jiang watched the video of Cassandra over and over again, each time pausing at different places. At last, she opened her notepad and wrote, "It isn't the killing that excites him the most. It's the power, the high he gets from holding another person's life in his hands. And he wants to make that feeling last as long as possible."

She paused. Yes. Cassandra's terror would go on for hours as she watched the water slowly rise around her— all the while knowing she couldn't escape. And he would be enjoying every minute of her suffering. Lien-hua put her pen to paper again, "Once the victim is dead, the thrill is over, so killing once isn't enough for him. He wants to experience it again and again. That's why he's taping her death."

When Lien-hua closed her eyes, she saw the face of a woman staring lifelessly through the water. A face pale, and shaded with death. She'd seen a face like that floating in the water once.

A long time ago.

She opened her eyes, rewound the video to the beginning, and started watching it again.

*   *   *

I felt the familiar tug in my heart: dad vs. FBI agent.

I needed to pull away and be a dad for a couple minutes. I tried Tessa's number. No answer.

Of course not.

I was a little worried about her, so I punched a few buttons on my cell phone to see if I could find her. Then I stood to stretch and clear my head, walked around the room twice.

When I took my seat and looked at my screen, my video chat icon was flashing. I clicked it and Terry's face appeared. "There you are, Pat. Good news. The video of Cassandra isn't on the Internet."

"How can you be sure?" I asked.

"Angela's team scanned the Web with their latest image-based search engines. We don't have to type in text anymore, just grab an image and go. It's like worldwide facial recognition. Web looks clean."

"Good. What else?"

"We deciphered the encrypted files. It's mostly all shark research, something about the ampullae of—"

"Lorenzini." I was getting antsy. "I got that too. Anything else?"

The clock on the wall.

Five forty-nine p.m.

"Well, there's a Project Rukh and some guy named Dr. Osbourne. I looked him up. He works for Drake Enterprises. First thing we thought—maybe the kidnapper, right? We did some checking on him, though, he's speaking at a convention in Boston. Been there for the last three days. Won't be back in town till tomorrow."

I thought through flight times and time zones and realized he couldn't have flown to San Diego and then back to Boston during the night to be part of the abduction. But I wrote down his name. I could follow up on him later. "What's Project Rukh, Terry? Do we know?"

"Looks like a DARPA project, although the Pentagon is pretty guarded about its defense contracts, and my intel is patchy. All I could come up with is that Drake Enterprises landed the contract."

Drake Enterprises again.

So, Cassandra did have a grant from the government after all.

In my mind I flew through a few of the things I knew about DARPA: theoretical weapons research—technology that's still twenty to fifty years out, sometimes they subcontract weapons systems to civilian organizations. But why an aquarium? Why a biotech firm? "Terry," I said, "DARPA. Talk to me. Quick summary."

"They're way out on the lip, Pat. If I wasn't here I'd be there. NASA grew out of DARPA, so did modern computer operating systems, artificial intelligence, voice recognition . . ." He must have been a bigger fan of DARPA than I thought. He continued to rifle through his list: "Hypertext, virtual reality, laser technology for space-based defense systems, submarine technology, and the Internet—all DARPA babies."

For just an instant I felt like saying that I thought Al Gore invented the Internet, but this wasn't the time to joke around. "So, what are you thinking?"

"DARPA doesn't just subcontract the big projects like jets or armored vehicles anymore. They use private firms to develop lots of smaller, high-tech items."

I thought back to my conversation with Maria at the aquarium. "What about killer ray guns?" I asked.

Silence. "What's going on here, Pat? This isn't just an abduction case, is it?"

That's when the door banged open and Ralph burst in. "Hunter struck," he said. "There's been another fire."

Five fifty-three p.m.

"Terry," I said. "Keep looking into the DARPA connection. I'll talk to you later. I have to go." I closed my computer and directed my attention on Ralph. "Casualties?"

"Unknown."

"Dirty bomb?"

"Doesn't look like it."

I slipped my computer into its bag and gathered my notes. "How do we know it's Hunter?"

"Aina can explain when we get there."

"So where is it?"

"You're not gonna believe this: Coronado Island. One of the buildings on the Navy SEAL Amphib Base. They call it Building B-14."

I was already halfway to the door. "Game on."

*   *   *

General Cole Biscayne paced to the window and stared into the night. Sickly moonlight wandered over the hills surrounding his West Virginia home.

He'd seen someone out there in the yard last week, just on the edge of the tree line. He knew he had, even though he couldn't be absolutely sure, even though the military police he'd brought in to investigate the area hadn't found anything. Still, Cole knew he'd seen someone. And he had a feeling he knew who it was.

Sebastian Taylor.

Years ago they'd worked together in the CIA, back when Cole served as the handler for a team of covert agents in South America. He'd trained Sebastian himself. Honed him into one of his unit's top operatives. But since Taylor had disappeared last October, the ex-assassin had contacted the general twice and made it quite clear that he blamed him for his fall from grace. Cole had done everything in his power to track down his protégé.

And had failed.

Cole scanned the yard again and saw nothing unusual, nothing out of the ordinary.

He was turning away from the window when the dogs began to bark.

47

Lien-hua, Ralph, and I skidded to a stop in front of the huge, slithering blaze that had all but consumed Building B-14. The ocean stretched like a dull smear of oil in the background.

A cluster of military personnel, firefighters, and even a smattering of what appeared to be privately hired security detail scurried around the burning building. Thankfully, the fire's location on the amphib base precluded a crowd of civilian onlookers.

Ferocious bursts of flame crackled and flared from the building, and the air all around us was scorched hot with soot and ash. The rigid heat from the flames kept us at a distance, but I caught sight of the Navy Fire Suppression Unit doing their best to direct their streams of water at the flames licking out of the windows. They aimed four hoses at the heart of the building, but in reply, the fire just ate the roof and roared toward the night sky.

Austin Hunter had made it out of the building just in time.

He crouched low, scanned the area. Clear.

Now, to get off the island and save Cassandra.

General Biscayne crept down the stairs and peered between the curtains, the revolver he always kept under his pillow gripped tightly in his hand.

A car in his driveway.

A man walking up the stone path to his door.

Military uniform.

Not Sebastian Taylor.

But who?

Then Cole recognized him: Sergeant Bier, one of his assistants in the Department of Defense. Cole lowered his gun. Opened the door just as Sergeant Bier was about to knock.

The sergeant saw the gun in Cole's hand and froze. "Are you all right, sir?"

"Yes, of course. What is it, Sergeant?"

"Project Rukh, sir." The sergeant kept his eye trained on the general's gun. "There's a problem. There's been a security breach in Building B-14."

"What?"

"A fire. I was told to deliver the message in person. They believe the fire was intentional, sir."

The general felt his gut tighten.

It had to be Victor Drake. It had to be.

So, Drake wanted to play it like this, huh? In order to hide his failure in completing the project, he decides to burn down the research facility that the military was providing him. Then he could just use the fire as an excuse for not delivering the device.

It sounded exactly like something a spoiled, self-centered billionaire would try. *OK. You want to play hardball; it's time to play hardball.*

"Contact the members of the oversight committee," General Biscayne said as he spun away from the door. "And arrange for an immediate flight to San Diego. It looks like I'll be meeting with Mr. Drake a day early."

48

Dusk was over, night was here.

It took me a few minutes to locate Lieutenant Mendez, but finally I found her talking with one of the base liaisons. They'd spread out the blueprint of the building on the hood of an MP's car.

I hurried to her. Just as I arrived, she finished her briefing with the senior chief petty officer and then gave me a quick rundown: no known casualties. The base had received an anonymous bomb threat two hours before the fire. They'd cleared Building B-14, swept for explosives, found none, and were just about to let the staff return when the fire alarms went off. Because of the bomb threat, there was some confusion about whether to send in the bomb squad or the firefighters. Ten minutes later, it didn't matter. The building was in flames, and all they could do was try to control the blaze.

"He was really quite clever," Aina said. "He got everyone out of the building, plus he created enough confusion to give the fire time to ignite."

"You're sure it's our guy?"

"Pretty sure." She drew my attention to the blueprint. "Fire started here, on the east wing, near the A/C center."

I immediately saw why she thought it was our arsonist.

"Fits the pattern."

"*Sí.*"

I traced my finger along the blueprint. "Just like the

first fourteen fires, he used vents and airflow to direct the blaze."

Aina picked up on my train of thought. "The building's main air-conditioning vents blew directly on the fire, feeding it a steady stream of air, here—"

"Creating a giant blowtorch that shot the fire through the building's air ducts. Building B-14 didn't have a chance."

"You think like an arsonist," she said.

"No," I said, turning to face the fire. "If I did, I'd know why he chose this building."

Creighton Melice grabbed the new cell phone he'd bought half an hour ago. Time to leave the warehouse and meet with Hunter to make the exchange.

Well, to be more accurate: to get the device. There wasn't going to be any exchange. There was only going to be a dead ex-SEAL.

He didn't want to worry about Cassandra somehow escaping, so he double-checked the security of the cotter pins that locked the metal bars in place at the top of the tank. The pipes passed through holes drilled into the glass, and since the cotter pins that secured the pipes were outside the glass, there was no way for her to get out, even if she were able to break the chain.

"See you soon, Cassandra," he called. "I hope I make it back in time to say good-bye."

The water was up to her chest. Cassandra shouted at him, a muted, hollow cry, and spit at the glass. Creighton waited a moment to watch the saliva slide into the water, and then he left her, locked the warehouse door behind him, and stepped into the cool San Diego night.

Time was ticking away. Already we'd been on-site for almost twenty-five minutes.

While Lien-hua went to speak to some base personnel about the nature of the bomb threat used to clear the building, I met with Aina and Ralph to try and narrow down where Hunter might be hiding.

"He could be in the crowd," Ralph said.

"We thought of that," said Aina. "We're checking on everyone who's here."

"No," I said. "Not this guy. He leaves. Remember? The

trolley system. He likes to disappear fast, and he knows how to do it. He's not going to stick around. Besides, he needs to get to shore. He wants to save Cassandra."

I tried to figure out what the best entrance and exit routes would be. *How would I get off Coronado Island?*

Obvious choice: drive. Either the Coronado Bridge or the Silver Strand, the narrow strip of land that leads from the island to Imperial Beach. Aina seemed to read my mind. "The military is treating this as domestic terrorism," she said. "They're stopping all traffic leaving the island."

"Boats?" I asked her.

"Already on it. We took a few people in for questioning. It doesn't look like anything though."

I heard the sound of a helicopter and noticed a news chopper hovering above the shore of the mainland. Hmm. It was possible. "See if there's been any base air traffic in the last hour. Helicopters especially."

"You serious, Pat?" said Ralph. "You think he flew out?"

"Just trying to eliminate the possibility."

Aina spoke into her walkie-talkie. "No air traffic," she said. "Not in the last two hours."

"Then there's only one option left," I said.

"What's that?" she asked.

I pointed to the dark ocean. "He swam."

Austin Hunter threw his arm out of the water and grabbed the edge of the dock. It had taken him longer than he expected to get to shore, but he knew there would be too much attention drawn to this fire to get off the island any other way.

After he'd hoisted himself onto the dock, he slipped out of his swim fins and then yanked off his face mask and snorkel. Normally he would have used a scuba tank and a rebreather to eliminate bubbles, but tonight he'd needed to pull something with him.

In his black hybrid wet suit he doubted anyone passing by could see him, but he needed to make sure. He gave the area a quick visual.

OK.

Clear.

Austin glanced at his waterproof watch: 1839 hours.

He needed to hurry; he was supposed to have checked in nine minutes ago.

The rope that was tied around his waist tugged at him, telling him that the five-foot-long inflatable sack containing the device was floating past him toward shore. Before it could bump into any of the dock's pilings, he pulled the floating waterproof bag toward him, and carefully lifted it onto the dock.

49

I spent a minute studying the water, gauging the wind. The currents. "Ralph, how far do you think it is to shore?"

He surveyed the distance. "I'd say about a mile, mile and a half."

"You were in the special forces; how long would it take a Navy SEAL to swim that far?"

"A SEAL, with this wind ... maybe thirty-five, forty minutes." As I stepped toward Aina I heard him mumble, "Take a Ranger twenty-five." I took a moment to compare the swim time with the time of the fire's origination.

"He's on the mainland," I said. "Aina, we need to send out an APB, have officers start sweeping the shore. Get some. Wait—" As I stared at the shoreline I saw the news helicopter again. This time I could read the writing on the side: Channel 11. "They're filming this. Ralph, see if you can get us a feed. Pull some strings if you have to. I want to see if they've caught our guy on camera." I saw Lien-hua coming toward us, picking her way through the crowd.

"Maybe we could have the helicopter crew help look for him," Aina suggested.

"No good," I said. "I don't trust the media, and the more control they have, the worse off we are. We need to get in the air ourselves."

Lien-hua arrived, and while Aina and Ralph made the calls, I ran with her toward the amphib base's landing pad.

The man on the phone had been very clear that if the device was not intact they would kill Cassandra. So, before delivering it, Austin decided to take a quick look and make sure it hadn't been damaged during his swim across the bay.

He bypassed the zipper and instead tore open the waterproof bag and pulled out the black duffel bag inside. He didn't rip this open, though, but unzipped it carefully. The device was enclosed in a protective foam wrap, which he gently unfolded.

The device looked a bit like a video camera supported on an extendable tripod base. The unit's body had a laser focus and a satellite dish the size of Austin's hand. An eight-inch video screen was mounted in the front, and a large removable battery pack with radioactive warning labels hung from its belly. If he didn't know better, he'd say it was some kind of laser tracking unit or remote listening device, or maybe a high-tech thermal imager. But he did know better; he'd seen those two men use it the previous night.

Austin thought this thing might have something to do with the research Cassandra was doing, but he couldn't be certain. One time she'd mentioned a project she was working on for the government, but he hadn't pried. After fourteen years as a SEAL, he knew that keeping secrets meant keeping your job. Now, he wished he'd asked her more about it. In any case, the device didn't seem to have retained any damage from its trip across the bay. No way to tell for sure, but it looked intact. He folded the foam around it and zippered the duffel shut.

Time: 1844 hours.

Cassandra would be dead in seventy-six minutes unless he delivered this device.

Austin pulled his combat knife out of its sheath, cut the rope off his waist, and tossed his snorkeling gear into the ocean. Then he strapped the device to his back using two elasticized ropes as shoulder straps and sprinted up the pier.

I smacked my hand against the stucco siding of the air transport building.

Two stern MPs blocked my path. "I'm sorry, sir," one of them said, "orders from the admiral."

Ralph appeared beside me. "Aina sent out an APB, they're scouring the shipyards—" Then he saw the expression on my face. "What's the problem here?"

"They won't get us a bird," I said. "We're on a military base, not civilian soil, so they said they would take care of this themselves."

"What?" He glared at the MPs. "Let me talk to your superior officer."

"Wait," said Lien-hua. "Time's not on our side anymore. Finding the right person, going through the right channels, getting clearance, we don't have that kind of time. What did Channel 11 give you?"

Ralph shook his head. "We got nothing," he said. "They were filming the fire, not the shore . . ." He looked toward the sky. "What the—"

I followed his gaze. The news helicopter had changed direction and was heading back along the beach of the mainland. "Oh no," I said. "They're going for an exclusive. They'll spook him. Ralph, can you—"

"I'm on it," he snarled, pulling out his phone again. Before speaking into his phone, though, he told Lien-hua and me, "You two get to the mainland. Now."

Catching up to Hunter was the key to finding Cassandra, and we had just over an hour to do it. Lien-hua and I hurried to the car.

I pulled out the car keys, but she grabbed them from my hand. "I'll drive."

•

50

As far as Austin Hunter knew, he'd never killed anyone. Never eliminated any targets.

That's how they put it in the special forces—eliminating targets. His friends had. Some of them had made a career out of it. But not Austin Hunter.

How had this happened?

How had he dragged Cassandra into this?

Oh, if they hurt her in any way.

If they do anything to her.

It was because of the fire last night. He knew they were doing this because he hadn't started the fire last night.

Austin had investigated each of the fire locations to make sure there were no occupants in the buildings. All were empty. No people. No casualties. No targets.

After the first six fires, he'd started to think that Drake was just a rich pyro who was too much of a coward to start his little recreational fires himself. And that's what Austin told himself for the next eight fires.

But then last night came, and everything changed.

Once again Drake had told him to come at the specified time—that was always part of the deal; he wouldn't get paid if he arrived early. But last night Austin had gotten a bad feeling after talking to Drake. The billionaire sounded really torqued about something, and Austin didn't want to be a part of any job that went sour. So he decided to arrive an hour early to check things out.

And that's when he saw what those two men did.

And in that moment, Austin realized that he'd gotten

himself in way over his head. The men had probably used the device at each site before he arrived. That's why he'd been brought in to start the fires.

And that's why he'd been told not to arrive early—so he wouldn't see them in the act.

Now they could set him up for everything.

Austin figured Drake's men would come after him, but he never thought they'd go after Cassandra.

The news helicopter rotated toward him, and Austin dashed past a marina and slipped into a gap between two buildings. He needed to avoid the sight lines of the chopper, but all the evasiveness was slowing him down and he didn't have time for that.

Victor Drake was behind this. He had to be.

But Drake had messed with the wrong man.

Austin waited a moment for the helicopter to pass, then edged into the street and ran toward the primary rendezvous point.

Earlier in the day, when he first saw the video of Cassandra in the tank, he'd thought about going after Drake, doing whatever it took to get him to talk, but he was afraid that if he did, Drake's hired guns would find out and kill Cassandra before he could save her. And, of course, Austin couldn't go to the authorities because the kidnappers would definitely kill Cassandra then, and afterward Drake would turn him in for starting the fires.

Really, Austin had no bargaining chips—except for his skills.

So. Mission objectives: burn down the building, retrieve the device, save Cassandra.

Then when it was all over: deal with Drake.

Yes, as far as Austin Hunter knew, he'd never killed anyone.

But if they hurt Cassandra at all, if they even touched her, that was going to change.

Creighton Melice waited anxiously by the docks for the call from Shade. According to the plan Shade had e-mailed him, Hunter should have found the cell phone taped beneath the park bench over twenty minutes ago. Shade was supposed to call Hunter first and then contact Melice to finalize where the exchange would take place. But so far, nothing. Creighton didn't like it when things didn't go according to schedule.

A thought crawled into his mind. An awkward, uncomfortable itch.

What if Hunter had retrieved the device and decided to keep it for himself?

No. He wouldn't do that. He loved Cassandra. That was the key to everything—his love for her. He wouldn't leave her alone at the deadline. He wasn't that kind of a man.

But then again, maybe Shade had read him wrong. Maybe Hunter loved something else more than his girlfriend.

Creighton decided to give Shade five more minutes and then, if he didn't call, return to the warehouse and switch to Plan B.

7:05 p.m.

Austin heard the phone ringing and sprinted the last sixty yards at full speed to the park bench, but by the time he arrived, the ringing had stopped.

He scoured the bench, found the phone, and snatched it up.

But when he opened it all he found was dead air.

No.

Too late.

They'd been very specific about the time, and he was too late.

No, he couldn't be too late. He couldn't be. He slammed a fist against the bench.

Maybe they were here, somewhere close by. He looked rapidly in every direction.

No one.

No!

And that's when he heard the sirens coming his way.

51

7:11 p.m.

I braced my hand against the car's ceiling as Lien-hua swerved around a corner and jammed on the brakes at the edge of a semicircle of spinning lights. In the middle of the road, surrounded by more than a dozen police officers, stood a lone man wearing one of the new breed of Kevlar-sewn body armor that doubles as a wet suit. He wielded a jagged combat knife and was turning in a cautious circle so the officers wouldn't rush him.

Austin Hunter.

They had him cornered.

And I had to assume that they didn't know about Cassandra.

Lien-hua and I jumped out of the car and rushed past the ambulance parked behind one of the police cars.

"Drop the knife!" one of the officers yelled. "Hands above your head!"

Hunter began to slowly raise his hands, and then in one lightning-swift motion yanked a Kimber Tactical Custom II .45 out of a holster slung around his chest and aimed the weapon at his own head before anyone could react.

There he stood. Knife in one hand, gun in the other.

This guy was brilliant. If he would've aimed the gun anywhere else—anywhere at all—the cops would have fired. And if he turned himself in, his abductors would think he'd gone to the authorities and would undoubtedly kill Cassandra. The only way to save himself and his girl-friend was to buy time by threatening to take his own life right now. Maybe get the authorities to listen to him. To help him.

"Drop the gun!" hollered one of the officers. "Now. Drop it!"

"They've got her," Hunter yelled. "They're gonna kill her."

I whipped out my ID, showed it to a sergeant who seemed to be the site commander. "We're federal agents," I said. "Stand down."

Hunter swiveled and looked at me, the gun still aimed at his own head. "They made me do it. I didn't want to. I need to find her."

I heard another officer shout, "Put down the gun!"

"They're gonna kill her," Hunter yelled.

"Relax, Austin," I said. "We're here to help."

The sergeant, whose badge read "Newson," was hesitating. Something you can't do at a time like that. This was rolling downhill fast, and there was only one outcome in sight.

Think fast. Think fast.

"Drop the gun!" someone hollered.

"Sergeant Newson," I said. "The field office sent us." I pointed to Lien-hua. "She's a negotiator." It wasn't quite true, but she was the best hope we had of reining this in. "Let her talk to him, now, before someone gets trigger-happy."

"FBI field office sent you?" Newson asked.

"Lieutenant Graysmith requested it," said Lien-hua.

Yes. Good thinking, Lien-hua.

"Graysmith?" Then he shrugged. "OK. It's his butt, not mine." He seemed relieved to hand the situation off to us. "Hold your fire," he shouted into his vehicle's built-in PA system. "Hold positions, but hold your fire."

"OK," I said to Lien-hua. "You're on."

In the tense silence, Hunter scrutinized Lien-hua and then me. "I didn't want to hurt anyone."

She slowly set her gun on the pavement. "I know."

"I just want to save her. We don't have much time. She dies at eight o'clock."

She stepped toward him. "We know about Cassandra," she said. "We want to help. Do you have any idea where she is?" Lien-hua had wisely kept the conversation on Cassandra's situation, rather than Hunter's, focusing on the one thing that mattered most to him.

He shook his head, the gun still aimed at his temple. "They're gonna kill her. Drake is gonna kill her."

Drake?

Victor Drake?

Lien-hua raised her hands, palms up, and took a gentle step toward him. "How will you get in touch with them, Austin? Can we contact them—"

"No. It has to be me. They contact me. They're watching. They'll kill her."

"Drop the gun!" blared one of the cops.

"Quiet," Lien-hua yelled. She took another step toward Hunter, her hands still open, showing she meant no harm.

He moved the gun closer to his head. "Stop. Stay there."

She paused. "Please, Austin. We want to save her. We know she's in danger. We saw the video."

He stared at her. "I didn't kill them. I swear." His voice cracked. "I didn't even know."

"No. You cleared the building. You saved them. No one was killed." She took another small step.

"Not them."

"No one died in the fire," she said. Then another step. And another.

"No, no. Of course not. I made sure—for all of them, I made sure. All fourteen." He twisted to the right to see if any of the officers were creeping up on him. "But I didn't start the fire last night, and I had nothing to do with that homeless guy."

"Homeless guy?" She was only a meter from him.

And then he stared past Lien-hua toward me. "Her abductors want it. They said we could exchange. It's over—"

And then Austin Hunter made his fatal mistake.

He might have survived the night if he hadn't pointed the knife at Lien-hua as he said those last two words.

52

As soon as Austin tipped the knife toward Lien-hua, the shooting began. "Stand down!" I yelled.

Austin's body jerked uncontrollably as the bullets slammed into him. "Stand down. Hold your fire!" A bullet blazed past my face and punctured the windshield of one of the patrol cars near me, sending dark splinters of glass mushrooming into the vehicle. I ducked. "Stand down!" I stooped low. Rushed through the gunfire toward Lien-hua, who'd dropped to the pavement and lain prone on the ground.

A moment later the shooting stopped, but with the number of bullets Austin took, even the Kevlar suit couldn't save him.

But my attention wasn't focused on him. I was kneeling beside Lien-hua's motionless body, reaching my hand toward the blood on her neck. "Get a paramedic over here, now!"

Austin Hunter knew he was dying. He tried to point to the device. Tried. Tried. It was Cassandra's only chance. He tried to move his hand but couldn't.

As his consciousness began to dim, he softly begged Cassandra and the negotiator woman who'd been shot and looked like she was dying—her too—he begged them both to forgive him. He'd failed Cassandra. And it was his fault the cops had shot the Asian woman. He'd been too slow getting to the rendezvous point.

Too slow. And now both of those women were going to die.

*   *   *

I feared the worst, touched Lien-hua's shoulder with a trembling hand, prayed that she would be all right.

Please, O God, please.

"Lien-hua." I pressed my hand against the wound on her neck to stop the bleeding.

She stirred.

"Lien-hua, are you . . ."

Then she rolled to face me and opened her mouth. My heart was racing. "I think," she murmured. "I think I'm OK."

"You were hit. Your neck is bleeding." I turned to the officers beside me. "Where's that paramedic!"

The last thing Austin Hunter saw before the final darkness chewed across his vision was a man walking toward him grinning, the very man he'd seen the night before aiming the device at that homeless man.

And the grinning guy was a cop.

As I pulled my hand away, I could see that Lien-hua's wound didn't appear serious or life-threatening. Maybe the bullet had only grazed her.

I hoped so. I prayed so.

As the paramedics helped her, I looked at Austin Hunter. A trickle of blood seeped from his half-open mouth, his body twitched one last time as he tried but failed to say something, and then Austin Hunter died.

53

One of the officers stepped into the pool of blood beside Austin's body and kicked the gun away from his motionless hand. "Suicide by cop," he mumbled. "Always hate to see that."

I knew it was standard operating procedure to use lethal force in a situation like this, especially for a suspected terrorist. And I knew it wasn't uncommon in a gunfight to have dozens of rounds fired, especially with this many officers. It's called survival stress reaction, it's just the way your body reacts, especially if you're inexperienced. You just keep firing. But still, I hated that it had happened. I hated that Austin Hunter had been killed.

Another tragedy. Another death.

I checked my watch.

Seven sixteen p.m.

In less than forty-five minutes, Cassandra would be joining her boyfriend. I felt the screws of anger and grief tighten around my heart. "This man wasn't trying to commit suicide," I exploded. "He wanted to live."

A paramedic leaned over Lien-hua. Two other EMTs knelt to attend to Austin, but nothing could help him now.

"He didn't want to live," the cop said. "He had a gun to his head."

I felt like decking this idiot. "That was to stop you from killing him. Couldn't you even see that? He just snuck onto the Navy SEALs' training base and burned down a secure military installation to save the woman he loves. A man like that doesn't kill himself before he can finish the job."

"You saw the guy," the officer responded. "You heard what he said: 'It's over!' This was his endgame."

I couldn't believe how stupid this guy was. I read his name tag. "Listen to me, Officer Rickman. He wasn't going to shoot anyone. He was scared. He was trying to—"

"Pat," Lien-hua called from where she sat beside me on the pavement.

I knelt beside her. "What? Are you OK?" I saw that the paramedic had wrapped a gauze bandage around her neck.

"We need to focus on Cassandra, now," she said. "Please. Let it be. Don't get tangled up in this. Let's not lose her too." Lien-hua began to stand up.

"Take it easy," I said, placing a hand on her arm.

"I'm OK. Really. It's just a scratch."

"Lien-hua, I think you should—"

"Patrick." Steel eyes. Steel will. "Stop it. I'm OK. Let's go find Cassandra." Yes, this was the woman I knew. The one who never failed to impress me. I offered my hand, and she let me help her to her feet.

I looked at the ground. The officer who'd been arguing with me had stepped back, leaving a bloody imprint of his shoe's sole on the road.

Then Detective Dunn appeared and strode across the street. He stared at Austin Hunter's body. "Who shot first?" Dunn scanned the faces of his men. No one replied. "Who fired the first shot!" he roared.

No one responded. Lien-hua asked for my latex gloves, I pulled some out of my pocket and after she'd tugged them on, she picked up Austin's gun, ejected the magazine. It was full. "He didn't even have a chance to fire his weapon."

I was still staring at a bloody shoe print next to Austin's body. "You work many fires, Officer Rickman?" I asked.

"Huh?"

"Fires. Arsons. Did you work the one this morning?"

"I'm a cop, not a firefighter." He spit out the words.

"Hunter was trying to tell us something," Lien-hua said to Dunn, interrupting my exchange with Officer Geoff Rickman.

Dunn leaned over, felt Austin's pulse. Unnecessary, but symbolic. "This man could have helped us find a missing woman," he said. "And now he's dead."

Rickman muttered something indecipherable as he started back to his car. I had some suspicions about Rickman, but they were still vague and unsupported, and right now I needed to lean on evidence rather than instinct. We needed something solid, and we were running out of time.

"All right," said Dunn. "We sort it out at headquarters. Let's get this mess cleaned up." He gazed at an abandoned car beside me, and then, in a burst of rage, kicked the tire and yanked out a pile of parking tickets stuffed under its windshield wipers. His reaction might have been fierce compassion, or maybe anger that he hadn't been the one to fire first. It was impossible to tell. "Get this freakin' piece of crap out of here. Take it to impound." Then he stared at me. "You two really get around for a couple of federal agents." He kept his words flat; I couldn't tell if they were spoken with respect or disdain.

"And you really get around for a homicide detective," said Lien-hua.

"That I do," he said. "That I do."

"Detective," I said. "Send some men to talk to Victor Drake right away. Hunter mentioned his name. He might know something about Cassandra's abduction."

Dunn didn't look happy about it, but he agreed and then walked away.

While everyone else drifted around the scene, seeming to breathe a collective sigh of relief, I thought of Cassandra and of Austin Hunter's last words: "It's over."

I could only hope he wasn't right.

I took a moment to kneel beside his body. It shouldn't have ended like this. He didn't need to die tonight. "I'm sorry, Austin," I whispered, and I really was sorry. Sorry he died for no reason. Sorry he'd been coerced into committing another crime. Sorry we hadn't found him earlier in the day so we could have stopped this. Sorry about so many things.

Despite the mistakes Austin had made, despite the laws he'd broken, he had served faithfully in the special forces for fourteen years. I laid my hand on his shoulder in honor of the service he'd given our country. He was just like so many people I know—a hero in one area of life, flawed and all too human in another. In the end, though, he'd died doing the noblest thing of all, trying to save another person's life. And though I might not have taken the same steps he did, I respected the value he seemed to place on human life—clearing Building B-14 before starting the fire, planning his fires to avoid casualties. I wondered how I would have reacted if someone had sent me a video like that of Lien-hua chained in a tank. I could only imagine the things I would have been willing to do to save her.

As I was rising to leave, I saw the end of a cheap, pre-paid cell phone jammed beneath the strap of his shoulder holster.

What?

"They contact me," he'd said. This phone must be how!

Everyone else had left me alone with the body, so nobody was close by. No one else had seen the phone.

I slid my hand down, cupped the phone, and then slipped it into my pocket. Maybe, just maybe, this could lead us to Cassandra.

"I'll find her, Austin," I said, even though the corpse beside me couldn't hear the words. "I'll save Cassandra. I promise."

I looked at my watch. I had only forty minutes to keep my promise.

Then I stood up to find Lien-hua.

54

During a short break, while Lachlan and Riker grabbed a smoke outside the studio, Tessa noticed the time and sent Patrick a text message that she wasn't feeling the greatest, which was true, and that she would just grab supper on her own and then go to bed early, but that she'd see him in the morning for their walk with Dr. W. at ten thirty.

Then Lachlan returned to the tattoo room to finish inking her arm.

He alternated between two different tattoo needles attached to two different machines. He used the narrow needle with his machine cranked to its highest speed to do the outlining, and then he used the wider needle to color in the main body of the tattoo. All Tessa knew was that the wider needle hurt way worse than the outlining needle.

He'd laid out a set of tiny caps beside the sink, a different color in each cap.

Blue. Black. Silver. Gray.

Dip the needle in the water. Then the ink.

Then against her skin.

Repeat.

When he'd first started, every time he touched the needle to her skin it felt like a hot scratch. But as he worked on her arm, her skin must have started to swell or get numb because she couldn't feel the needle anymore, just a dot of tight pressure.

"Now," he told her, "I gotta go back and fill in the rest of the color on the tail feathers. The skin on the inside of your arm isn't gonna be numb anymore. It'll be even more sensitive than ever, plus with that scar . . . well, just be ready."

She nodded.

Then Lachlan began to fill in the color, and she realized he hadn't been lying about the tenderness of her skin.

No, he hadn't been. Not one little bit.

After a minute or two of etching her arm, Lachlan said, "Hey, listen. I got a puzzle for you. This one usually takes people like a half hour or so to figure out. Should take you through to the end."

"I like puzzles," she said, trying to sound casual.

"Me too," said Riker, who was pulling up a new playlist on the stereo's digital display.

"OK," Lachlan said. "So there's these two guys rob a bank and they're figuring out the cut, right? And the first guy says, 'Hey, it's not fair. You got way more money than me'— You know this one, Riker?"

"Naw, go ahead."

"OK, why don't we see who figures it out first, you or Serial-Killer-Stabber-Girl?"

"Right on," he said.

"I suppose I can give it a shot," said Tessa.

"So," Lachlan continued. "Like I was saying, the first guy says, 'You got way more than me. If I gave you one of these stacks of bills, you'd have twice as much as I have.' But the other guy is like, 'Dude, check it out. I planned the job, so quit complaining, it's a fair cut. Besides, if I gave you one of my stacks, we'd have the exact same amount.' So, question is, how many stacks of bills does each of the—"

"Got it," said Tessa.

"—guys have." Lachlan stared at her. "You didn't figure it out already. There's no way."

"Give me a sheet of paper."

Lachlan dug a pen and a yellowing sheet of paper out of a drawer and handed them to Tessa. She wrote something on the page, then folded the paper in half, gave it to Riker, and then set down the pen. "After you figure out your answer," she said, "look at mine. Then ask Lachlan which is right."

"You heard it before," Lachlan said.

"Puh-lease."

"So you never heard it before?" said Riker.

"No."

"You figured it out that fast?"

"You'll have to wait until you unfold that piece of paper to find out."

Riker looked at her slyly. "But what if I don't figure it out until after your tattoo is done and you take off?"

Tessa felt her heart beating like a rabbit as she said the words, "Then we'll have to compare answers the next time we see each other."

"Deal."

55

7:25 p.m.

With his television tuned to Channel 11 news, Victor Drake watched Building B-14 crumble to the ground.

Hunter. It had to be Hunter.

But how did he know which building to torch?

Maybe Hunter had followed Geoff and the doctor last night, after they left the fire site and were returning the device to the base.

Victor could feel a migraine coming on. Not just any migraine either, a big one. Half an hour ago he'd gotten a message from Biscayne's cronies that the Project Rukh Oversight Committee meeting was moved from Thursday at two p.m. to tomorrow morning at eight a.m. A major-league migraine.

His cell phone rang.

He answered it. "Yeah?"

Geoff's voice. "Hunter's dead."

A glint of hope. "What?"

"I'm afraid he was killed in a tragic shoot-out. Suicide by cop. Always hate to see that."

Oh, this could be good. This could be very good. "Okay. Listen. Make sure there's nothing on his body that could tie him to the project. I'll contact you later. We'll need to meet again to clean up this mess."

"I'm on my way to your place now."

"What?"

"As a cop. They want someone to interview you. I volunteered. So let's practice: You don't have any connection to this man Hunter, do you, Mr. Drake?"

A slight pause. "No, of course not, Officer."

"Good. When my partner and I get there, just remember that."

"Good work, Geoff. Thanks."

A pause. "I'm putting in a lot of overtime for you this week."

"I'll give you an extra fifty grand."

"One hundred."

"What?" How dared this underling make demands of Victor Drake! "Absolutely not."

"I'm not doing this for humanitarian reasons, Drake. I only care about one thing: money. You give me a hundred grand in cash tomorrow and I'll spend tonight making sure this little problem goes away. Otherwise, I bail."

Victor felt his teeth grind, his head spin, his heart rate shoot through the roof. He hated himself for saying it, for doing it, for giving in, but at last he said, "All right. A hundred. But only if you can get this cleaned up before the general arrives in the morning."

"Done."

Lien-hua and I tried to back-trace any calls that might have been received on or dialed from Austin's phone, but found that it was brand new. Never been used. The kidnappers must have left it somewhere for Austin. "Let's hope he was still waiting for their call," I said. Then a moment later I was startled when my own phone throbbed. I took a quick glance to see a text message from Tessa canceling supper. I was a little disappointed but also a little thankful since I couldn't really get away right now anyway.

"OK," I said. "Let's forget the phone for a minute. It's no good to us unless they call. What else do we have?"

"Some officers are going to talk to Drake. Otherwise . . ." Lien-hua thought for a moment. "Ralph had an agent checking to see if the tank had been shipped to this part of the country. Did we ever hear anything from him?"

I shook my head. "Not that I know of."

Then the alarm on my watch went off.

"What's that for?" Lien-hua asked.

"Thirty minutes," I said. "We only have thirty minutes left until Cassandra dies."

"I'll call Ralph." She stepped away to make the call and

while she did, I tried to think of any clues, any clues at all, that I was missing. Anything that could lead us to Cassandra's location.

Nothing.

Nothing came to mind.

Seconds, minutes passed by.

Nothing, nothing, nothing except the thought of Rickman's shoe print. The impression patterns—

And that's when Austin's phone rang.

I flipped it open, held it to my ear. Waited, waited for whoever was on the other end to speak first. The silence was unsettling; maybe Austin was supposed to initiate the conversation.

Nothing.

I began to fear that the caller might hang up. "It's done," I said. I spoke in a low voice and hoped he wouldn't notice I wasn't Austin.

"So, Austin." An electronically altered voice. "You did find the phone."

The kidnapper ... and he doesn't know Austin Hunter is dead.

"Yeah."

"We weren't sure you made it. You were supposed to check in over an hour ago."

He said "we" ... how many are there?

"Cops all over the place."

A brief pause. "My name is Shade, and I have some instructions for you."

Shade? A code name ... Why is he introducing himself now? ... He must not have spoken with Austin before. Test it. Find out.

"Let me talk to the guy from before. I don't know you."

"He's busy with Cassandra. I want to thank you for what you did. But now, it's time for you to deliver the device."

So, there are at least two of them ... This one doesn't know Hunter's voice, hasn't spoken with him before ... And there's a device ... What device? I tried to think of something, anything to say in response, but there was too much at stake, and too little information. Too many wrong things I might say.

"Are you there?" Shade said.

"Yeah."

"The deal was: the building and the device for the girl. So, do you have it?"

What device is he talking about?

"Yeah, I have it." I had to say something. "Where do you want to make the exchange?"

"Same place you were told before. Be there in ten minutes."

Oh no. Oh no.

"Can't. Too many cops around there."

A pause. Shade must have been considering what I'd said. Maybe he was on to me. For Cassandra's sake I hoped not.

"I'm there right now," said the person calling himself Shade. "There aren't any cops. You just killed Cassandra Lillo, Dr. Bowers."

56

The line went dead.

No, no, no.

I'd killed her.

How did Shade know my name?

I'd killed Cassandra.

I spun, checked the sight lines. Did he see me? Was Shade here? I saw no curtains quiver shut, no movement, no glint of a scope or binoculars. No one in the crowd of officers was on a cell.

I tried to redial, nothing. Tried Terry's number for a trace. Busy. Called Angela Knight: she would get on it, but it would take some time—the one thing we didn't have.

"Pat." Lien-hua came rushing toward me. "I think we caught a break. A big one."

"The tank. They found the tank?"

She shook her head. "No." She was running toward the car now, and I was hurrying to keep up with her. "There's a woman named Randi who says a guy drove her to a warehouse by the shipyards last night and started talking about how he was supposed to pick up some other woman. That the plans had changed and it was time to get her. Things like that. Then he left Randi there."

We climbed in. "That's not enough." I said. "It could refer to anything."

Lien-hua started the engine. "Somehow Channel 11 found out about Cassandra's disappearance, and an un-named police officer gave them Hunter's name. A few minutes ago they did a news flash, and listed Austin Hunter and Cassandra Lillo as persons of interest in the terrorist attack at the base—they're calling it a terrorist attack—and asked for people to call in with any information." She backed up the car, then pulled into the street.

"I still don't see the connection." The nightscape of San Diego flashed past us in swirls of blurred light, street lamps, and restless palm trees.

"Randi phoned the station, and Ralph followed up with her. Apparently, she took the wrong phone and someone named Shade called her this afternoon and mentioned the fire at Building B-14 before she could say a word."

"What! Where is she?"

"Shade is probably one of the—"

"That's who I just talked to."

"Someone called the phone?" she gasped. "Why didn't you say so?"

"I would have, it's just—listen, I'll tell you on the way. Where are we heading?"

"Randi gave Ralph the address. It's by the shipyards. She's not there though—she's scared."

Maybe, just maybe, we could still save Cassandra. "Drive like you mean it," I said.

And in reply, she did.

57

Ralph was waiting for us in a neglected parking lot that sprawled between two abandoned warehouses.

"This is the address, but I don't know which building it is," he shouted as Lien-hua and I rushed out of the car. "I called SDPD; they're sending some cars. But we've got less than five minutes, there's no time to wait." He scanned the buildings. "It could be either building, there's no way to tell."

"Yes, there is," I said. "Remember the video? Natural light. Second- or third-story windows. Shadows appeared on Cassandra's right side, so based on the sun's position at the time of day—"

Ralph pointed. "That one's only got first floor windows." All three of us turned to the remaining warehouse, saw the rows of third-story windows, and began sprinting across the parking lot.

Ralph drew his gun. "Pat, you take the right side, Lien-hua, go left. I'll take the front."

We flared out. I ran along the west end of the building but found only one steel door, and that was chained shut. The graffiti-covered building straddled nearly an entire city block, so there wasn't time to backtrack. Rusted pipes and gray air ducts stuck out of the warehouse's side at odd angles, and I had no idea what most of them would ever have been used for. All of the windows high above me were cracked and splintered and reminded me of great, blood-shot eyes.

Time, time, running out of time.

I glanced up at the windows again. They were maybe eight meters up. A few pipes snaked out of the building and then curled around the edge of the warehouse. I saw that one of the air ducts terminated within a meter and a half of the windowsill.

You got it, Pat. It's the only way in.

I jumped up, snagged a handhold, and heaved myself up.

A small ledge to my left gave me just enough of a foothold so that I was able to stretch across the wall, slide my fingertips between two strips of metal, do an undercling with my left hand, and then swing myself over a thick vent. Hundreds of thousands of pull-ups paying off.

Handhold. Foothold.

Now halfway up to the window, I studied the wall above me, searching for fingerholds, finding my rhythm again. All the time smearing my shoes against the gritty exterior of the building and clinging to ridges in the wall with my fingertips. Smoothing out my moves. Finger jam. Feel the rhythm. Foothold. The vertical dance.

There.

The window.

I looked inside and caught sight of a catwalk that skirted the inside of the warehouse. Most of the window's broken glass still clung to the frame like great serrated teeth. I punched out some of the knifelike projections, pulled out my SIG, and leapt onto the catwalk.

Looked at my watch.

Eight p.m.

Apart from the smear of city lights seeping through the windows, the interior of the warehouse was only a dark pool stretching before me. I pulled out my Mini Maglite and swept the cavernous room. My light didn't reach the far wall, but it did reach a metal staircase about thirty meters away that descended into the black cavity of the warehouse.

In the video there was a concrete floor; the tank is on the first level.

I raced toward the staircase, trying to keep my light steady as I ran.

At the top of the stairs my circle of light glanced across

an industrial-sized light switch. We didn't have any time left for sneaking around. We needed to find Cassandra now. I clicked on the lights as I clanged past the switch and then flew down the steps three at a time. A few stray fluorescent bulbs on the ceiling high above me flickered to life but then winked on and off, creating an eerie strobelike effect.

Ground floor.

Dust-covered manufacturing machines, tools, and broken conveyer belts littered the main section of the warehouse. I didn't hear either Lien-hua or Ralph. Maybe they were still outside the building.

Or maybe they'd found Cassandra.

"Hello?" I called. I checked my watch.

Eight oh two.

I heard a thunderous *crack* and guessed it was the sound of Ralph busting down a door. "Ralph?"

"It's me!" called Lien-hua. I threw my light toward her. She'd kicked the door down. "Got anything?"

"No." I swung my flashlight, but the beam hardly made a dent in the darkness. "Wait . . ." The fluorescent lights blinked on, off, on. Dim light washing around me. Off, on. I caught the sight of something, a glint of glass. I started bolting across the void. "Over here." Yes, yes. I did see something.

The tank.

Off, on. Off, on.

I'd found it.

It lay twenty-five meters ahead of me near the corner of the warehouse. Faintly, in the hesitant light, I saw a body in the tank. *Cassandra!* I couldn't tell if she was alive or dead.

58

8:03 p.m.

Time sprinted with me through the warehouse.

"Here!" I yelled. "Over here."

Alive. Water up to her neck. Reaching, reaching for air.

I stumbled over something, crashed into a piece of abandoned machinery. Slammed onto the concrete.

Back to my feet.

Running again.

Others too. Others running.

Who? I couldn't see.

"I see her!" Lien-hua yelled.

The echo of footsteps around me.

Flickering light. Flickering light.

I heard the slap of my Nikes. Ralph's steady, pounding boots. Lien-hua's fluid stride.

But another set of steps too. A fourth set.

Then something clattered against the floor to my left, and I aimed my light toward the sound. Saw a figure bolting toward the other end of the dark warehouse.

"Stop. On your knees!" I yelled. The lights high above me flickered, flickered. "Now!" Thin light dancing across the interior of the warehouse.

A macabre dance.

"Stop!"

But he didn't stop. I needed to make a decision.

Chase him or save Cassandra.

Easy choice.

Cassandra.

I heard Ralph and Lien-hua. "There!" I yelled. I pointed. "He's getting away."

"He's mine," Ralph shouted while Lien-hua leapt with the grace of a doe over a dead conveyor belt and arrived by my side.

Water poured from the pipe that led down the wall of the warehouse and spanned the meter-long gap to the top of the tank. The water wasn't just dripping anymore. The valves must have been opened all the way.

Cassandra Lillo pounded and slapped against the glass as the churning water reached her chin. She was screaming, still screaming as the water began to cover her mouth.

"Where's the valve?" I yelled to her, holstering my SIG. "The valve?" But Cassandra was too busy trying to stay alive to answer.

Lien-hua pounded on the glass. "We're going to get you out. Hold on."

The water bubbled over Cassandra's lips.

"Pat." Desperation rose in Lien-hua's voice. "You have to stop that water."

I ran to the back of the tank, pocketed the flashlight, jumped up, and grabbed the water pipe. I swung my weight, hard, trying to jar the pipe loose from the side of the building, but it held firm. I wedged my feet against the wall and twisted with all my strength.

Nothing.

Yanked. Yanked.

Nothing.

Cassandra tugged against the chain, took a gulp of air. The chain looked slack, but she didn't notice. "Relax!" I yelled. "You'll be OK!"

But it didn't help. She was panicking.

"Hurry, Pat." Lien-hua found a lead pipe and swung it against the glass, but only faint slivers of cracks appeared. "We're losing her!"

I dropped to the ground, and Maglite in hand, I scanned the area surrounding the tank. My flashlight sent spatters of light across the walls, but I didn't see any way to release the water.

The valve must be outside the building.

A memory of my river rafting days flashed through my mind. Once a man who'd fallen from a raft got his leg wedged beneath a submerged tree branch. His head was a meter below the surface, but a friend of mine and I kept him alive by swimming down and passing him air, mouth to mouth, until he could get rescued twenty minutes later. If I could get into the tank, I could do that for Cassandra.

But when I studied the top of the tank, I saw that the metal bars were held in place with thick, curved metal pins. I'd never be able to remove them fast enough to save her.

Fluorescent lights on. Then off. Darkness and light. Darkness and light.

"Relax, Cassandra!" I called. "We're going to get you out!" But her long struggle had exhausted her. She flattened her hand against the glass and opened her mouth slightly, sending a fresh burst of bubbles to the surface, swallowing, gagging on a mouthful of water. For a moment she beat on the glass with a desperate fist, but then her fist uncurled.

Her fingers drifted back in the water.

Now, Pat. Now. Help her. Save her.

"Lien-hua." I said. "Step back." I unholstered my weapon, angled it so I wouldn't hit Cassandra if my plan actually worked, and began to empty the magazine at the hairline fractures Lien-hua had created. As soon as she saw what I was doing, she followed suit. The bullets ricocheted off the glass and flew into the psychedelic darkness of the warehouse. I hoped the bullets wouldn't bounce back toward us, but there was no way to tell and no time to worry. Light and sound flashed and echoed, reverberated through the vacant air.

Lien-hua and I fired at least sixteen rounds before the growing web of cracks imploded and water rushed into the room carrying the shattered glass with it. The force of the water slammed into us, knocking both of us off our feet while Cassandra's limp body dropped to the ground beside us amid a storm of clanging metal pipes.

My flashlight had flown from my hand and skittered across the floor, sending curling beams of light spinning around the room. I looked toward Cassandra and saw that Lien-hua was already at her side. "She's still alive, Pat. Get an ambulance."

I yanked out my phone and dialed 911 while Lien-hua leaned over, feeling Cassandra's pulse, checking her airway. Dispatch told me an ambulance was already en route, but to save them time when they arrived, I relayed as much as I could about Cassandra's condition and confirmed the warehouse's address. In the meantime, I retrieved my flashlight and saw that Lien-hua had rolled Cassandra onto her side to help clear her airway. Miraculously, Cassandra seemed to be breathing reasonably well on her own.

"You're going to be OK," Lien-hua told her. "It's over. You're safe now. It's over."

Cassandra nodded feebly, letting Lien-hua hold her, reassure her. Then I remembered that Ralph was pursuing a suspect—but that there were at least two people involved in the kidnapping. Shade and someone else. I flicked the light around the area.

"How many?" I asked Cassandra. "How many people were here?"

She shook her head. She didn't know.

I swept my light around the room, scanning, scanning. My heart beating.

What's taking those officers so long?

I set my phone beside Lien-hua in case EMS needed more info. "I'm taking a look around."

"Be careful," Lien-hua said.

I slid a new magazine into my SIG and began to search the creases of throbbing darkness all around me.

59

I'd made it halfway to the warehouse's far wall when I heard footsteps to my right. I crouched low. Shooting stance. My heart hammering. "Stop right there."

"Pat," Ralph's voice shot back. "I lost him." Then Ralph let a string of curses color the air.

"We found Cassandra," I said. "She's OK."

Just then, a flash of movement in the shadows caught my eye. I swung my light. Saw a glimpse of pale skin.

A face.

"Hey," I yelled. The guy jumped to his feet. Bolted. Closer to Ralph than to me. I pointed my flashlight. "Ralph, take him down!"

Without hesitation Ralph exploded toward the cluttered center of the warehouse. I hurried toward the nearest door to block the suspect's escape but kept my light trained on him as best I could.

From outside the warehouse, the whine of ambulance and police sirens told me the officers and paramedics had finally arrived. As the suspect neared the staircase I'd descended earlier, he grabbed a tool of some kind from a nearby workbench. "Ralph, he's got a weapon!"

The man stopped suddenly, whipped around, and swung a clawed hammer at Ralph's head. Instead of ducking, Ralph stuck out a hand, snagged the hammer in midflight, and wrenched it from the man. Tossed it into the blinking darkness.

That would have intimidated me, but not this guy. Unfazed, he leapt at Ralph and unleashed a vicious packet of swift karate chops to Ralph's neck and chest that stunned him for a moment, but Ralph landed an uppercut to the guy's jaw that sent him toppling backward, and then Ralph was on him, crushing him to the concrete. A moment later Ralph had rolled him over and cuffed the guy's hands behind his back.

Law enforcement and medical personnel were streaming past me. Ralph heaved the suspect to his feet, and the SDPD officers swarmed around him. "Nice timing," Ralph said sarcastically, handing the guy off to them. Then he rubbed his neck where the guy had karate chopped him. "He's a frisky little fellow."

As Ralph brushed himself off, I shook my head. "Ralph, why didn't you just pull your weapon on him?"

Ralph held up a huge meaty fist. "I did."

As he held up his hand, I noticed that his little finger was angled sideways, dislocated either from punching the suspect, or perhaps from tackling him. I pointed toward the finger, and Ralph stared at it for a moment. Then he wrapped his other hand around it and, with a slight grimace, yanked the finger forward and then sideways, popping the joint back into place. "Just the way I like it," he said. "Fast and clean."

I think Ralph needs to get a hobby. Yoga maybe. Or one of those little Japanese rock garden deals. That, or a good therapist.

Then he jogged toward Cassandra and the shattered tank, and I noticed Detective Dunn coming my way. "What do we have?" he asked.

"There's at least one more," I said. "Could be anywhere in the building."

"Flare out," Dunn ordered his men. "Cover the space. Bring him in." Immediately, the officers spread out across the warehouse to secure the premises.

I took advantage of the moment to settle my breathing. To calm down, to begin processing what had just happened. Austin Hunter was dead. Cassandra Lillo was alive. We had a suspect in custody. Yes, breathe, breathe.

Breathe.

Tessa slipped into her hotel room with her secret, fresh raven perched on her arm. Her skin was so sore that it really did feel like the bird's claws were clenching her. She winced as she closed the door.

Before she'd left the studio, Riker had given her a half-used bottle of antibacterial soap to wash her raven. "You can put a little hand lotion on it too," he said. "But not too much or it'll draw out the color." Then Lachlan had wrapped her arm with gauze and told her to wait an hour before removing it.

But now that she was in her room, she was anxious to see her tattoo, so she gingerly shed her shirt and peeled off the soft gauze covering.

Her skin was red and swollen. And tender. Very tender. But the raven really was beautiful.

Lachlan was as good as Riker had said.

Tessa gently washed her tattoo, and then curled up on a pile of pillows on the bed, pulled out her notebook, and began to write about the deep blue depths of Riker's eyes.

As two officers began reading the suspect his rights, someone found the main set of lights and snapped them on. A flood of fluorescents woke up, the warehouse came into view, and for the first time I was able to get a good look at the suspect. Late twenties, early thirties, five-ten, one hundred seventy-five pounds. Light brown hair. Sable eyes that reminded me of the dark stones you might find at the bottom of a northern lake. Jeans, sweatshirt, leather boots. A number of discolorations and scars on his neck and face. No jewelry or visible body art or piercings. And bobcat tough, even against Ralph.

Then I noticed that near the wall of the warehouse, beside the shattered remains of the tank, pools of water were sloshing lazily across the concrete, feeling out the grooves of the uneven floor. The water had probably helped remove any trace evidence from the area, but breaking the glass had been the only way to save Cassandra.

Years ago I'd learned to pick locks, so I decided to help free Cassandra from the shackle on her ankle, but when I looked up I saw that the paramedics were already wheeling her toward me on a gurney. Maybe Ralph had helped pry the chain loose to free her.

One of the EMTs walking beside Cassandra placed an oxygen mask over her mouth and began adjusting the dials. The doctors would need to check Cassandra out, of course, but it looked like we'd made it just in time. She appeared to be conscious and responsive. Lien-hua was walking beside her, holding her hand. Thankfully, Cassandra was lying down and didn't see the suspect standing ten meters away. I could only imagine what her reaction would have been if she would have looked up at that moment.

As the paramedics neared the door, the suspect called something to Lien-hua that I couldn't hear. She stopped. Turned. "What did you say?" She let go of Cassandra's hand and approached him. "I couldn't quite make that out." I thought he might be taunting her so I started walking in his direction to put an end to it.

But before I could get there, he spoke again and I heard him this time. "That sure is a nice dress she has on," he said. "I hope the water didn't ruin it." Without hesitation, Lien-hua stepped over the discarded clawed hammer, whipped around, and gave him a lead leg punch to the abdomen, driving him out of the clutches of the two SDPD officers beside him and sending him careening to the ground. Then she rushed him, and it took both Ralph and me to hold her back. She fought against us with a fierce strength that startled me. It was the first time I'd ever seen her lose her cool. The guy might sue or press charges, but I don't even think she cared. Her reaction was so much like mine when Basque mocked Sylvia Padilla's death thirteen years ago that it gave me chills.

"Easy," I whispered to her as she pulled against my grip. I felt the ropes of tension in her muscles. "Easy," I said again. Finally, she began to relax, and Ralph and I let go of her, but we stayed close beside her, just in case.

Dunn motioned for the officers to lift the suspect to his feet, and then stared at him toe-to-toe. "I can't wait to get you downtown."

But the man just eyed Dunn coolly, as if the detective were the prey and he were the predator. "Sorry, Detective." He threw a glance toward Lien-hua. "But I'd rather dance with the lady. She's going to be my next girlfriend."

Dunn got right in the guy's face, and I thought we might have to restrain him too, but thankfully he held back. "Get this slimebag out of here." Then, in a moment of uncharacteristic gentleness, he walked over to Cassandra, brushed some of the wet hair from her forehead, and said, "It's all over now. Everything's going to be OK."

I took it all in. Took everything in.

One of Dunn's officers returned. "The warehouse is empty."

"Search it again," I said. "We believe there were at least two abductors."

Dunn watched the paramedics wheel Cassandra away. "All right," he said. "Scour it. Set up a perimeter. We'll grill this guy about his partner once we get him to the station." The officers all began their duties of searching and investigating and securing the scene.

"Did we get anything from Drake?" I asked Detective Dunn.

He shook his head. "He doesn't know anything. We'll follow up tomorrow."

I wanted to talk more with the suspect, find out Shade's identity, learn what the device really was and why part of their demands involved burning down Building B-14. So many questions. And I wanted to talk to Cassandra too. Listen to her story of what happened at the Sherrod Aquarium, ask her about her research, and find out how much she knew about the fires Austin Hunter had set.

But now wasn't the time for any of that. The police needed to process the suspect, the doctors needed to treat Cassandra, and the criminalists needed to set up their crime scene perimeter, no doubt using the parking meters and stop signs on the streets surrounding the warehouse to string up their caution tape. As I was thinking about all these things, I heard Ralph mention offhandedly to Lien-hua that Executive Assistant Director Margaret Wellington had arrived in town and wanted to swing by the scene. Great.

I realized that all in all, there wasn't much else for Ralph, Lien-hua, or me to do here tonight, so we gave our statements, filled out the prerequisite paperwork. I turned in Austin's cell phone as evidence, and then, as we were leaving, Ralph said to Lien-hua, "I bet that felt good. Kicking him like that."

"No," she said. "It didn't feel good. None of this feels good. None of it at all."

Her words sent my thoughts flying back to Basque yet again. That unforgettable night in the slaughterhouse. How it felt to hit him, to step over the line. And then, in light of

Lien-hua's words, I felt a dark surge of shame, because, unlike her, part of me had enjoyed the descent into the darkness. Part of me had wondered what it would be like to live on the other side of the line. And part of me still wondered, even after all these years.

Only after Lien-hua and I had stepped outside the warehouse and were climbing into the car did I notice that some of her blood was still on my hand from when I'd tried to stop the bleeding of the gunshot wound on her neck.

I laid my palm flat against my leg and held it there all the way back to the hotel.

60

10:02 p.m.

Tessa finished her poem about Riker, the guy who'd told Lachlan to give her whatever she wanted. Then she closed up her notebook and pulled out a book of nineteenth-century French short stories that she'd been wanting to read.

But after only a few minutes, her eyes weighed themselves down, and Tessa found sweet sleep coming to her in a tumble of dreams of ravens and sharks and dark waves kissing the shore.

10:14 p.m.

General Biscayne's military escort plane leveled off for its final approach to the North Shore Naval Base on Coronado Island. He figured he would have just enough time to drive to his sister's house in Carmel Valley, and still manage seven hours of sleep before returning for the Project Rukh Oversight Committee meeting at 0800 hours—the meeting during which he would terminate the DARPA contract with Drake Enterprises.

10:26 p.m.

Back in her hotel room, Lien-hua Jiang checked beneath the bandage on her neck. Thankfully, the wound didn't look serious, and overall she felt remarkably good, despite how unnerving the night had been.

Her leg was bothering her, however. She'd felt a stiff achiness stretching across her right thigh ever since the water from the shattered tank had knocked her down, but it wasn't until she pulled off her jeans to change into sweatpants that she discovered the deep and wicked bruise on her thigh. One of the metal bars must have speared her as it fell to the ground, and with all of the adrenaline in her system she hadn't noticed how serious the contusion was until now.

Ice. That's what she needed. Ice down the leg before going to bed. She grabbed the ice bucket, opened the door, and almost ran over Pat Bowers, who was standing in her path, his hand poised in midknock.

"Hi," he said, his hand still in the air.

"Hi," she said with a smile. "Are you practicing tai chi?"

"Hm?"

"Your hand."

"Oh. Right." He dropped his hand. "Sorry, I um . . . I just wanted to check on you. Just wanted to make sure you're OK."

"Well, thank you. I'm on my way to get some ice for a bruise on my leg." She stepped past him, expecting him to ask if he could walk with her.

"Hey, can I walk with you?"

Absolutely. "Sure."

They walked side by side.

Her hair was draped across the gunshot wound on her neck, and it surprised her when he gently slid some of the hair to the side. "Is your neck going to be all right?" Then his hand fell away.

"I think so. The bullet just grazed me." They reached the ice machine, and she placed the bucket onto the tray beneath the ice chute.

"Here, I'll help you." He punched the button.

"Wow. Thanks, Pat. I don't think I could have managed that on my own."

"No problem." He stood awkwardly beside her as the ice rattled and tumbled into the bucket.

It seemed to take forever.

Then, when the machine was cycling back to sleep and the bucket was finally full, Pat reached for it. "I can get that for you."

She'd already reached for it, however, and his hand barely missed glancing across hers as she picked it up. "I know it looks heavy, Pat, but I think I can manage." For a moment she thought that if this night were being made into a movie, their hands would have touched. Guaranteed. And in a way she wished they had, even though it was a cliché, cliché, cliché.

As she led the way back to the room, she found herself walking slower than she needed to.

"You were good out there tonight," Pat said. "Really good. Talking with Hunter. Helping Cassandra. Keeping us focused on finding her . . ." She could tell he was fishing for the right words, and it was kind of cute. "And this afternoon too," he continued. "At the briefing . . . Very thorough. Very . . . professional."

"Well, thank you, Dr. Bowers. You were very professional today too." They reached her door. "I could see you piecing things together, almost thinking like a profiler."

He let a smile drift to the corner of his mouth. "Lienhua, here I come to check on you, and you insult me." His five-o'clock shadow lent a deep masculinity to his face. "What possible motive could you have for that?"

"I thought you didn't believe in motives?"

"Oh, I believe in them. I just think sometimes we have more than one influencing us at a time."

The question begged to be asked, and so, trying not to anticipate the answer, she threw it out there. "So, what ulterior motives did you have stopping by here tonight, Pat?"

In reply, he lifted his hand as if he were going to knock on the door. "You guessed it before. Tai chi." He began to move slowly through a series of tai chi moves. "Health benefits. Gotta stay fit."

"Well, I hope that works out for you," she said. "And once again . . ." She flattened her right hand, lifted her fingers to her chin, then lowered them slowly.

"That's sign language, isn't it?"

"Yes, it means 'thank you.'"

He repeated the sign. "You'll have to teach me more sometime. I'd like to learn."

"OK. Sometime." She slid the key into the lock and pressed the door open. She wanted this conversation to go on. She wanted to invite him into her room, but instead, she simply said what she was supposed to say to a coworker who'd showed appropriate concern for her well-being. "Good night, Pat. I'll see you in the morning. Really, I'm glad you stopped by to see how I was doing."

He gave her a slight nod, tapped the door with his finger, and said, "OK, see you in the morning. Take care of that leg. Your neck too."

She stepped into her room, eased the door shut, stood beside it for a moment, counted to five, then cracked it open to see if he'd left. When she saw that he had, she closed it again and went over to tend to her vase of dying flowers.

Nearly ten minutes had passed before she noticed that the ice was melting in the bucket and the bruise was still throbbing on her leg.

I'm an idiot.

That's all there is to it.

A complete idiot.

Oh, you were very professional today, Lien-hua. I stopped by at this time of night to tell you how professional you were. Here, let me stand in the hallway with my fist stuck in the air like a bad mime for a few more minutes.

Did I actually say, "Health benefits. Gotta stay fit"? Did I actually say that?

Just shoot me now.

Well, at least I didn't say what I was really thinking when she mentioned that she needed to ice down her leg. At least I didn't say, "I could do that for you." At least I didn't say that.

I'd kinda been hoping she might invite me into her room just to debrief the day.

Yeah, right—debrief the day.

Just chill, Pat. Get some sleep.

I tapped on Tessa's door, but she didn't answer. I figured she was either asleep or listening to her iPod. Probably both. I pulled out my phone to see if she'd left me another text message and instead found a voice mail: "I'll see you in the morning, Patrick. Just don't be all, 'Let's get an early start on the day!' or anything. It's annoying."

All right then, tomorrow we would catch up, and she could fill me in on how she'd spent the rest of her day.

Although, based on a couple of the phone calls I'd made

earlier in the afternoon, I thought I already knew. And she hadn't spent much of her time at that Internet café that served imported coffee, or walking around Balboa Park. Instead, she'd spent nearly five hours at one of the seedy tattoo studios over on Market Street.

Well, I could talk to her about that in the morning. For now, I needed some sleep.

61

Creighton Melice lay on the cot in his cell and let himself relax into the deep unknown. He dreamt of spiders, as he often did, but tonight, with the end so close at hand, the images seemed as real to him as moonlight and blood.

And so. Now, his dream.

A spider the size of a baby's fist wriggles up his neck and across his face, brushing her feet against his lips, his cheeks, his eyelids, the soft indentation beneath his nose. In his dream he's paralyzed, so he can see her dark body pause on his cheek, but he can't move, can't brush her away. It repels him and excites him at the same time, sending shivers of secret pleasure running all through his body.

The spider rears back and lands with a prick in the middle of his cheek. He wants to scream but can't make a sound; can't brush her away. He feels the pressure, the widening wound, the gentle ripping sensation as she burrows into his cheek and the skin kisses open to receive her eggs.

She deposits her skinned offspring, then, in one moist plop. And he can feel the small wet sacks soak onto his tongue.

In the cocooned heat of his mouth it won't take the eggs long to hatch.

Time passes. How much? A moment. An eternity. Impossible to tell. Impossible to know.

And then they hatch.

It's a dream. It's all a dream.

Their whisper-thin feet explore his tongue. Some of the babies roll down his throat, while others manage to squeeze up and out the narrow passages of his nostrils. A few of the tiny spiders crawl out his mouth, nimble legs stepping over his teeth, across his lips, and then spreading out to scurry around his face. Always examining, always probing.

Of course, it's just a dream.

It's only a dream.

The rest of the babies descend deeply into him. Moist bodies sliding, wriggling against the tight, confining space of his throat. Down. Down.

A dream. A dream.

All the way down.

Deeply, deeply.

They land in his stomach. They're still alive.

Then he feels them wriggling inside him, and senses the quivering sensation as they begin to work their tiny mandibles and chew. Devouring him from the inside out.

And he imagines how all of this would feel, should feel, how much it should hurt; but he notices only textures, light and airy; only pressure, blunt and numb.

Then Creighton Melice awoke, pleased by his dream, and rolled to his side. And there, in the solitude of his cell, he began going over tomorrow's plan as he scratched at the small wound on his left palm that none of the cops who arrested him had bothered to inspect. Wouldn't they be surprised.

Wouldn't they all.

62

The next morning, after a quick workout at the hotel's fitness room and a brisk shower, I walked to the Internet café Tessa had told me about to buy some of what she called "weird-sounding coffee."

The place featured mostly South American blends, and I grabbed a cup of some gracefully nutty Peruvian coffee from the Chanchamayo Valley. The high regions of the Andes produce a light-bodied, aromatic, and slightly sweet coffee, perfect for the morning.

I could taste that the coffeehouse had roasted the beans just a bit too long, but I was feeling generous and didn't even mention it to them. I added a little cream and honey, no sugar, just like always, and sipped my way to heaven.

Since I expected to have some company for breakfast, I picked up a couple extra cups to go.

On his way to the Project Rukh Oversight Committee meeting, Victor Drake stumbled upon a realization so simple, so obvious, he was amazed he hadn't thought of it sooner. Who cares why Austin Hunter started the fire? It didn't matter. He was dead. He couldn't hurt Drake Enterprises anymore. And the fire had been effective. That's all that mattered.

Everything had been destroyed.

Everything.

Yes, this would work out to his advantage, after all. He could get the remaining files from Dr. Osbourne and shred them as soon as the doctor got back into town. Yes, yes, yes. And because of the fire, he could get out of the contract gracefully and there would be no board of directors inquiry and no public backlash.

Victor couldn't help but congratulate himself on how brilliant he was. He began to hum as he drove, as he thought about the look he would see on the general's face in less than an hour when he regrettably explained the unfortunate situation to him.

After leaving text messages for both Ralph and Lien-hua, inviting them to join me for breakfast on the hotel restaurant's veranda, I brought my computer to an empty table, and pulled up my notes about this case. A flock of questions flew through my mind.

It was time to get them to fly in formation.

First of all, before Austin Hunter died, he admitted to Lien-hua that he'd started the first fourteen fires but not the one on Monday night. OK, so that solved one mystery, but left us with another. The geographic distribution of the fires supported the premise that the same person had chosen all the fire locations, so I typed, "Why didn't Austin start Monday's fire? Who did?" I thought for a moment and then added, "Does John Doe's death have anything to do with the previous fires?"

I gazed across the beach. A distant dog-walker. Two children looking for shells, trailing behind their mother. An older couple walking hand in hand. The ocean lay beyond them, gentle ripples on the surface, dark currents underneath. High above the world's only ocean, a circle of patient clouds held up the sky, while on the eastern tip of Coronado Island, smoke from the remains of Building B-14 sloped southward, bent by the morning breeze.

Building B-14.

Cassandra's abductors wanted that building burned down—why? I added three more questions to my list: "What is their connection to Building B-14? What device were the kidnappers after? Where is it now?"

Nearby, a pair of anxious gulls greeted the morning with their screaking chatter, reminding me again of Tessa's comment Monday night about squeals in slaughterhouses. Reminding me once again of Sylvia Padilla's wet screams . . .

Of Cassandra Lillo's silent ones . . .
Of Austin Hunter's desperate struggle to save her life.
What else had Austin told Lien-hua last night?
Oh yes. That he hadn't killed the people. But which people? Who killed them? Where were the bodies? When were they killed?

Too many questions. I sighed, but entered the growing list of mysteries into my document.

My mind sifted through the facts of the case, rotating them, holding the investigation's complex prism up to the light. An enigma with so many intersecting angles.

Cassandra Lillo, shark researcher . . .
Austin Hunter, arsonist . . .
John Doe, transient . . .
Victor Drake, billionaire . . .
Shade, unknown kidnapper who somehow knew my name . . .

What did they all have in common? What tied them together?

As I looked over the list, I realized there was at least one rabbit hole I hadn't yet peered down.

I pulled up my Internet browser and cruised to the Drake Enterprises Web site, and a moment later found the person Terry had mentioned to me, Dr. Rigel Osbourne. I looked over his vita: BS in genetic engineering from UCLA, MS in microbiology from Biola, and two PhDs, one in neuropathology from Yale and the other in neuromorphic engineering from the University of Texas. Having jumped through graduate-level academic hoops myself—night classes, distance learning, independent studies, thesis, dissertation, all while still working in law enforcement—I knew how hard it can be to stick it out for an advanced degree, so I was impressed with Osbourne's academic achievements. But since I'd never heard of neuromorphic engineering, I was also confused.

A couple clicks later I found an online scientific encyclopedia and discovered that neuromorphic engineers attempt to use computers to mimic biological processes. The last paragraph of the article read:

Since its development in the 1980s, neuromorphic engineering has primarily been used in artificial intelligence research and in the development of advanced robotics systems. However, even though historically neuromorphic engineers have focused on ways to reverse engineer biological nervous systems to create artificial neural pathways, since 2003 the biotech world has been exploring many other uses for this quickly emerging field.

Many other uses, huh?

I went back to my Word document and typed, "What about killer ray guns?"

Then I checked my e-mail and found a note from Terry telling me that he hadn't uncovered anything more about the grant Cassandra was working on or DARPA's contract with Drake Enterprises. Angela Knight had also e-mailed to let me know that the cybercrime division hadn't been able to get a GPS location on the caller who referred to himself as Shade. I wasn't surprised. I had a feeling Shade was no amateur.

Finally, I made a list of three goals for the day: (1) talk with Dr. Rigel Osbourne; (2) find out what really went on in Building B-14; (3) follow up with Aina about the radio-active isotopes found at Austin's apartment.

Honestly, I didn't feel like an investigator who'd just hours ago helped save a woman's life and apprehend a suspect. Despite our progress on this case, despite the apparent closure, I felt more like a rat in a maze in which someone was opening and closing portions of the wall. Leading me steadily into a corner.

And I had a feeling I knew who it was.

Shade.

I entered one last question: "Who is Shade?"

I was poring over the notes on my computer, thinking about how much the gulls were really starting to annoy me, when Ralph showed up wearing the same set of clothes he'd had on yesterday.

"No suitcases, huh?"

He plopped down beside me. "On their way to Miami. Can you believe it? Miami!" Then he let out a deep sigh and provided me with a colorful description of what the airline baggage handlers ought to do to themselves with his retractable-handle fold-over garment bag. I wasn't sure it was anatomically possible to do what he recommended, but it certainly brought an interesting picture to mind. "Plus," he added, "I tried making coffee in my room this morning. I'm telling you, Pat, avoid anything with 'o-matic' in the title. I don't care if it's a toaster-o-matic, a pizza-o-matic, a jambalaya-o-matic, or a urinal-o-matic. Doesn't matter. If they couldn't come up with a better name than that, their product stinks. You can be sure of that."

I wasn't really in the mood to talk about urinal-o-matics. "Well, here." I offered him a cup of Peruvian coffee. "This is pretty good, except I think they might have used a roaster-o-matic." After he'd swallowed a Ralph-sized gulp, I asked him if he'd heard how Cassandra was doing.

"Talked to the docs. She's stable, but they told me one-third of the people who survive a near-drowning like that end up with nervous system problems, or lung and heart complications, so they want to keep her at the hospital today. Monitor her progress."

"Maybe I'll head over there before she leaves," I said. "See if she can help untangle some of my questions about this case."

"Better hurry. Docs say she's not too excited about being there." Ralph took another draft of coffee, finishing off the cup. "A couple more tests scheduled for this morning. Then she'll probably take off."

The way he phrased that, "probably take off," reminded me of our theory that she and Austin might have been trying to get out of town quickly yesterday morning. "Ralph, do you know if anyone has told her about Austin's death yet?"

"I asked the hospital the same thing, but since Austin didn't have any ID on him last night, they said they're waiting until his body can be positively identified before telling her. It's just a formality, but it's enough to hold things up—and after what Cassandra went through yesterday, they don't really want to make her do it. I think they're trying to contact a family member somewhere in Arkansas. Hey, did you eat already?"

"Just some oatmeal."

"I need some flapjacks."

And before I knew it, I was in line behind Ralph to get a second breakfast.

*   *   *

Ralph's mention of the search for Austin's family member brought to mind a question I'd wanted to ask him, but I waited until we had our plates stacked high with pancakes smothered in maple syrup and were on our way back to the veranda. Then I said, "Ralph, you've been a parent almost ten years longer than I have. How do you know how much freedom to give Tony?"

"Oh. So Tessa did something stupid."

"Snuck off to get a tattoo. Does that count?" We found our seats. "I just don't think I can trust her to be here in San Diego without supervision. She's at a tough age. She asks for more freedom, and I want to give it to her, but when I do, more often than not, she acts irresponsibly."

Ralph attacked his pancakes with gusto. "Sounds pretty normal for a teen."

"I know she wants to stay in San Diego, but I don't want to reward her for doing things behind my back. So I decided earlier this morning to send her back to Denver and have her stay with my parents for a day or two until I can close up some things here and get back home."

"The freedom thing, Pat, no one knows the answer to that." Ralph didn't let having food in his mouth stop him from passing along his parenting advice. "It's always a balancing act between trusting 'em and setting 'em up for failure. They'll push the limits, you'll end up stepping on their toes. You're both gonna make mistakes, I guarantee you that. You just need to keep loving her and be patient. That's about all I know. Where's the butter?"

I handed him some mini butter tubs. "One more thing."

He stuck his fork into his pancakes. "What's that?"

I wasn't quite sure how to phrase this. "Ralph, something happened to Lien-hua. Something in her past. A couple times she's hinted to me about it, but when I follow up and ask her about it, she backs off. Do you know what it is?"

The edge of his jaw twitched. "No. It was something before I met her. I wondered for a while, and then one day I just decided to let it go and let her have her secrets. You better believe I've got mine."

"Yeah," I said. "We all do."

He swallowed a forkful of pancakes and then draped a giant paw across my shoulder. "Pat, I know what you're thinking. Don't do it."

"Don't do what?"

"Investigate her. Just let it be. You push her, you might hurt her. I know her heart's been broken before. Don't pry. She deserves better than that."

"Ralph, you know I don't want to hurt her. That's the last thing I want—"

"Good morning, boys." Lien-hua appeared beside me and set down a plateful of fruit and a bowl of yogurt sprinkled with granola. "What were you saying, Pat? What's the last thing you want?"

"To eat yogurt," I said, staring at her plate. "If I ever tell you I want some yogurt, hospitalize me. That and quiche. I'm obviously not in my right mind."

"Yogurt-a-matic," mumbled Ralph.

"Health benefits," she said coyly. "Gotta stay fit."

I passed her a cup of coffee and noticed that she'd tied her hair back into a thick, rich ponytail, and had placed a wide plastic-strip bandage across the wound on her neck. I nodded toward her neck. "How is that this morning?"

She pulled out a chair. "Doesn't really hurt." She was wearing a lightweight, body-hugging turtleneck and tan shorts. Not what she might wear to the office in Quantico, but pretty typical for San Diego.

When she sat down, her shorts rode up just enough for me to see the deep, purplish bruise on her right thigh. My eyes wanted to loiter on her leg, or on her turtleneck, but I made them stare at the yogurt.

She grimaced a bit as she situated herself in her chair, and Ralph's look of concern told me that he'd noticed. "Bruised my leg last night," she explained. Then, she extended her lean leg in our direction. "I mean, would you look at that thing?"

I figured that since she'd invited me to, I'd better do what she asked. I stared thoughtfully at her leg. "Wow. Yeah. That's something else, all right."

Ralph glanced at her bruise, then at me, then asked Lien-hua, "How's it feel?"

"It's OK," she said. "It was pretty stiff this morning, but I did some tai chi in the hallway, that really helped."

"The hallway?" Ralph said.

"Never mind," I mumbled and stuffed some pancakes into my mouth.

*   *   *

General Cole Biscayne brushed a fleck of lint off his uniform, slid his glasses up the bridge of his nose, and checked the time: 0809 hours.

Good. He liked the fact that they'd had to wait for him before beginning the meeting. He threw open the doors to the conference room and saw that the other members of the Project Rukh Oversight Committee were already assembled. They saluted, shook his hand, or offered him a slight nod depending on their rank and how well they knew the head of the Pentagon's research and development agency.

He motioned with one finger to a woman standing at attention by the door. "Petty Officer Henley, the shades."

"Yes, sir." She walked to the wall of windows and closed off the panoramic view of the ocean and the line of smoke tilting into the sky. Then she left the room. This was not a meeting for someone of her rank.

General Biscayne chose to stand while the others sat. "Let's cut to the chase." He scanned the room. No one looked happy; most looked scared. Seated around the table were two other DARPA members, as well as North Island Naval Air Station Base Commander Admiral Norval Tumney, FBI Executive Assistant Director for Criminal Investigations Margaret Wellington, half a dozen other top-ranking defense department and intelligence agencies officials, and Victor Drake, president and CEO of Drake Enterprises.

"Gentlemen," General Biscayne said, and then with a nod toward Ms. Wellington, he added, "and ladies. The police caught and killed the arsonist from last night's attack. Good. I'm sure the investigation will go on for months and we'll eventually find out all we need to know about him, but for right now, here's what I want: will someone please tell me that the Project Rukh research wasn't compromised before the facility was destroyed? Tell me we have confirmation that the prototype wasn't stolen. Tell me I flew all the way out here for nothing, that I can relax, and then go back to Washington, meet with the president tomorrow, and inform him that neither the research nor the prototype has gotten into the wrong hands. Tell me those things and I will leave this room a happy man."

No one moved, except for those who averted eye contact with the general. Victor Drake began tapping his fingers rhythmically against the table.

"Let me be clear." Anger prowled through the general's words. He yanked back the shades and pointed at the smoke. "The Department of Defense has invested nearly three billion dollars in this program, and we are not about to let all that go up in smoke because some rogue SEAL had a vendetta to pay."

Still no answer from the group.

General Biscayne looked directly at Victor Drake. "How close was the device to being fully operational?"

"It was completed, but I'm sad to say it really doesn't matter anymore. All the files, as well as the prototype, were destroyed in the fire."

The general let the shades fall shut again. "All the research?"

"I'm afraid so. Nothing could be salvaged. We kept only hard copies of the research so it wouldn't be possible for someone to hack in to the computer system and steal the findings. At this point, though, it looks like we may have made the wrong decision."

"And the prototype as well? Destroyed? Are you certain?"

"Yes. No doubt about it."

General Biscayne considered all this for a moment. If Victor was behind the fire—and it only made sense that he was—he probably *had* made sure to destroy the device. It was the only way to cover up his failure, the only course of action that made sense. So, maybe the fire was a good thing after all. The Department of Defense could get out of its dead-end contract with Drake Enterprises, blame the fire on terrorists, capitalize on the public outrage, and then use the incident to lobby for a substantial increase in the national security budget for the next fiscal year.

FBI Executive Assistant Director Margaret Wellington coughed softly and then spoke up. Her voice reminded the general of a ratchet set. "General Biscayne, we are all aware that this project is of the utmost importance to you and the rest of your team at the Pentagon. Fine. But I'm new to this committee and I haven't been adequately briefed on the exact scope of Project Rukh. The way in which all the pieces of research fit together still remains—"

"Classified," he interrupted her. "And it does so for a reason."

She tensed, folded her hands in front of her. Refused to be intimidated. "Do not interrupt me, General. I'm a civilian. That means you work for me."

Silence squeezed its arms around the room. Squeezed it tight, until Admiral Norval Tumney, a man whom the general thought would have been more aptly named "Tummy" or "Tubby," said, "The navy will do everything in its power to assure that this situation is resolved promptly and professionally."

"I'm sure you will, Norv," said General Biscayne. "It's the only way to save your butt from a court-martial after letting this guy, Hunter, sneak onto the base and burn down B-14."

The admiral's face darkened with disdain, but General Biscayne didn't care. "I want the remains of that building gone through with a tweezers. If there's a shred of paper the size of my fingernail that survived the fire, I want it found. Am I making myself clear?"

Everyone except for Margaret Wellington nodded.

"And verify that the prototype was destroyed. I don't need to tell you that it had better not fall into the wrong hands." He riveted his eyes on Victor Drake. "And Drake, whatever paperwork you have stashed away in your office somewhere—and I know you have some—I want that as well. I want it all. We're pulling the plugs on this. The DOD is finished with Drake Enterprises." Then he stomped past the conference table and was halfway to the door before he threw one word back into the room: "Dismissed."

63

Lien-hua, Ralph, and I let the breakfast conversation wander into sports and the weather and politics and Ralph's struggles to conquer his son at video games and Lien-hua's upcoming trip to visit her brother in Beijing, and it felt good to let our friendship explore other topics than just murder, death, and abductions. But soon, like always, our conversation cycled back to the case.

"Well," said Ralph. He spoke tenderly, with respect for the dead. "With Austin Hunter dead, Cassandra in the hospital, and the suspect from last night in police custody, I think you two might be able to head home. Margaret arrived last night. Lucky me. I get to spend the day with her."

"We still have a lot of unanswered questions about this case," said Lien-hua. "Plus, we still need to find Shade."

"Lien-hua is right," I said. "At this point there are a lot more questions than answers, and we need to address some of them before we can wrap anything up." I folded down my computer screen. "I'm going to visit Cassandra before Tessa wakes up for our meeting with Calvin."

"Werjonic is here?" Ralph exclaimed. Dr. Calvin Werjonic is a household name among investigators, especially those who track serial offenders.

"We're meeting at ten thirty."

"Well, say hi to the old buzzard for me." Ralph nodded with deep respect. "He's a good man, that Werjonic. Smartest guy I ever met."

Lien-hua stood. "Pat, I think I'll come with you to talk

with Cassandra. Hopefully, it'll shed some light on this case before we close things up."

I had a feeling that closing things up was not on the day's agenda, but I just stood and said, "Sounds like a plan. Let's go."

64

After all that Cassandra had been through, Lien-hua hadn't wanted her to see the bruise on her thigh, so she changed into jeans before we left the hotel.

When we arrived at the hospital, Cassandra's doctors told us that the police hadn't been able to contact any of Austin Hunter's relatives, but that she was packing to go and they didn't want her to leave before someone told her about Austin's death. A severe-looking nurse standing beside a gurney informed us that she was on her way to the room to tell Cassandra the news right now.

When I was a detective in Milwaukee, I'd had to tell people this kind of news all too often. It's not something I enjoy, but at least it's something I have experience with. "No," I told the nurse. "I'll do it. I was there. I know the circumstances surrounding the shooting."

The doctors agreed, and the nurse looked relieved as she led us to Cassandra's room.

On the way, Lien-hua touched my shoulder lightly. "Let me tell her the news. I was the last person Austin spoke to. She needs to know he died thinking of her. I'd like to be the one to give her the news. I'm a woman. It'll be better coming from me."

Maybe Lien-hua was right. "OK," I said. "Just let me ask her a couple questions before you tell her."

A few minutes later we knocked on Cassandra's door, and when she called for us to enter, I saw that she was already gathering her things together to leave.

Maria, her coworker from the aquarium, was standing beside her and must have brought her some clothes, because an overnight bag lay by the windowsill and Cassandra was wearing jeans, flip-flops, and a beige blouse instead of the red dress. Maria's face held a mixture of both anxiety and relief. I assumed she was relieved that Cassandra was OK, and probably anxious because Lien-hua and I had shown up.

We introduced ourselves to Cassandra, and as we did, I noted that she was about five-eleven, just as I'd guessed. I asked her how she was doing.

Still distracted with her packing, Cassandra said, "I spent twelve hours chained to the bottom of a tank that was filling with water." Her voice was cold and distant, as if she were speaking to us from another place. "I almost drowned. How do you think I'm doing?"

"Cassandra," Lien-hua said softly. "We were there with you last night. Do you remember us?"

She looked at us closely then, for the first time. "Of course, I . . . You broke the tank, didn't you?"

Lien-hua nodded.

At that, Cassandra let out a heavy breath. "Oh. Thanks. I'm sorry . . . I didn't . . . I didn't recognize you at first. I thought you were just a couple more cops. Really, thanks for saving me."

"You're welcome," Lien-hua said.

"I mean it."

"Cassandra," I said, "I'm wondering if we could talk with you for a few minutes. We won't be long, I promise."

She tossed her hospital gown onto the bed. "I really need to get going."

"We wouldn't be here if it wasn't important," I said.

"Maybe later. In a couple days. A week or something."

"Please," said Lien-hua. "It'll be helpful in building a case against your abductors."

Cassandra hesitated for a moment and then spoke to Maria. "Um, can you go get me a Coke or something? Just give us a couple minutes, OK? Thanks."

Maria looked as if she were about to say something, but swallowed her concern and stepped quietly past us into the hall. I closed the door behind her.

As soon as Maria was gone, Cassandra said softly, "So, you got him, right?" Her throat constricted, her voice wavered. "I mean, you caught the guy who put me in there, didn't you?"

"We apprehended a man at the warehouse," I said. "Yes, he's in custody now."

"So, good. You got him. He's in jail?"

The man we had in custody was innocent until proven guilty, but that's not what Cassandra needed to hear at the moment. "The police are talking with him today, and we're in the process of gathering more evidence," I explained. In light of the news we needed to give her about Austin's death, I decided to keep my questions focused on her abduction rather than her possible involvement in starting the earlier files. "That man, had you ever seen him before?"

She shook her head.

"And why did you go to the aquarium so early?"

"I'd stopped by to grab some things." She paused to shake her head. "I guess he must have drugged me. I don't really remember. One of the officers told me it was a dart. The guy shot me with a dart. Can you believe that?"

"Did he ever mention any kind of device?"

She thought for a quiet moment. "Yeah, I guess he did talk about something when he was on the phone with some other guy. They were talking about getting it out of a building. I don't know. Why? Is it something important? Did you find something?"

"No. We're still looking into that," I said. "Do you know what it is?"

She shook her head and Lien-hua asked, "The other man on the phone, do you know who he was? Did you get a name?"

She thought for a moment. "I think I heard the guy call him Shay or Dade. Something like that."

"Shade," I said.

"Sure. Maybe, I don't know."

Time to move into specifics. "Do you think your work on Project Rukh might have anything to do with your abduction? Could they be related?"

She blinked, let her eyes bounce back and forth from me to Lien-hua to me. "How do you know about that?"

"While we were looking for you, we found some references to it in your computer files."

She cornered her lip between her teeth. "I can't really talk about that. Copyrights, patents, things like that. But I don't see how it could be related. Listen, I just want to go see my boyfriend." She grabbed the overnight bag and glanced at the door, undoubtedly looking for Maria.

"Please," said Lien-hua. "Can you tell us anything about the project? Anything at all?"

"You'd have to talk to Dr. Osbourne for—" She caught herself. Never finished her sentence. "I'm sorry. I've said too much already. I could lose my job. I don't want to talk about this anymore. I just want to get out of here." She glanced at her watch.

Lien-hua stepped toward the window. "Would you recognize the man who attacked you if you saw him again? Could you pick him out in a lineup?"

Her jaw tensed. "I'd recognize his face anywhere. I'll never forget it. Never. But I'm not looking at any lineup. I never want to see that face again. I just want to move on with my life."

I wanted to keep questioning her and explain to her in no uncertain terms that we needed her to identify her abductor and testify against him, but in light of Austin's death, I knew this wasn't the time for that. I did have one more question, and, even though I knew it might be a hard one for her to hear, I had to ask it—I had to find out if she knew about the video her abductors had sent to Austin Hunter. "Cassandra," I said. "Do you know what the man was doing while you were in the tank?"

"What do you mean? No. He was just waiting for me to die. I saw him come out and check on me a couple times, but otherwise he just left me there alone." Her voice began to tremble. "I just want to put this whole horrible thing behind me. That's enough questions. I'm done now." Then I heard the door open behind me and noticed that Maria had returned. In her hands, she held a can of Coke and a set of car keys conspicuously dangling from her fingers.

"There's something else I need to tell you," Lien-hua said. "Maybe you should sit down."

"No. I'm leaving. I was supposed to meet my boyfriend yesterday for breakfast. I need to find him. I need to talk to him. I can't seem to get him on the phone. Good-bye.

Thanks again for helping me last night. I mean it. I just . . . I don't want to do this anymore. It's too soon."

Lien-hua and I shared a glance and then I handed Maria a couple dollars. "Could you get something for Agent Jiang and me as well? We're almost done. It'll only be a few more minutes." Then I leaned close to Maria and whispered, "We didn't say anything about the things you told us at the aquarium. We're not going to. Don't worry." At first she hesitated, but finally she took the money and left for the soft drink machines again.

Cassandra watched her friend exit the room. "What's going on?"

Lien-hua gently guided Cassandra to sit beside her on the bed. "You need to know that Austin Hunter burned down a building in order to meet your kidnappers' demands. Afterward, the police caught up with him."

"What? They arrested Austin?" Cassandra pulled away from Lien-hua and stood up brusquely. "Why didn't you tell me! Where is he?"

"I'm afraid they didn't arrest him. The officers thought he was a threat, thought he was going to hurt me."

"You?" A heavy darkness began to drape over the conversation. "Why you?"

Lien-hua stayed seated and spoke softly, patiently, like a mother might. "I was talking to him, trying to find out if there was anything he could tell us to help us find you." Lien-hua paused to find the right words, but there are no right words for telling someone that the most important person in her life is dead. "You have to understand, the police thought my life might be in danger. Austin had a gun in his hand, and he was pointing a knife at me."

I could see that Cassandra was slowly coming to the inevitable conclusion, slowly grasping what Lien-hua was saying beneath her words. "He's dead?" Her voice split in half as she spoke. "That's what you're telling me, isn't it? That Austin's dead?"

Lien-hua answered by standing and enfolding Cassandra in her arms.

Finding out that kind of news is shattering, gut-wrenching. If you're there with a person when she hears it, you want to comfort her, hold her and tell her that things will be OK, but all the while, deep inside, you know that whatever you say will only come across as hollow and trite. Comfort doesn't come from words at a time like that. It mostly comes from silence.

I saw a cup of water on a nearby dinner tray and thought of handing it to Cassandra, but realized how ridiculous that would be. That it wouldn't help anything at all.

She was trembling as Lien-hua and I supported her weight and helped her sit on the hospital bed once again. "He loved you," Lien-hua said. "Saving you was the only thing that mattered to him in the end. He loved you more than anything else in the world."

Soft tears began to drop from Cassandra's eyes. Her chin quivered. "He did this." Lien-hua sat beside her, an arm around her shoulder. "The one who took me," she continued. "It's his fault. I want him dead." And then her voice grew in pain and volume. "I want him dead." Her shrieking lament filled the room. "I want him dead. I want him dead!"

She repeated her sentence over and over, sending the words reverberating off the bright walls of the hospital room as Lien-hua held her tenderly and let her weep and wail and tremble against her shoulder.

Lien-hua and I waited until two of the hospital's counselors arrived and Maria returned to the room. Then, with the three of them there to console her, Lien-hua closed the door and we stepped into the hallway.

I think Lien-hua would have liked to stay and help, but Cassandra needed to work though her grief with people who'd be around to help her long-term, not with a couple of federal agents who'd be flying out later in the week.

As we drove back to the hotel, the meeting with Cassandra weighed on me, but I reminded myself that she was getting the help she needed and there wasn't anything more Lien-hua and I could do for her. Part of living is acknowledging people's pain and grief, but not letting it take over your heart. Though it's always nighttime in the depths, the waves still reflect the day.

Life is both eerie and beautiful.

It's both.

By the end of the drive, I'd started to put the pain into perspective. I packaged up the moments I'd spent with Cassandra and set them aside so that I could deal with them one by one when the time was right. I made a quick call to Ralph asking if he'd heard any more about Victor Drake and his possible connection to the abduction, but he hadn't. He promised he'd check on it though, and get back to me after his meeting with Margaret.

Then, after dropping off Lien-hua at the FBI field office, I picked up Tessa from the hotel to introduce her to Dr. Calvin Werjonic.

65

Tessa and I bought a few more cups of Peruvian coffee on the way to Balboa Park and then parked in the lot beside the Alcazar Garden to wait for Calvin. We were a little early, so we took a walk through the nearby Palm Canyon, and on the way Tessa informed me that Balboa Park is the largest urban cultural park in the U.S. "There are more than a dozen museums and performing arts venues here, as well as the San Diego Zoo."

She seemed unusually awake and perky today, and I wondered if maybe she was under the weather. I'd never thought I would put the words *Tessa* and *perky* together in the same sentence, unless the word *despises* appeared between them. I decided to try a little conversation, see how she responded.

"You know, Raven." I pointed to her freshly touched-up black fingernail polish. "I like that color on you. I didn't used to like black so much, but I think it's growing on me."

"Thanks, but black isn't a color. It's the absence of all color."

"Oh, really? Well, I've got you now. Look in a box of crayons. Black is definitely a color. It says so right on the crayon."

"Wow, on a crayon. You know what? I think you're right, Patrick. I guess black's a color after all." There was sarcasm in her voice, but it was light. Decaffeinated derision. "I mean, despite what the laws of physics say about black not reflecting light waves, if a box of crayons says black is a color, we should probably revise our understanding of how light travels through space."

Well, I guess she was feeling all right after all. Both perky and sardonic. A killer combination.

As I was thinking about how I might defend Crayola, a woman with a stroller approached, and I put my hand gently on Tessa's arm to guide her off the sidewalk, but as soon as I touched her arm, she grimaced and ducked away.

"Sorry. Are you OK?" After I touched her I realized I'd grabbed the same arm Severn Adkins, the serial killer who called himself the Illusionist, had sliced last fall. But that scar was pretty much healed by now. *That must be where the tattoo is.* I didn't mention the tattoo though. I wanted to give her the chance to tell me herself. "Did I hurt your scar?"

"I'm OK. No, you didn't do anything, really. It's just . . . I must have slept on my arm wrong or something. That's all."

She quickly changed the subject and asked what had happened with the case last night, and I couldn't think of any good reason to invite her to peer over the police line at someone else's pain, so instead of telling her about Austin Hunter's death and Cassandra's near drowning, I simply told her that Cassandra was OK and that we had a suspect in custody related to her abduction.

"What about the arsonist?" she asked.

"He was stopped by the police," I said. "He won't be starting fires anytime soon."

"So, is your case over then? Are we gonna be able to hang out today?"

"We'll have to see." Her flight to Denver didn't leave until two twenty-six p.m. I wanted to wait as long as possible before telling her I was sending her home.

"So I never asked you," I said. "How was your drive with Lien-hua yesterday? Did she pull out all the stops or drive like a mortal?"

"She drove pretty much like she did when she took me back to the hotel Monday night. Pretty normal." And then, just as I took a sip of coffee, Tessa asked, "So, what's up with you two, anyway?"

"What do you mean, what's up?"

"C'mon. Don't even act all innocent. I've seen the way you two look at each other. Besides, she was the first person you thought to call after that guy jumped in front of the trolley and you needed someone to come get me. What's the deal with you two?"

"Nothing. Nothing's the deal—"

"Yeah, right. You *so* stink at lying. Besides, whenever people say 'nothing,' it's always something, but they're just afraid of admitting it."

"I'm not afraid of admitting anything—"

"So what's up then?"

Perhaps a slightly different approach. "All right. I can't tell you how she feels about me, but I enjoy working with her, I respect her, I wouldn't mind getting to know her a little better—"

"You think about her all the time, when you're alone with her, you feel more alive than any other time in your life, whenever she talks to you, your pulse races and—"

"OK, OK. That's enough. So, maybe it might be something, but it's not really anything."

We chose a path leading back to the parking lot. "Well, are you seeing her? And don't be, like, 'We've been working together a lot lately,' or something, because that's totally different. Besides, she already tried that on me."

"What? You talked to her about this? You didn't really, did you? You're just saying that, right?"

"Maybe, maybe not," she said evasively. "But that's not the point. Now I'm talking to you, and you're avoiding my question."

Part of me wished that Lien-hua were here so I could make sure we were on the same page with anything I said. On the other hand, I was glad she wasn't hearing any of this. "Tessa, maybe we could discuss this later?"

She paused and turned so that she was directly facing me. "Naw. Now's good."

Since Christie's death, Tessa and I had never really talked about the idea of me dating again. And since my relationship with Lien-hua hadn't progressed to the point where it seemed like an issue, I'd never brought it up.

"So," Tessa persisted. "Are you seeing her? And please don't say 'sort of.' Like you're 'sort of' seeing her."

"What's wrong with saying 'sort of'?"

"It's a cop-out. Very lame. For people who are afraid to commit."

"Oh."

"Well?"

"Well, it's like this, Tessa . . . you see . . . it's . . . it's complicated."

"It's complicated?" She slung her hands to her hips. "A question that requires a yes or no answer is too complicated for you, Dr. Bowers? Are you seeing Agent Jiang: yes or no?"

Just then my phone rang, and Tessa stared at my pocket. "You have got to be kidding me. You dialed that yourself, somehow, didn't you? Pressed a redial button or something?"

"I'm good," I said. "But I'm not that good."

I checked to see who it was. Lien-hua.

"So, who is it?" Tessa peeked at my phone's screen. "Oh, you can't be serious."

"I think I need to take this, OK?"

Tessa folded her arms, cocked her head in a teenage way, and glared.

"Hi, Lien-hua." As I spoke, I kept the phone cradled close to my ear so Tessa couldn't listen in.

"Pat, we need you back at the station."

"What's up?"

"The suspect won't talk to the police, but asked to talk to me. By name."

I knew Tessa was good at overhearing conversations so I stepped away and lowered my voice. As far as I could remember, no one had mentioned Lien-hua's name while we were in the suspect's presence at the warehouse. "How did he know who you are?"

"We're not sure. Margaret's talking with his lawyers now. Ralph's meeting with her in a few minutes. They want you here by noon."

"Well, I can't be there by then. I need to . . ." I could see Tessa straining to listen in. I rephrased what I was about to say just in case she heard me. "I need to take care of a few things. I can't get there until one at the earliest."

"OK. I'll call you if I find out more."

"OK. See ya soon."

As I hung up, Tessa asked suspiciously, "What was all that about?"

The case had just become a little more complex, but I couldn't get into all of it with Tessa. "I'm afraid this investigation is going to eat up some of my time today. I won't be able to leave until tomorrow afternoon at least."

Her eyebrows awoke. "But I thought we were staying until Friday, right?"

"That was the plan." *Before you tackle that conversation, finish up this one.* "Anyway, where were we? Oh yes. I was just about to make you promise not to talk to Agent Jiang about all this are-we-seeing-each-other stuff."

"No, you were just about to tell me if you're seeing her. But I'll make you a promise if you give me a straight answer."

I collected my thoughts. "Tessa, listen, how about this: if Agent Jiang and I ever decide to move from something that's nothing to anything that might be more than sort of something, I'll let you know."

"You didn't think I followed that, but I did."

"I believe you. Now, promise."

"I promise."

"You promise what?"

She sighed, took a deep breath, and said, "I promise not to tell Agent Jiang how much you like her and how badly you want to start seeing her. How's that?"

I rubbed my forehead as a cab pulled up and a tall, lean gentleman unfolded himself from the backseat. He handed some bills to the driver and turned to face us.

Dr. Calvin Werjonic had arrived.

66

Calvin couldn't have chosen a more unusual outfit for visiting San Diego. He was wrapped in a wafer-thin London Fog trench coat—I'd rarely seen him wear anything else—and he wore a crumpled fedora even though they'd gone out of style forty years ago.

"Patrick, my boy!" Considering all the long talks and late nights we'd shared together over the years, a handshake didn't seem like enough to me, but I knew Calvin wasn't a hugger. He pumped my hand warmly. "So good to see you. And this must be the lovely Tessa Ellis?"

"Hello."

"Patrick has told me all about you."

"I'll bet. He didn't tell me so much about you, but I read about you in his two books."

"Hmm . . . I fell asleep reading those sections."

"Those were the only parts that kept me awake."

"Eh-hem." I handed him his coffee. "You look good, Calvin."

"Your stepfather is a very poor liar, Tessa."

"Well, that's OK. I make up for it."

"Tell me about it," I said.

Calvin took in a deep drink of San Diego air and then gave me a quick once-over. "So Patrick, you look as fit as ever. Still doing those press-ups?"

"We call them push-ups in the states. But usually for me, it's pull-ups."

"Ah yes, of course." He lifted his coffee to his lips, took a sip.

I watched for a reaction. "What do you think of that coffee? Nice, huh?"

"A bit tart for my taste, I'm afraid." He took off the lid, poured the coffee onto the sidewalk, and dropped the cup into a nearby trash can. "Come along, then." He started walking up the trail at a brisk clip.

Tessa saw the look on my face as I stared at the tragic coffee stain on the sidewalk. "Don't cry, Patrick. It'd embarrass me."

"Come, come," said Calvin, who was already twenty meters ahead of us. "I don't have all day."

Calvin and I took a few minutes to catch up on each other's lives, and then Tessa quizzed him about some of his cases. She wanted as many details as she could get as long as he stayed away from mentioning blood or dead bodies. Then he took some time to ask her about the best Web site for downloading ring tones, what this week's hottest YouTube videos were, and how many friends she had listed on her Facebook page.

After about fifteen minutes, I asked Tessa if she wouldn't mind if Calvin and I discussed some cases that involved lots of blood and shootings. Immediately she offered to wait for us up ahead at the SDAI Museum of the Living Artist, and after she was gone, Calvin said softly, "Smart girl, that one."

"You have no idea."

Then Calvin filled me in on some of his current consulting work with the National Geospatial-Intelligence Agency, a little-known combat support agency that provides geospatial intelligence to the Department of Defense. The NGIA emphasizes military use of geospatial intelligence, but over the years Calvin and I have both worked with them to help find ways to integrate their GEOINT into law enforcement. However, last year I bowed out when they started pushing for an international cyberinfrastructure that would include an integrated global video array between our spy satellites, private firms, and the GEOINT of our allies.

Calvin and I had never seen eye to eye on this issue.

"But, Patrick," he said earnestly, "even now the Department of Defense is designing the next generation of satellites. By integrating current technology into the satellite systems, we will be able to zoom in close enough to read text off a document, numbers off a cell phone screen, even verify identities through retinal scans. And with laser targeting there's been talk of—"

"Calvin, please," I didn't mean to sound impatient, but I'd heard all this before. "Law enforcement personnel need probable cause to stop a car, tap a phone, enter a house, search a suspect, or even follow someone home. With global video, all that would go out the window; the government could follow anyone, anywhere, anytime. No privacy. We have a right to live our lives without someone looking over our shoulders every minute of the day. We should use technology to find the guilty, not monitor the innocent."

"But think of it, my boy. A crime occurs, say perhaps a child is abducted, we review the global video at the time and place of the crime, then follow the offender from the scene, use live tracking, and locate him in a matter of minutes. This is the zenith of environmental criminology. It's what we've been working toward for decades. It will revolutionize the investigative process."

"We arrest voyeurs and Peeping Toms, but now the NGIA is proposing creating one giant webcam for intelligence agencies all over the world so they can peek into the lives of innocent people. I still say it's not right. Maybe we can debate this another time. I know you need to catch your flight—"

"Yes, yes, of course." He brushed a gaunt hand against the air as if he were erasing the words we'd just spoken to each other. "Please forgive me. Your case. Tell me about your investigation."

Calvin quickened his pace, and I summarized the current case, changing the names and some of the details so that I wasn't revealing information that might compromise our investigation. Calvin listened astutely, nodding at times to show that he was following what I said, and then at last he asked, "Patrick, have you explored the connection of Monday night's fire to John Doe's death?"

"So far all I have is the nexus of time and location."

"Hmm. I know you don't typically venture into motive, but has Agent Jiang plumbed your arsonist's motivation for the previous fires?"

"Ralph assigned one of the field agents to look into the

arsonist's bank records, and she found that the man had made a twenty-five-thousand-dollar deposit within a few days of each of the previous fires. So, if you're looking for motive, it appears that he did it for the money."

"Yes, but the money from whom?"

"We don't know."

"And regardless, that's not what the abductors wanted from him in the end."

"Apparently not."

"Obviously, you'll need to follow up with your elusive Dr. O."

"He's still out of town. It's on my list for later today."

"Yes, of course. And Shade, what do you know of this Shade character?"

"Not much. He might be the man we took into custody, but I doubt it. Shade told me on the phone that he was at the rendezvous point and it seems unlikely that would have been the warehouse. Whoever Shade is, he knows how to mask his GPS location and he knows me. He positively identified me during our brief phone conversation so I'm afraid he might be someone from a previous case, or maybe even a personal acquaintance."

"Quite so." Calvin walked in silent repose beside me for a few minutes and then said, "It's an intricate case to be sure, but I'm confident you'll be able to unravel it, my boy. I'll certainly consider all that you've told me, and if I have any additional investigative recommendations, I'll contact you promptly. One word of advice . . ." Then he began speaking to me as if I was still a doctoral student at Simon Fraser University, and he was still my professor. "Remember, Patrick, the devil is not in the details, but in how the details relate to each other. Sometimes you need to stop looking at the facts and start looking at the spaces between them. One cannot adequately understand the movement of the planets through a solar system until one has identified what they all orbit around."

I was reflecting on his comments when he added, "And now for the personal matter you were reticent to mention on the phone."

I knew he would be able to tell if I were hiding anything from him, so I didn't even try. "Calvin, at times my job really eats away at me. The human potential for evil is, well ... it's staggering."

He read between the lines. "But it's your personal potential for evil that troubles you most."

"Yes."

"We're all capable of the unthinkable, Patrick."

"I know. Maybe I know that too well."

We paused in the shadow of a thick palm tree, and Calvin said, "I believe the more acutely aware we are of our human frailty, the less vulnerable we are to our base instincts."

"It's those base instincts that frighten me the most—not just the inclination we have toward evil, but—"

"The subtle enjoyment of it."

"Yes."

He contemplated my words for a few moments. "So, to put it in mountaineer's terms, how do we know we're not going to slip off the escarpment when we're all living on the edge of the cliff?"

"Yes," I said. "And how do we know we're not going to push someone else off the arête?"

We stepped back into the bright day and continued along the trail.

"The simple answer, Patrick, as you've already deduced, is that we don't. We can never be sure we won't jump or push someone else. But that's not a satisfactory answer because we all want to think that we're different, that we would never do those things—and yet the edge is within reach of all of us. Nietzsche wrote, 'Whoever fights monsters should see to it that in the process he does not become a monster. And when you look long into an abyss, the abyss also looks into you.' You have looked long into the abyss, my boy. And you've seen how alluring it is."

I thought for a moment. "You're right, Calvin, except I don't fight monsters and neither do you. We track offenders who are just as human as we are. Killers, rapists, pedophiles—they do monstrous things and their actions make them more guilty than others, but not less human. The more you search for what makes 'them' different from 'us,' the more you find that, at the core, we're all the same. Offenders aren't monsters any more than we are."

"Then, perhaps," Calvin said with disturbing resignation, "we are all monsters."

Just what I needed to hear. "It's such an encouragement talking to you, Calvin. If Dr. Phil ever retires, you ought to apply for his job."

"I'll keep that in mind."

Tessa was waiting for us across the parking lot from the Museum of the Living Artist, in the Casa del Rey Moro Garden. "What took you two so long?"

"I'm afraid we're still a bit befuddled by this case," Calvin said.

"I thought it was almost solved?"

"A few remaining conundrums, as it were," he replied.

"Well, I think your problem is, you two need to start thinking more like Dupin."

"Dupin?" I said.

And then Tessa taught Dr. Werjonic and me how to investigate a crime that, by all appearances, could not possibly have occurred.

67

"Dupin," Tessa repeated. "Haven't you ever read 'The Murders in the Rue Morgue'?"

"Probably . . . A long time ago," I said. "Maybe when I was your age."

"That would be a long time ago," she muttered.

The truth was, I did remember reading some of Poe's writings when I was younger, but I'd never been that interested in him. Now, I suspected I would regret that. "Tessa," I said, "who is Dupin?"

"Monsieur C. Auguste Dupin. Poe created him. Wrote three stories about him. In the first one, 'The Murders in the Rue Morgue,' there's these two people who get killed— a woman and her daughter. But they're not in a morgue, though. It's the name of a street. Anyway, the detective is this guy named Dupin, but he's not really a detective exactly, more like a profiler or something."

"Hmm, a profiler," Calvin muttered.

"Yeah," she said. "And he ends up solving the crime."

"Well, there you go," I said. "You can already tell it's fiction."

Tessa gave me a headshake. "If Lien-hua were here, she'd drop-kick you for saying that."

"Quite so," remarked Calvin, who had chosen to lead us north along the path that led past the Botanical Building. "But I'm sad to say, my dear, this Dupin fellow, he seems to be a pale apograph of the inimitable Sherlock Holmes."

"Holmes?" Tessa recoiled. "Do not even *go* there with me. Sir Arthur Conan Doyle, if I can even call him 'sir,' totally cripped Poe. 'The Rue Morgue' was written in 1841;

Doyle wasn't even born until 1859. And then, in 1885 when Doyle decides to start writing detective stories, he makes Holmes a complete carbon copy of Dupin. Holmes thinks like Dupin. Acts like him. Talks like him. Relates to the local police in the exact same way. And Watson is totally based on the guy who narrates Dupin's cases." She was getting really riled up. Passion looked good on her. "And then, despite all that, in the first Holmes story, *A Study in Scarlet*, Doyle has the effrontery to have his pseudo-creation Sherlock Holmes dis Dupin by calling him 'a very inferior fellow.' Doyle is lame. Poe rocks."

Calvin, a connoisseur of detective stories from the other side of the Atlantic, cleared his throat slightly. "Did you just say 'effrontery,' my dear?"

"You'll get used to it," I told him. Then I faced Tessa. "Not that I don't find all this very interesting, but how does this relate to us solving this case?"

"Hold on. I'm getting to that. So, here's what Dupin does in 'The Rue Morgue' . . . ." She counted on her fingers all of Dupin's investigative techniques, one at a time. "He looks over the facts, collects physical evidence, studies the wound patterns, analyzes hair samples, does a preliminary autopsy, evaluates the statements from witnesses, interrogates a suspect, and then gets a sailor to confess his involvement in the incident."

"Sounds like you, Patrick," said Calvin, "on one of your better days."

A jogger passed us, pounding up the trail, palm trees on his right, cacti on his left.

"Actually," Tessa said, looking at me, "Dupin was kind of like you."

"How's that?"

"He visited the scene—that was a big deal to him—and he studied how the killer got into and out of the room."

"Nice," I said. "Entrance and exit routes."

"He called them ingress and egress, but whatever. And he also managed to get on the nerves of the local authorities."

"Sounds like my kind of guy." The trail began its long circuitous loop back to the Alcazar Garden by curving around the outer fringes of the San Diego Zoo. Inside I could hear the chatter of birds and the roar of some large jungle cat.

"The whole entrance/exit thing is actually what helped him solve the case. See, it looks like a robbery, but Dupin, he considers other options. Instead of just looking at the evidence that supports his theory, like the police do, he tries out different ideas that don't even seem to make sense."

"The mark of a true investigator," said Calvin.

"That's not even all of it. So then, Dupin thinks about the size, body type, and special skills of the killer—who could do this crime, right? And then he uses that to help narrow down the suspects 'cause he knows the killer has to be really strong, *extraordinarily* strong, to cause the kind of injuries the victims had, but also, the killer's gotta be very *agile*."

As she spoke, Tessa became more and more animated, like a natural-born storyteller. I'd never seen her this excited about anything, and I didn't want to stop her. It might have been her way of showing me that I wasn't so innovative after all, since Poe created Dupin nearly a hundred and fifty years before I was even born, but whatever her reasons, it was good to see her so enthusiastic about something. I let her keep going.

"And as Dupin studied the wound on the dead girl's neck, he even built, like, this tube to see how big someone's hand would have to be to make the bruises."

"Crime reconstruction," mumbled Calvin. "This chap should teach at Scotland Yard."

Tessa wavered her finger against the air in front of her. "But, here's the thing, the wound wasn't caused by a human hand."

I suspected Poe had created some type of fictional monster to commit the crimes. An easy solution to the problem. "So, what caused the bruises?"

"Well, instead of just looking at what happened, Dupin, see, he focused on what happened that was unique to that specific case."

"The more unique a crime, the easier it is to solve," I mumbled, quoting a maxim I often shared at my seminars. I used to think I'd made it up. Maybe Poe did.

"But this wasn't a crime," said Tessa.

"I thought two people were murdered?"

"No, two people were *killed*."

"Just a moment, my dear," said Calvin. "I believe you have yet to explain the bruises."

"The killer gave them to her."

I still didn't get it. "OK, wait. So the sailor did it?"

"No, the ape did."

"The ape?" Calvin and I both exclaimed.

"Yes, an orangutan from Borneo who was trying to shave the people and accidentally nearly sliced the woman's head off with a straight razor." She shook her head slightly. "That part of the story's not quite as good."

"What about the sailor?" asked Calvin.

"He owned the orangutan. It escaped."

"You're kidding me, right?" I said. "An orangutan who was trying to shave the victims?" I didn't remember ever reading that.

"Hey, you gotta cut Poe some slack. FYI: 'The Murders in the Rue Morgue' was the first detective story ever printed, the first locked-room mystery, the first crime fiction story, and the first example of criminal profiling to appear in literature. With just one short story, Poe created four genres of literature that are still around today. Still *popular* today."

"Well, in that case," Calvin said, "consider the slack cut."

Tessa stepped over a clutter of tumbleweed that had blown into the path. "That," she said, "and the cool thing is, Dupin actually used the fact that it seemed so unsolvable to solve the case. As impossible as it seemed, it *did* occur, so it must have been possible. But the police made the mistake of *de nier ce qui est, et d'expliquer ce qui n'est pas.* But Dupin didn't."

I stared at her. "You can't be serious. When did you start speaking French?"

She looked defensive. Shy. Embarrassed. "I'm just learning. Why? Did I pronounce something wrong?"

"No," Calvin said. "I don't believe so."

I sighed. "Can you translate for me? My French is a little rusty."

"*De nier ce qui est, et d'expliquer ce qui n'est pas,*" she said again. "'Ignoring what is and explaining what is not.' The cops saw a robbery and two murders in a locked room. But in the end, there was no robbery, no murders, no crime, no motive, and the room wasn't locked."

I'd never seen Calvin as confused as I did now. "My dear, I'm afraid you're going to have to walk me through that."

"The ape didn't steal anything, so no robbery; he didn't

have a motive, unless you count trying to shave someone; and he didn't murder the people—killed them, sure, but he wasn't human, so it wasn't a murder, and that's also why there wasn't any crime. And the room wasn't locked when the ape climbed in, it's just that the window latched itself shut when he bumped into it while egressing—that's actually a word, by the way, but I don't remember if Poe actually uses it. Anyway, there you go."

Calvin beamed at her with admiration. "Well done, my dear. Well done, indeed."

"Nothing was as it appeared to be," I said softly.

"Right," she said. "And at the very end of the story, Dupin is talking about the idiotic police detective and says, 'I am satisfied with having defeated him in his own castle.' I like that part."

"Defeating him in his own castle . . ." Calvin mumbled. "I'll have to remember that. It might make a good title for my next book."

As we approached the Alcazar Garden, I could see that Calvin's cab had returned and was already waiting for him. He gazed at his watch and announced, "I do need to be getting on my way. Tessa, my dear, it's been a pleasure. I look forward to my next lesson in American literature."

"Read more Poe," she said. "'The Mystery of Marie Rogêt' and 'The Purloined Letter,' the other Dupin stories. You'll like 'em."

He patted her shoulder, then gripped my elbow in his hand. "Good luck with this case, my boy. Remember: trust the evidence wherever it takes you. Keep disproving your theories until you uncover the truth."

"Thanks," I said. "It was great to see you."

Then, we said our hurried good-byes, Calvin left, and I realized it was time to confront Tessa about her tattoo.

Lien-hua watched Margaret Wellington pace stiffly back and forth across the conference room floor. Thirty minutes ago, Margaret had asked her to brief her about the case, share her preliminary profile of the abductors, and explain how her foot happened to land in the suspect's abdomen last night in the warehouse while he was still standing up. It was in light of Lien-hua's explanation that Margaret had started pacing.

The silence in the room was finally broken when Ralph stepped through the door and announced that the criminalists were processing the warehouse and the suspect's condo. "Guy's name is Neville Lewis. Police still haven't gotten a word out of him. His record comes up clean, but so far we haven't been able to find any actual people who can vouch for him."

"Did you run his prints through AFIS?" Margaret asked.

Ralph nodded. "We got nothin'. As far as I can tell he never even jaywalked or cheated on his taxes."

"Wait," said Lien-hua. "A man who built his own torture chamber and was involved in this sophisticated of a kidnapping has no priors?"

"Doesn't fly, does it?"

Lien-hua shook her head.

"Well," said Margaret, "I tend to trust the Automated Fingerprint Identification System over your intuition, Agent Jiang. AFIS doesn't lie."

Lien-hua considered that. "Let's say his records were falsified. How good would someone have to be to pull off an electronic identity package like that, good enough to fool AFIS?"

"Good," said Ralph. "Really good."

"What about witness protection?" Lien-hua glanced back and forth from Ralph to Margaret. "Is it possible Mr. Lewis might be in the program?"

Ralph deferred to Margaret with a shrug.

"Well," she said. "I doubt it, but I will look into it. Meanwhile, Agent Hawkins, find out from the navy if they've removed any additional evidence from the site of last night's fire. If you run into any trouble, just tell them you're working directly for me."

"I won't run into any trouble."

"And Agent Jiang"—Margaret gave her an innocuous-looking smile—"I would like you to go over the events of last night one more time. Just for the record."

68

After Tessa and I left Balboa Park we returned to the hotel, and I invited her to take a short walk with me along the beach. Obviously she wasn't going to bring up her tattoo, so I would have to. The day was sunny, but my mood had turned overcast.

"So, Tessa, tell me about your afternoon yesterday, after we left the aquarium."

"I don't know. I walked around for a while. I visited some shops and stuff."

"I thought you hate shopping?"

"Well, I do, but I was just curious, you know, exploring stuff downtown."

I gave her a chance to say more, but she didn't take it. "What about last night? Where'd you have supper?"

"I just ate here at the hotel and then I wrote for a little while, read some stuff, and went to bed."

I waited, wishing she would just tell me. I wanted to hear it from her. "So that's all you did, then?"

"What is this? Like, an interrogation?" Her voice was becoming surly. "I told you. That's it."

I took a tense breath. "Can I at least see the tattoo?"

Confusion ghosting across her face. "What?"

"The tattoo on your arm. I'd like to see it." I felt my anger rising, not so much that she'd gotten a tattoo—I'd been expecting that for months—but I was getting fed up with her half-truths and evasions and disobedience. "You got your nose pierced without asking me. You got your eyebrow pierced without asking me. And now you get a tattoo, which is, by the way, illegal in this state unless you're eighteen—and not only did you not ask me, but just now you lied to me."

"I didn't lie to you!"

"You told me you just went walking around."

Her eyes flashed with resolve. Independence. "Oh, so I get it. It was a setup, huh? Your nice little questions about what I did yesterday. Silly me, I thought you were actually interested in my life. Well, I won't make that mistake again."

"Stop it, Tessa. It wasn't a setup. I was giving you the opportunity to tell me the truth. To be straight with me."

"Oh. An opportunity. Is that what you call it? And how do you know I went to a tattoo place anyhow?"

"I was worried about you after that deal at the aquarium—"

"I told you that those sharks ate this fish and I went looking for you! Why won't you believe me? All I knew was that you were in the back somewhere and I was scared."

"So I decided to check on you," I continued. "To monitor where you were."

"To monitor me? Ex*cuse* me. Am I two years old?" She paused to regroup. To catch her breath. She only needed a moment. "Oh!" Then, she smacked her satchel into my side, sending her personal items scattering across the sand. "You had me followed!"

"No, Tessa. I didn't have you followed. Nothing like that." I bent down to help her gather her things, but she pushed me away.

"Oh, you didn't have me followed? Then how did you . . ." As she was sliding her things back into her purse, her hand fell on her cell phone. "Oh . . . You didn't . . . Tell me you did not . . . Yes, you did—you tracked my cell. The GPS!"

"I wanted to make sure you were OK."

"You didn't trust me. I cannot believe you!"

"Trust you? Why should I trust you? You wander around in places I specifically tell you not to go in. You sneak off to get a tattoo. You don't tell me where you are. You don't return my phone calls. I'm concerned about you. Don't you understand? You're my responsibility."

"I am not your responsibility!" She snatched up her satchel. "I'm my own responsibility, OK? I grew up without having any dad around to tell me what to do or where to go or whether or not I could get my nose pierced or get a tattoo or whatever. I did fine without a dad before, and I can do fine without—"

"Don't even say it. Do not say it, Tessa. I thought we were trying to rebuild a family here, and a family depends on trust."

"But you don't trust me!"

"Because you haven't earned it."

The air bristled between us. She grabbed her sleeve, yanked it up to her shoulder. "You want to see my tattoo? OK, here it is. I got a raven, OK? I got a raven because you sometimes call me Raven and I like it, 'cause it makes me feel special—or at least it used to. But now, you know what?" Her words were filled with so many kinds of pain. "I wish I would have gotten something else."

My heart felt like it was going to explode and wither at the same time. "Tessa, I'm sending you back to Denver this afternoon." The words felt like acid against my teeth.

"What?"

"I already talked to my parents. They'll pick you up at the airport. I'll fly home at the end of the week, and we'll deal with all this then. I can't leave today. I would if I could, but I have to complete my obligations on this case, and I can't do that with you here in San Diego if I can't trust you."

"Oh, really?" She swung her satchel over her shoulder and set her jaw. "Well, you know what? I'm glad you want me to go back to Denver because I'd rather go there than spend *another minute* here with you." Then she spun and stormed off.

And my heart broke to splinters.

And I was thankful she didn't turn around.

Because that way she couldn't see the hot tear sliding down my cheek.

69

Victor Drake parked his Jaguar in front of the seedy box-
ing gym where Suricata and Geoff normally worked out. It
was time to dissolve the team, but first, he needed to make
sure that all the jobs were satisfactorily completed.

This whole part of town disgusted him. It wasn't for people like him, and he could hardly believe that he was even
here. What if someone saw him?

But then again, since no one would expect a man of his
stature to show up here, it was less likely anyone would recognize him. He didn't bring the money with him, of course.
He wasn't going to drive into the heart of Barrio Logan
with two hundred and fifty thousand dollars cash in the
trunk of his car.

Victor locked his car and then slipped inside the crusty
building. The place was just like he expected it would be:
dark, rank, and filled with the barbaric sounds of large men
pummeling each other into unconsciousness. What a wonderful place to spend your free time.

Geoff and Dr. Kurvetek were already there, waiting for
him beside a large punching bag. Suricata was finishing
battering the face of a man fifty pounds heavier than him.
Victor had always known Suricata was good with knives,
but he'd never seen Suricata box before. It was disturbingly
impressive.

"Do you have the money?" asked Geoff.

"Don't be ridiculous. No. Not with me."

An edge of anger. "I thought you were bringing it?"

"I'll get it to you, OK? But first I want to know if you can
keep the cops off my back and tell me where the device is."

"The cops won't bother you. I took care of all that," Geoff said. "And Hunter didn't have anything with him when he was killed. I looked all over the area, the pier, everything. It wasn't there. It's gone. And I checked his body. There's nothing to connect him to us."

By then, Suricata had joined them. Victor allowed him a brief glance. The man was panting. Perspiring. And he smelled revolting. What else was new?

Dr. Kurvetek peered at Victor through the sweat-soaked air. "It appears the device truly was destroyed in the fire. Hunter didn't know anything about it. Why would he have removed it? Everything ended with his death."

"Yeah," snarled Suricata. "Now, what about our money?"

"Tonight," Victor said. "I'll have it at my house. All of it. Be there at eight thirty. I'll give it to you then. But for now, bury all the evidence, the reports, do what you need to do to pin everything on Hunter. No slipups." And then, before the three men Victor had grown to despise could respond or object, he strode past them and removed himself from that filthy place.

He would have the money for them tonight. Yes. After all, he was a man of his word. But then, as soon as this nightmare was wrapped up, he was going on a little vacation until the dust settled again.

He finished off his bottle of pills, pulled out his cell, and called his travel agent. Then he drove as quickly as he could away from the part of town he never should have ventured into in the first place.

I was standing in the hallway outside Tessa's door waiting for her to get her suitcases packed when Ralph called. I answered, hoping maybe he could encourage me that I was doing the right thing by sending Tessa home, but before we could even get to that, he said, "Pat. Nothing more on Drake. He looks clean."

"What else?"

"Margaret's taking over the case. Suddenly, she seems very interested in it. We have a briefing at police headquarters at two o'clock, and she's insistent that you be there."

Executive Assistant Director Margaret Wellington was the last person I wanted to see right now. She doesn't believe in environmental criminology or geospatial investiga-

tion and tries to discredit me and cut funding for my work
every chance she gets. Needless to say, we don't get together
to play Scrabble on the weekends. Having to deal with her
would put me right over the edge. "Listen, Ralph. You tell
her I'll be late, if I come at all. You tell her that, OK?"

He processed that for a moment. "Didn't go so well with
Tessa, huh?"

"Not so good. We're heading to the airport in just a few
minutes."

He paused, probably to weigh what I'd just said against
the consequences of me not showing up at one of Margaret's meetings. "All right. I'll cover for you. And if you can't
make it to the meeting, I'll tell Margaret you're on an assignment from me."

"Thanks. And, hey, tell me I'm doing the right thing here
with Tessa."

"You're doing the right thing, Pat."

"Thanks, Ralph."

"I think."

And before I could say another word, Tessa's door
swung open and she stepped past me, carrying her hastily
packed bags. After she'd taken four steps, she called over
her shoulder, "You can take me to the airport now, Patrick.
I am *so* ready to be out of here."

Ralph and I ended the call, and I led my stepdaughter
and her illegal raven to the car.

70

12:39 p.m.

Neither Tessa nor I spoke much on the way to the airport. I'm sure we both had things we wanted to say, needed to say—I know I did—but the conversation just never got started.

We parked. Unloaded her stuff. Walked inside, all in silence.

Finally, at the ticket counter I said, "Tessa. You know I love you and I want what's best for you."

Silence.

"I'll be home sometime in the next couple days. We'll straighten this all out then."

"OK," she said. And that was all.

After she had her boarding pass, I walked with her to the security checkpoint, although she made sure she was a few steps ahead of me the whole way. The line was short, and before she could enter it, I stepped in front of her and said, "Good-bye, Tessa."

I didn't think she would reply, but she did. She said one simple, final word: "Good-bye." Then she brushed past me and walked over to show her driver's license and boarding pass to the TSA agent.

The words "I'll see you soon" didn't quite make it to my lips. I wanted them to, but they didn't. I couldn't stay and watch her walk away like that. I just couldn't do it.

So at last, without saying another word, I returned to the car.

*   *   *

Tessa dropped her satchel onto the conveyor belt, emptied her pockets, and waited for the bored-looking TSA guy to motion for her to step through the stupid metal detector. She'd avoided eye contact with Patrick so he wouldn't see that she was about to cry. She didn't want him to know how much she hurt.

Hurt because of what she'd done.

Hurt because of what he'd said.

He didn't trust her. She wanted him to, but he didn't. And it was at least partly her fault.

The security guy waved her through. The way her day was going she expected the thing to beep. That would have been just brilliant.

But it didn't.

Thankfully.

But then, as soon as she got to the other side, one of the other worker guys picked up her satchel, shuffled through it, and took out the antibacterial soap for her tattoo because he said it wasn't 3.4 ounces or less and besides it hadn't been placed in a quart-sized resealable plastic bag and he threw the soap into the trash and all that did was make her think of the tattoo again and of Riker and Patrick and what had just happened between them and how badly she just wanted to be alone, alone, alone.

Tessa plucked her satchel from the TSA guy's hands and huffed past him to the gate. She escaped into the restroom, locked herself in one of the stalls, pulled out her notebook, and let the words that were raging inside her bleed onto the page:

> *in the bin of a*
> *thousand heartaches, i place*
> *my feathered pain.*

Then she stuffed her notebook back into her satchel and snapped rubber bands against her wrist until all the ones she had with her were broken. And then Tessa Bernice Ellis began to cry where no one else could see her, locked inside the shiny steel walls of the bathroom stall.

71

It was hard for me to leave the airport.

After dropping Tessa off, I'd sat in the parking garage for nearly fifteen minutes, wondering if I should go back inside to try and talk with her some more. But I finally realized that I was doing the hardest thing, but the best one. If I went back in there, she wouldn't learn her lesson. I needed to be firm and stand my ground. Over this past year I've been learning that being a dad is a much harder job than catching serial killers. Much, much harder.

And sitting there in the parking garage, I began to realize something else: sometimes when you're a parent, your love has to be tough and uncomfortable, and it has to sting if it's going to prove to be real and last for the long haul. Love that's too timid to ache isn't love at all.

However, as I left the airport, I knew I wasn't ready to meet with Margaret yet. So, I decided to do the thing I do best—instead of going to police headquarters, I drove back to the site of Austin Hunter's death to have a look around.

When I arrived, I parked in the same place Lien-hua and I had parked the previous night when we rushed here to try and find—and then to save—Austin Hunter. I stepped out of the car and visually scanned the area, checking sight lines, comparing the scene now to what it had looked like last night.

Why here? Why did Hunter die here?

I closed my eyes and pictured the roads of San Diego, the arteries of the city, intersecting, interconnecting. I knew Hunter's cognitive map of the city better than anyone, and now, despite my natural tendencies, I tried to climb into his mind, to think like he did.

But I couldn't do it.

I tried layering in the locations of the fires, and the address of his apartment, and the trolley depots he'd used to leave the scenes; then I mixed in the wind conditions last night, and the most likely place he would have come ashore after swimming across the bay . . .

But as hard as I tried, I just couldn't figure out why Austin Hunter had let the police corner him where they did. He was too smart to get trapped in the middle of a road by mistake. This man had spent two years teaching survival and evasion tactics to Navy SEALs, and this location didn't seem to make any sense. I knew he wouldn't have led them to the rendezvous point, that much was for sure. So why here?

I opened my eyes and studied the area again.

The device. He wouldn't have left Building B-14 without the device.

But he didn't have any kind of device with him, except for the phone, when the police surrounded him. We could certainly analyze it, but when I'd used it, there didn't seem to be anything unusual about it. I couldn't imagine that all this fuss was about a prepaid cell phone.

Austin was a pro.

A pro.

I didn't know what the device was, or exactly what it did, but if Austin was going to steal it, the device would need to be mobile and, if the size of an MEG machine was any indication, the device would have to be at least large enough to be easily seen.

So, if Austin had it with him, where would he have hidden it?

A place it would be safe.

A place he could get to later.

Just before he was killed, he'd tilted his knife at Lien-hua. I walked to the place where I'd been standing; I pictured where Austin and Lien-hua had been.

"It's over," he'd said, but I didn't think he was talking about his life, and I didn't think he was threatening Lien-hua.

It's over.

What's over?

I glanced at the empty stretch of curb beside me. A car had been there last night. The car with the parking tickets, the one Dunn kicked.

The one he'd ordered taken to impound.

It's over . . . It's over . . .

Could Austin have been talking about the device? *The device is over . . .*

Austin pointed. He pointed.

Oh.

The device is over . . . there.

Austin had put it in the car.

It was time for me to pay a visit to the police impound yard.

When Tessa finally stepped out of the restroom and walked to her departure gate, she heard the poofy-haired airline lady who was working at Gate 24 announce that their departure time was delayed because of mechanical problems.

Great. Just great.

Tessa pulled out her cell phone and slouched into one of the airport chairs, ergonomically designed to cause permanent back problems. She tried not to think about how stupid the TSA rules about soap were, how stupid this whole trip had been, or how much her tattooed arm was hurting. Or her wrist where she'd snapped the rubber bands.

Or any other part of her body, like specifically, maybe, hello, her heart.

So some of it was her fault. So what? Patrick still wasn't being fair. He wasn't. He just wasn't.

She pulled out her phone, scrolled through some of her e-mail, and was texting a couple friends to tell them she was coming back two days early when a white-haired woman sitting in the chair beside her said, "Good afternoon, dear."

Tessa didn't want to be rude. "Hi."

"Are you going to Denver too?"

You think? Could that possibly be why I'm sitting at this gate?

"Um, yeah."

"I wonder . . ." The woman had tender wrinkles around her eyes and a soft grandmotherly smile. "I wonder if you wouldn't mind letting me leave my purse and my bag here. If you wouldn't care to watch them for a few minutes." Tessa saw a cane resting beside the woman's leg. "It's such a task taking them to and from the bathroom."

"Yeah, no problem."

The woman handed her a smile. "Thank you. That's very sweet of you."

Then the lady, who was starting to remind Tessa of her second-grade teacher, stood up slowly. And, using her cane for balance, she left her purse and her carry-on bag beside Tessa's chair and walked gingerly toward the restroom.

At the impound yard, I learned that a video camera had been found in the abandoned car's trunk and had been handed over to the evidence room at police headquarters. I had a feeling it was much more than a video camera.

When I arrived at headquarters, I took my laptop with me to the second floor, walked past the infirmary, and found room 211: the evidence room.

At most police stations, everyone calls this facility "the evidence room" rather than "rooms," but nearly always, the "room" consists of a mazelike series of many narrow rooms, packed with shelves that are piled high with boxes labeled by year, by case, by type of crime.

The officer in charge of the evidence room, a bearded man named Riley Kernigan, who appeared to be serving his last stint with the force before retirement, lowered his newspaper and greeted me with a languid smile.

As he glanced halfheartedly at my FBI badge, I asked him if I could see the sign-in sheet for the video camera. "Sure," he said. "But it's empty. You're the first guy interested in this thing."

"Can I see the camera then?"

"Camera, yeah," he said with a touch of sarcasm. "I'll show you the video camera." Obviously Kernigan didn't believe it was a camera either. He pushed himself to his feet and led me past two narrow hallways to the storage room for current, unsolved cases. I saw the device sitting on the table beside a large duffel bag—the same kind of bag I'd seen the man carrying at the site of John Doe's suicide. A thick, foam protective wrap lay beside the duffel bag. I figured Kernigan had unwrapped the device when he checked it in.

The device that the impound guys thought was a video camera didn't look like any video camera I'd ever seen. It had a digital display screen, laser targeting, radioactive stickers. I didn't know how it worked, or what it did, but someone thought it was important enough to kill to get, and that was enough for me.

Officer Kernigan stood beside me, stared at it, and then shook his head. "Darndest thing I ever saw."

The facts of the case were folding in on themselves like a great origami figure. I just wished I could guess what the final shape would look like.

"Can I have a few minutes?" I asked him.

"Take as much time as you like. Stay all afternoon if you want." He gave the device one last lingering glance and tossed his newspaper onto the table beside it. "I get off at five thirty, though. Shift change. Just be done by then 'cause I gotta lock up back here. Do me a favor and stick it back in the bag when you're through."

"Thanks, I will."

Then he returned to the front desk.

I needed to make a decision. This device was stolen from a secure military base, but, as far as anyone else knew, it had been destroyed in the fire. The only other person who knew it had been removed from the base was Austin Hunter, and he was dead.

No one else had signed in to look at it yet, but I knew that a lot of people would be looking for this thing. Most likely the military, maybe people from Drake Enterprises.

Maybe the men from Monday night.

And Shade, whoever he was.

It might be good to see who comes searching for it first . . .

I set my laptop up in the corner of the room, turned on the video chat camera and the computer's digital video recorder. Even after the screen went to sleep, the built-in camera would continue recording. With the amount of battery life and memory on my computer, I could take six to eight hours of video if I needed to. I didn't think any visitors would be suspicious of a computer in the corner of the room, nor would they notice the tiny display light indicating that the camera was on.

Before putting the screen to sleep, I changed the computer's system settings to allow me to remotely access the hard drive through the Internet. This way I'd be able to run any of my programs even if I wasn't able to retrieve the computer from the evidence room until evening.

Then, so that we wouldn't lose track of the device again, I decided to hide it in plain sight . . . so to speak.

Wearing latex gloves, I carefully wrapped it in the newspaper Officer Kernigan had discarded beside me and then slid it behind a dusty box of evidence from a 1984 grand theft auto case. I needed to put something back into the black duffel bag but didn't want to compromise the evidence from another case, so I rooted around in the drawers and the custodial closet of the evidence room, found a roll of duct tape, and set to work.

72

Fifteen minutes later, when I arrived at the third-floor conference room, I was pretty certain Margaret's two o'clock meeting would have started already, but something had delayed them and they were still waiting to begin.

Oh, I was overjoyed.

Detective Dunn was sitting at the table, along with Lien-hua, two agents from yesterday's meeting, and Lieutenant Aina Mendez, who'd probably come because of the connection between Cassandra's abduction and the fire on the base. Officer Geoff Rickman stood in the corner talking with a man wearing a lieutenant's badge. I suspected he might be Graysmith.

I took a seat, and a few moments later Ralph entered and settled into the chair beside me. "Well," he said quietly. "How did it go with Tessa?"

"About as well as I expected."

"She at the airport?"

"Yeah." I glanced at my watch. "In fact, the plane's probably boarding right about now. She's got a layover in L.A. so she won't get to Denver until almost seven o'clock tonight. I guess I'll talk to her then."

"Her bags'll probably end up in Europe."

"Maybe."

"Good luck with all that. Let me know how things work out."

"I will."

I noticed that Officer Rickman wore his watch on his

right wrist, and when he sat down, he picked up his pen with his left hand. *The discarded leather glove at the arson site was from a left-handed person . . . Aina mentioned that a police officer's prints had been found on it . . .* I saw Ralph's eyes shift toward the door, and then I heard Margaret enter, her heels clattering over top of, and then taking over, the quiet conversations happening all around the room. I would have to follow up on Rickman later.

Margaret chose to stare at me while the people around us took their seats. "Dr. Bowers," she said, her teeth gleaming. "FBI director Rodale told me all about your tactfulness in dealing with the SDPD. Congratulations. You've kept your reputation firmly intact."

"Thanks, Margaret. I've been listening to these self-help podcasts. It's good to know they're paying off. If you ever want to know the link, just say the word."

She drew in a tight breath, looked at the clock on the wall, and then strode to the head of the table. Cleared her throat. "We have a lot to do, and we don't have a lot of time to do it." She paused and gazed around the room like an irritated librarian until everyone had stopped shuffling papers and had turned their attention to her.

"So far the only thing tying Neville Lewis to Cassandra Lillo's abduction is his presence in the vicinity of the crime. But as you know, that's not enough. In order to get a conviction we'll need either incontrovertible eyewitness testimony, a confession, or irrefutable physical evidence."

"Cassandra doesn't want to testify," Lien-hua said. "She doesn't even want to look at a lineup. She was quite traumatized. I'm not convinced she's going to change her mind."

"Without Cassandra we don't have an eyewitness," grumbled Detective Dunn.

"Wait, maybe we do," I said. "Let's bring in the woman who led us to the warehouse. Randi. Let's talk to her."

Ralph spoke up, "We've been trying to find her. Surprise, surprise, she seems to have disappeared."

"All right," said Margaret impatiently, "we'll work on that, but for now let's move on to confession. Mr. Lewis says he's afraid to talk to the police."

Dunn grinned. "Of course he is. He knows if he talks to us we'll get the truth from him and send him away to a prison full of guys who are always thrilled to have new mates to play with."

"No, Detective," Margaret said. "You missed my point. His lawyers say he doesn't trust the police for his *safety*, that after he was in their custody at the warehouse, they failed to protect him." She glared at Lien-hua. Something passed between them. "They say that after he was cuffed and read his rights, one of the federal agents assaulted him. His lawyers brought in a doctor who says he has a bruised rib."

Ralph leaned over, and I heard him whisper to Lien-hua, "That really was a nice kick."

I don't think Margaret heard his comment, but she cleared her throat once again regardless. "With all due respect to the San Diego Police Department, so far all of their efforts to get Lewis to talk have been unproductive. However, in return for not pressing charges against Agent Jiang or filing a civil suit against the FBI or the SDPD, Mr. Lewis's lawyers informed us this morning that he would talk, but only to Agent Jiang. He requested her by name."

That's what Lien-hua had told me on the phone while I was at Balboa Park talking with Tessa, but it didn't make sense. "How does he know Lien-hua's name?" I asked.

"Well, I'm just speculating here . . ." Margaret blew a channel of stiff air between her teeth, making the sound of a machine leaking steam. "Maybe his lawyers told him her name while they were encouraging him to press charges against her for assault and battery. Now, if we could get back to the reason we're here, we need to make a decision—will we accept their offer or not?"

"That's easy," Lien-hua said. "We accept. I'll talk with him. I'll find out what we need to know—"

"Excuse me," said Detective Dunn. "We arrested this guy in our jurisdiction. This is a local law enforcement matter. We'll take care of it on our own."

"I'm afraid it's not as local as it appears," Margaret said. "Tell them about the DVDs, Detective Dunn."

He sat staring. Wouldn't respond.

"Go on," said Margaret. "Tell them that your criminalists found seven DVDs in the back room of the warehouse, each with the video of another woman wearing a red evening gown drowning in that tank."

I heard shocked murmurs ripple around the room.

Margaret's eyes left Dunn and she addressed the group as a whole once again. "So far we've been able to identify women from three different states, based on missing persons reports since November. We're working to identify the other four women, but this is unequivocally not a local law enforcement issue. This is a federal matter. And that's why the FBI has taken over jurisdiction of the case."

Seven murders since November would be an average of one murder every week or two, a remarkably high number. Usually serial killers have a cooling off period in between crimes. But not always. Jeffrey Dahmer, who killed seventeen people, Gary Ridgeway, who killed at least forty-eight, and the nineteenth-century Chicago businessman Herman Webster Mudgett, who may have killed over two hundred, all averaged a victim or more per week during certain months of their criminal career. I was thinking of these grim statistics when I noticed that Dunn's hands, which had been lying flat on the table, were now curled into tense fists.

"Margaret," I said. "Were the videos posted online?"

"I was getting to that, Dr. Bowers," she said tersely. "The answer is yes. The cybercrime division is removing the links, shutting down the sites, but I'm afraid that already, over four hundred thousand people have watched those women die."

Twenty-first-century rubbernecking. Just thinking about it made me sick. "Did the criminalists find DNA, fingerprints, any physical evidence tying Lewis to the crime?"

Margaret shook her head stiffly. "The water from the tank you blew apart washed away any evidence from the area surrounding the scene. Imagine that? And Mr. Lewis was smart enough not to leave fingerprints on the DVD cases or the cameras. We tried voice recognition with the video of Cassandra but came up dry since the only audio was heavy breathing. Right now, to build our case, we need this man's confession."

"Then it's settled," Lien-hua said. "I'll do it."

"Then it's not happening here at police headquarters," Dunn said, "unless we can have an observer, namely me, present."

"Well, then," said Margaret. "We'll move Lewis to the FBI field office."

The lieutenant, whom I assumed to be Graysmith, finally spoke up. "I'm not sure FBI director Rodale would appreciate how this investigation is being handled, Executive Assistant Director Wellington." He laced the words *assistant director* with rich sarcasm.

Hmm. Maybe I could learn to like this guy after all.

"I'd like a few things clarified . . . ," he continued, "since the matter will likely come up this weekend while Director Rodale and I are on the links in Phoenix. Just so I'm clear, explain to me why we can't have one of our detectives present for the interrogation of a suspect who lives in our city, kills in our city, and was apprehended in our city? I'm a little fuzzy on that part of this whole deal you're striking with the suspect's lawyers, and I want to have my facts straight when Director Rodale asks me to fill him in on the case."

Margaret gave Lieutenant Graysmith's words a moment of quiet deliberation, tapped the table twice with her index finger, and said, "All right. Dunn, you observe. Lienhua interrogates. And we put this guy away. I'll have his lawyers draw up the papers relinquishing his rights to file any charges."

She glanced at her watch. "The interrogation will start promptly at three thirty-five p.m., exactly fifty minutes from now. In the meantime, I want everyone in this room pulling up whatever they can on Mr. Neville Lewis so that our interrogator can go in prepared. This meeting is adjourned." And then, as people stirred from their chairs, Margaret added, "Agent Jiang, I'd like you to remain for just a moment."

73

While I waited outside the door for Lien-hua to appear, I asked Aina to follow up on Officer Geoff Rickman. "I think he was at the fire," I said.

"Rickman? But Dr. Bowers, I've already spoken with him. His fingerprints were on the glove."

"There you go. That's him then. He was there."

"No," she said. "He wasn't assigned to the fire, but he received the gloves from the two criminalists and delivered them to the evidence room. Officer Rickman says that he made a mistake and touched the glove. He apologized."

I'm sure he did. "He stepped in Austin's blood yesterday, Aina, and his shoe prints matched one of the patent prints left in the hallway. If he wasn't assigned to the fire, it's possible he was one of the people responsible for starting it."

"You memorized the shoe-print impressions in the soot?"

"Of course."

She paused for a moment. "Well," she said. "I'll see what else I can learn."

"Thanks."

She disappeared down the hall, and as I was considering the implications to the case if Rickman really were Monday night's arsonist, the door beside me banged open and Lien-hua fumed into the hallway. "What is it, Lien-hua? What did Margaret say?"

She spun, her eyes narrow, her lips drawn tight. "Margaret said that even if Lewis doesn't press charges, it doesn't change what I did. She said she can't have an agent in the field who cannot control herself. She told me that after the interrogation, she's putting me on administrative leave. Indefinitely."

"What? You can't be serious?"

Lien-hua stepped away. "I'm going to get ready for the interrogation, Pat. I need some time by myself."

Margaret wasn't there last night. She didn't see how things played out.

I thought back to the Sherrod Aquarium and the sharks' feeding schedule. I wondered how long it would take them to devour a bony forty-seven-year-old woman.

Tessa's flight was supposed to have left thirty minutes ago, and the whole time she'd been waiting she'd been wondering just how long it would take before Patrick called to "monitor" her some more.

She figured that when he did, he would probably apologize all over the place for sending her back home.

Good.

He should.

She pulled out her cell phone and set it on her lap.

In the last fifteen minutes the grandmotherly lady had left for the restroom two more times, and Tessa felt bad for her. The woman looked pale and queasy, so Tessa wasn't surprised when, once again, only a few minutes after taking her seat, she asked Tessa if she wouldn't mind to watch her bags just one last time. "Is there anything I can do for you?" Tessa asked.

The woman shook her head. "That's so kind of you to ask. Just the bags, dear. I think perhaps something I ate isn't agreeing with me. I'm not used to this flying business, you know. I'll be back in just a few minutes." Then she looked warily out the window toward the runway. "You don't think they might start boarding the plane?"

Tessa saw that the gate agent was faithfully earning her pay by reading a novel with a windblown, shirtless hunk on the cover. "Doesn't look like it. I promise I'll come get you if they do."

"You are a dear. Thank you."

Then, the woman ambled toward the restroom again, and Tessa stared out the window at the wide-bellied planes asleep on the tarmac.

A moment later, when Tessa's phone rang and she saw

that it was from an unknown number, she thought it was probably one of Patrick's FBI friends. *So, he's too scared to call me himself. Ha.* She took a moment to recall some of the choice phrases she'd overheard Uncle Ralph use a few times, and then answered the call. "Who is this?"

"Hello, Raven." At first she thought it was Patrick, since he was the only one who ever called her Raven, but the voice wasn't right. "This is you, right?" the voice said.

Oh, oh, yes.

That voice.

The cute guy from the tattoo studio.

Tessa was flustered. Wasn't even thinking. "Riker? How'd you get my number?"

"Your permission form. You wrote it down for me."

Hello, Tessa! Sometimes you are so dense!

"So," he said. "Whatcha doing?"

She slumped back in the slick plastic airport chair. "Nothing. You?"

"Just hanging." He took his time before continuing. "Trying to figure out a puzzle."

"Still didn't get it, huh?"

"No, no, not the bank robber one. A different one."

"Which one is that?"

"A black-haired one. A sly little smile one. A raven-inked one."

A thrill scampered through her. "Yeah, well, I've heard that kind is pretty tough to figure out."

"Good, I like a challenge."

She twisted in the chair to try and get comfortable, but it wasn't humanly possible. "So what do you know so far? Any pieces filled in?"

"I think I need to do a little more research first. Gather some more information . . ." He let his voice trail off and then he added, "Maybe look over the board again."

She wasn't quite sure she liked the way he phrased that. But maybe she did. She didn't hang up.

"I'm heading to a club tonight," he said. "Why don't you come help me with my puzzle?"

She looked around the airport. "I don't think I can make it."

"Oh, blowing me off, huh?"

"No, it's not like that." It was exciting, so exciting to

have a guy, an older guy, interested in her. "Trust me. If I could come, I would."

Riker took a couple of moments before responding. And when he finally spoke, it sounded to Tessa like he was reading: " 'Then this ebony bird beguiling my sad fancy into smiling, by the grave and stern decorum of the countenance it wore.' "

Oh man.

" 'The Raven,' " she said. "By Poe. You looked it up."

"Yeah. Like I said, I'm trying to solve a puzzle."

"So is that your favorite line?"

"Maybe. I'd have to spend a little more time with the ebony bird to know. There's another line I like too. Hang on . . . Here: 'And the silken sad uncertain rustling of each purple curtain thrilled me—filled me with fantastic terrors never felt before.' I like that phrase: 'fantastic terrors never felt before.' "

"Yeah."

"What about you? What's your favorite line?"

Tessa didn't even have to think about it. She'd first read the poem soon after her mother's death. " 'Eagerly I wished the morrow; vainly I had sought to borrow from my books surcease of sorrow . . .' "

He waited. "Is that the end? It doesn't sound like the end of the line."

That's one way to put it.

"For a long time it seemed like it was." Tessa watched the grandmotherly lady emerge from the restroom and start returning cautiously to her seat. "We'll have to see."

We do what we have to do.

Surcease of sorrow.

Riker interrupted her thoughts. "Hey, c'mon, hang out with me. I want to see how your tattoo is doing."

Man, she could tell this guy was totally into her. "Well . . ." she said. *This grandma lady trusts you. That couple next door in Denver you catsit for, they trust you—even the other kids at school trust you when you edit their stuff . . . Everyone trusts you.*

Except Patrick. Nope. Not him. Not at all.

A flurry of soft warnings blew through Tessa's mind, but she ignored them. "Maybe I could meet you after all. But not tonight. Now. This afternoon."

"Righteous. Where are you?"

Make up something. Don't tell him. Take a shuttle. "The Hyatt, the one over by the airport. I'll meet you in the lobby. Half an hour." The elderly woman was about ten feet away. Tessa wished she didn't have to use that cane.

"The Hyatt by the airport," Riker said. "But I need a little time. Let's make it three forty-five. I should be able to be there by then."

"Oh, and bring me some more of that soap stuff for my tattoo."

"I'll bring you a whole bottle."

"OK, I'll see you there."

"I'm looking forward to it, Raven."

"Me too." She cradled the phone in her hand for a long, sweet moment before finally snapping it shut and turning the ringer off.

"Thank you, dear," said the second-grade-teacher-woman as she lowered herself into her chair.

"You're welcome." Tessa reached down for her satchel and discreetly slid her cell phone into the woman's purse. Just in case Patrick decided to monitor her again.

Then Tessa picked up her satchel and headed back through security to the curbside pickup area for hotel shuttles.

74

Ever since leaving the meeting with Margaret nearly half an hour ago, I'd been sitting in a secluded, vacant cubicle watching women die.

I'd requested copies of the seven DVDs, and, using one of the police station's computers, I accessed my laptop. Then I uploaded the videos of the women into CIFER and used it to play them simultaneously on the screen, just as I'd done with the trolley depot videos the day before.

Any one of these videos might give Lien-hua some tangible evidence to use in the interrogation, so I forced myself to watch even though it was gut-wrenching and deeply troubling.

The shortest of the death videos was about three minutes in length, the longest was over an hour, so I knew I wouldn't have time to watch all of them through to the end, but by playing the videos at twice their normal speed, I could look for similarities in how they were filmed, in the camera angles, in the responses of the women.

I found that all of the women were dressed in the same style dress. All were chained to the bottom of the tank, although the chains appeared shorter than the one used on Cassandra. All were barefoot. All were terrified. Lewis didn't move the cameras around the warehouse, but preferred filming from the same location. Some of the videos had been edited in numerous places, just like Cassandra's, and some included fast-forward footage to get to the final ghastly conclusion, but what struck me the most was the resiliency of the women. All of them stood with their bodies turned sideways to the camera, in the direction of the warehouse doors, facing freedom. Always looking toward freedom. And of course at the end of each of these videos, the women all died.

The whole time I watched, I was wrestling with a deep swirl of anger and frustration with Margaret, with Tessa, with myself. After all, no matter what anybody is doing, there's always a lot going on beneath the surface of our lives. Maybe it's better that we can't shut off our feelings and our dreams and our regrets in one area of life when we're trying to concentrate in another, but it would certainly make life easier if we could.

Finally, with only fifteen minutes left before the interrogation, I realized I was overlooking the obvious: the tank hadn't been constructed just for Cassandra but had been used in at least seven murders. That meant it'd been there since November. So whoever owned that warehouse would be a good person to talk to.

I pulled up an Internet browser and began going through plat books and city registries.

But as time ticked away, I ran into yet another series of dead ends.

The property was owned by Richardson and Kirk, Inc., a company based in Austin, Texas.

Which was a subsidiary of Briesen Industries, located in Detroit, Michigan.

Which was owned by a multinational manufacturing conglomerate based in Germany.

Which didn't seem to help us one bit.

At least I did find out that Richardson and Kirk, Inc., bought the warehouse on November 2—seven months after the arsons started, and nine days before the first woman disappeared.

At last, with only five minutes left until the interrogation, I was gathering up my notes when I heard Ralph's heavy footsteps pounding down the hall. His form shadowed the doorway. "Margaret found something on our guy," he said. "Looks huge. C'mon."

We found Lien-hua, Margaret, and Lieutenant Graysmith all gathered in the lieutenant's office, and Margaret got right to it. "I don't want to hold up the interrogation, but we have some new information that I believe will be helpful."

We waited. She looked us each in the eye, savoring the power her long pause had over the conversation. "I followed up on Agent Jiang's suggestion about a possible connection between our suspect and the witness protection program. No connection—I wasn't surprised. However, I did have the cybercrime division do an Internet facial search using Mr. Neville's mug shots from last night, and fifteen minutes ago we found out his name is not Neville Lewis. His real name is Creighton Melice—history of battery, assault with a deadly weapon."

She slid a file folder to Lien-hua, who started paging through it.

Margaret continued. "After posting bail in November for a second-degree murder charge in DC, he failed to show up for trial, and the only eyewitness was later found dead in the backseat of a car, tied up, gagged, and strangled. The ME concluded she'd been tortured prior to her death. No suspects."

I noticed Lien-hua place her digital audio recorder on the table and press "record."

"Our man, Creighton Melice, has a condition," Margaret said. "That will be important to monitor throughout the interrogation."

"What condition is that?" Lieutenant Graysmith asked.

"He doesn't feel pain."

Ralph leaned forward. "What?

"Is that even possible?" asked Graysmith.

She pointed to the folder. "It's extremely rare, but yes. It's possible. He has congenital insensitivity to pain with anhidrosis, or CIPA. The sensory neurons that register pain never developed. It's so rare there've only been ninety-eight cases ever diagnosed in the United States. Creighton Melice is number fifty-four. Apparently, it's almost unheard of for someone with CIPA to survive until adulthood. And the ones who do rarely make it unscathed—bone fractures, burns, infections that all go untreated."

She consulted her notes again. "Last year a teething baby in South Dakota chewed off two fingers before her mother noticed. Three years ago, an eight-year-old boy in Pakistan tried washing his face with boiling water. Recently, a thirteen-month-old boy from Scotland broke his ankle and ran around the emergency room with his foot flopping sideways on the floor, giggling, as he was waiting to be seen by a doctor—"

"OK, that's enough," Graysmith said. "We get the picture."

I was amazed that Margaret and her team had been able to pull up all of this information on Melice and his condition in less than twenty minutes.

She went on. "No one really understands what causes it, but the gene responsible for it has been identified as . . ." She looked down one more time. "TrkA1. Apparently mutations of that gene block the growth of certain nerve endings."

"Can he feel anything at all?" Graysmith asked. "Or was he born with only four senses?"

Margaret flipped to the third page of her notes. "It seems people with CIPA can feel different textures and pressure on their skin, but that's all. And they show no change in blood pressure, heart rate, or respiration when exposed to painful stimuli. They can undergo surgery, including amputations, without anesthetic."

"Congenital insensitivity to pain with anhidrosis," I mumbled. "It's congenital, so people are born with it, and it would tend to run in certain families."

"And anhidrosis means you can't sweat," Lien-hua added. "So, the condition must disable the body's ability to feel temperature."

"That is correct, Agent Jiang," said Margaret. It looked like it pained her to say it, to actually affirm Lien-hua. "People with CIPA don't feel either hot or cold stimuli. So, not that you would do this anyway . . ." She paused . . . paused . . . paused . . . finally concluded, "But it would do no good to threaten Mr. Melice during your interrogation. The man you're about to interview has never felt pain in his entire life."

"Only caused it," Ralph muttered.

"And that means he didn't feel anything when Lien-hua kicked him," I said. As I was considering what, if any, significance that might have, the door opened, and Dunn leaned into the room. "He's ready."

Lien-hua grabbed her notepad and her digital voice recorder. "So am I."

75

I thought that before Lien-hua went into the interrogation, she should know I'd found the device. I didn't know if the topic would come up, but I wanted her to be armed with as much information as possible. So, as Lien-hua and I followed Detective Dunn to the interrogation room, I slowed my pace a little until I was sure he couldn't hear me, and then, in a whisper, told her about the device. "I don't know what it does, but it's in a safe place," I said. "Still in the evidence room. We can take care of it later. I just wanted you to know."

"Good. Thanks."

As we stepped onto the elevator, Dunn said, "I got the room all set for you. We'll interrogate him in room 411."

"Actually, no. We won't interrogate him," Lien-hua said. "I will."

"I'll just sit in the back and observe—"

"I go in alone," Lien-hua said.

Dunn folded his thick, snakelike arms across his chest. "The deal was, I get to observe."

"You can do that from behind the two-way mirror. I'm going in alone."

"Last night you attacked the man," said Dunn.

"If you're concerned for his safety, I can assure you he'll be in fine shape when you send him to the prisoners who, how did you put it, 'are always thrilled to have new mates to play with.'"

The elevator door opened; she took a step forward. Dunn refused to move aside. I was ready to take action, but Lien-hua stared him down. "Perhaps you misunderstand,

Detective. I'm not asking for your permission. I'm asking for your cooperation. If I have it, you can stay and watch. If I don't, I'll contact Lieutenant Graysmith and have you transferred from this case. Which will it be?"

He ground his teeth for a moment and then finally relented. "All right. Fine. But I don't care if you're an FBI agent or the freakin' president of the United States, if things go south, I'm coming in there."

He pounded off to the observation room, and I stayed with Lien-hua for a moment. I wanted to go into the room with her, to stand by her side, to protect her. Maybe I'm old-fashioned that way, but I wanted to slay a dragon for her, even though I knew she could slay dragons as well as anyone. "Are you sure you don't want anyone in there with you?"

"I'm all right." A flat fury had taken over her voice. I knew it wasn't directed at me.

"Is it because of the seven women?"

Lien-hua has a slim, captivating face, but now the muscles in her jaw constricted, bringing an intensity to her that I'd never seen before. "He filmed their deaths."

"I know."

"Posted them online."

"That's why—"

"I'll be fine. Really."

"I just wanted—"

"Enough, Patrick!" She stepped back, her slender arms taut. "Enough. Please. Sometimes you don't know when to stop. You push things too far. It builds walls, OK? Don't do it. Not with me. I'll be all right. Now please, excuse me." Before I could respond she brushed past me, leaving me reeling in the swirl of her words.

I had a sense that I should apologize, but I wasn't sure I'd done anything wrong.

In the span of just a few short hours, I'd managed to make both Tessa and Lien-hua, the two women who matter the most to me, angrily turn their backs on me and walk away.

At last, when I realized I wasn't going to apologize or even go after her, I headed off to join Detective Dunn in the observation room down the hall.

*   *   *

Tessa didn't have a compact so she was using the curved reflection of a lamp in the lobby of the Hyatt to touch up her eye shadow. Riker would be arriving in just a couple minutes, and she wanted to make sure she looked all righ—

"Hey." Riker stepped into view, startling her. He must have come in one of the side doors rather than the revolving door at the main entrance to the hotel.

She noticed he was wearing jeans and a cotton, button-down untucked shirt. She brushed at a strand of hair that had fallen in front of her eye and put her makeup away. "Hey."

He smirked and held out a full bottle of antibacterial soap as she stood up. "Will this do ya?"

"I sure hope so." She accepted it, stuffed it into her satchel. It barely fit.

He watched her and grinned playfully. "So, is the raven ready to fly away?"

"That would be a yes."

They walked together toward the door. "My bike's out back. No valet parking for motorcycles."

A cycle. How cool was that. "What kind do you have?"

"Honda ... Not quite a Harley, but they ride forever." He opened the door for her. "So, you gotta tell me. That poem by Poe, is that why they call you Raven?"

A white fire fueled by regret and anger and a strange kind of homesickness flared up inside her. "It used to be sort of a nickname."

"Your friends at college give it to you?"

Now a blush whispered across her face. So he really did believe she was over eighteen. He thought she was in college! "Naw. Someone I used to trust."

He led her to his bike. "Ouch. Had to be a guy. Typical for those losers over at SDSU. That where he went?"

"I go to school in Denver." It was true, it just wasn't the whole truth. "I'm just visiting San Diego."

"That's cool." Riker stowed Tessa's satchel, then climbed onto his bike, and she slid on behind him. "So," he said. "You ready to ride?"

"I'm ready to ride." Tessa wrapped her arms tightly around his waist, he fired up the bike, and they peeled away from the curb.

76

Over the years Lien-hua had seen some terrible, unthinkable things. And she'd always kept her cool, kept her wits about her. But today she wasn't sure she'd be able to.

Ever since hearing about the DVDs, she'd been thinking about the accident no one in her family ever spoke of.

Bruised innocence.

Stay focused, Lien-hua. Don't get distracted.

The arrangement would never be the same again.

She paused, leaned against the wall just around the corner from the interrogation room, and tried to pull herself together.

Why couldn't Pat just stop trying to protect her?

OK. Fine. It was flattering, but it was starting to tip her perspective, cloud her objectivity. She needed to focus and not let her feelings for him distract her.

I don't need protecting. I can do this on my own.

She took a moment to slide Pat out of her mind and order her thoughts, then walked around the corner and motioned to the two officers stationed outside the interrogation room.

They unlocked the door, and she stepped inside.

I threw open the door to the observation room.

Maybe I was angry at Lien-hua, maybe at Tessa, maybe at myself. I couldn't tell. I just knew I never should have let myself have feelings for Lien-hua. That was the problem. It made it harder to be objective. Harder to step back and see things clearly.

Detective Dunn was already seated at the table, facing

the two-way mirror, musing over a pile of notes and file folders.

I wasn't in any mood to talk to him, so instead, I stared at Creighton Melice through the glass. Lien-hua had just entered the room, and Melice was eyeing her coolly. His obsidian eyes tracking her every step. I could see him, but he couldn't see me.

Everyone knows the bit with the two-way mirrors—that the big mirror on the wall is really a window for law enforcement personnel, but still, it's surprisingly effective for getting suspects to talk. People tend to forget that others are watching them when they're busy watching themselves.

Melice was seated, his ankles shackled together, his wrists cuffed and attached to the table by a short chain.

A collection of maps with crime scene photos hung on the wall to Lien-hua's left. She took a chair from the corner of the room and dragged it to the table so that she could sit facing Melice.

Detective Dunn stood abruptly, walked to the two-way mirror. "I need to tell you I'm not comfortable with this."

"Agent Jiang can take care of herself."

"That's not what I mean."

"Oh." I walked to him. Leaned my arm against the glass. "What exactly do you mean?"

He glared at me. "She's a woman."

Oh, man. He was pushing things too far. Way too far. "Yes, she is, Detective. And you better be careful what your next few words are. That's a friendly warning because I'm a nice guy, but I do have my limits. Now, please. Go on."

He gestured toward the interrogation room. "This guy, Melice, he manipulates women. Seduces them, tortures them, kills them. He'll feel more powerful, more in control, with her in there. I don't want him toying with her."

"You don't know Agent Jiang."

"You're right," he said. "I don't. And that's what I'm worried about."

Lien-hua took her seat on the other side of the glass, pulled out her notepad, and started the interrogation.

77

Black holes.

That's what Lien-hua thought of as she looked across the table and into the dark pools of Creighton Melice's eyes. She searched them for a clue to his feelings, his state of mind, but they remained emotionless and blank. As she looked him over, she noticed that he had a gauze bandage wrapped around his left hand. Possibly he'd been injured the night before in his fight with Ralph. The doctor who examined his ribs earlier in the day must have treated his hand.

Everything that happened in the room was recorded by a video camera on the other side of the two-way mirror, but Lien-hua had discovered over the years that the visible presence of a recording device helped shake people up. Sometimes she left her recorder behind because of that. Today, she set it directly in front of her. Just out of his reach.

Melice looked down at the digital recorder resting between them on the slablike table, then back to her. He wore a smirk. Still didn't speak.

You're here for one reason, Lien-hua. To find out what he knows about the murders. Stay on track.

She pressed "record."

"I'm Special Agent Jiang, with the FBI."

"I know who you are, Lien-hua. I requested you."

"Well, good, then we can save time with lawyers and introductions. Because I know who you are too."

"I doubt that." He grinned slightly. "As you probably heard, I decided not to press charges against you for assaulting me. A few inches to the side and you would have broken a couple ribs, maybe punctured my lung. Not a bad kick for a girl." To Lien-hua, his voice seemed to seep from his mouth as if it were coming from an open sore.

She ignored him and spoke into the digital recorder. "The date is February 18, 2009. Time: 1553 hours. I'm interviewing Neville Worchester Lewis. Mr. Lewis, I would like to confirm that you are here under your own accord, that you have not been pressured or coerced in any way, and that you have chosen not to have legal counsel present. Are all of these statements true?"

"They're true. I've been read my rights, and I know that anything I say can and will be used, blah, blah, blah . . . all that crap. Let's get started already."

Lien-hua leaned back in her chair. "She's going to be all right, Neville. We got to her in time. You failed."

He feigned confusion. "I failed? Oh. I see. Well, I'm not sure I know what you mean by that, Special Agent Jiang. My lawyers told me this morning that seven women were killed. How tragic. Have they all been found, then? The bodies, I mean?" He paused, waited, but she refused to reply. "Agent Jiang, a baseball player who bats .350 is an all-star. If I really did connect seven out of eight times at bat, I'd have a batting average of .875; not to mention the hits I might have gotten in the minors. I wouldn't be a failure, I'd be one of the league's greatest stars."

I wanted to smack this guy, take him down right now. "We need to find out how he knows her name," I said, speaking my thoughts aloud. "See if he has any connections to the Bureau."

"Sorry," said Dunn. "I'm just here to observe."

Frustration.

Building, building.

I watched through the glass. Lien-hua didn't seem at all fazed by Creighton Melice's batting average comments. She just jotted something on her legal pad, flipped it over so that he couldn't see what she'd written, and then stood up.

The image of Cassandra in the tank rose in Lien-hua's mind, but she wrapped the shroud of her professionalism around it, folded her arms, and leaned against the wall. "Neville, tell me what you know about Cassandra Lillo."

Silence.

"Where did you first meet her?"

Silence.

"Would you like to give up your accomplice now, or wait until we catch him and let him blame everything on you?"

Silence again.

"Are you Shade, Neville? Or is Shade someone else?"

He smiled. "Now that I'll answer."

She waited.

Every syllable became a slow drumbeat: "I don't know who Shade is."

Lien-hua approached the table and looked directly into his chilling eyes. "Oh, I think you do."

I watched Lien-hua walk to the table, press "pause" on the digital recorder, and then lean close to him and say, "Let me explain something to you, Neville. Just so we're clear here. I know this game better than you do and you will not win. You're not in control anymore. I am. And I am a woman."

Oh, nice line, Lien-hua.

That's what I'm talking about.

I noticed Melice's left cheek twitch. *He can't stand the thought of a woman having control over him. Sweet.*

She lowered her finger and pressed "record" again.

78

Lien-hua watched Creighton Melice force a smile onto his face, but a sneer lurked beneath his words. "Well played, Agent Jiang. Well played. Did they teach you that at the Academy? Classic Power Plays and Intimidation Techniques? Let me guess—do whatever it takes to keep the suspect talking: threaten him, play to his ego, pacify, feign interest, become whatever he desires most in order to gain his trust—a friend, a confidant, an admirer, a mother figure, a seductress . . . How am I doing?"

She let the glimmer of a smile pass across her face. "We must have taken the same course."

Move, countermove.

A short silence from Melice. Yes, she'd struck something there. *Maybe he has taken classes in criminal science. Maybe he was in law enforcement.* I made a note to check on that.

She flipped her notepad faceup, wrote something down. I couldn't see what she was writing, and neither could she, since she kept her eyes trained on Melice the whole time.

I noticed him stare past her to the crime scene photos Dunn had hung on the wall. I don't like those kinds of gimmicks. The idea is to make the suspect think the authorities have mountains of evidence against him. The problem is, sometimes when innocent people see the array of evidence they get so unnerved that they start confessing to things they never did. Fear often makes people do and say things they later regret.

Melice seemed to read my mind through the glass. "Are those pictures supposed to make me nervous, Agent Jiang?

Get me to confess? Sorry to say, but I'm not interested in confessing any of my sins today. I'm not Catholic . . ." He let a sly smile play across his lips. "And you don't look like a priest."

"Do you normally confess your sins, Neville?"

"Only to God."

"So, you believe in God?"

"Yes."

"And you believe in sin?"

A pause. "Do you know what the Lord said to Cain, Agent Jiang?"

"What did the Lord say?"

"The Lord told him that sin was crouching at his door. That it desired to have him, but that he had to master it."

"And did he?"

"No. It mastered him. The firstborn of our race murdered the second. Quite a legacy."

Without missing a beat: "Is that what happened to you, Neville? Did sin master you? Is that why you killed the women?" He refused to reply. She waited, waited, and finally said, "Neville, why didn't you want a lawyer here today?"

"Maybe there's something I want to tell you that I don't want my lawyers to know."

"I'm listening."

"Come closer."

She didn't even hesitate. She walked to him, set both of her hands on the table, and leaned over so that her ear was beside his lips.

Dunn stood and walked to the two-way mirror. "What's she doing?"

"She's getting him to talk," I said. "It's what we sent her in there to do."

Lien-hua could smell Melice's sour breath.

"Drowning," he said, his voice coarse and low, "would be a terrible way to go, don't you think, Agent Jiang?"

Her thoughts spun sideways.

The image of Cassandra in the tank.

The fabric of that crimson evening gown wafting around her like curious red smoke, embracing her with a strange mixture of beauty and death.

An elegant, designer shroud.

Cassandra choking on water. Gasping for breath.

And then it wasn't Cassandra's face anymore, but her own. Staring up pale and lifeless through the water. A dead reflection of herself.

Lien-hua shook the thought loose. Shook it loose. "Is that why you do it, Neville?" she whispered. "Because you think drowning would be a terrible way to go?"

They were whispering to each other. I couldn't hear what they were saying, but I figured I'd ask Lien-hua about it later. They spoke for a couple moments, and then Melice smirked and Lien-hua stepped back.

"I have an idea," he said. "You're interested in the way a killer thinks. Why don't we play a little game? You ask me questions about the murders, and I'll tell you what I think might have been going on in the killer's mind. All hypothetical, of course; we'll call it my best guess."

I'd seen this before. It's not uncommon for killers to give their confession in the third person, recounting the events as if they were observers of, rather than participants in, the crime. Verbally distancing themselves from the crime seems to make it easier for them to confess.

Then Melice stared directly into the two-way mirror. "How does that sound, everyone? Sound like fun?"

He knew we were watching and he seemed to relish the attention. This guy would not be easily rattled.

"All right, Neville," she said. "Tell me what it's like. I've talked to dozens of killers. Let's see if you can do as well as they did, if you can articulate the experience eloquently enough for me to feel what a killer would feel."

A slow smile creased Melice's face. He shook out a cigarette and began to fondle it in his bandaged hands. I wouldn't have given him the pack, but Detective Dunn apparently had a different strategy.

"Oh, I think you misunderstood me." He massaged the table with his bandaged hand. "I don't want you to feel like the killer. I want you to feel like the victim."

"OK, I'm ready," she said. "Make me feel like the victim."

"I'll do my best."

79

Lien-hua waited while Melice licked at his cigarette. He didn't have a way to light it, and she wasn't about to offer him one.

Get him talking about what he likes, and he'll tell you what he's done.

"So," she said. "Tell me. The killer. What does he enjoy most? Let's start with that."

"I'll bet that, more than anything else, the killer enjoys the moments that lead up to the end. Watching his victims. Following them. Stalking them, and then acting like it was a chance encounter when they finally meet. To him that would be loads of fun."

"How does he choose them?"

"He prefers it when they choose him."

Detective Dunn and I listened as Melice spun his elaborate "hypothetical" stories about a killer being in the right place at the right time to find new "girlfriends."

I kept telling myself he was innocent until proven guilty, but it was hard for me to believe. Everything he said was consistent with the confessions of other predatory killers I'd encountered. They're always on the lookout for potential victims, always trolling, seeing who they can lure in.

As he spoke I couldn't help but notice that Melice was being careful to make his observations vague enough to be interpreted different ways. He didn't actually confess to anything but couched everything in terms of what a killer *might* think or *might* do. He was good at this game.

But I was banking on the fact that Lien-hua was better.

I heard the door behind me open and recognized Ralph's heavy footsteps.

"What do we know?" I kept my eyes glued on Lien-hua and Melice.

I heard Ralph flop a stack of papers onto the table beside me. "Good news and bad. The handwriting on the wall of the warehouse doesn't match Melice's. Based on his writing style, the analysts say he wouldn't have made those strokes when painting the words."

"Is that the good news or the bad?"

"Both. Good: it confirms there was another abductor. Bad: the second guy's still at large. Next, criminalists' reports. You're not gonna like this. The metal pipes, computer in the back room, cameras, the whole freakin' place is clean. No prints from this psycho, just a few partials on the keyboard, but they're not Melice's. We ran 'em through AFIS and got nothing."

Why didn't that surprise me.

"The criminalists are at his condo now," Ralph continued. "But so far, zilch."

A thought wandered past me. The idea seemed utterly unlikely but still possible. "Maybe it wasn't him," I said softly.

"What?" said Dunn.

"Maybe he was just passing through the warehouse, he heard the shots that Lien-hua and I fired, and came running to see if anyone was hurt."

"You're kidding me, right?" he said.

"Let's just be careful what we assume," I said. "Things aren't always what they appear."

"I don't buy it," Dunn said. "Melice told Lien-hua he was batting .875 and now he's telling her all about what it's like to kill women."

"I'm with Dunn on this one, Pat," said Ralph. "I think this is our man. But let's see what else the criminalists turn up."

My phone trembled, and when I checked it, I saw a text message from the airline notifying me that Tessa's flight had been delayed. Since I was the one who'd booked the ticket, they were using my phone number rather than hers. Her flight had been scheduled to leave over ninety minutes ago and just now they were sending me the message. How helpful.

I shook my head. Then I left a quick voice mail for my parents, letting them know to check the flight schedule first, before leaving for the airport, and then as I was pocketing my phone again, I noticed that Melice was scratching at a moist wound beneath the bandages on his left hand. "Did you two see that?" I asked Dunn.

"What?" asked Ralph.

"Why do you think he's picking at his hand like that?"

Dunn pretended to be seriously thinking about it, but his sarcasm was evident. "I don't know ... let's see ... because it itches?"

"I'm growing tired of your attitude, Detective," I said, and I was ready to say a lot more, but before I could, Ralph asked me, "What're you thinking, Pat? About the scratching?"

"Margaret said people with CIPA can only feel pressure and texture, right?"

"That's right," Ralph said.

"Well, do they itch?"

He was silent for a moment. "I don't know." He looked at Melice through the mirror. "It looks like it."

"We need to find out," I said, leaning toward the glass. "I want to know for sure why he's scratching that hand."

"What's wrong with you, Bowers?" grumbled Dunn. "Maybe this ... maybe that ... we can't be sure about this ... You have boatloads of evidence staring you in the face and you question everything."

"Thank you," I said.

Ralph stepped around the table. "I'll get someone to check on that itching thing."

I stared through the glass. "I'll be right here."

Lien-hua felt a prick of warm sweat beneath her arm. The room was hot, too hot. The police had probably cranked up the heat to make Melice uncomfortable, without even realizing that he didn't feel either heat or cold. She could sense droplets of warm moisture forming just above her eyebrows, and she hoped he didn't see it as a sign that he was getting to her.

"And then," Melice went on, "after he meets her, he finds a way to get alone with her—maybe coffee, maybe dinner, maybe a hotel room. Who knows? And then it either happens or it doesn't, and he's prepared either way."

"How does he get them into his car?"

"Maybe he just asks them, maybe he forces them. I'd say he likes it better when the women climb in by their own choice."

Flowers. She thought of flowers in full bloom.

"So it's her fault if she gets hurt?"

Petals, bruised and withered. Lying dry and brittle on the table.

"You see? Your problem, Agent Jiang, is that you're thinking like a profiler and not like a killer. It's never about those things—fault or guilt or shame. It's about control. Everything's about control." He rolled the cigarette between his fingers. "How do you think a handful of hijackers took over those planes full of people on 9/11?"

"They threatened the people onboard. Threatened to hurt them if they didn't comply." She knew that wasn't the reason, of course, but she wanted to see how he'd respond.

"There. You see? You don't understand people as well as you think you do. The hijackers didn't threaten the passengers, they reassured them."

"How do you know?"

"Because they were successful." He paused long enough to scratch at his hand. "The way to control the frightened is to give them hope. So that's what your killer would do. My father was in the army, and one of his drill instructors used to say, 'Always leave your enemy an escape route. Never corner him. Even a mouse will fight fiercely when it's trapped in a corner.'"

He laughed at this; maybe he was mocking the saying. It was hard for her to tell.

"Your killer would know this," Melice continued. "He'd know that allowing people an escape route is the best way to corner them for good. Lead them along slowly, baiting them with hope, until at last they're in the position where they think the corner is safe. Then, you snatch all hope away. To the killer, that moment would be the best one of all. Just like it was for those hijackers when they slammed into the buildings."

As Melice talked about baiting people with hope, I could see he'd let down some of his guard. Lien-hua probably knew this would happen. She'd gotten him talking about the things he loved most—abducting, overpowering, and killing young women. He was opening up. Enjoying the spotlight.

I heard Dunn flipping through some papers.

"His dad wasn't in the army," he said. "He's playing her."

"No," I said. "I think she's playing him."

80

As disgusting as Melice made her feel, Lien-hua couldn't help but agree with much of what he said. He understood people, their motives, how to crawl past their defenses and take advantage of them. After less than an hour alone with him she could see he was an expert at it.

"So," Melice said. "The woman makes the choice, and then he takes that choice and twists it around her, overpowering her with her own mistakes. Seeing the look in a woman's face when she realizes she can't escape, will never escape, and that she could have avoided this but that she brought it all on herself by trusting someone she never should have trusted . . . well, that's the most delicious moment of all." And then he added, "To a killer."

Lien-hua tried to distance herself from Melice's chilling words. Tried to step back into clinical objectivity, but she was a human being. She was a woman, just like the women he'd lured in and tortured and murdered. And because of her work as a profiler, always trying to see the world through the eyes of others, she could imagine with disturbing clarity what it must have been like for those women. She felt it all as if it were happening to her: the deep and final death of hope as the cold handcuffs closed around her wrists, the ropes tightened around her ankles, the gag smothered her screams.

And then, the moment when you realize you're not going to get away. That no matter how hard you struggle you'll never be able to break these chains, escape from these bindings, keep your head above the rising water.

She felt it all.

Experienced it all.

Powerless. You can scream. Yes. And you do. But no one except your murderer will ever hear you again. And even your screams will just bring him more pleasure. Because this time, no one is coming to save you.

The vase is falling.

Shattering on the floor.

She felt her throat clench. She shuddered. Hoped Melice hadn't seen it.

But the brief flash of satisfaction in his eyes told her that he had. He brought his hands together in slow-motion applause. "Yeah," he said. "You get it. Exactly. Just like that. To him, that moment is better than the one when she stops twitching. 'Cause in the end, after it's all over, that look in her eyes when she realizes there's no escape—that moment when hope dies forever—that's the one he holds on to and savors. That's what brings him back for more. That look in her eyes." He licked the edge of his lips and said the next few words as sweetly as a lover whispering across a pillow. "That look in your eyes, Agent Jiang. That look in your eyes."

Lien-hua let a moment flicker by, used it to bury her thoughts, her feelings. "So, is that your confession?"

"That's my conjecture." His eyes slid to the clock on the wall. "And now I'd like to go to my cell."

Lien-hua felt the bruise that she'd gotten on her leg yesterday stiffening. She shifted her weight to relieve the pressure, winced a little, and then leaned against the wall again. "Your hand, that must really hurt." She motioned to the blood-soaked bandages.

"Yeah. And it hurts where you kicked me."

"No, it doesn't."

"Of course it does."

"Don't lie to me, Creighton."

An extra blink. "My name is Neville."

"Your name is Creighton Prescott Melice. Born September 9, 1977, to Leonard and Isabelle Melice in Wichita, Kansas. You attended George Washington Carver Elementary School. You have two younger brothers named Trenton and Isaac. You began attending the University of Michigan in 1995—do you want me to go on? I told you when I first came in here that I know who you are."

Silence. His eyes narrowing.

"Did you kill the eyewitness in DC too? Torture her and then leave her body in the backseat of that car?"

In a sudden burst of rage Melice yanked at the chain fastening his handcuffs to the table. It clanged, but held fast. "You have no idea what you're dealing with here."

"Then tell me—what am I dealing with, Creighton?"

He refused to meet her stare.

"You have it, don't you?" she asked.

"Have what?"

"The device. I know you do. Hunter gave it to you, didn't he?"

His mouth flattened into a wicked line. "A minute ago I saw you shift your weight, Agent Jiang. Pressure on your hip, maybe? Or, maybe relaxing the muscles in your leg to get comfortable? That doesn't happen to me. No muscular strain, no discomfort, no stress on my joints. None of it. I've never been comfortable or uncomfortable in my life. I've never screamed. Never cried. Never been hot or cold. Only existed."

A primeval fire ignited in his eyes, blazed as he went on. "Did they tell you about my sister Mirabelle? Or haven't they found that out yet? She had CIPA too. And when she was eleven she woke up paralyzed. She'd twisted her spine as she slept, cut off the circulation to her legs and laid like that until the nerves could no longer be repaired. You see, our bodies don't tell us when to move. So, we don't roll over when we sleep. I've had to train myself to do it. Mirabelle died in that same bed two years later. As you know, most of us die young. I guess I'm one of the lucky ones. If you choose to look at it like that."

Lien-hua sensed his motive. Honed in on it. "You dream of pain, don't you, Creighton? I'll bet you do. I'll bet you fantasize about pain, about finally being fully human."

Nice, Lien-hua.

Very nice.

Melice's lip quivered, his eyes shifted. He didn't reply.

"What's she trying to do in there?" Dunn asked.

"Her job."

Melice's voice tensed. "Of course I dream of pain. All my life I've been dreaming of pain, hoping to feel this thing that makes people cry and scream and beg for mercy. That's the only thing I live for: the hope of one day suffering before I die."

"Baited by hope," she said. "You're the little mouse in the corner, aren't you, Creighton? Shade put you there, didn't he? And one day he's going to snatch that hope away."

Melice held out his arm as far as his handcuffs would allow. "Hurt me. If you can find a way to do it, let me taste what it feels like to suffer. Yes, I dream of pain. Some people call CIPA a painless hell." Then he added, "Who wouldn't dream of leaving that?"

She didn't move.

"Well, if you can't think of a way," he said, "how about I do?"

And then, Creighton Melice lifted his left hand to his mouth, closed his teeth around his little finger, and bit down.

81

I sent my chair sprawling across the floor as I rushed to the door, beating Dunn into the hallway.

Then, around the corner to room 411.

Two officers stood sentry outside the interrogation room. "Open the door," I said.

Confused looks.

"Now!" At last one of the officers, a brawny man with a pockmarked face, pulled out a key, fumbled with the lock, and as soon as the door was open, I pushed past them both. Lien-hua had slipped off one of her socks and wrapped it around Melice's left hand to stop the bleeding. Quick reaction time. Very quick. "Are you OK?" I asked her.

"Yes."

Dunn crashed into the room. Stared at the glistening blood splattered across the floor. "Look at this mess." Then, before I could stop him, Dunn grabbed Melice by the hair, wrenched his head back, and slammed his face against the table. Then Dunn leaned close and sneered. "Too bad you can't sue me, scumbag."

"Back away, Detective," I said.

He glared at me, then at Melice.

"Back away."

At last he did, slowly, and muttered to the two men who'd been guarding the door, "Get this piece of garbage out of here. Take him to the infirmary."

Melice, his face bloodied, just stared at him. "Sorry, Detective. Nice try, but I didn't feel a thing. Kind of a letdown, huh? When you want to hurt someone that badly and you just can't do it?"

"Just wait," said Dunn. "Your day is coming."

One of the officers who'd been standing guard unlocked Melice's cuffs from the table and dragged him to his feet. Recuffed him. The other officer gingerly picked something up from the table. "They might be able to reattach this," he said.

Dunn's eyes fell on the garbage can in the corner of the room. "Give me that."

I could see where this was going. "No," I said to the officer. "Take it along. Give it to the doctor, see what he can do."

Dunn's anger flared at me. "If he wanted to keep his finger, he wouldn't have bitten it off."

"Go on," I told the officers. "Take care of that guy."

They manhandled Melice toward the door, and Dunn slammed his foot into the steel leg of the table and stormed past them out of the room.

I put my hand on Lien-hua's shoulder. "You sure you're OK?"

She nodded.

As the officers led Melice into the hallway, I heard a scuffle and saw him wrestle against them for a moment, then spin from their grip. I ran over to help restrain him, but by the time I got there, they'd already been able to grab him and were pulling him back into the hall. "One last question, Lien-hua," Melice called as they dragged him away. "Do you feel like a victim yet?"

"Sorry," she said calmly. "Not yet."

"Give it time," he called, his words echoing down the hallway. "You will."

Then the door swung shut and their footsteps began to recede down the corridor.

I glanced at her to see her reaction. The gears in her mind seemed to be turning. She narrowed her eyes and mouthed several different words as she stared at the gray table now splayed with fresh streaks of Melice's blood. "Give me a couple minutes, OK? I just need a chance to think."

Once again I wanted to stay with her, but her words from earlier echoed in my head: *You push things too far. It builds walls, OK? Don't do it. Not to me.*

"Sure," I said, and stepped into the hallway where I saw Dunn having words with the officers taking Melice to the infirmary. And a few thoughts of my own began to form in my head.

All during the interrogation, Lien-hua had known that Melice was trying to get to her. And although she didn't want to admit it to herself, he'd succeeded—at least a little. Killers know how to play mind games, and they're usually better psychoanalysts than the doctors the state hires to analyze them. Lien-hua just didn't like considering the possibility that Melice was better than her.

She took one more look around the room, then picked up her recorder and notepad and flipped to the last page of her notes.

For the most part, she'd been watching Melice as she took notes, and had hardly looked down at the paper. And, while it was true she'd scribbled a few words on the page, that's not what caught her attention. Instead, in the center of the page, surrounded by a clutter of cryptic words and shorthand phrases, Lien-hua had sketched a picture. Without even realizing it, she'd drawn a scissors snipping off the head of a chrysanthemum.

She held the notepad against her chest and went to join Pat.

82

Creighton found that it wasn't easy to walk with his feet shackled together and his hands cuffed in front of him, and he stumbled a little as the two cops led him into the elevator. Well, at least he wouldn't have to put up with the restraints for long. He'd be free soon, in just a few minutes, as a matter of fact. And when he died later tonight it would be worth losing the finger. It would be worth everything.

He discarded Lien-hua Jiang's sock in the elevator and watched the blood from his hand drip and form bright patterns on the tiled floor.

His little meeting with her had gone well. Yes, very well.

Despite the fact that the feds had somehow found out his real identity, things had still ended the way Shade had planned.

The elevator clanged to a stop, the doors slid open, and the three men began their long walk to the room at the end of the hall.

Creighton could tell he'd shaken something loose inside of Special Agent Lien-hua Jiang. And he liked that very much. It brought him a tingle, a promise, a cool inviting shiver. He'd brushed up against that secret little something hidden in her past, deep in her psyche. And touching her pain in that way tasted sweet to him. Sweet and strong.

The lotus flower had begun to unfold, just as Shade said it would.

Lien-hua had tried to hide it, they always do, but you can see it in their eyes. Eyes never betray you. Inside of every woman lives a needy little girl wanting to feel pretty, loved, secure. Expose her to her imperfections, toy with her desire to feel loved, rattle her sense of security, and you bring that needy little girl to the surface.

And during the investigation, Agent Jiang's eyes had told him how fragile the girl inside of her was, and of course, Creighton already knew why. Actually it was one of the reasons Shade had chosen him.

Probably the main one.

They reached the infirmary door and one of the cops grunted for Creighton to stop. So he did.

Creighton Prescott Melice stood still and submissive between the two men he was about to kill.

83

Tessa had never been on a motorcycle before, and with the wind whipping through her hair, it really did feel like she was flying. After spending the last hour or so driving up the coast with her arms snugged around Riker's waist, everything felt right in the world.

And now that they'd stopped to watch the sun set, she climbed off the motorcycle and followed him toward the beach. To a special place he knew.

She was with a guy.

She was on her own.

And there was no way for Patrick to check up on her.

She was a raven spreading her wings, and it felt so, so good.

Tessa walked with Riker to a deserted section of beach, and there, on a dry spot of sand near a flat gray boulder, they sat down together to watch the sun sink into the sea. Tessa wanted to lean against Riker, to let his strength support her, but she resisted and just sat close instead. "So," she said. "Did you ever figure out Lachlan's puzzle?"

He patted his pocket. "Got my answer right here."

"Let's see it."

He tugged out two sheets of paper—his sheet as well as the yellowed sheet she'd written her answer on. "So, remember, there's two guys," he said. "If the first guy gives one stack of his money to the second guy, then he ends up with half of the second guy's amount, but if the second guy gives the first guy one of his piles, then they have the same amount."

"Unfold the paper," said Tessa. "See what I wrote."

Riker spread it across his hand. "Five and seven."

"Right," she said. "If the guy with five stacks gives the other guy one, they'll have four and eight, and if the guy with seven gives the first guy one of his stacks, they both have six."

"And you figured that out on the spot?"

On the horizon, scalloped clouds growing dark, welcoming the night.

"Yeah." She was a little embarrassed, because admitting that she'd figured out the puzzle so quickly made Riker seem kind of dumb. "Let's see your answer. What did you write?"

The sun was melting lower and lower, a small slice of melon against the base of the sky.

Riker held up the paper, but as Tessa reached for it, he pulled it away. She reached again, and he rolled onto his back. She leaned across him to grab it, and finally, when their faces were only a few inches apart, he let go. "Unfold it," he said softly. Tessa caught the scent of his inviting cologne mixing with the wild ocean air.

The sun was a sliver . . .

She flattened the crinkled paper against his chest and read what he'd written: "You." Her heart trembled.

. . . and then the sun was a dot . . .

"That's my answer," he said. "You are." Tessa felt wanted, loved.

. . . and then the sun was gone, swallowed by the waves.

She lay by his side until the night's cool fingers closed around them; then Riker took Tessa's arm and helped her to her feet. "Let's go. There's still a lot I want to show you tonight."

84

When Lien-hua and I returned to the conference room to meet with Margaret and debrief Melice's interrogation, we found her sitting at the head of the expansive table waiting for us. Even before we could pull out our chairs, Margaret said, "Agent Jiang, talk to me about this man." Her voice was unusually cool and reserved. After what had just happened in the interrogation room, her even tone surprised me. "From a profiler's perspective, what are we looking at?"

"It's the perfect storm," Lien-hua replied as we took our seats. "A psychopath with CIPA. He feels no pain in his body and he feels no pain in his heart. Here is a man who has never felt discomfort or guilt or shame or suffering of any kind—either mental or physical." As she spoke, I thought of the astronomical odds against a psychopath also having CIPA, but then I remembered Tessa's comments about the way Dupin approached his case: as impossible as it seems, it did occur, so it must be possible.

Lien-hua went on. "Psychopaths don't feel either empathy or compassion and never develop close enough relationships to feel heartache. Instead, they just look at other people as objects to be used and then discarded when they no longer enjoy them. Often they become addicted to controlling people, and when they get obsessed with something, their obsession can go on for decades."

I took Lien-hua's words to heart and wondered what it would be like to live, as Melice put it, in a "painless hell." How different would that be from a "joyless heaven"? Maybe no different at all.

"What about the interrogation?" asked Margaret. "The things he told you?"

"A classic example of 'semantic aphasia,'" Lien-hua said. "That is, using the words that your listeners want to hear. It's a way of manipulating people. Career criminals are experts at it. They only care about getting their way, exerting power. So it's tough to say how much of what he said could be taken as a confession. I'd need to talk with him more. But I can say this much—he knows the mind of a killer. And he likes fantasizing about death."

"Or maybe," I said, "he just likes watching people do the one thing he can't do—suffer at the hands of others."

Then Margaret folded her arms and looked back and forth from Lien-hua to me. "Now," she said coolly. "Tell me what you two know about Project Rukh."

85

What? Where did that question come from?

"Project Rukh?" I said. "What do you know about Project Rukh?"

"I'm the one asking the questions, Dr. Bowers," Margaret said in a clipped voice. "Kindly address them or refrain from participating in the conversation."

OK.

A moment earlier I might have considered mentioning that I'd found the device, but since she was acting so Margarety, I decided to keep that information to myself for the time being. The device was safe, and until I knew more, it seemed like a good idea to keep its location a secret, so instead, I told her the sketchy facts that I'd discovered about Cassandra's shark research, Dr. Osbourne's neuromorphic engineering studies, and the possible connection to MEG technology.

"There is a device," she said. "Do you know anything about a device?"

"Shade mentioned something," I answered. "I believe it was from Building B-14, but I don't know what it's used for. Do you?"

"Was it destroyed in the fire?"

"If you don't mind me asking, Margaret—"

"I do mind you asking."

Lien-hua held out her palms. "Help us out here, Margaret. What are we looking at?"

Margaret folded her hands, looked at her watch, and then to my utter amazement, spoke with stark candor.

"Most of what I was told is classified, of course, and eyes only for people above your pay grade, but, since I believe this may bear some relevancy to the case, I can tell you that Drake Enterprises was contracted to design a device that would use electromagnetic imagery to find bodies in rubble or in buildings where thermal imaging can't reach."

Electromagnetic sensory location, just like sharks do with buried fish.

Remembering the radiation warnings on the device and the trace radioactive isotopes found in Hunter's apartment, I said, "Does it use radiation? Radioactive isotopes?"

Margaret's eyes became inquisitive. Maybe suspicious. "It does. Cesium-137. It's found in certain medical devices and gauges that are used to treat cancer, but it's also used to measure the thickness of materials—metal, stone, even paper. That's what helps the device 'see through'"—her tone of voice laid quotation marks around the last two words—"matter to find the electromagnetic signals."

"Wait." It was Lien-hua. "It can see through buildings?"

"It can't exactly see through matter," Margaret explained, "but it can sense the location of the electromagnetic impulses of muscle twitches and brain activity of people who are buried in rubble."

"It makes sense," I said. "Remember? Sharks can locate prey buried in the sand. Thermal imaging is similar, but this would simply register magnetic or electric impulses rather than heat. By using neuromorphic engineering it could be possible to replicate the sixth sense of sharks."

Margaret's impatient sigh was her way of asking for another turn to speak. "I was told that the purpose of Project Rukh was to develop a device that could be used to find terrorists in caves, miners in cave-ins, skiers in avalanches, and so on. After the towers fell on September 11 and the government had to resort to tapping on metal pipes to search for survivors, they began looking for more efficient ways of finding survivors in wreckage or debris."

I weighed what she was saying with the facts of the case. The pieces just weren't adding up here. "No, that's not big enough," I said. "It has to be something more. It has to have another use."

Margaret leaned forward. "Dr. Bowers, it may surprise

you to hear me say this, but in this case, I agree with you wholeheartedly."

Just then, a knock at the door. Ralph.

"Come in, Agent Hawkins," Margaret said. "And close the door behind you."

86

As Ralph entered and shut the door, Margaret said, "I believe that Building B-14 was burned down to mask the robbery of the device that Drake Enterprises was contracted to develop."

"Terrorists?" asked Ralph.

"No," she said. "I think it might be someone related to the research, someone in the government or the intelligence community, or possibly—"

"Detective Dunn," said Lien-hua.

All three of us turned toward her. "Dunn?" asked Ralph.

"I've been thinking." Lien-hua flipped through her notepad, read some of her scribbles. "Detective Dunn was at the scene of the suicide Monday night. He showed up at the Sherrod Aquarium—the site of Cassandra's abduction. He was also at the warehouse, and he made sure he spoke with Cassandra before the paramedics wheeled her away. He prepared the room for Melice and demanded to be present during the interrogation."

"Was he ever alone with Melice?" asked Ralph.

"I saw him, just a few minutes ago," I said. "Talking in the hallway with Melice and the officers who were taking him to the infirmary." A thought began circling, like a buzzard, through my mind. "Wait . . . Melice specifically asked for the FBI, asked for Lien-hua by name, and agreed not to have a lawyer present?"

"That's right," said Margaret. "Now, if we can get back to—"

"Wait a minute, Margaret—"

"Dr. Bowers, might I remind you that I'm—"

"Sure," I said. "Tomorrow." As Margaret opened her mouth to respond, my thoughts zoomed back to the previous night, and before she could lay into me, I said, "Ralph, at the warehouse, Lien-hua and I were by the tank, you were sweeping the north side of the building. The door that Lien-hua kicked open was between us. Melice could have left, could have slipped out the door, but he didn't. He doubled back. Why didn't he just leave?"

"You think Melice wanted to get caught?" Lien-hua asked.

"Maybe," I said. "His lawyers stalled until this afternoon. Why?"

Melice decided when the interrogation would end by biting off his finger . . .

Timing, location. Timing, location.

I stood, started for the door. "The infirmary, Ralph. He wanted to go there."

"Why?"

Psychopaths only care about getting their way . . . exerting power.

"They would have to take off his cuffs to treat his finger," I said. "He planned this all along." *At the end of the interrogation Melice looked at the clock . . .* I glanced toward Ralph. "Do people with CIPA itch? Did you find out?"

"They don't itch." Ralph saw me throw open the door, and he rose as well. "What's going—"

"Move." I bolted down the hallway. "Shift change, five thirty. He's going to try to escape—"

And that's when the police headquarters' intruder alarm began to squeal through the halls.

87

I raced down the stairs to the second floor, took a quick glance through the infirmary doorway, and saw that, although there was at least one officer down, five people had already come to his aid. But that's not where I expected to find Melice anyway. No, he had another destination in mind.

I ran to the evidence room, whipped out my SIG, and kicked the door open. "Riley?" I said. No one at the counter. "Are you here?"

No reply.

"Creighton, you're not going to get out of the building," I called. "I know what you're after."

Amidst the wails of the intruder alert, I swept the series of tightly packed rooms just like I'd been taught at the Academy, letting my gun lead me around each corner.

Run the walls, dig the corners.

Clear.

It's never like you see in the movies. You don't blaze into a place waving your gun in the air.

Run the walls, dig the corners.

Clear.

Any moment someone might shoot you, rush you, attack you. Not knowing what lies around the corner is the most frightening thing of all.

Heart beating. Heart beating.

The last room. I stepped in, scanned it. Saw my computer in the corner, the duffel bag missing. No other people.

Clear.

Then a moment to breathe.

So, Melice was gone. So was Kernigan.

How did Melice know the device was here?

Shade must have told him.

Shade. Shade.

Dunn? Kernigan? Melice's doctor? Well, whoever Shade was, if Melice did get away, the two of them would be getting a little surprise when they opened their duffel bag. After all, before I exited the evidence room earlier today, I left my card wrapped up with my lovely makeshift contraption, along with a note scribbled on the back of the card: "If this one doesn't work, give me a call and I'll let you play with mine." I had a feeling it wouldn't be long before either Shade or Melice contacted me

The tables were beginning to turn.

I saw the duct tape I'd used still lying on the counter. Wait. The custodian's closet. One more door.

I steadied my gun and edged to the closet. "Creighton? Are you in there? Come out."

No response.

My heart beating and my gun ready, I threw open the door.

Inside, I found Officer Kernigan alive but unconscious. His uniform was missing.

Melice is dressed as an officer.

Even if the clothes didn't fit well, even with his bloodied face and hand, Melice might still be able to slip away in the confusion. I rushed to the hallway and pulled a sergeant to the side. "Don't let anyone leave the building. Melice has an officer's uniform. Make the announcement over the PA system. Do it now." She looked at me quizzically for a moment. "Go," I said, and at last she hurried off.

I ran back to help Officer Riley Kernigan and found he'd been pistol-whipped. Probably had a concussion, but he looked like he'd be all right. He was stirring, so I helped him sit up and lean against the door. "You're going to be OK, Riley," I told him. He nodded.

After making sure he could sit up by himself, I verified that the actual device was still hidden safely behind twenty-five years of evidence. Then I located an officer who'd been trained as an EMT, and I asked him to attend to Officer Kernigan.

Before leaving the evidence room, I went to the log-in forms to see if anyone had stopped by to look at the "video camera" since I'd first visited the room. After Lien-hua's suggestion that Dunn might be Shade, I wondered if I might find his name.

But I didn't.

I found Margaret's.

And the facts of the case began to spin apart once again. I retrieved my computer. I could review the video in a few minutes to see if Margaret knew more about the device than she was letting on. But first, I needed to stop by the infirmary to see the extent of the pain Melice had succeeded in causing.

88

The second floor hallway of police headquarters was filled with scurrying officers, shouted vows of what would happen to Melice when they got their hands on him, and the incessant whine of the intruder siren.

I found the exam room overflowing with police officers, FBI agents, and medical personnel, so rather than crowd them any more, I stood beside the door and surveyed the scene. One of the downed officers appeared to have been stabbed in the neck, and since the paramedics weren't working on him, I realized that, tragically, his wounds had been fatal. The other man was fading into and out of consciousness and had a thick bandage with a stain already spreading across it wrapped around his left eye.

Only after the siren finally stopped did I hear the announcement that the suspect was wearing an officer's uniform, but I suspected the announcement had come too late. Too much time had passed, and Melice's escape had been too well planned.

I saw Graysmith and approached him. "What do we know about Melice?"

"We're sweeping the building," he said between clenched teeth. "We set up a six-block perimeter."

"Video?" I asked.

"No, not in the exam rooms. Privacy concerns." His voice became taut with resolve. "This is a police matter now. He killed one of my men. We'll take it from here."

"No," I said. "We're all on the same team, Lieutenant. I don't care who gets the credit, let's just nail this guy. Once we have him, I'll have Ralph do all he can to give you full custody."

He hesitated.

"Trust me," I said. "I keep my promises."

After a moment he gave me a tight nod. "All right."

He began to step away, but I called him back. "Just a second. Can you tell me why Dunn was at the site of John Doe's suicide the other night? It might help us out. It's one piece that still doesn't fit."

Graysmith took a cautious breath, then said softly, "We've had more and more suspicious suicides near trolleys over the last year. I started wondering if there was someone out there who likes tossing homeless people to their deaths. I wanted Dunn to look into it." Graysmith's explanation didn't resolve all my questions, but considering the circumstances, it did seem plausible. Then he added, "Now, let's get this creep."

He left to find Margaret to coordinate the search for Melice, and Ralph's eyes found me from where he stood in the middle of the room. "Pat, what do you think?" He stepped closer to me. "Melice waited until he was in here because it was easier to escape? Less security?"

"Probably." I lowered my voice. "Plus, it's right beside the evidence room. Melice stole the device, or at least he thinks he did. But I've got the real one. Listen, he knew it'd be in there. And I think he knew the shift change was at five thirty."

"Someone told him," growled Ralph.

I thought of Dunn speaking with the officers who were leading Melice to the infirmary, and then of Margaret's sudden interest in the device. "Yes. Someone did."

While Ralph and I were talking, a number of the officers stepped past us, leaving the room to join the search for Melice, so I was finally able to approach the dead officer and study the wound on his neck. "Does anyone know what he was stabbed with?"

"Piece of metal," someone said. "A shiv of some kind. Parkers told us that much before he passed out." I assumed Parkers was the man with the battered face.

"All right," hollered Dunn. "He was cuffed. Where did he get the shiv?"

I examined the dead officer's neck more closely. A thin tip of metal protruded from the wound, but it hadn't passed all the way through the man's neck. Using my hand, I measured the diameter of his neck . . . about fifteen centimeters. Then, I compared that to the size of my hand . . . about ten centimeters.

"I think," I said, "Melice might have had it with him, hidden in his hand, probably embedded at the metacarpophalangeal joint. That's what he was picking at. He wasn't itching, he was digging at the skin, pulling it away. We missed it. And now this man is dead."

"Who inspected this guy?" Ralph's fists tightened. "Who processed him?"

Detective Dunn took a flat breath. "I did. I processed Melice." Then he stared at the two officers, one dead, one seriously wounded. "And I'm gonna be the one to kill him." Then Detective Dunn thundered out of the room.

Could Dunn be Shade after all? What about Margaret? Graysmith?

More evidence, less conjecture.

Eliminate your theories, don't try to prove them, try to disprove them one by one.

I didn't know who to trust, but I figured as long as I had the device, Shade would come looking for me. "Ralph, meet me in five minutes at the work space I was in earlier."

He agreed, and I went to get set up.

I'd recorded over three hours of video, but thankfully, my laptop's media player allowed me to slide the cursor along the control module to quickly scan the footage until I came to the image of a person dressed in civilian clothes. At that point, I played the video at normal speed and saw the lights in the room blink off and then a person stepping cautiously into the darkness.

Since the person was starkly backlit and walking through the dark, I couldn't make out a face. Unbelievable. Shade was smart. Very smart. I had to give him that.

He took only three steps into the room, then eased backward and left, keeping his face in the shadows the whole time. Whoever it was, he was probably just verifying the presence of the device. I checked the time on the video marker—two fifty-eight p.m., the time we were all off by ourselves researching Melice. Anyone might have slipped in here.

Wait. Not anyone. I highlighted the footage, opened CIFER, and analyzed it.

Weight distribution, pace, posture.

Male.

That eliminates Margaret. *Someone else must have signed her name onto the log.*

I placed a call to the evidence room to see if Officer Kernigan could identify the person, but whoever picked up the phone told me Riley Kernigan had slipped back into unconsciousness and had been taken to the hospital.

All right then, I knew what I had to check on. It was time to decipher Project Rukh. I made a call, and then, before I could close up my computer, Ralph arrived.

"Do they need you here at the station right now?" I asked.

He shook his head. "Margaret can run the FBI teams, Graysmith'll coordinate the police. What do you need?"

"I want to find out what this device really does. And there's one person who I think might be able to help us."

"Who's that? Drake?"

"No. Dr. Rigel Osbourne."

"Wasn't he at some kind of conference?"

"He's back," I said. "A telemarketer just called his house. He picked up."

Ralph grinned. "What were you selling?"

"Luggage."

"That's not even funny."

"Let's go pay the doctor a little visit."

89

Twenty minutes after escaping from police custody, Creighton Melice rounded the corner in the car he'd jacked off some lowlife crack dealer two blocks from police headquarters, and cruised down India Street. Shade had given him the time and place to meet after his escape, and it looked like things were right on schedule.

The escape had gone just as planned.

Inserting the six-inch shiv into his hand last night at the warehouse had been easy. He'd just positioned it against the base of his left middle finger and pressed. It went right in. Just like sliding an oven thermometer into a turkey.

Of course, digging it out meant peeling back a layer of meat from his palm during the interview. For anyone else it would have been painful, but of course he didn't feel it. He didn't feel anything. Then, on the way to the exam room, he used the shiv to pick the lock on his handcuffs, and when they arrived and the pockmarked cop was on the phone calling for the doctor, Creighton simply grabbed the guy's hair with one hand and shoved the shiv all the way into his neck with the other.

It went in clean and smooth. Just like sliding a thermometer into a turkey.

Then he smashed the handcuffs into the other cop's face. The guy howled in pain and, based on his reaction, Creighton guessed that having your eyeball flattened into paste was a painful experience. He took note of that as he swung the cuffs at him again and again, sending him reeling into the wall.

At that point, though, he realized he needed to hurry, so

he'd decided not to take the time to kill the guy, but instead grabbed the keys to his ankle chains, unlocked the shackles, helped himself to a new gun, and walked casually and confidently to the evidence room.

Creighton let the car roll to a stop inside the auto body shop. A moment later he'd pulled down the garage door and locked it. He swept his hand across a nearby workbench, scattering the tools, discarded car parts, and a pile of greasy rags to the floor. Then he retrieved the black duffel bag from the backseat of the car and carefully set it in the center of the area he'd just cleared.

His fingers were trembling.

This was it. The moment he'd been waiting for.

Tonight, after they'd finished with the woman, Shade would use the device on him and he would finally feel pain. Finally realize what it's like to suffer. What it's really like to be a human being.

Creighton closed his eyes and let his mind wander into his elaborate fantasies of pain. The spiders were just the beginning. He thought of blades and screams, of tender flesh so easily torn, and of splintered bones piercing meat. He dreamt of finally feeling that elusive ghost called pain.

Before Creighton could unzip the bag, he heard a swift whish of air and saw the wood of the bench explode less than an inch from his hand. A bullet.

"Don't turn around," said the electronically altered voice from behind him. "Unzip the bag."

"Don't tell me what to do," Creighton barked. A tense moment passed where neither of them spoke, and then finally, Creighton unzipped the bag, unwrapped the foam, then stared down at a tripod of three broken mop handles with a radio, a can of solvent, and a broken coffeemaker all duct-taped together onto the end. He felt his teeth clench. "No." Grit. Grind. "No. No!"

"Pick it up," said the voice.

Creighton didn't just pick it up, he grabbed the fabricated device and smashed it, smashed it, smashed it against the workbench until only a shattered array of broken pieces remained.

"So," said Shade. "Someone has decided to get creative with us."

Creighton snatched up a business card that had flown to the floor, read it to himself, then said, "It's from a federal agent. Bowers. He's got the real device. He's taunting us."

"I know Agent Bowers," Shade said. "I'll take care of him. You'll need to leave here quickly and lie low. I'll call you in one hour. Don't worry. We'll get the real device. Trust me."

Creighton Melice probed the corner of the shop with his eyes. He couldn't see Shade.

Shadows, always in the shadows.

Creighton didn't want to play these stupid games anymore. He'd had enough. "Before, you told me not to trust you."

"And now, I'm telling you to trust me. Follow my instructions or you won't get what you want when this is over."

Creighton still had that cop's gun.

Take care of this freakin' creep. Do it now.

He drew the gun, but as he did, Shade put a bullet through his right hand, sending the gun clattering to the floor. "Careful, Creighton," said Shade. "I'd rather you stay alive and assist me, but I'm prepared to deal with my disappointment if you choose not to let that happen."

"I'm tired of all this spy bullcrap." Creighton stood tense, ready for a fight, blood dripping from the shredded flesh of the wounds that he didn't feel in each of his hands. "Show me your freakin' face. Kill me if you want to, but my guess is I'll be able to do you some damage first. If we're going to do this, if we're going to end this tonight, let me see your face. That or I'm done."

And then, after a brief moment, the shadows parted and a figure stepped out, and Creighton stood frozen, staring, his jaw gaping. It really was the last person Creighton would have ever expected.

"We finish this, tonight." No masked voice anymore. Finally, finally standing in the light. "We finish it together."

90

Ralph and I each carried the oversized laundry bags we'd scavenged from the police headquarters gym to our cars. I had the real device, Ralph's bag was weighted to look just like mine.

Just in case anyone was watching us, we each chose a different route to Dr. Rigel Osbourne's house, and after making sure we hadn't been followed, we carried our bags to the door.

"How do you want to play this?" I asked him.

"Cassandra Lillo is dead. Anyone implicated in her abduction will be tried for murder." He knocked on the door. "Improvise."

"Have you sent a car to Cassandra's place yet?" I heard footsteps from the other side of the door. "It's possible Melice will go after her, to finish what he started."

"Already done," he said.

A moment later, the door opened and Dr. Rigel Osbourne stared at us through the crack. "Yes?"

Ralph put a hand on the door and pressed it open, sliding Dr. Osbourne to the side. "FBI," Ralph said with a quick flip of his badge. "You don't mind if we come in, Rigel? We just need to ask you a few questions." Ralph and I both set the laundry bags on the floor. Then I swung the door shut behind us.

"Who are you?" Osbourne's eyes were twitchy. His lower lip looked like it was used to being chewed on. "What's this about?"

"A shark researcher," I said.

"Found dead," said Ralph ominously.

Osbourne's face grew pale. "I don't know anything about a dead shark researcher." He wet his lips several times and began to eye the door. Neither Ralph nor I spoke. "How . . . how did she die?"

"We didn't tell you the researcher was a woman," I said. This guy was obviously not used to interrogations. I hoped that would help us find out everything we needed.

Ralph busied himself with opening one of the laundry bags and removing the device. "It's a federal offense to lie to an FBI agent."

Osbourne was watching Ralph pick up the device and lay it on the couch. "I just assumed, I mean . . . I didn't know. Where did you get that?"

"Doctor Osbourne," I said. "We're here to find out everything you know about this device. We don't have a lot of time, and neither of us is in a very good mood." Then I nodded in Ralph's direction and lowered my voice. "Especially not him."

Dr. Osbourne shook his head. "He told me it was destroyed. He told me—"

"Who told you?" asked Ralph.

"Victor Drake."

Was Drake Shade?

"I'll go get him," said Ralph.

"Wait." I pulled him aside and whispered, "We need everything we can get on Drake first. Let's finish with Osbourne. Then we'll go talk to Drake. You know how it works: the more evidence we have when we get there, the more evidence we'll have when we leave."

Ralph considered that, then nodded and said to Osbourne, "All right. Talk. This is your only chance. And if I don't like what I hear, I'm taking you in as an accessory to murder."

"Murder! I didn't . . . I don't know—"

"Listen to me," I said. "Let's just take it slow. Start at the beginning. Tell us everything you know."

General Cole Biscayne rolled to a stop in the driveway of his sister's beach house, and sighed.

Ever since the PROC meeting earlier in the day, he'd been fielding phone calls from the state department, the Pentagon, and even the White House, trying to assure them that the prototype had been destroyed. After all, the fire had completely consumed Building B-14, nothing was found at the scene or on the shore, and the police reports confirmed that the arsonist did not have the device with him when he threatened the federal agent and was subsequently stopped by means of lethal force from attacking her. So, it looked like the satellites' development might be pushed back, but in the long run things would work out.

Cole's sister Beverly was working late but had told him to make himself comfortable, to grab whatever he wanted out of the fridge, and that she would see him about ten o'clock. He was glad for the space. It'd been a long, tedious, stressful day. He needed some time to relax and unwind.

The evening had cooled, and the general's Windbreaker snapped to attention around him as he stepped out of the car. Out of habit, he glanced at the shadows lurking around her house, remembering the form he'd seen outside his home in New England.

But there was no one there in the shadows. Of course there was no one there. This whole business with Sebastian Taylor had gotten blown completely out of proportion. Taylor had been on the run for almost four months. If he were going to make a move, he would have done it by now.

And so, General Cole Biscayne reassured himself with these thoughts as he walked up the stony path to his sister's home and slipped a key into the lock.

91

Dr. Osbourne had swallowed all the spit in his mouth, so before he could begin telling us what he knew, he poured himself a glass of water, downed it in one great tenuous gulp, set down the glass, and then said, "I never met the shark woman, Cassandra Lillo. I swear. All I did was use some of her findings. We're not allowed to meet each other."

"Who's not allowed to meet each other?" Ralph asked.

Stone silence. Dr. Osbourne had already told us more than he was supposed to. His hand was shaking. "All I know is that we each have one person to report to. One contact person. We pass our research along to him; he passes it along to someone else." Dr. Osbourne bounced his nervous gaze from Ralph to me to Ralph again. "There's nothing illegal about it."

It seemed like a highly unusual and inefficient way to do research, but it wasn't unprecedented. In World War II only a select few people knew exactly what was being developed at the Oak Ridge National Laboratory in Oak Ridge, Tennessee—the parts and fuel for an atomic bomb. Only when the bomb was completed did the staff find out what they'd made. *So it's possible Osbourne is innocent, just another pawn.*

I wondered what kind of weapon would warrant this kind of secrecy today, but decided for the moment to follow up on the process, not the product. "So," I said. "Cassandra sent you her findings. Who did you send your findings to?"

"A man named Kurvetek. Dr. Octal Kurvetek."

"What do you know about him?"

"Nothing, except he works closely with Victor Drake."

"Figures," said Ralph.

"And you worked out of Building B-14?" I said.

Osbourne nodded.

"Listen carefully," I said. "I want you to tell me what went on in Building B-14. Why would someone burn it down?"

"It's where we collated the findings, kept all the files, all the research." He motioned toward the device. "And that thing. The prototype. We kept everything in hard files, so no one could hack the system. The government was worried about the Chinese."

In my mind I tried to gather up the fragments of information I'd collected so far, but they were still in disarray. "This prototype," I said, "it does more than just sense faint neural electromagnetic impulses, doesn't it?"

He nodded nervously but didn't say anything.

"I'd suggest you be a bit more forthcoming," Ralph said to Dr. Osbourne, who rubbed his fingers anxiously together in response.

"Tell us about the connection to MEG technology," I said.

He eyed Ralph, who was leaning forward, his shirt straining against his thick, corded neck muscles. Dr. Osbourne's eyes quivered as he continued. "The device uses the same basic principles as magnetoencephalography, or as you said, MEG technology. An MEG machine is too big to be used in the field, and a patient needs to sit beneath it without moving for several hours. Also it needs cryogenic temperatures and a shielded room to block other magnetic—"

"So that's where the sharks come in," I said, speaking my thoughts and inadvertently interrupting Dr. Osbourne. "Sharks don't need any of those things. They can identify the signals instantaneously, on the fly, using the jellylike substance in their electrosensory organs."

"Mucopolysaccharides," he said with a nod.

"My point is, sharks don't need cryogenic temperatures or shielding devices. And they do it over long distances."

"Exactly," said Dr. Osbourne. "So by combining a laser-guided targeting device with the neuromorphic and biogenetic engineering developed from electrosensory research on sharks, and including magnetoencephalography technology, we created an inorganic version of the shark's ampullae of Lorenzini receptors and neural pathways."

Surprisingly, I was following what he was saying. But there was more, there had to be more.

"What about the cesium-137?"

"That's been one of the problems." He walked over and pointed to the device. "See this removable pack?" He took a moment to slide the cesium-137 unit from the bottom of the device. "We weren't able to figure out how to stop minute quantities from escaping—just during use, you understand. We're perfectly safe right now." He reattached the cesium-137.

"OK," I said. "I know that when the neurons in our brains fire synapses, they create minute electromagnetic impulses. That's what the MEG records. But how does all this fit together?"

"With the recent strides in understanding how hemodynamic and electrophysiological signals relate to each other—"

Ralph threw his huge hands to his hips and stood like a drill sergeant. "He's wasting our time, Pat." The more irritated Ralph appeared, the more Osbourne seemed to open up. Ralph might have noticed that and been playing into the scenario, or he might have really been getting annoyed. Hard to tell.

"Talk us through the brain signals," I told Dr. Osbourne.

He rubbed his fingers nervously together and edged back slightly from Ralph. "Hemodynamic and electrophysiological signals are different processes within the brain, different ways we respond to stimuli. By studying the spatial and temporal correlation of the two different processes, we can better understand which neural impulses relate to which cognitive tasks."

"Wait a minute." I stared at the device lying on Dr. Osbourne's living room carpet. "You're not saying this machine can read people's minds?"

"No, no, no. Nothing that specific."

"So not at all, then? Not even in a broad sense?"

"No." He paused though, and his eyes wandered across the far wall. I had to believe he was at least considering the possibility. "Theoretically, I suppose . . . this line of research might explore the possibility, but that would still be decades out." I thought of DARPA and their research on the theoretical weapons systems of the future. I felt like

I was slowly seeing all the threads weave together, but I hoped I was wrong.

Ralph scrunched up his face. "But you are telling us it can map the way someone thinks?"

"That's one way to put it, yes, by identifying specific neural patterns."

By mapping a person's unique neural signature the government could identify someone by the one thing no one can cover up or mask or disguise—his brain waves.

Ralph must have shared my thoughts. "Law enforcement could use this instead of facial recognition," he said. "Install it anywhere."

A tense thought began scratching at the back of my mind—what if this device could be installed on the National Geospatial-Intelligence Agency's next generation of spy satellites? The NGIA would be able to map people's neural patterns, and since the technology could "see through" buildings or rubble, it would be able to locate and identify someone whether he was indoors, or outdoors, or hiding in a cave. It was Calvin's global video project taken to the most extreme level.

Ralph's ringing phone jarred me back to the conversation. He looked at the number and stepped into the other room to take the call.

And then the final hammer blow fell in my mind. It would still be theoretical, of course, but if it ever became possible . . .

I remembered what Tessa had said.

Think like Dupin.

As impossible as it seems, it did occur, so it must have been possible.

I had to consider it. "Rigel," I said, opting for familiarity and hoping it would keep him talking. "Could the device be calibrated to do more than simply identify and map the pattern of neural impulses?"

He furrowed his eyebrows. "What do you mean?"

"Could it be used to affect those neural signals? Change them? Disrupt them in some way?" He shook his head. With added urgency I rephrased my question. "Think. Is there any way at all this device could be used to identify a person by the unique neural signature of his brain activity, and then somehow disrupt that activity?"

"You mean cause a cerebrovascular accident?"

"Yes, give the person a stroke. Or maybe cause other irreversible brain damage that might affect behavior?"

"I can't see how . . ." He shook his head. "No."

"Are you sure?"

"Absolutely. I can't think of any way you could . . ."

Ralph stepped back into the room.

"Maybe with the cesium-137?" I said. "Or somehow through the laser targeting? I'm not saying is it possible now, but is it theoretically possible? You have a PhD in neuropathology. Could it ever be possible?"

"No, of course not. You'd need . . ." He stared into space for a long frozen moment, and then at last his eyes quivered, and his face grew ashen. "Oh . . ."

That was it. That's all I needed to hear. "Ralph, we need to get Dr. Osbourne out of here."

"What? Why?"

"This is my home," Dr. Osbourne exclaimed. "I'm staying right—"

"It's for your safety. They'll come after you. You know too much. Listen, do you have any of your research here, or did you send it all to Building B-14?"

"I had some files with me at the conference. I was—"

"Where are they?"

"Mr. Drake," he was stammering now. "He stopped by thirty minutes before you arrived. I gave him everything. Oh no . . . I can't believe I've—"

I motioned to Ralph. "Take Rigel to the field office, assign some agents to protect him, and then go find Drake and this guy Kurvetek. Find out who the other researchers are. We need to get them all into protective custody. But keep this as quiet as possible. We still don't know who's involved, and it might be someone in the Bureau, or maybe the police department."

"You think Drake might be Shade?" Ralph said.

I grabbed the device, slipped it back into the oversized laundry bag. "No. I've got someone else in mind. Just get Dr. Osbourne to the field office, make sure he's safe. Then go find Drake. Get Margaret to help you, she's the only one we can trust."

"Margaret?"

"She's not Shade."

"You're not really making a lot of—"

"Trust me on this, Ralph."

"Where are you going?"

"To find Lien-hua." I tied up the laundry bag with the device inside and carried it to the door. "Melice asked for her by name. They know her. She's not safe."

On the way out the door, my phone rang. An electronically masked voice said, "You have something I want, Dr. Bowers."

"Shade," I replied. "I've been expecting your call."

92

"I can assure you," said Shade. "I'm not the only one look-ing for it."

"Good. Let's get together. You bring some of your friends; I'll bring some of mine. We'll have a party." I started the engine and pulled into the street.

"Dr. Bowers, please. I don't want to have to hurt you."

"Oh, now see? That wasn't so smart, threatening a fed-eral agent. After I catch you, that won't bode so well for you at the trial."

Shade ignored what I'd said. "You need to know this goes much deeper and much farther than you could ever guess. The only way to protect yourself and the people you care about is to hand over the device. I'll give you a time and a place. If you do as I say, you'll never hear from me or my people again. But if you make me come and get it, this will not end well for you."

"Bring it on," I said.

And then I hung up the phone.

Cliché or not, it sure felt good to say it.

Things were beginning to get interesting.

General Cole Biscayne grew tired of the mindless reality show he was watching and turned off his sister's television. The instant the volume died, he heard a voice behind him, and it wasn't his sister speaking. "It's been a long time, Cole."

And that was the last thing Cole Biscayne ever heard, because then Sebastian Taylor, the assassin Cole had trained more than thirty years earlier, the man who had once been the governor of North Carolina and was now on the FBI's most-wanted list, fired the Glock he was holding. The bullet entered the back of the general's head and exited through his right eye socket, and General Cole Biscayne's fresh corpse slumped forward onto the lush lemon-colored carpet of his sister Beverly's living room.

Sebastian Taylor holstered his gun.

There.

That was finally taken care of. The general's sister would find him later when she got home. Too bad he'd made such a mess of the place.

Now it was time to visit Cassandra Lillo and finish up one more piece of business.

I phoned Lien-hua and found out she'd gone back to the hotel. I told her to wait for me there, and then I dialed Tessa's number but was only able to reach her voice mail. I left her a message to call me as soon as she could.

I hadn't wanted to check on Tessa's location again, but if Shade was threatening the people I cared about, I needed to find out where she was. So, even though I knew she would hate me for doing it, I called cybercrime to have them check her phone's GPS, and after a couple minutes on hold, found out she was still thirty-three thousand feet in the air, forty-five minutes from Denver. Good. I was actually glad her flight had been delayed. Tessa was safe.

The main arteries of the city were clogged and traffic was only inching along, so I left the highway behind and began to pick my way through the backstreets of San Diego.

I speed-dialed my parents and found out they were already at the airport. "Listen," I told my dad, "I'll have some officers meet you there. When Tessa arrives, go with them until things settle down here. I'll try to make it home tomorrow." He agreed, we hung up, and as I cruised through a yellow light, I called my friend Lieutenant Kurt Mason with the Denver Police Department and explained what was going on. "Kurt, have two officers meet Tessa and my parents, Martha and Conor, at the airport. I'll be back as soon as I can, probably a day or two. I'll take care of everything when I get there. Guarantee me Tessa and my parents will be safe until then. If for some reason they're not at the airport, send a car to their house."

"You have my word, Pat. I'll pick them up myself."

"Thanks."

I was almost to the hotel. I'd be with Lien-hua in a matter of minutes.

As they approached the club, Riker slid his arm around Tessa's waist. His tight muscles flexed against her side, and it felt good to be so close to a guy. She didn't pull away.

It felt good.

So good.

She wondered if this was how a young bird must feel, leaving the nest. Independent and free, spreading her wings against the wind.

Exciting.

So exciting.

The thrill of walking on the edge of the forbidden.

At the door, a mound of a man with a cement-block head held up his hand. His voice sounded like it came straight from a subway tunnel. "IDs."

Riker pulled something out of his pocket, leaned over, and slipped it into the big guy's hand. Tessa caught a glimpse of green paper. The man closed his mitt around the bills and waved them through.

Now inside. "Thanks," she whispered.

"No prob."

Pulsing, pulsing music roamed through the air and pumped and echoed all around Riker and her as they walked through a dark throat of a hallway. On each side, the shadows held impatient lovers groping each other in the cyclical winking light.

A few of the guys nodded toward Riker from the recesses of the hall as he and Tessa strolled to the dance floor. Then Riker spoke to her, raising his voice loud enough to be heard over the sound of the music. "They know me here. I come here a lot."

Techno music throbbed through the air, through the walls, vibrated up through the floor. Tessa loved it. Loved it all. "This place rocks," she called out.

"One of my favorite clubs."

She saw a few surfer types, but most of the people in the club seemed to have a darker edge to them. Partly Tessa felt at home. Partly she felt unsure. Then Riker took her hand and pulled her onto the dance floor, into the swirl of sweaty, swaying, leather-clad bodies. Tessa had been to clubs before, but never one like this. Never so intense.

Exciting.

So exciting.

The trancelike beat of the music rolled over her and through her. Seemed to course through her veins. She watched Riker shut his eyes and rise into the music, his whole body finding the driving rhythms of the song. She wanted to feel his arms around her again so she glided closer to him. Let the side of her leg nudge against his.

His eyelids parted, he smiled in a roguish way. Drew her close.

Exciting.

So exciting.

Tessa trembled. Maybe it was his touch.

But maybe it was the distant echo of her mom's voice that day on the frozen lake in Minnesota. That warning, faint with the years, telling her to turn around, to stop wandering out so far onto the ice.

Tessa closed her eyes to the laser lights, ignored the muffled warning from her childhood, and danced in time to the music pulsing beneath her skin.

93

I needed to make sure that both Lien-hua and the device were safe, but I also wanted a way to draw Shade into the open. I figured I could use myself as bait, but not if Lien-hua and I were at the FBI field office or police headquarters. Besides, I still wasn't exactly sure who to trust.

So after considering my options, I decided it made sense for Lien-hua and me to find a place to rest and regroup for a few hours where we could wait to hear from Ralph about Victor Drake, and also see if Shade would contact me again. After all, I'd invited him to bring it on and I figured he would be more than willing to take me up on the invitation.

So after Lien-hua and I picked up some fast food, we located a beachside hotel on the outskirts of San Diego called the Surfside Inn.

Along with the small suitcases of clothes we each carried, she brought in the food and I toted the laundry bag containing the device.

At the front desk, we checked in under phony names.

"One room?" asked the man behind the counter.

"Yes." I glanced at Lien-hua and whispered so that only she could hear me, "For security reasons."

"Oh, I see," she whispered back. "So you need me to protect you?"

"That's not exactly what I—"

She turned to the man behind the registration counter. "Can we make that a two-room suite?"

"Yes, ma'am."

A few moments later he handed us each a room key,

and as I followed her onto the elevator she said, "Security reasons? I've never heard that one before."

"What can I say? I'm a safety-conscious kind of guy." I heard her mumble something about ulterior motives, and a couple moments later the doors opened and we exited to find room 524.

Once inside the suite, Lien-hua and I took a few minutes to check for intruders or listening devices—you can never be too careful. Then we sat down to finish supper. "I'm glad Tessa's not here," I mumbled, after swallowing a mouthful of cheeseburger. "Sometimes it's nice to eat something that never had roots or leaves and not feel guilty about it."

Lien-hua took a sip of her Diet Coke and worked at her chicken Caesar salad while I began summarizing the visit with Dr. Osbourne. I'm not a fan of briefings, so I tried to make my synopsis as short as possible, but before I could start explaining the connections between the different branches of scientific research, Lien-hua said, "Wait. I'm still confused about how the device ended up at police headquarters. Dunn just happened to kick the car containing it and then ordered that car be taken to impound? Doesn't that seem a little too convenient?"

"You know, I've been wondering the same thing. Let's check the plates, see who that car belonged to."

I pulled out my laptop, but Lien-hua touched my arm to stop me. "Are you sure you should be using that? What if Shade's able to track your computer use?" She removed her hand.

"Not possible," I said. "Remember CIFER? It's designed for field operatives. Masks the user's location. I'll just use that to access the Internet." I tapped at a couple of keys. "Let's find out who owns that car."

Using my federal ID access number I logged onto the police archives and searched through the impound records; and a moment later Lien-hua nailed a finger to the screen. "It's Austin Hunter's car!"

"Unbelievable," I said. "He was one step ahead of us the whole time."

I tapped a few more keys. "The parking tickets are real. He managed to get them all since leaving the SEALs. He must have saved them up, stuck 'em on the car so it would get noticed."

She thought for a moment. "So, Hunter must have known that if he got caught, the car would eventually be impounded because of the parking tickets. The device would be confiscated and stored safely at police headquarters and he would still have a bargaining chip to save Cassandra. Simple but elegant."

"It's just that Dunn's impatience helped the process along."

"Very impressive."

The mention of Austin brought a somber mood to the room, and only after working on our meal silently for a few moments did it seem right to get back to business.

At last I continued my explanation of neural mapping, identity tracking, and the technological possibility of inducing brain damage or giving someone a stroke with the device. I ended by saying, "I know that at first glance this whole thing sounds unbelievable, like some kind of science fiction movie, but—"

Lien-hua shook off my skepticism. "Pat, cell phones were science fiction thirty years ago. So were mp3 players, DVDs, personal computers, smart bombs, spy planes, digital photographs, the list goes on."

"True." As I thought about her words, I realized that nearly all the technology I need in order to do my job had been invented in my lifetime.

"Even a decade ago," she continued, "who would have thought we could implant electrodes into the brains of people with physical disabilities that would allow them to type, simply by thinking of the letters?"

"What's impossible today is commonplace tomorrow," I mumbled. I tried to imagine what types of technological, medical, and weaponry advances we'd see within the next thirty years, but it was too mind-boggling to even imagine.

"Besides," she added, "if what Dr. Osbourne told you is true, the technology for this device has been around for years."

"It just took someone to pull it all together," I said. "To make the connection."

"Yes," she said slowly. "I'm almost surprised no one has tried creating something like this before."

Our conversation brought me back to the troubling thought that I'd first had at Dr. Osbourne's house, but in the rush to find Lien-hua and get to an out-of-the-way location, I hadn't had the chance to look into it. "Lien-hua, what's the hardest thing to do in a murder?"

Without even hesitating. "Getting rid of the body."

"Right. So, what if you don't have a body?"

"How could you not have a body?"

"By not murdering someone."

She took a small sip of her cola. "I'm not sure I'm following you here."

I surfed to the online archives of the *San Diego Union-Tribune*. "Remember when Hunter said he didn't kill the people?"

"Yes."

"I've been thinking about that. Who was he talking about? Which people? I figure that, since he was the arsonist, whatever deaths he was talking about would seem to be related to the fires, right?" As I spoke, I found what I was looking for. The obituaries page for April 22, 2008.

"That follows, yes." She scooted closer to get a better look at the screen. "So, what are we looking at here?"

"The first of the arsons was reported at two thirty-one a.m. on the morning of April 22, 2008." I pointed to one of the obituaries. "And look. An unidentified woman was found dead that night on Euclid Avenue, within a block of the fire."

"And that proves what?"

"Nothing. But let's see if there's a pattern." I surfed to the obituaries for the date of the next fire, the one in Chula Vista. "Obits for suicides and natural deaths won't necessarily list location, but they should list the time of death ... And here we are ..." I read it off: "'May 17, an unidentified man died of natural causes sometime between nine and ten p.m.,' that's one hour before that night's fire was reported."

I scrolled to the date of the next fire. "And here, on June 16, Rene Gonzalez died at approximately eleven p.m., two hours before a fire was suppressed on the same street. And ..." I surfed to another date. "Here we have a Jane Doe on August 1 at one a.m., ninety minutes before the fire—"

"You memorized the dates, times, and locations for all the fires?"

"It's easier that way. Then I don't have to keep looking things up. So, see?" I kept scrolling. "Here's a suicide, within three blocks of the fire."

Now that I knew what I was looking for, it went faster, so I whipped through the remaining obituary pages, summarizing as I went. "Another stroke . . . two suicides . . . and two more unidentified deaths." I finished scrolling through the dates of the fires and then said, "It doesn't happen at every fire, but there are enough incidents to establish a high correlation."

Lien-hua's voice fell into a soft lament and she said the words I was thinking, the words I hoped couldn't possibly be true: "They were testing the device on the homeless population."

"Yes," I said, "I think they were."

94

I hated to admit it, but all the evidence so far told me we were right. "So, use the device on someone and either induce a stroke or give him severe enough brain damage to cause him to consider suicide."

"Probably to the frontal cortex," she mused. "Controls inhibitions, language production, judgment. Destroy that and we're little more than animals."

"And remember? Hunter chose sites near trolley stops so that he could get away. So if Drake's men were testing the device nearby, that would explain why Graysmith and Dunn noticed the high rate of suspicious deaths among the homeless near trolley tracks."

"Don't murder someone," Lien-hua whispered. "Let him die from natural causes. Think about San Diego, Pat: a biotech hub with hundreds of thousands of undocumented immigrants. What better city to test this in? Here you have all the scientists you need, all the technology and biotech resources you need—"

"And all the test subjects," I added. "People who would never be missed: immigrants, transients, the homeless." It was terrible to say, but I knew it was true. "The system doesn't care if a few vagrants or illegal aliens end up dead. The nameless don't make the news. To the system, they don't exist."

"And with the high occurrence of mental illness in the homeless population, who would notice if the test only caused slight brain damage?" She paused. "This device would be the perfect weapon for an assassin."

"Wait," I said, staring at the deadly device lying right

beside us. "Think big here, Lien-hua. We can already use satellite-based lasers for tracking and targeting, and soon we'll be able to do retinal scans from our defense satellites. If the government were able to install this technology on the next generation of satellites, they'd have the ability to track people either through global video or by neural synapse patterns, and then, anytime they wanted, give a person permanent brain damage or a stroke and leave no trace evidence behind. No bullets, no DNA, no fingerprints, no physical evidence of any kind left at the scene of the crime. No murder. No crime. The person just died of—"

"Natural causes."

"Yes."

A long silence. Then Lien-hua said, "If what we're talking about is actually possible, it could tip the balance of world power. Nearly all of our current security measures would be useless. Bodyguards, locks, security systems, bulletproof glass, body armor, Kevlar vests, all worthless. A government could assassinate anyone, at any time, for any reason, and never be implicated."

We were both silent again. I wasn't sure I wanted to explore the possibilities any further. It seemed like the more I did, the more disturbing the implications became.

"But, Pat, I'm still wondering ... why do you think Shade wanted Building B-14 burned down? Why not just steal the device?"

"The research. The government could just make another device. The files all went up in smoke. That's why I wanted Dr. Osbourne and the other researchers in protective custody. Now that the files and the device are gone, I figured Shade might go after the researchers next."

We both reflected on everything for a few moments, and then she said, "But why the other fires? What's the connection?"

Truthfully, even with all the puzzle pieces I'd been able to slide together so far, I couldn't see a reason for the previous fires. "I don't know. It seems like it would draw more attention to the scene than just letting the victim die. It doesn't make sense. That part's still a mystery to me."

We discussed different possibilities, but neither of us could untangle any more threads of the case with the facts at hand. There was a lot to process, a lot to think through.

And even though much of what Lien-hua and I had discussed was only a working hypothesis, I felt like we were on the right track. After all, John Doe's death fit the pattern: brain damage, suicide, then a fire.

I thought once again of Dupin and the orangutan from Poe's story. I didn't remember the French saying Tessa had quoted, but I did remember the translation: ignoring what is and explaining what is not. We needed to explain what did happen, however impossible it might seem. And the working theory we were exploring did just that.

Lien-hua stood. "I need to let all this sink in. I'll see you in a bit. I'm going to take a shower, get cleaned up."

As she stepped into the bathroom, I started wondering once again how Shade and Melice found out the device would be at police headquarters. Using CIFER to mask the origin of my call, and using my computer's internal microphone, I phoned Angela Knight. "Can you check to see if anyone has accessed the satellite imagery of the showdown with Hunter?" I said. "Using infrared thermal imaging it might have been possible to view Hunter stashing the device. I'll e-mail you the exact street location."

"I'll check," she replied. "I'll get back to you as soon as I can."

While I waited for her reply, I contacted Ralph. His phone was off, but I left him a brief message summarizing what Lien-hua and I had discussed. Then I called Graysmith: still no word on Melice, although they did find a car he'd stolen and the remnants of my little creation in an auto body shop on India Street. I tried Tessa's number again, no answer. I left another message.

By the time I was done, Angela had sent me an e-mail explaining that Terry Manoji was the only one who'd logged in to the network. "He must have had the same idea you did, Pat," she wrote.

Another dead end. I let out a sigh.

Both Lien-hua and I had been going almost nonstop since yesterday morning, and I could feel the stress and fatigue catching up with me, so I went to the suite's other bathroom for a shower of my own, and it gave me a chance to think things through.

Lien-hua was safe, Tessa was safe, and, although Shade and Melice were still out there, the FBI and SDPD were on

Melice's tail, Osbourne was on his way to protective custody, and soon Ralph would be on his way to talk to Victor
Drake.

For the moment at least, it seemed like Lien-hua and I
had stepped into the eye of the hurricane. All around us,
the winds were swirling, but we'd found a brief pocket of
calm air. Maybe it was just the calm before the storm.

About fifteen minutes later, Lien-hua and I found ourselves
in the suite's living room. Showered. Refreshed. Beginning
to relax.

I'd put on my typical jeans and a T-shirt; she was wearing
jeans and a pile pullover. "So, Pat," she said, taking a seat
in the recliner. "I'm impressed with your work on this. Very
thorough. Very professional."

"You too. Very professional. By the way, how's your
leg?"

"Good. Your arm, where the guy bit you?"

"Good. Your neck?"

"My neck is good too," she said.

"That's good."

"Yes."

"I'm glad we're both good," I said.

"Right."

"Good."

Brilliant, Pat. You are one stunning conversationalist.

The moment tumbled into silence, the kind of silence
that asks you to turn a corner in the conversation. "So," I
said. "I guess Ralph will be calling soon."

"Yes."

"And until then it looks like we have a little time to . . ."

"Time to what?"

"Ourselves." I could hardly believe I'd said it, hardly believe I'd let it slip out, but I had, and in the moment it felt
right and I didn't regret it.

Just the two of us.

"I think I'd like some fresh air," she said, rising from the
chair to open the sliding door to the veranda.

"I'll get it." I walked past her, pushed the glass door
open, and let in the cool San Diego night.

I heard her voice behind me. "Wow. Thanks, Pat. I don't
think I could have managed that on my own."

I turned around in time to see her untie her ponytail and shake her hair free. It fell like an inviting waterfall across her shoulders. "No problem," I said. A touch of her perfume curled around me. I motioned toward the open door. "Do you want the curtains open too?"

She looked like she was about to answer, but then curled her hand into a loose fist and nodded it at me.

"Sign language?"

She nodded with her hand again.

"And that means 'yes'?"

One more nod with her closed fist. I pulled back the curtains.

Though it was February, the breeze drifting past me tasted like a sweet summer dream. I signed "yes" back to her. "Teach me some more signs. I think it'd be good to know them."

"It takes a while to learn."

"Don't sell yourself short, Lien-hua. I'm sure you're a very good teacher." I walked over and sat on the edge of the couch. "At least teach me the alphabet. Maybe I could fingerspell words and communicate with people who're hearing impaired. If I ever needed to."

She glanced through the open doors toward the sea, then back to me. "It's just as hard as learning any foreign language."

"Tessa's good at foreign languages. She knows Latin. She's learning French. Maybe it runs in the family."

That elicited a slight grin. "She's your stepdaughter, Pat."

"Oh yeah. I guess you got me there. So then, how's this?" I squiggled my fingers rapidly in the air, making up my own indecipherable language.

"Not so good."

"See?" I said. "I need help."

"Funny. Margaret told me that exact same thing just last week."

"Now that, I believe."

At last Lien-hua sighed and sat down on the other end of the couch. "OK, Pat, watch. 'A' is like this." She slowly curled her fingers to form the sign language letter for A.

I imitated her gesture.

"Then B."

Again I did as she did.

"C."

I repeated "C."

Then she showed me D, and then E, and then on through the rest, each time waiting just long enough for me to repeat the sign. After we'd gone through the entire alphabet she said, "OK, now you try. See how many you can remember."

I made it to Q before stumbling.

She reviewed the alphabet for me, but this time I only made it to M.

"See? I told you it wasn't easy."

"Work with me. I'm a willing student."

She held me with a gentle gaze. "The best way to learn is to close your eyes."

"Really?"

"Yes. Go ahead."

I closed my eyes and waited for her to tell me to begin. I couldn't quite understand how this would help, but as I was puzzling over it, I heard the soft shuffle of movement as she slid closer to me on the couch.

And then, I felt her warm hand on mine. Her fingers gently, carefully shaping mine to form the next letter. "N," she said, and then the next: "O ... P ..." One letter at a time, her fingers guided mine through the remainder of the alphabet.

"Let's start over at the beginning," I said, my eyes still closed. "I'm not sure I've quite got hold of it yet."

Without a word, Lien-hua took my fingers slowly through the entire alphabet. Every letter she formed made the rest of the world retreat farther and farther away. And every time our fingers flexed and curled together, my heart raced faster. And when we were finished, I opened my eyes.

"Close them again," she said softly.

I didn't want to be disagreeable, so I did as I was told.

With my eyes closed, my other senses seemed more acute. I could hear the soft waves bumping against the shore five stories below us, and the tender rustling of palm branches in the breeze. All around me, I smelled San Diego's ever-present scent of spring swirling, coloring, covering the night. And of course, with my sense of touch, I could feel Lien-hua's knowledgeable fingers guiding, teaching mine.

After we'd finished the alphabet, she said, "Keep them closed." She made me wave my hand. "This is 'hello.'"

"That's an easy one." I waved to her.

"That was good." I heard a smile pass through her words. "I hope you can remember it."

"Might be tough. I'll do my best."

"And this is 'How are you?'" I felt her fingers, full of confidence, full of grace, glide across mine. I repeated the words as I did the gesture by myself.

"This is 'please.'" She led me through the sign. I repeated it, and then she paused for a long moment, her hand resting on mine. I heard her soft breath beside me in the night, and I caught the scent of her shampoo, herbal and rich with the smell of meadow flowers. I could almost sense the beat of her heart, rising through the dark expanse of my closed eyes. "This," she said, "is the sign for 'come closer.'" Her voice had fallen to a whisper.

"Come closer," I said, I signed. Lien-hua's hand remained on mine. A touch of discreet wind whispered against my cheek and the anxious trembling of my heart sent chills riding across my back.

"And this," she said, "is 'I'm here for you.'" She let her fingers teach mine.

"I'm here for you," I said with my words and my fingers.

She didn't take her hand away from mine at all anymore. "I need you," she said, and she took her time teaching me the sign.

"I need you," I repeated with my mouth, with my hand.

Her fingers curled lightly around mine, didn't let go, although now she'd stopped teaching me sign language. She placed her other hand gently against my closed eyes. "Don't open them," she said. "Not yet." The feelings for her that I'd been trying to quiet for months rose, climbed through time, and became a restless melody drawing me deeper and deeper into the moment.

"Monday night, after I brought Tessa back to the hotel and I saw you in the hall . . ." Her voice was a cool caress that calmed me and thrilled me. One of her hands on my hand, the other across my eyes. "That's what I wanted to tell you, Pat, but I couldn't find the words. I wanted to tell you: 'I need you.'"

My heart was on fire. The world became a sprinkle of joy
and wonder and promises as new as dawn. "I need you,"
I whispered the words, and then added two more: "Come
closer."

I said the words and I signed them. "Come closer." I repeated them again.

And again.

Until she did.

And that's when I heard the knock at the door.

Victor Drake had just finished printing out the boarding
pass for his flight to the Philippines and was busy shredding papers when the three men arrived at his home. Victor hated the word *henchmen*. He hated the idea of using
henchmen. And even more, he hated giving money to his
henchmen. But that was exactly what he was about to do.

He saw their cars pass across the video monitor of the
surveillance cameras at the front gate. Then he headed
downstairs to usher his three henchmen into his home.

95

A moment ago, when we heard the knock, both Lien-hua and I had leapt off the couch, pulled our weapons, and approached the door to the hallway.

Now we covered both sides of the door. I silently counted to three with my fingers. Then I threw the door open, grabbed the person standing outside it, pulled him into the room, and had him on the ground and restrained before the door even banged into the wall.

It was the man from the front desk. In his hand, he held a manila envelope. Lien-hua scanned the hallway and then, finding it empty, quickly closed the door.

"Hey!" the guy cried. "It's just me. It's just me."

I eased my grip, holstered my SIG, saw Lien-hua do the same. "Who's the envelope from?"

"I don't know. Some homeless guy brought it in, told me someone gave him fifty bucks to deliver it to me. That's it. That's all I know. Now, please."

I took the envelope from him and then I stood back. "Did he tell you the room? Did he tell you which room to deliver it to?"

The man from the front desk climbed to his feet, shaking his head. "No. Just said the Asian lady and the guy who needed a shave. That's it. I swear."

My name had been printed on the front of the envelope. "All right." I dug a few bills out of my pocket and handed them to him. "We'd rather not be disturbed."

"I'll keep that in mind," he mumbled as he passed back through the door and walked away rubbing his wrist.

I closed, then dead-bolted the door. "Someone knows

we're here, Lien-hua, but it doesn't look like they know which room."

"Shade."

I nodded. "Probably. He may have followed the doorman; let's be ready either way."

She eyed the envelope. "Do you think you should open it?"

"No, but I don't always do what I should." Carefully, I took it into the bathroom and held it over the sink just in case there was powder or poison inside. But it felt like only a few slips of paper.

I unclasped the metal brad, cupped the envelope open, and one piece of paper and a photo of the shattered tank in the warehouse slid out. The piece of paper read, "You missed something, Dr. Bowers." It was signed, "Shade." The handwriting appeared to be the same script as the words on the warehouse wall.

As I stared at the photo of the tank's remains, I had a thought. "Lien-hua, back in the interrogation room, Melice whispered something to you. What did he say?"

"He asked me if I thought drowning would be a terrible way to go." She was quiet for a moment then added, "The truth is, someone close to me drowned a long time ago and I got the feeling Melice knew it and that's why he asked me the question."

"What did you say to him?"

"I asked him if that's why he drowned the women. Because he thought it would be a terrible way to go." Then she gazed at me. "Why, what are you thinking?"

"I'm thinking things aren't what they appear to be." I pocketed the photograph. "I have to go back to the warehouse."

"What?"

"I think I might know who Shade is."

"Who is it?"

"I need to check first."

She started to tie back her hair. "I'll come too."

"No, no. You have to stay here with the device."

"You can't go alone, Pat."

"Lien-hua, I'm still not sure who to trust in the police department or even the FBI. If Melice and Shade see a big team coming, they'll disappear and this'll go on and on. They might go after Tessa. I can't let that happen."

"But it might be a trap."

"Of course it's a trap. That's why we shouldn't both be there, and that's why we definitely shouldn't bring the device. You need to stay here with it. Besides, if one of them is at the warehouse and one comes here, we can get them both. Divide and conquer. I'll be all right. This ends. And it ends tonight."

"But Pat—"

"Shh." I touched my finger lightly to her lips. "That's sign language for I'll see you soon, don't worry about me, we'll talk more when I get back."

She looked like she was going to argue with me, but at last, she repeated my newly invented sign and pressed her finger against my lips. Then she gave me a quick kiss on the cheek. Just on the cheek, that was all. But it was a kiss, and it felt intimate and familiar and natural. And it gave me swift courage and it sharpened my resolve.

"I'll see you soon," I said.

"I'll be here." Then she added, "Don't worry. I can take care of myself."

"I know you can."

I went into the suite's closest bedroom, looked over the device one last time. I thought perhaps it would be better if Lien-hua and I didn't have all of our eggs in one basket, so, I removed the cesium-137 pack from the bottom of the device just like Dr. Osbourne had shown me. Then I slipped the device and my cell phone back into the laundry bag, and, taking only the cesium-137 unit with me, I went to go find Shade.

In his home office next to his library, Victor was handing the suitcases of money to Geoff and Dr. Kurvetek when a man built like an NFL linebacker burst through the door, and aimed a gun at his head. "FBI," the guy said. "Shut up. Lie down. And I might not shoot you."

Victor dropped to the floor as the two henchmen in the room simply gazed at the agent.

"I said down," the big guy growled, leveling his weapon at Geoff. Then, from his position on the carpet, Victor saw Suricata, who had slipped to the bathroom a few minutes earlier, pull a long knife from his jacket and take another silent step closer to the FBI agent's back. But Victor must have stared at Suricata a moment too long because the agent noticed Victor's eyes and pivoted to face his assailant.

Suricata was quick, knocking the agent's gun away and swiping at him with the knife, backing him into the room. Dr. Kurvetek took advantage of the brief scuffle and ran past them into the hallway. Meanwhile, Geoff rose, pulling a gun of his own.

Victor wanted to leave but he really needed to shred the rest of those papers. Of course, if his henchmen could stop this guy, he could shred them in a few minutes. Two against one.

He decided to wait it out.

Suricata raised his ten-inch custom-made dagger and sneered at the FBI agent. "I'm Suricata. It's important to know the name of the man who kills you."

"Oh. Well, in that case, I'm Ralph," the guy said. "Let's dance."

Suricata flipped the knife around in his hand, tossed it into the air, then snatched it out of its rotation and feinted toward the FBI agent named Ralph. Geoff was aiming his gun, but as Suricata and Ralph ducked and turned, he couldn't seem to get a clear shot at the agent. Suricata jabbed the knife at Ralph, and for an instant it looked like he was going to bury it in the agent's chest, but Ralph spun away from the blade and sunk a massive fist into Suricata's stomach, catching him by surprise. Two more blows to the stomach, one to the back, and Suricata was down.

"Stop right there," said Geoff, taking careful aim at Ralph and grinning. "Hmm ... homicide by cop. Always hate to see that—"

But an intense-looking woman stepped out of the library and cut him off in midsentence, "Drop your gun, Officer Rickman." Victor recognized her from the PROC meeting. Another FBI agent.

Geoff hesitated and the woman continued. "Don't tempt me. I don't like dirty cops, and shooting you would save the taxpayers a lot of money. Drop it now."

Geoff made eye contact with her, slowly set down his gun, and Victor began sliding along the wall toward the door as Ralph cuffed Suricata and the woman cuffed Geoff.

Victor was almost to the library. He might still be able to slip away.

"What took you so long, Margaret?" said Ralph.

"I wanted to let you have a little fun first, Agent Hawkins."

"Well, there's a first time for everything. Thanks. Someday I'll return the favor." Ralph picked up the knife. "This is nice. I needed a new knife."

Margaret saw Victor beside the door. "Going somewhere?"

Victor froze. "No, no. Just wanted to thank you. Those two men broke into my house and were about to—"

"Help you finish shredding those papers?" She gestured toward the stack of research beside the shredder. Victor watched her begin paging through the files. Then she said, "I think we'll need to confiscate these as evidence."

Ralph picked up the boarding pass from Victor's desk. "The Philippines, huh? I hear that's a nice place. And no extradition treaties with the U.S. How convenient."

And in that moment, Victor Drake wished, oh how he wished, he hadn't used up his bottle of pills.

One song ended, or so Tessa thought, and another began. It was hard to tell. Every song rolled effortlessly into the next.

The music and the gyrating dancers made it nearly impossible to talk, so eventually, when Riker signaled for her to follow him, she clung to his fingers and let him lead her through the sea of people, to a bar located around the corner from where the band was jamming. The bar was just far enough from the heart of the music so people could actually call out their orders to the bartender and be heard.

Riker straddled a chair. "Whadd'ya want?" he asked Tessa.

For a moment, Tessa thought about having a drink. It wouldn't have been her first one, but she didn't like how alcohol clouded her thinking, made reality fuzzy. No, she didn't want that. Not tonight.

Tonight she wanted to savor every moment.

She shook her head.

"C'mon." He signaled with a finger to the bartender and pointed at a Corona. "I'm buying."

"I don't want any," she said again.

He looked at her, eyes smoldering. The lights from the

club flickering, dancing across them. "Don't ravens drink?" Then he put his hands on her forearms, gently. So gently. A light touch. An endearing smile. "The night's just getting started," he said.

The little girl inside of her felt herself drifting farther onto the ice.

He cared about her. He did. His tenderness proved it. She could trust him. It would be OK. He would hold her tonight and she would hold him and her heart would have a safe place to go.

"OK," she said at last, when the long, tremulous moment was over. "But just one."

96

The warehouse loomed before me like a giant coffin in the night.

Shade or Melice was probably waiting for me. Maybe both of them. But I can do pretty well fending for myself when I have to, and I knew that if they were here, this would be my best chance at catching them.

Watchful, cautious, I stepped from my car and leaned beneath the crime scene tape. Then I pulled out my SIG and my Maglite and approached the great black coffin.

The criminalists had chained the door to the warehouse shut, but it didn't take me long to pick the lock. I creaked the door open, entered the dusty stillness, and took in the scene. High above me, the jagged windows let only slivers of city light into the building.

No sign of Shade or Melice.

With my flashlight, I located the window I'd climbed through after scaling the outside wall. Then I swept the light along the wall to find the staircase I'd descended.

Missing . . . what was I missing?

I moved the light toward the area where I'd first seen Melice.

Ralph was to your left . . . the tank with Cassandra was at the far end of the warehouse.

Swinging the light like a giant saber, I walked warily forward. I could hear the faint sound of dripping water from somewhere. The lonely air around me took the sound and toyed with it, magnified it, making the innocent drops of water sound like the soft, wet heartbeat of the building. Other than that, complete silence.

No sign of Shade or Melice.

After a few moments, I found the remnants of the tank where Cassandra had been imprisoned for over twelve hours. I stepped inside the tank's remains and stood where she stood. *This is where she screamed. Where she wept.*

The rusty ring beside my feet.

Gently dripping water.

The camcorders used to record the women had been hidden in the wall about four meters away. I shone my flashlight on the area.

The camera angles in all eight videos were consistent, so the cameras had been mounted in the same place for all the shots. I'd read in the criminalists' report that Melice had used two cameras, one of which he'd moved subsequent to filming Cassandra's video. I walked to the room where the cameras had been located, made sure no one was waiting in ambush for me, then found the cameras' original positions. After checking the sight lines, I returned to the tank and saw that Melice had done an amazing job of concealing the cameras' locations. Both were set in shadowed recesses in the wall and wouldn't have been visible from inside the tank.

Just two tiny holes in a wall full of shadows.

Four meters away.

I tuned my ears to listen for any hint of movement, but heard nothing. If Shade or Melice were here, so far they'd been deathly still.

Windows, high and off to the left . . . the glint off the windows . . .

You're still missing something, Pat. Think.

The chain lay beside my foot, still attached to the metal ring. The last link of the chain was bent, opened, scratched. I guessed Ralph had used a tool of some kind to wrench it open. I studied the chain, counted the number of links. I bent low, aimed the beam of my light at the place where the metal ring was attached to the bottom of the tank. Then turned and looked up at the writing on the wall.

Remembering the water fingering away from the tank and into the room, I let my light follow the cracks in the uneven floor as they spread away from the tank.

What was I missing?

I thought of John Doe's suicide, the fires, the abduction, the death of Austin Hunter.

Once again, I wondered what I would have done if someone had been threatening to hurt Lien-hua. Even before having her hand on mine, even before feeling our fingers intertwine or receiving her gentle kiss, I would have done anything to save her.

Anything.

As I let myself think of her, the last couple days became more vivid to me, colored richer by my feelings. I pointed the light at the place on the floor where she had leaned over to help Cassandra.

As far as we knew, Cassandra was the only one to survive this tank. Seven other women had died right where I was standing—all within the last four months; beginning about the same time the Illusionist attacked Tessa, the same time Sebastian Taylor disappeared. The same time Lien-hua first flew to San Diego to profile the arsonist.

Motives. Dripping water. Echoing.

Thorough. Professional.

Lien-hua found the exit door at the aquarium.

She was also the one who found the gloves at the site of Monday night's fire.

I aimed my light at the now-broken chain once again.

Melice asked for Lien-hua by name. She was the one who tried to make the case for Dunn being Shade.

Fact. Fiction.

Fiction. Fact.

Someone had to tell Melice about the device. *You told Lien-hua the device was in the evidence room. She whispered something to Melice during the interrogation.*

The note from Shade said, "You missed something, Dr. Bowers."

I missed something.

No, no, no.

Lien-hua was the one who offered to tell Cassandra about Hunter's death. She held Cassandra. Let her weep against her shoulder.

Psychopaths just look at other people as objects to be used and then discarded . . .

Everything I knew about the case was beginning to split apart.

Lien-hua was the one who quickly bandaged Melice's
hand with her sock. So quickly. That's where he'd hidden
the pick—in the hand she wrapped ...

*There was no robbery, no murder, no crime, no motive,
the room wasn't locked.*

I grabbed the chain. Yanked it.

The room wasn't locked.

The eyewitness to Melice's trial in DC was killed ...
Lien-hua knows DC. She used to be a detective there ...
What had Osbourne said? The government was worried
about the Chinese ... *She's Chinese. She's planning a trip
to Beijing.*

Defeating him in his own castle.

Every thought was a betrayal to my feelings, to my
world, to all I'd come to believe about the woman who told
me she needed me.

*Semantic aphasia ... using the words that your listeners
want to hear. It's a way of manipulating people.*

Lien-hua was the one who led us to the warehouse, and
both times Shade had called me, Lien-hua wasn't beside
me, wasn't in view. Reality began to splinter apart.

No, it couldn't be.

Yes, it could.

Nothing was as it seemed.

I bolted for the door with one thought ripping through
my mind: Lien-hua was Shade and I'd just left her alone
with the device.

Creighton Melice set the garment bag on the edge of the
reception desk at the Surfside Inn. "Excuse me," he said to
the man working behind the counter. After he had his attention, Creighton flashed the FBI badge Shade had given
him at the Blue Lizard Lounge in November. "I'm looking
for two people who checked in here earlier today. They're
suspects in the terrorist bombing yesterday at the naval
base. I assume you've heard about it?"

The man's nervous nod said it all.

"All right, then. You'd recognize them. A very attractive
Asian woman and a man who—"

"Yeah. I know 'em. They're in room 524. The guy nearly
wrenched my arm out of its socket."

"That would be him. Room 524, got it. We'll bring in one

of our men to watch the front desk while I go up there. I
need you to wait in the back room and lock the door. Give
us at least thirty minutes. Am I clear?"

More nods, and then the man backed away from the
desk and, rubbing his wrist, disappeared into the back
room while Creighton picked up the garment bag, entered
the elevator, and pressed 5.

Lien-hua pulled the curtains shut and took the device to
the far room of the suite.

She let her mind walk slowly through all that had happened over the last couple days. Every moment became
another flower, and in her heart she placed them in a vase
and began to arrange them in a way that caught all the light
she'd ever known.

She untied the laundry bag.

This is what she'd wanted, wasn't it?

A new beginning? A chance to fall in love again?

She slid the device out. Just to see it. Just to look at it.

In Pat's arms she felt stronger and weaker than she had
in years. Was that a good thing or a bad one? Who could
tell? Feelings do that, twist and change our motives, our
dreams. She heard the door to the hotel room creak open.

A flicker of excitement and apprehension caught hold
of her. She reached for her gun just in case it wasn't who
she expected.

"Hello?" she called. "Is that you?"

97

I skidded around a corner, then punched the accelerator again.

Maybe I was wrong. Maybe it wasn't Lien-hua.

I had to be wrong. Yes. I had to be.

A good investigator doesn't look for evidence to prove his theories, but to disprove them.

And I'd never wanted to disprove myself more than I did right then.

I needed to trust the evidence.

Evidence. Yes. Not conjecture. I was doubting Lien-hua only because of circumstances, events that could be read different ways.

Trust the evidence wherever it takes you.

My thoughts spun backward, funneling hours and hours of our investigation into a few brief seconds.

I had to be wrong. I had to be.

The chains. The cameras. The angles. The videos.

Blind spots.

The evidence room.

Wait. The person who checked on the device in the evidence room was a man. Not a woman.

Not a woman. Not Margaret. Not Lien-hua.

But I needed more than that. I needed more.

You missed something, Dr. Bowers.

Yes, I did.

The handwriting on the envelope, on the wall. I'd seen Lien-hua's handwriting a hundred times, and even though handwriting analysis has never been my specialty, I could tell it wasn't hers. And the analysts already determined it wasn't Melice's, so unless there was another abductor we didn't know about . . .

Not just the handwriting, the video.

And then, everything about the case unraveled again. All the facts began to mount in a new order. My head was finally starting to clear.

The AFIS records were altered.

The thermal satellite imagery showed Hunter slip the device into the car. That's how Shade knew the police had the device.

Terry mentioned Sebastian Taylor had been sighted.

Crease after crease, my preconceptions unfolded.

Mental origami.

Dupin. Think like Dupin.

The video of Cassandra in the tank was exactly one minute and fifty-two seconds long.

Yesterday Calvin told me to stop looking at the facts and to start looking at the spaces between them. "One cannot adequately understand the movement of the planets," he'd said, "until one has identified what they all orbit around."

So what did everything orbit around?

The video.

Yes. That was the key to everything. The one-minute-and-fifty-two-second-long video of Cassandra in the tank.

And in one crystallizing moment, the final shape of the case became clear. No, Lien-hua wasn't Shade after all. I'd been wrong, I'd been wrong. Thank God I'd been wrong.

No, she wasn't Shade.

An old friend of mine was.

No reply from the other room.

Lien-hua called again, "Pat? Is that you?"

No reply.

She steadied her gun, crouched. Listened for movement. "Pat?"

No reply, except for the click of a closing door.

To get to the suite's main room she needed to walk through one more bedroom. She glided in, made sure the room was clear. Quickly checked the closet.

Empty.

Bathroom. Shower.

Nothing.

Under the bed.

Clear.

Now to the main room of the suite.

She eased around the corner and saw Creighton Melice standing placidly beside the desk.

"Down," she shouted. "On your knees!"

He was holding her vase of dying flowers. Both of his hands wrapped in bloody, shredded gauze, the untended wounds smearing blood against the glass. "Nice flowers." He set down the vase beside her notepad.

"I said get—"

But before Lien-hua could finish her sentence, the dart entered the back of her neck.

Someone else. There's someone else in the room. Shade.

Lien-hua's hand involuntarily flew up to her neck, and she tugged out the dart as she whirled around to see if she could identify the other assailant, but the ripple of the curtains told her the person had disappeared onto the veranda. By the time Lien-hua had turned back to Creighton Melice, he was on her with a vengeance, chopping his hand at the gun, sending it spinning to the ground. Then, he came at her with a stylized uppercut and back fist.

He'd studied martial arts.

But she knew the form: Choy Li Fut.

And knowing it, she could counter it. She leaned into this punch and used the force of his momentum against him, driving him backward, then twisted his wrist behind his back. He yanked free, but not until after she'd hammered his side with two brutal alternating straight punches that would've brought most men to their knees. He didn't even flinch, just pivoted backward and brought an elbow into her face. She tumbled against her vase and sent it smashing into the wall.

He feels no pain. You have to knock him out.

Moss began to grow across her field of vision.

The dart. She'd been drugged.

The whole world tipped sideways, sounds and colors came to life, time began to stretch thin and then wrap around her, and she couldn't be sure what was real anymore.

Then Melice grabbed her arm, slammed her into the wall, and yanked her backward by the hair to smash her head into the mirror hanging beside the closet, but she sensed him standing behind her just to her left side. It would be a tough kick, but she'd done it before. She kicked up, doing the splits vertically, and slammed her foot into his face. She heard the crunch of impact but no cries of pain, though his grip did loosen and she was able to twist free.

He faltered backward, and she faced him, kicked him once in the side of his left knee, and as he crumpled, she connected another kick to his head, and then she felt her legs giving way, her strength seeping.

"Don't fight it, Lien-hua," he said as he shook off the kick and readied himself to come at her again. "It's better if you just let yourself go. Only a few more seconds and you'll be like me. You won't feel anything."

Her thoughts stumbled over each other, looking for a place to stand, but found no footing. Lien-hua rushed him, gave him a front kick to his abdomen, and a roundhouse kick to the ribs, and he was down.

Still conscious, though.

And now he was getting up.

If you can get to your gun, if you can just get to your gun.

But a smothering weakness washed over her. The world around her turned in a wide, hazy circle for one lingering moment that was somehow both slower and faster than real time. Then, despite her best efforts to stay standing, she began to drift to the ground.

Melice rose to his feet, retrieving her gun and sliding it beneath his belt. "You can feel it, can't you? It's taking over everything. I'll bet you're wondering what we're going to do with you when you finally pass out."

Lien-hua's legs melted, and she collapsed onto the carpet. She blinked. Tried to focus. The paralyzing sedative was climbing over her quickly. She couldn't move. Too weak. Powerless. Melice walked to her, stood beside her. Leaned close. "Do you feel like a victim yet? If not, you will. I have quite an evening planned for you."

He stepped out of the edge of her vision, and Lien-hua tried to rise to her feet, but it was all she could do to roll her head to the side. She saw Melice bend over a chair in the corner of the room and pull something out of a garment bag.

"She's almost ready, Shade," Melice said.

Then, a shadow fell across Lien-hua as someone else approached and stood behind her.

The world was being swallowed by a hungry, sweeping numbness. But before the gray sleep could cover her, she saw Melice turn and step toward her.

A red, silk evening gown in his hands.

98

Tessa and Riker talked for a while at the bar, then danced some more, returned to the bar, then danced again. Time meant nothing in here. Only moments mattered. Shared moments.

And so, Tessa had no idea how long they'd been in the club when Riker led her up a wooden staircase located in the belly of the building. She found that she needed to use the railing to keep her balance. It'd only been a couple of drinks, but still, the world seemed to be slowly tilting to the side.

With every step, she could feel the music pulsing through the floor, but more distant now. The top of the stairs was another world.

They arrived at a hallway lined with doors, high above the throbbing club.

Now alone and no longer under the pounding spell of the music, Riker grinned. "It's quieter up here, huh? This way we can talk." For a moment she was afraid he was going to direct her into one of the rooms, but he just sat at the top of the stairs and patted the floor beside him. She joined him.

"So, if you go to school in Denver," he said, "what are you doing here in Diego, anyway?"

The music. The world. It was all slightly askew. A little off balance. "Um. Just visiting some friends at SDSU."

"Oh. Well, you should have told me. They could have come too."

Her heart was beating.

Beating.

Pulsing music rising through the air. She was alone with a guy. An older guy. A cute guy who liked her.

She let her gaze climb his chin, his cheek. Until her eyes found his. "Maybe I didn't want anyone else around."

Then she closed her eyes and kissed him deeply, and as she did, in the back of her mind, far beneath the thrill of the moment, a little girl felt the ice cracking underfoot.

I sprinted through the hotel lobby. Too many people waiting by the elevator. I flew up the stairs.

Fifth floor.

Then into the hall. Drew my gun. Room 524.

Key out, I slipped it into the lock. "Lien-hua?" Gun ready. Door open.

A broken vase on the floor and a scattering of dead flowers on the damp carpet. A Sabre 11 military issue dart beside them. "Lien-hua!"

I scoured the entire suite. Empty.

They had her and they had the device.

No!

I grabbed the room phone.

Earlier in the day when I was in the evidence room, I hadn't thought to stick some kind of tracking device in the bag with my contraption. But now, I called Angela Knight to have her track the GPS for my cell phone, which I'd left in the laundry bag.

Let it never be said I don't learn from my mistakes.

She told me it would only take a few minutes, and then put me on hold before I could tell her I didn't have a few minutes.

As I waited I had a disturbing thought. I remembered the video Melice had made of Cassandra. *What if he made one of Lien-hua?* I flipped open my computer to see if Shade or Melice had e-mailed me anything. I found nothing except a message from Calvin:

Couldn't reach you on your mobile, my boy, but you mentioned that radioactive isotopes had been found at the arsonist's apartment. I've been wondering if perhaps the fires were never intended to cover up a crime at all, but maybe the smoke was. Ring me.
—Calvin

The smoke?

I thought about the device, the fires, their locations. Why there? Why then?

What about this: Drake's men would test the device, emitting trace amounts of cesium-137. And after they'd left, Hunter would arrive. *That's why he didn't know about the tests*... But since Drake's men had used the device, when Hunter arrived at the arson sites he would be exposed temporarily to the cesium-137, and that's why MAST found the traces of it at his apartment...

The smoke.

Yes, of course.

The smoke would disperse the radiation so MAST wouldn't be able to identify the tests during their radiation sweeps of the city.

Yes. I could finally see it. The fires weren't meant to distract, the smoke was meant to disperse. It made sense. It fit, but in that moment I didn't care.

All I cared about was Lien-hua.

And Angela was taking too long, way too long to help me.

Lien-hua shook her head. Everything was bleary, dim. The world lay shrouded in a misty dream. Her hotel room. She remembered that. Melice. The dart. And now, she was lying on her side, that much she could tell.

But she wasn't on a bed. No. Something else. Something stiff and cold.

She took a quick inventory of her body, moving her limbs slightly. Nothing seemed broken. She wasn't tied up. That was good. But where was she?

She shook her head again, tried to clear her thoughts. Opened one heavy eyelid. Bleary. Bleary.

Blinked twice.

No, not a bed. She wasn't on a bed; it was concrete.

She slid one tired hand along her leg but didn't feel the fabric of her jeans. Instead she felt the silky grace of the evening gown.

Both eyes open.

She saw what she was wearing. Elegant and red.

Lien-hua's head still pounded. Dizzy. So dizzy.

She eased her hands forward, and as she began to sit up

she felt a cold ring encircle her left ankle and then heard
the sound of a lock snapping shut.

As I waited for word on my cell's location, I noticed Lien-
hua's notepad on the desk, a bookmark toward the end.
I flipped it open and saw that she'd drawn a flower being
snipped from its stem.

Below it she'd written "June 17, 1999."

The date meant nothing to me, and before I could wonder about it any longer, I heard Angela's urgent voice on
the other end of the phone. "We've got it, Pat. Your cell's at
the Sherrod Aquarium."

I was all the way to the door by the time I heard the
phone's receiver hit the desk.

Lien-hua twisted around and saw Creighton Melice kneeling beside her bare feet. And in one terrible instant she
realized where she was—the empty shark acclimation pool
at the Sherrod Aquarium, her ankle now shackled securely
to the drain. The dizziness was fading. Her head began to
clear. She pushed herself to her feet.

Melice stood up and smiled. "Drowning will be a terrible way to go, don't you think, Agent Jiang?"

Though Lien-hua was still somewhat disoriented, her instincts took over, and with years of honed quickness, she leapt
toward him, using the chain to add a few inches to her leg's
reach. In the air, she angled her right foot at his jaw, reached
full extension, and connected, hard, sending him smacking
into the glass wall of the pool as the angry chain snapped her
back to the ground. Her ankle cried out in pain, but she was
on her feet again in seconds. Arms locked, ready to fight. Melice stood and shook his head. His legs were wobbly. It hadn't
been one of her best kicks, but it wasn't her worst either.

She lowered herself into a ready stance. "Come here,
Creighton Melice, and I'll make you wish you could fight
like a girl."

As Tessa kissed Riker, she felt a warm tingle rising within
her, swallowing any uncertainty she might have had about
the direction her choices were taking her tonight.

Below her, in another world, the music pounded, thumping like a distant heart.

Exciting. So exciting.

Over the course of the last few minutes, half a dozen couples had stepped past them either on their way to, or from, one of the rooms in the hall.

Finally, Riker pulled away from Tessa's lips just far enough to speak to her. He held her close, so close. "It looks like we're a little in the way here by the stairs." His words held both a promise and an invitation. "No privacy. C'mon. Let's grab a room."

Exciting.

So exciting.

The sweetness of his kisses overcame her flicker of hesitation, and she stood, took his hand, and followed him to a room at the far end of the hall.

99

Lien-hua's thoughts were still foggy, but she stood her ground, waited to see if Melice would fight her. "Are you that scared of me, Creighton? Scared of a chained-up girl? Maybe now I won't beat you as badly as I did at the hotel, but I doubt it. You're not nearly as good as you think."

Out of the corner of her eye, she saw a tripod on the edge of the deck above her. For a moment she thought it might be the device, but then she saw that it was a video camcorder.

Oh, not good. Definitely not good.

"I don't want to fight you," Melice said. "I want to watch you. See how you do compared to the others. And tonight the whole world will be watching. Lots of people out there with my taste in entertainment. An FBI agent? At the world's largest aquarium? We'll get at least eighty thousand hits by tomorrow. Maybe a hundred."

Lien-hua yanked her foot against the chain.

"That's good. Keep that up. The more you tug the better the video will be." He began to climb the ladder that led out of the pool, leaving bloody prints from his wounded hands on each rung. "You broke my tank at the warehouse, but this should work just as good, don't you think? Sorry to say, it won't be a live feed, though. I don't want us to be interrupted by any cops." When he reached the deck he gazed around the animal husbandry area. "Kind of ironic, huh? That we're back here where everything started yesterday morning."

Dread dripped into Lien-hua's stomach. *Be brave. You need to be brave.* "Where's Shade? Still too afraid to show his face?" she asked.

"Shade is taking care of a few loose ends."

She worried that Melice might be referring to Pat, but she didn't want to appear weak or scared so she didn't let her concern reach her face. Melice glanced at his watch and then continued. "Be here in thirty minutes. I'm sorry you two won't have the chance to meet. The filming will be done by then."

Then she had it. She realized Melice's primary motive. "Pain. Shade's going to kill you with the device. Make you feel pain."

"Oh yes." He looked to the side, across the deck. "It's already set up and waiting for me." Then, he let his eyes roam back toward the acclimation pool and walk across Lien-hua's body. "You look good in that dress, by the way. I'm sure your viewers will appreciate that you've kept yourself in shape."

Lien-hua looked around, tried to think of some way to escape, but saw no viable options.

Not drowning. Please, no. Anything but drowning.

Melice positioned the camera. "Now, you may need to work with me a little here. I'm not sure how quick that pool is gonna fill. I'll probably have to shoot this a couple times, let some water out, and then refill the pool again, before I can get all the footage I need. So, do your best to hold your breath and you might last two or three takes."

And then, Creighton Melice stepped out of sight and turned on a valve somewhere, and the thirteen-foot-deep shark acclimation pool began to fill with water.

100

I came screaming to a stop at the aquarium's little-used exit door near the two rusted Dumpsters, leapt out of the car, and found the door locked. I might have been able to pick it but I didn't want to waste the time. I shot out the lock, then slipped into the building.

Melice's face appeared beside the video camera. "You're starting to feel it, aren't you, Lien-hua? What we talked about in the interrogation room? The door to hope beginning to close. You'll yank at that grate until your ankle is chafed and raw, you'll try to unhinge the clasp, maybe try to pick the lock somehow. But all the while the water will be rising and then, finally—reality check—you're not gonna get away. You're going to die right there, tonight, while I watch."

Water to her knees. The pool was filling faster than she'd thought it would.

Melice continued. "Don't be upset. Just remind yourself that over the next few months you'll be providing entertainment to hundreds of thousands of eager viewers." Then he added, "Who knows, you might even make it to a million downloads by summer."

Tessa sized up the room. Wooden floor. Plaster walls. A queen-sized bed pushed into the corner, strewn with a tangle of filthy, rumpled sheets. There on the far wall, faded blue curtains in front of a narrow, airless window. The place smelled like the back room of a bar, and the only stirring of air came from a small oscillating fan beside the bathroom door.

No overhead light. Just a small lamp beside the bed. Riker walked over and snapped it off, so that now the only light in the room came from the murky yellow haze climbing through the window and resting expectantly on the bedsheets.

Then Riker came to her, took her hand, and, speaking soft and comforting words, led Tessa toward the bed.

I hurried through the dizzying maze of filtration tanks. I didn't know if Lien-hua was dead already; I could only pray she was still alive. When we arrested him, Melice had said that she would be his next girlfriend, and I knew all too well what he did to them.

That's why I was heading for the shark acclimation pool. It seemed like the logical place for him to bring her. And I was close. Just a few more turns and I'd be there.

Tessa's heart trembled with exhilaration and fear. The fan's twitching air brushed across the curtains, they rippled faintly, and Tessa thought that in the dim light, the bluish curtains appeared purple. And with that thought, Poe whispered to her, his words riding through the centuries, rising from the grave, *"And the silken sad uncertain rustling of each purple curtain thrilled me—filled me with fantastic terrors never felt before."*

Fantastic terrors.

Never felt before.

Tessa had never hooked up with a guy. Not like this. It was something her mom had been really intense about, and ever since she died, despite two close calls, Tessa had honored that wish. No. It wasn't supposed to happen like this.

Terrors never felt before.

"So, I was thinking . . ." Riker said.

"No." She pulled away from him but stumbled a little. Off balance. Everything was off balance. "No. I need to go."

"We just got here."

She backed away. "I need to go. I have to leave."

Riker came toward her and grabbed her forearm. "Whoa, whoa, whoa, Raven. Not so fast." His grip was tighter than it needed to be.

"I said no. Now, let go of my arm."

No, this can't be happening.

He held her.

"Let go!"

He let go slowly but stood with arms flexed ready to grab her again. "I've been thinking it's time we made a little trade."

Terrors never felt before.

"What kind of trade?" She reached for a rubber band on her wrist. Found none.

He let a smile wander across his face, but it wasn't really a smile. "You don't really believe I'd let you have a tattoo like that, five hours of work, for $180. Lachlan's the best around. You're wearing over $700 worth of ink and time."

Though faint, the music was pounding behind his words. A dark heartbeat. "You told him to give it to me." Tessa was edging toward the door. "To give me whatever I wanted."

"That's right. I did. I gave you what you wanted, and now it's time for you to give me what I want. And the way I figure it, I've got at least a couple hours coming to me."

Her stomach filled with ice. She rushed for the door but was too slow. Riker beat her to it and nailed it shut with one strong arm. She began to back away from him slowly, toward the window.

It was the only thing she could think to do.

To jump.

Jump.

101

I stepped past the wet suits hanging behind the staircase and saw Lien-hua chained to the bottom of the shark acclimation pool, water to the middle of her thighs. When she saw me I pressed a finger to my lips to signal for her to keep my arrival a secret, and then with the other hand I finger-spelled, "How many?"

With her hand hidden behind her leg she finger-spelled back to me, "One, maybe two."

I could hear Creighton Melice's voice. "Do you miss your sister, Lien-hua?"

Sister?

"What did you just say?" she called to Melice, her voice cold, unyielding.

"Weapons?" I asked her with my fingers.

"Gun. Darts. Device," she signed to me while she stared at him.

"Your sister. Chu-hua. Do you miss her? I miss Mira-belle. It must be different for you, though. I hear identical twins share a special connection."

Lien-hua never mentioned a twin sister.

"When one twin feels pain," Melice said, "sometimes the other one does too. That's what they say. When one dies, the other feels like half of her life is gone. Is it true? I've heard it is. I've always wondered." I began to creep up the steps.

Eliminate the greater threat first.

Melice or Shade?

"So, Agent Lien-hua Jiang," Melice went on. "How does it feel to know that you're about to die the same way she did?"

* * *

The moment Creighton Melice mentioned Chu-hua's name, it all came back. The memories, the regret, the terrible images burned in Lien-hua's mind, they all came howling at her from her past, found the moment, and blistered apart inside of her.

Chu-hua facedown in the pool ... Maybe she was still alive ... She might have been ... Maybe Lien-hua could have saved her if only she'd tried. If only she'd known how to swim. If only she hadn't been afraid of the water.

Lien-hua slid her fingertips between the metal bars of the grate and yanked until the metal began to groove through her skin, but the grate didn't budge.

"You never believed it was an accident, did you?" Melice went on. "That's what the cops told you, but you wouldn't believe it."

He was right, and she hated that he was right. It's why she'd become a detective, then a profiler, to give others what she'd been denied—the truth.

Pat, you need to hurry.

"It's too bad we don't have time for me to show you the footage," Melice said. "She was my first home movie. My first real girlfriend."

Creighton smiled. Yes. Shade, his friend, his fan, really had been following his career, really had found the blog entries.

Really had chosen him for a reason.

It was all so perfect.

A complete circle.

"I hadn't thought of the chain back then," he called to Lien-hua. "It's a lot better this way, though, don't you think?"

The next few events happened in only a matter of seconds.

Tessa backed up all the way to the window. Tried opening it.

Locked.

Riker just watched her. Then he came at her, fast, grasped both of her shoulders, and shoved her against the wall.

"No, no, no." Tessa felt queasy, tired. Why did she have to have those drinks? It was hard to focus, to know what to do. She tried to kick her knee into his crotch, but he must have been expecting it because he turned his leg to the side, and all she caught was his thigh.

Riker slid his hand from her shoulders to her upper arms and squeezed his right hand into her tender tattoo. A flare of pain sent bursts of sharp light sprinkling across her eyes. She wanted to cry out, needed to cry out, but refused to make a sound. Refused to give him the satisfaction of making her cry. He squeezed harder, and a tear eased from the edge of her eye, but Tessa didn't let herself cringe.

"I was hoping to do this the easy way." His voice was low and filled with malice. "But we don't have to. It's your choice."

Think fast, think fast, think fast. "I need to get ready."

"You look ready to me."

Stall, Tessa. Stall. "No. I'm serious. I just need a minute in the bathroom, OK?"

"No, you don't."

"Shut up. I do. It's girl stuff. Let go."

She wasn't sure he would do it, but at last he slowly released his grip.

Thank goodness. The screaming pain in her arm began to quiet itself.

"All right. Five minutes. Get yourself ready. But if you don't come out in five, I'm coming in. And I won't be so gentle then."

Tessa snatched up her canvas satchel, pushed past him, and slammed the bathroom door shut behind her.

Here she could be safe.

Here she would be safe.

She reached to lock the door but found that the doorknob had no lock. She spun around. No window. No other door. No way out.

And then a chill, raw and deep.

"They know me here," Riker had told her just after they entered the club. *"I come here a lot."*

"Oh, no, please God, no," she whispered, and as she said the words they became a terrified prayer. "I'm not the first one."

Now at the top of the stairs.

Go for the greater threat. Look for a gun.

With one smooth motion I stepped forward onto the deck and swung my gun at Melice. "Hands to the side where I can see them, get on your knees." I didn't see a gun in his hands, but eight meters away I did see the world's most perfect assassination weapon device, aimed right at my head. The removable cesium-137 pack was in my car, but I wasn't sure; the device might still work.

There's one person, maybe two.

Eliminate the greater threat first.

I put three bullets into it, shattering the device and sending it tottering back into one of the quarantine tanks, where a steamy sizzle of water told me it hadn't been designed to be waterproof.

"No!" Melice roared. I leveled my gun at him, but I could see I was too late. He'd drawn on me and now fired, a bullet ripped into my left thigh, and the impact sent me sprawling back down the stairs, tumbling, spinning, reeling, crashing to the bottom.

"Raven, I'm waiting," Riker yelled. Fire had crept into his voice. "Three minutes."

Tessa needed to come up with a plan.

But she had absolutely no idea how to get away.

I stared at the ceiling, trying to gather my wits and mentally separate myself from the pain coursing up my leg.

I'd been shot, the water was up to Lien-hua's waist. I needed to save her and I needed to do it fast.

I inspected the gunshot wound. The bullet had entered the front and exited the lateral side of my quadriceps. Missed the bone. Missed the femoral artery. I've never believed in luck, but at that moment I was tempted to start. I might be able to walk, but it would be dicey and very painful. I pressed one hand on the entrance wound, the other on the exit wound. *You need to find a way to control that bleeding.*

"No," Melice was raging from the deck. I imagined him fondling the shattered device. "No. No. No!"

Good. So he could feel pain after all—the pain of having all of his hope snatched away. I wondered if experiencing pain was all Melice had dreamed it would be, but by his furious cries it sounded like the pain of slaughtered hope wasn't exactly a dream come true.

It was never pain he wanted, but freedom from a painless hell.

"You're dead, Bowers!"

My gun. Where was my gun? I'd dropped it. Yes. But where? *You dropped it when you jerked backward. When you hit the side of the stairwell.*

It might be on the deck. I hoped not. I scooted around the corner from the stairs in case Melice or Shade decided to come down to finish me off. I scanned the area for my SIG.

Nothing.

Then I looked through the glass at Lien-hua and saw her tugging at the grate, and I realized my gun was lying at the bottom of the acclimation pool. A SIG will fire even when underwater, but it was too far away. She couldn't reach it.

"Hey, Bowers." A razor blade cut through Melice's words. "I'm coming for you and I'm gonna kill you slowly, but first I want you to watch her die. That's your reward."

Weapon. I needed a weapon.

If only I'd called for backup before I left the hotel!

Assess the situation: I had no phone, no gun, the water would be over Lien-hua's head in a matter of minutes, and I'd been shot. Before I could do anything I needed to control the bleeding.

I scanned the area and saw the wet suits hanging behind the stairwell.

Neoprene is waterproof, it'll seal off the wounds.

If there was a weight belt with the wet suits, I might have a chance.

As quickly as I could, using one hand I dragged myself around the stairs. With every movement deep jolts of pain flashed through my leg. But I kept moving. I had to.

After flipping four wetsuits aside, I finally found a neoprene weight belt hanging on a hook. I dumped the weights from it and cinched it around my thigh, not tight enough to be a tourniquet but snug enough to act as a pressure bandage. The bleeding eased. I could think again.

I clicked through my options in my mind. None of them was good. *Melice has the strategic position. Even if you make it up the stairs, he'll shoot you on the spot. If you try to get to the car to go for help, it'll take too long, Lien-hua will drown.*

From the other side of the glass, Lien-hua finger-spelled "Hurry," then flashed the sign for "I need you."

"I'm coming," I signed.

I pulled myself to my feet, and, with my leg rebelling against every step, I shuffled through the doorway to the foam fractionator tower that rose past the offices on the deck above me.

Access. There was access to the husbandry area.

Then I grabbed the ridged edge of the tower, and with my left leg hanging as dead weight, I began to climb.

"Two minutes," yelled Riker.

Tessa scanned the bathroom. Toilet paper. Toilet. A single lightbulb in the center of the room. No mirror—why wasn't there a mirror? There should have been a mirror! Paper towel dispenser. Toilet plunger. Bath towel draped over a towel rack. She looked under the sink for some kind of cleaning chemicals that she could splash in his face. Nothing.

The ceramic lid of the toilet?

She checked again—a floor-mounted model, no lid.

Wait. Towel rack.

Yes, maybe.

She threw off the towel, grabbed the bar of the rack. Wrenched at it.

But it held fast. It must have been anchored into the studs.

C'mon. C'mon. There must be something. There has to be.

She could maybe hit him with the plunger, but she wasn't really strong enough to hurt him, so that'd just make him madder.

Tessa emptied her purse into the sink. She had to have something in here that she could use as a weapon. She had to!

So: a stubby pencil, her notebook, a stick of gum, a flash drive, the big bottle of antibacterial soap from Riker, her iPod, some lipstick and mascara, her wallet, some loose change, a small bottle of the lotion she'd been smearing on her scar, a pocket-sized dictionary.

She heard movement from the other room. Maybe he was coming for her.

"I'm not hearing you getting ready."

Tessa reached over and flushed the toilet. "Just a minute, already!" She tried to make her voice sound confident.

This can't be happening. It can't be.

But it was.

I climbed with fire in my fingers and hatred in my heart. I could feel the tangle of rage and fear, the constant struggle. The dark currents welling up, calling my name.

Anything to save Lien-hua. Anything.

Vowing to save her whatever it took, I climbed.

102

Lien-hua kicked with all her might but only managed to gouge the shackle into her Achilles tendon and send a searing clutch of pain rocketing up her leg. The grate didn't budge, the chain didn't break. It wasn't going to break. There was no way it would.

You're going to die. Right here. Right now. At the hands of the same man who killed Chu-hua.

Hope fleeting.

Fleeting.

Maybe she didn't want to live. Maybe it was better if she died.

Freedom or pain?

Pain.

Death.

The two flowers. Lien-hua, the lotus. Chu-hua, the chrysanthemum. Both snipped from the stem by the same man.

Yesterday Lien-hua had told Tessa that she'd seen too much corruption to believe in purity, in enlightenment. And it was true.

We can't rise above who we are.

"I'm sorry I couldn't save you," she whispered to the ghostly memory of her sister as the water rose above her chest. "I was afraid, afraid of the water."

Bruised petals.

The arrangement will never be the same.

No, we can't rise above ourselves.

But what had Tessa asked her? What had she said?

Can someone else lift us?

In that moment the question brought its own answer

and from deep inside her bruised heart, Lien-hua prayed, cried out to the God she wasn't sure was there. Begged him to lift her from her past, from herself, from the stinging regrets she'd been carrying since June 17, 1999, when she found her twin sister floating facedown in the family's swimming pool.

"All right. That's it," yelled Riker. "I want to play with my raven now." And then he dared to quote Poe, " 'Only this, and nothing more.' "

"I'm coming. Just a minute!"

Soap. Plunger. Towel.

Yes, yes. It was the only thing Tessa could think of. She grabbed the plunger and turned on the faucet.

I made it halfway up the tower, saw Melice four meters below me. I gauged how far out I'd need to jump and, relying on my good leg, turned on the tiny lip of a ledge so that I was facing him.

And leapt.

Creighton Melice felt the impact, the pressure of a sudden weight crush him to the ground.

As he connected with the deck, he knew it was Bowers. Somehow it was Bowers. The force knocked Creighton's gun away, and it went sliding across the deck and landed out of reach in one of the recessed view ports to the Seven Deadly Seas exhibit.

Creighton rolled free.

He rolled free. He was quick. He ran for the food prep area, and I rose awkwardly, painfully to my feet. My left leg throbbed with nearly unbearable pain, and the floor was slick, making it even harder to stand. With the gunshot wound, I wouldn't be able to chase him down. I glanced toward the shark acclimation pool. The water was up to Lien-hua's chin.

Air. I needed to get her air.

The scuba tanks were by the wall.

I started toward them as Melice stepped out of the food prep area wielding one of the long, slender skinning knives.

I would need to get past him to save Lien-hua's life.

                    *   *   *

Lien-hua took a long sip of air. It would only be a matter
of seconds now.

Seconds before she joined her sister.

She stretched for the surface one more time.

But found it out of reach.

Tessa finished getting ready, jammed the soaking wet towel
into her satchel, and swung it at the lightbulb. Shattered
it. Then she backed into the corner. Riker threw the door
open and blocked the doorway. "This stalling is gonna cost
you," he said. She didn't reply. She saw him step forward
and reach for his belt buckle. "It's time to come back to the
nest, my little Raven."

Quoth the raven, "Nevermore."

"I'm ready," she said. "Come and get me."

103

"Oh, I'm gonna enjoy this," said Melice, raising the knife, both of his hands dripping blood from their gruesome wounds.

The water was rising fast. Fast. "Where's the release valve for the pool, Creighton?" My leg was growing numb. It was tough just to stand. "Help me get her out of there."

A man has a knife; a woman is dying.

Basque. Melice.

Melice. Basque.

"I'm afraid I already smashed the valve." Melice motioned toward the food prep area. "Turned it up all the way first, though." He leered at the shark acclimation pool. "Oh, this is the best part, right here, when the water rises above her head. I always rewind it and watch it over and over." Then he grinned at me. "So, Bowers, what's it gonna be? Stop the bad guy or save the damsel in distress?"

You have to get past him to get to the air tanks.

"Both," I said, and I rushed toward him as fast as my shrieking leg would take me.

Riker stepped into the darkened bathroom and for a moment Tessa wondered if he'd be able to see what she'd done. But then he took one more step and she heard a startled cry as his face collided with the plunger she'd suctioned to the wall, and then she heard the welcome crash as he lost his balance on the water and liquid soap she'd spread across the floor.

As Riker tried to stand, she swung the satchel, weighted with the saturated towel, down hard against his head,

smacking his face onto the tiling. Then she planted one foot
on his back, leapt over his legs, and ran for the door.

I dodged a swipe of the knife and crashed into Melice, driving him toward the wall, but he grabbed my arm and threw
me to the ground. He was amazingly strong and, with the
wet, slick floor, he was able to sling me into the middle of
the husbandry area. I hobbled to my feet and gasped, "The
tank was already constructed when you got to San Diego,
wasn't it?"

A brief hesitation. "How did you know?"

*Hold your breath, Lien-hua. Hold your breath. I'm
coming.*

"And Shade was there, right? At police headquarters?
He had your lawyers tell you about the device."

"None of that matters now." He came at me with the
knife. Came at me fast.

I tried to fight him off, but with my injured leg, I lost
my balance. He kicked his steel-toed boot hard against the
gunshot wound. The pain was crippling. I tried to stand, he
kicked me again, this time in the stomach. As I struggled
to get to my hands and knees, he pressed his foot against
my side, rolled me to my back. Kicked my wounded thigh
again.

As I started to fade, dizzy from the pain, he grabbed my
wrist and dragged me toward the acclimation pool. "Well,
looky here. I guess you were too late to save her."

I rolled my head to the side and saw Lien-hua's beautiful dying eyes staring up at me from below the water's
surface.

*Without oxygen she has maybe four minutes, max, before
brain damage. That's all. You have to get her some air.*

I tried to pull free from Melice so I could go for the gun
in the pool, but his grip was solid. He took a slow look at his
knife and then at the door that led to the path around the
Seven Deadly Seas exhibit.

Then he yanked me away from the pool and dragged me
toward the Seven Deadly Seas. "I think, Agent Bowers, that
it's feeding time."

To Lien-hua, air was a memory. No matter how hard she
tried, she couldn't reach the surface.

She knew she'd just taken her last breath. Her last one ever.

Stay calm. Stay calm. You'll use less air.

But it was hard to stay calm, so hard. A burst of air escaped her mouth and bubbled toward the continually rising surface of the water.

Tessa decided not to waste any time trying the other doors in the hallway. She didn't need to hide. She needed to get out of this club.

Down the stairs, then to the bar.

But when she yelled for help, her words were met only with disinterested looks and the grinding rhythm of the music. Out of the corner of her eye, she saw Riker crashing down the stairs behind her. She squeezed forward into the melee of people and moved as quickly as she could toward an exit door.

I tried to roll free, but once again, Melice paused, kicked my wounded leg, and then he hauled me through the doorway that led to the path around the Seven Deadly Seas. I felt the sheathed Maglite that hung on my belt digging into my back.

He held my left wrist, but I had my right hand free. Twice I tried to grab him but failed.

I had to get away. Now. A few more seconds and it would be too late.

Wait. My Maglite. My belt.

Get him to the ground. You have to get him to the ground.

As he dragged me, his back was turned so I was able to unclasp my belt buckle and pull my belt free from my jeans without him noticing. I curled it into a loop, and as he stopped near the edge of the water, I rotated to my side, threw the loop up to my other hand, and grabbed hold of it.

Yanked.

Hard.

Since he was holding that wrist, the force pulled him off balance and he toppled onto the path beside me. I rolled, pulled myself toward him, and punched him hard in the face.

But he still had the knife in his right hand.

I snagged his wrist and was pinning it to the ground when he wrestled his other arm free, threw it across his body, and drove his palm down the knife's blade all the way to the hilt. Then he squeezed his hand tight to lock the blade in place, released his right hand's grip on the handle, and with the knife sticking through his spurting hand, swung the blade toward my face. I pushed back and he barely missed severing my neck.

"You can't hurt me, Agent Bowers," he hissed. "You can only kill me or die trying."

As he swung the knife at me again, I twisted to the side, flipped the belt around the blade and the handle, cinched it tight. Now I had control of his arm and the knife.

"Have it your way," I said.

Shock swept across his face. I clenched the belt and rolled toward the water, pulling him with me. At the ledge, I let go of the belt and let the momentum launch him into the Seven Deadly Seas.

Melice tried to pull himself out of the water, but the blood from his hands had caught the attention of half a dozen hammerheads. The largest shark curled toward him, rolled its eyes back, and before I could even consider trying to drag Melice onto the deck to cuff him, the shark used its ampullae of Lorenzini to locate its prey and then sank its ragged teeth into Melice's abdomen and dragged him under the water.

A burst of air and frothy blood came churning to the surface. Then the shark bolted, taking Melice deep into the Seven Deadly Seas tank, where a frenzy of other sharks were waiting to be fed.

I turned away so I wouldn't have to watch.

Creighton Melice finally got his wish. He was no longer trapped in a painless hell.

Lien-hua. You have to save Lien-hua.

I stood and then lurched toward the husbandry area. The acclimation pool lay ten meters away and was nearly filled by now. There was no time to go looking for the release valve, and I knew the air tanks were too far away for me to get to them in time.

I would need to get air to her myself.

104

With the number of people in the club, Tessa couldn't get to an exit door, so she headed for the wall and the next best thing.

A fire alarm.

The water was calmer now, as Lien-hua tried to relax and use less precious oxygen. Blood seeped out of the circular cut around the bottom of the shackle and drifted lazily up toward her face. Her body swayed in the water.

Without air, she knew what was going to happen next. In a few moments her heart would stop beating and her blood would stop flowing and her awareness would flicker and fade and then within three or four minutes, her brain would join the rest of her body in death.

She knew these things, realized them in one tightly packed moment.

She gazed up through the water.

The surface was out of reach.

Forever out of reach.

As the last dribbles of air ascended from Lien-hua's mouth, her lips formed one final word. The only word that mattered to her anymore.

Pat.

Then, in the final drifting darkness, she saw someone dive into the water and Lien-hua Jiang realized she could still move her fingers, so she did.

I swam to her. Desperately. Frantically.

She'd stopped struggling against the chain. With my

hand on her shoulder, I pulled myself to her face and saw her blink. *Yes, she's conscious.* I pressed my lips against hers and gave her all my air; then I swam to the surface for more.

Having gotten her some oxygen, I'd bought her some time.

Good, good.

Back to her. I passed her more air. Then up to the surface again. I was swimming too slowly, though, with my leg dragging me down.

You can do this. You can save her.

I gave her my air once again, my lungs burning. But I wasn't getting her enough oxygen. I knew I wasn't. Not quickly enough.

Then to the surface.

On my fourth trip down, I saw she was moving her fingers. Sign language. Three letters. Signing, what was she signing? She was weak, the letters indistinct.

I gave her air, then reached for her hand, felt her fingers, closed my eyes. Floated beside her. Remembered. Remembered.

D . . . A . . . E . . . D . . . Was she mixed up? Was she signing "dead"? Why would she sign "dead"? . . . D . . . A . . . and then her fingers stopped moving. Her mouth drifted open, a final bubble of air escaped, and though I shook her and shook her, she didn't respond. *Unconscious. Unresponsive.*

No more time. I had to get her out of the water and I had to do it now.

I swam to the surface, gulped more air, then swam down and tried to pull the chain free, but I couldn't do it. There wasn't time to pick the lock.

Wait. The gun.

With my air almost gone, I grabbed the SIG off the bottom of the pool, took aim at the chain and fired—a deafening noise—but underwater the velocity wasn't enough to break the link. I emptied the magazine, but the chain was too thick.

My ears ringing, I dropped the useless SIG, then tugged at the grate until I was completely out of air. But it did no good. The chain held.

I kicked to the surface, and as my head broke through

the water I saw the track high above the pool and the cable hanging from it.

And I knew at last how I could get Lien-hua free. I just didn't know if I could do it fast enough.

Tessa had made it to the fire alarm, but not to a door.

At first no one in the club seemed to notice the blare of the alarm or the strobing emergency lights. Maybe they thought it was part of the show. Then she saw Riker pushing his way through the crowd. His eyes found her. She tried to cut through the mass of people to a door. Couldn't make it.

Suddenly the room lights came on, and people were yelling and shoving toward the doors, pulled by the unstoppable force of panic. But there weren't enough doors. Tessa stayed pressed flat against the wall, and the wave of people tugged Riker away from her. But now she wasn't thinking so much about him but instead about how if anyone got trampled in the mad herd of people it would be her fault.

Now out of the water, I smashed my hand against the release button for the cable, grabbed the metal hook attached to the end, yanked on it to make sure the cable was loose, and dove into the pool. If this cable could lift a thousand-pound shark, it could pull up a metal drain.

Lien-hua's limp and unconscious body floated beside me, her face pale. Her eyes open. Sightless. Unblinking.

Two minutes. Maybe two minutes left.

I attached the cable's hook to the lowest link in the chain, pushed off the bottom, swam to the surface. I scrambled out of the water and over to the hydraulic control board. Pulled down on the lever and heard the motor engage.

The gunshot wound in my leg roared with pain, but I ignored it.

Come on. Come on.

As the motor began to whir and the cable started wrapping around the carriage drum, I grabbed the phone on the wall, called 911, and told dispatch there'd been a drowning at the Sherrod Aquarium—but that was all I had time to say because then the cable tightened and I heard a muffled crack as it pulled the entire drain loose from the bottom of the pool.

I stopped the crank, jumped into the water, unhooked

the cable, and, cradling Lien-hua's body, I swam to the
pool's side as best I could with my useless leg. I knew there
was a backboard hanging on the wall, but I didn't think I
could have used it by myself, so I decided to try and lift her
on my own.

But with the weight of the drain that was still chained to
her ankle, it was all I could do to hold on to the edge of the
pool while supporting her limp body. Even though I was
furiously kicking and lifting, I failed twice to slide her body
over the lip of the pool and onto the deck. Finally, with one
more desperate try, I succeeded.

Clambering out of the water, I knelt beside her and saw
her face, blank and cold, the color of death already falling
across her lips.

No, no, no.

I shook her, yelled her name, shook her some more,
yelled for her to wake up, to be OK, but she was unresponsive. Her head lolled to the side. Her bluish tongue visible,
her face ashen from lack of oxygen. I shook her again, still
unresponsive.

This isn't happening. It can't be happening.

The CPR training I'd received as a raft guide and later
reviewed as a federal agent took over, and I tilted her head
back and lifted her chin to open her airway. I felt for her
breath on my cheek, watched her chest to see if it would
rise. *No breath.* I gave her two breaths, two good strong
breaths, then felt for a pulse.

Airway breathing, circulation.

No pulse.

No breathing, no pulse, it's over.

No, it can't be. It's not—it's not.

*We live short, difficult, brutal lives and then die before
our dreams come true.*

No, not now. Please, not Lien-hua.

So much I needed to say to her. So much life I wanted to
live with her. So much.

I needed to keep oxygen circulating through her body. I
heard a voice in my head, *Begin five chest compressions.* I
interlocked my hands, pressed down against her sternum.
Count them off: One.

I leaned forward. Felt her chest sink beneath my hands.
Two.

She'd tried to tell me something, to communicate with me. Signed "D...A...E..." but I didn't understand. What was she trying to tell me? D...A...E...D...

Three.

I scrambled the letters in my mind. Unscrambled them. Rearranged them: ADE—*aid her?* ... EDDE—*an eddy in the water?* ... DEAD...ADD...AED...

Four.

Oh...AED.

Five.

AED: Automated external defibrillator.

Lien-hua knew she was about to die. She was telling me to bring her back. The only way to bring her back.

The defibrillator hung on the wall beside the backboard. I limped over, yanked it down, pulled out the defib pads, and crouched beside her. The dress Melice had put on Lien-hua had only thin straps, so I slid one to the side, placed a pad over her heart, and put the other pad on the left lateral side of her chest beneath her armpit, so the current would go through her body and be more effective. All the while, inside of me, I was screeching out a prayer, awkward and raw, a one-word prayer. *Please. Please.*

Tessa's words from yesterday about readers liking pain and the characters not always surviving at the end of the story haunted me. *"It doesn't always happen, you know,"* she'd said. And she was right.

Please.

The defibrillator is automatic—it's supposed to check for a pulse, then give the shock—but I knew we couldn't wait. I pressed the alternate button to deliver the shock manually. The defibrillator buzzed, Lien-hua's body arched, lurched. Dropped.

Again I checked her airway, her breathing, felt for a pulse.

Still no breath. Still no pulse. Glassy eyes. Open. Staring at me. A fixed blank stare.

No, no, no, no.

Four minutes. Brain damage after four minutes without oxygen. Irreversible.

I gave her two more breaths.

Checked for a pulse.

None. I needed to circulate the blood.

Beginning compressions. *One.*

This time as I depressed her sternum I felt a snap and knew I'd broken one of her ribs, maybe more than one. But I had to keep going.

Two.

I heard the broken bone grind and pop as I pressed down again. You almost always break someone's rib when you give CPR, but you have to do the compressions that hard. You have to go that deep.

Three.

I tried to ignore the awful grating sound as I pressed down. But she could live with a broken rib. She couldn't live without oxygen.

Four.

Crack.

Another rib. But I knew she'd forgive me, knew she'd understand. If only she survived.

Five.

I saw that the defibrillator had recharged. I pressed the button. Another shock. Her limp body jerked. I listened for breath again.

Nothing, no air. Still no breathing.

It had to have been four minutes by now . . . It had to have been . . .

I gave her two more breaths, her lips cold and claylike against mine. The water had been cool, maybe it had slowed her metabolism, maybe it would give her more time.

I felt for her pulse.

No, the water wasn't that cold. It wasn't cold enough. "Come on, come on," I whispered. She'd been under too long. *Please, please, don't die. Why did I ever doubt you, Lien-hua? I can't believe I ever thought you were Shade. I'm sorry. So sorry.*

Then. Wait. There. Faint. A pulse. Thready. Weak. A pulse.

Yes, oh yes.

Unconscious. Barely alive.

But alive.

Alive.

I gave her two more breaths, and her body quivered, her head jerked backward, and she spit up a mouthful of murky, bile-laced water. I quickly turned her to the side to help clear her airway. She shivered in my arms. More coughing, more sour water. Yes, yes.

Alive. She was alive. Thank God she was alive. Pale, but breathing. Her color coming back.

And then I heard footsteps behind me.

And I knew who it was.

Shade.

Without turning around I spoke his name, "Let me save her, Terry. Kill me if you want to, but first—"

"Back away, Pat," said my NSA friend Terry Manoji. "Do it now. I'm a good shot. Back away before I count to three or I'll shoot you at the base of the neck."

105

Tessa scanned the club. Didn't see Riker. Thankfully, didn't see Riker. The crowd was thinning. It didn't look like anyone was hurt. It looked like she'd actually gotten away.

"One," said Terry.

Lien-hua lay on her side, her eyes were open. I saw her throat shudder, and then she spit up another mouthful of water. It was touch and go. Her heart might stop again at any second. Her eyes touched mine. I pressed a finger to her lips, wordlessly telling her, *I'll see you soon, don't worry about me, we'll talk more when I get back.* A feeble nod. She understood.

"Two. Back away, Pat."

Back up or he'll kill both you and Lien-hua. Your only hope of saving her is to stay alive as long as possible. Do what he says.

"Three—"

"Wait! Listen to me, Terry." I eased back slightly. Faced him. "Do what you want with me. But she might die here. You have to let me help her."

"Farther."

"Terry—"

He leveled his gun. "Now."

I backed up some more. Lien-hua rolled limply onto her back where she might aspirate on water or vomit at any moment.

Terry walked past me so that now Lien-hua lay between us. "Farther, Pat. It's my turn to be with her." He waved me back with his gun and I slid back until he was out of my reach. "I'm sorry it has to be like this, Pat," he said. "But we warned you that things would not end well for you if you refused to give us the device."

Lien-hua's breathing was weak, her chest rising only slightly. The defibrillator lay a couple of feet from me.

Terry looked past me to the remains of the device I'd shot. "You cost me a lot of money there, Pat. You should have given it to me. You should have listened."

I could hear Lien-hua coughing, gulping for air. I wanted to make a move, to do something for her, but if I tried, Terry would kill me on the spot.

"Why, Terry?" I said, desperation rising. "Why are you doing this?" He kept the gun trained on me with one hand, caressed Lien-hua's cheek with the other.

"We're in a stalemate, Pat. Whether we like it or not, everyone's going to get nuclear weapons. It's just a matter of time. But it's a catch-22. No one wants to use them because then everyone else will. The world needs a new weapon, one that'll tip the scales of power once again."

He didn't just mean the world, he meant someplace in particular. Then I realized what he was saying. "Who, Terry? The Chinese?"

Lien-hua was still breathing shallowly, faintly.

"They're outpacing us. Even passing up DARPA." He smiled. "And I have to say, they pay much better than the NSA."

I could hardly believe it. "How long?"

"Two years now. It's amazing how naive the U.S. government is."

He knelt, reached over, and slowly removed the defib pad from Lien-hua's chest. "You won't be needing this anymore, Lien-hua—as Pat might say, I have more than one motive here tonight."

Lien-hua watched helplessly as Terry removed the defibrillator pad. Weakness shrouded everything. She felt just strong enough to move, but not strong enough to fight.

Then she thought of the defibrillator. Maybe she didn't have to fight Terry after all.

While he removed the other defib pad, Terry took a long lingering gaze at Lien-hua, then asked me, "How did you know it was me, Pat? A few moments ago. You said my name before you turned around."

At least if I was talking he wasn't killing either of us. "Melice's identity package, for one. Only a handful of people could hack into AFIS and pull that off. That was my first clue."

"That's not much."

"No, but then I realized that when you first watched the video, it only took you one minute and thirty seconds. I know, I remember glancing at my watch when you called me back. But the video was one minute and fifty-two seconds long, and the words on the wall didn't appear until the last ten seconds. Yet when you called me, you told me the deadline, but you couldn't have known it unless—"

"I'd seen the video before."

"Right. Or, unless you wrote the words yourself—which you did. I saw your handwritten notes during the video chat and I didn't realize it at first, but they match the writing on the envelope and the writing on the wall."

He gave me only a slight nod for a reply.

I saw Lien-hua's fingers speaking to me, spelling AED once again. Terry was staring at me; he didn't see her signing.

"Then when Angela informed me that you were the only one who'd accessed the satellite imagery of Hunter's death, the pieces fell into place. That's how you found out the device was in the car."

"Nicely done—but you missed the fact that I tracked you to the Surfside through CIFER. Remember? I designed it. I have the only other copy. I was monitoring you the whole time."

"I wondered about that." *Keep him talking. Keep him talking.* "But why didn't you just take the device from the evidence room? Why wait for Melice to steal it?"

"Never part of the plan. I was just sent in to confirm it was there."

What?

Sent? Sent by whom?

"What do you mean, 'sent'?"

He ignored my question. "You've always been good at your job. It's a shame you have to die."

"Who sent you, Terry?" I edged toward him, but he

raised his gun again. "Don't do it, Pat." Then he stared into Lien-hua's eyes. "I've been watching you, Lien-hua, ever since your sister died. Ever since the day I saw you at her funeral. I loved her, you know, even though we never actually met."

Obviously he wasn't going to answer my question, but he was going to hurt Lien-hua. I had to stop him. I eased forward but he fired a warning shot off the floor beside me. I froze.

"I watched her," he went on. "Followed her, planned a life with her. One day we would have been together. One day."

I was shocked that he could have been that fixated on someone for ten years, but then I remembered Lien-hua saying that when some people get obsessed with something it can go on for decades.

"Oh, you look just like her," he said to Lien-hua. Then his voice hardened. "I gave you the chance to be with me, but you refused."

Keep talking. Stall. The paramedics are on the way. "But, Terry," I said, "if you were in love with Chu-hua and Melice killed her, why would you work with him?"

"For over nine years I looked for her killer. I only found out it was him six months ago when I was searching the Web for a missing person. Stumbled across his blog. Don't you see, Pat? It was perfect. Getting the device was the only way I could punish him. The only way I could really hurt him. Just killing him wouldn't have been satisfying enough. He wouldn't have felt anything."

While he was distracted talking to me, Lien-hua was slowly reaching for the two defib pads.

"But," he said, "that device would have done it. I researched it. Even with the TrkA1 mutation, Creighton would have finally felt the pain he wanted. I would have given him a depth of pain few humans have ever experienced. And then I would have killed him, but only after I'd made him suffer like he deserved."

Here was a man I'd trusted, a friend I thought I knew. "But you let him drown those other women, Terry. How could you?"

"I had to keep him happy until the timing was right with Hunter, and Lien-hua was called back to work the case.

Timing and location, Pat. You should know that. It's always about timing and location."

Terry reached over, brushed Lien-hua's hair away from her eyes, but kept the gun trained on me. "You had your chance, Lien-hua. If I can't have you, no one can. One little kiss and you're going back in the water. I'd say you're still too weak to swim." He leaned over her. "Good-bye, Chu-hua."

Just before his lips reached hers, he closed his eyes for an instant and that was all it took. Lien-hua whispered, "Good-bye," and with weak but steady hands, she lifted the defib pads. I dove toward the AED. She stuck the pads to Terry's temples, his eyes snapped open, a moment of blank confusion crossed his face, and I pressed the button on the defibrillator.

An airless gasp rose from Terry's throat as the current jolted through his frontal lobe. I didn't know what kind of damage that current would do, but the way his body writhed and then convulsed, the defibrillator appeared to be even more effective than I would have guessed.

By the time I reached Lien-hua's side, Terry Manoji's body had swayed backward and slid into the acclimation pool, dragging the AED with him, sending up a hiss of drowning sparks. And that was when the ambulance sirens came coursing through the walls.

I held Lien-hua until two policemen and a team of para-medics burst through the door. Immediately, one of the EMTs called to me, asking if I was Dr. Bowers.

"Dispatch said you'd be here." He handed me a cell phone. "Lieutenant Mendez. She needs to talk to you."

Confused, I took the phone as the medical team leaned over Lien-hua. "Aina, what is it?"

"A few minutes ago," she said, "the fire alarms went off at a club, the Future Relic."

"I don't understand." I tried not to let the pain of my leg seep into my voice. "What's this about?"

"I'm at the scene, Dr. Bowers. Your stepdaughter is here."

"What? Tessa? How? She's supposed to be in Denver."

"She's here, Dr. Bowers."

I was stunned by the impossibility of what I was hearing. "Is she OK?"

"*Sí.* She is OK, but please. I need to tell you something. She's OK, but a boy tried to assault her, sexually assault her. She got away."

I felt the chills any parent would feel after hearing those words. "Is she there?" My voice cracked. "Put her on."

Then Tessa's voice. "Patrick—"

"Tessa, did he touch you? Tell me. Did he touch you?"

"No. I'm OK. I ran away. But I'm scared. I need you."

I looked over at Lien-hua. The paramedics were with her. She was safe. "I'm coming. I'll be right there."

"I'm sorry, Patrick. I—"

"Don't be sorry. I'm coming."

I shouted to the responding officers, "The Future Relic. The club. Can you get me there fast?"

One of the men nodded to me. "I got you covered. It's over by the Horton Grand Theatre where Triple Espresso used to play."

Tessa and I ended the call.

With my gunshot wound, the paramedics were adamant that I stay with them, but Tessa needed me and nothing was going to stop me. Finally, when they saw I was leaving anyway, one of the EMTs hastily dressed the wound and gave me a pair of crutches from the ambulance. "You still need to get to the hospital as quickly as you can," he said. I assured him that I would.

Before leaving, I told Lien-hua I'd see her at the hospital, and she nodded beneath her oxygen mask. I kissed her lightly on the cheek. Then, as I used the crutches to head toward the door, I heard one of the paramedics say, "He's still alive. Hurry, let's get him out of the water."

So, Terry had survived.

Well, I could deal with that later.

As we drove to the Future Relic I felt the tug of the undertow once again. The whole way there I imagined all the things I wanted to do to the boy who'd tried to molest my stepdaughter. And after fifteen years of seeing the most hideous things one human being can do to another, I had plenty of images to choose from.

When you look long into an abyss, the abyss also looks into you.

I imagined in vivid detail how I would make him suffer

and then I thought of how I would justify it all in my mind when I was done. The courts would probably be on my side too, at least to a certain extent, but even if they weren't, I'd find a way to live with myself.

I couldn't let him get away with this.

I couldn't.

When we arrived, I still wasn't sure how I'd react when I saw him, but as soon as I stepped out of the car, my thoughts shifted from him to Tessa. She saw me, came running, flew to my arms, and I held her. I held her with the fierce love and pride and dreams and disappointments and fire of a father. She told me she was sorry she'd skipped her flight, and I told her we'd talk about all that later; she told me she'd fought the guy off, and I told her I was proud of her, and then for a moment we were both quiet, and eventually she stopped trembling and stepped back.

She pointed to the police cruiser where her attacker was being held. "That's him over there."

"Can you give me a second?"

"Yeah."

Just then, Detective Dunn came stalking up to me. I was about to ask what he was doing here when he blurted out, "Heard your name on dispatch, thought I'd come to help." Dunn leaned close and pointed to the suspect. "You want me to give you a few minutes with him?"

I knew what he meant. "Yes. I do."

Dunn stepped aside, and I hobbled over to the kid sitting in the car. He looked at me through the window with a mixture of defiance and fright.

I felt tension growing in my shoulders, in my arms.

He was going to rape Tessa. You need to make him pay.

Tension. Tension.

I remembered Melice talking about Cain, and the Lord's warning about sin crouching beside him, wanting to have him. And as I stood there I could sense it crouching beside me too. *It's part of who we are, part of the human dilemma, but we must master it.*

I tried to. Really, I did.

But I couldn't.

Not after what this guy had tried to do to Tessa.

I reached for the door.

It feels good, doesn't it?

Yes, it does.

You're not like them, are you?

Yes, I guess I am.

My fingers found the handle.

Christie used to say we can't reach the Light on our own, but the Light can reach us. As I clicked the car door open, I thought of that, and of what Calvin had told me—that maybe we are all monsters.

He was right. We are. None of us makes it past the abyss without peering inside. Without stepping inside.

The dark space inside of the car spoke my name and I knew that I would kill this boy, tonight, right now, with my bare hands. I couldn't say no, not on my own. Not tonight.

I slid into the car and stared at him, cornered in the backseat, delivered to me. I felt rage.

Fear.

Horror.

Not just because of his choices, his abyss, but because of my own.

And in that moment my heart cried out for courage, cried out to the only one able to bring light to an abyss as deep as me.

We are all monsters, all of us, but we were meant to be so much more.

And as I reached for the kid and saw his trembling eyes, I made a decision.

I leaned back, stepped out, and closed the door. Dunn was standing close by, ready to block the view into the car's window. When he saw me leaving he gave me a quizzical look.

"I have a better idea, Detective," I said. "Let's book him. Prosecute him—"

A grin slithered across Dunn's face. "And send him to prison full of guys who are always thrilled to have new mates to play with."

"That'll work."

106

Lien-hua's hospital room.

I was amazed at how well she was doing for someone who'd just died the night before. Weak, tired, but recovering.

Now she slept and I sat by her side.

Ralph and Tessa had left to get some breakfast and run a few errands twenty minutes earlier, leaving me alone with Lien-hua. Before they took off, Tessa and I had agreed to wait until we returned to Denver to talk about her ditching the flight. We both knew she shouldn't have done it, but after what she'd been through last night, punishing her wasn't at the top of my to-do list.

Earlier in the day we'd also found out Ralph's luggage had arrived late last night—in twice as many pieces as it should have. Most of his clothes were shredded or missing, so he'd bought a Hawaiian shirt from the hotel gift shop and was wearing it proudly when he arrived at the hospital. "I like this style," he announced, rolling his shoulders back and forth. "Gives me an island mentality."

"It kinda looks like a rainbow threw up on you," Tessa said.

"Great," he mumbled, deflated. "Now I'll think of vomit every time I wear this shirt. Thanks for that."

"You're welcome."

I decided to intervene. "Maybe you can help Ralph pick out a suit," I said. "For the funeral this afternoon."

Tessa looked at his shirt again. "Well, it's evident he could use some fashion advice."

"You just don't appreciate good taste," Ralph muttered.

Then they left and Lien-hua slept and I let my thoughts meander back to the case.

Terry had been one of my best friends over the last three years. He was one of the few people I really trusted, one of the few people who knew just how much Richard Basque bothered me, haunted me. In fact, Terry knew me better than almost anyone. But now I realized I'd never known him. Not really.

I heard Lien-hua stir. "Pat." It was a relief to hear her speak.

"Shh," I said. "The docs tell me you're supposed to rest."

"Some water." Her voice was coarse but resolute. "Please."

I brought a glass to her lips, and after a small swallow, she reached for my hand. As she took it, she spoke again, her words intense and urgent, but also tender, "Thank you for last night. For all you did."

She was amazingly coherent for having just woken up. Maybe she'd been awake for a while but I hadn't noticed. "You're welcome," I said.

A faint grin. "I always wanted two broken ribs."

Well, at least her wit was on its way to recovery. "Don't mention it."

She took a thin breath. "Really, I wish I could find a way..." She swallowed some air. "To thank you. I don't know what to say."

"Maybe we can find a way that doesn't require words," I said. And I wasn't necessarily thinking of sign language.

That brought a smile. "I'm serious."

"So am I. Anytime you need someone to give you mouth-to-mouth again, just let me know."

Another smile, beautiful in its gentleness. "OK, I'll do that." She paused. "Margaret stopped by earlier."

"Margaret Wellington? I don't believe it."

"She brought me a card—"

"Incredible."

"And then told me I'm still suspended."

"What! No. I'm not going to let this happen." I went for my cell phone but Lien-hua stopped me with a squeeze of her hand and a shake of her head. "Leave it for now. It's OK. It'll give me a chance to visit Redmond."

Lien-hua had been born in Redmond, Washington. I wondered if that's where her sister was buried. "Chu-hua?"

She nodded. "I think I'm finally ready. I need to set a new flower arrangement on her grave. One that catches a little more light."

Then she asked for another sip of water, and after I'd given it to her, I realized there was one more thing I needed to say, but I wasn't quite sure how to do it. Finally, I decided to just be straight with her and get it out in the open. "Listen, I need to tell you something. For a short time I thought you might be Shade." I held her hand lightly. "I'm sorry."

I wondered if she would be upset or disappointed with me, and when she was slow to respond, I realized she probably was, but at last she whispered, "Don't be sorry. You were only looking for the truth."

"I know, but—"

"It's OK. It's who you are. It's what you do."

Hey, wait a minute. "Do you know, that's almost exactly the same thing Tessa told me the other night? Have you two been sharing notes?"

She smiled slyly. "Maybe we just think alike."

"That's a scary thought." I liked that she was still holding my hand. "So, still friends?"

She signed "yes" to me with the hand that held mine. And I signed back "thank you."

"OK," I said. "Now, you need to rest."

"Wait. One more thing. In the room . . . the hotel room . . . when I taught you the alphabet, you remembered the letters, didn't you? The first time through?"

"Yes."

"But you stopped at Q, then M. Why?"

"Honestly?" I asked.

"Honestly."

"I wanted the lesson to last as long as possible."

"Hmm," she said softly as she closed her eyes and relaxed back into her pillow. "Ulterior motives."

"Guilty as charged."

I held her hand and watched her drift back to sleep and wished I could do the same. Rest. Sleep. Relax. But as tired as I was, as much as the gunshot wound on my leg was bothering me, something else was at the forefront of my mind. Terry's words: "I was just sent in to confirm it was there."

Who sent you to the evidence room, Terry?

If only he weren't in a coma I could've asked him.

But he was in a coma. And according to the doctors, he wouldn't be coming out of it anytime soon.

A few minutes after Lien-hua fell asleep, Ralph and Tessa arrived. Tessa went in to sit with Lien-hua, and I tottered into the hallway to talk with Ralph about the case.

After we were alone I asked him about the Project Rukh researchers. "Are they all OK?"

"Yeah, I just talked to Margaret. They're all safe. Being debriefed as we speak. Except this one guy, Kurvetek. Osbourne mentioned him. We haven't been able to track him down yet."

I let that sink in.

"And, by the way, Margaret told me why it's called Project Rukh."

I didn't even want to think about Margaret, but I was curious about the name so I took the bait. "Why is that?"

"Turns out *rukh* is a Persian word. Back when chess was invented, it was the name of the piece we call a rook. It used to mean either 'war chariot' or 'hero,' and later, when chess made it to Europe, the piece morphed to look like a siege tower. The idea was the same, though—by using your *rukh*, you could slip past your enemy's defenses and then take him out before he even knew what hit him."

"And that's exactly what the device does."

"Right."

"Slipping past their defenses, taking them out unawares," I said. "Maybe they should have called it a Ralph."

"Kind of you to say so." He drained the last few drops of his extra-large breakfast Mountain Dew. "Oh yeah. I almost forgot. Graysmith and Dunn are looking into another homicide—General Cole Biscayne was shot in the head last night. No leads yet, last I heard. One bit of good news though. That girl, Randi, she was just hiding out at a friend's place, afraid of the 'terrorists.' She's all right."

"Good. What about the device?"

"You're a good shot, Pat. It's destroyed. And, although most of the files are gone, Margaret is going over the ones Drake didn't have a chance to shred."

"I'm sure she is. And Cassandra?"

"She's fine. Spent last night and this morning in a safe house. I guess she's gonna take some time off work to recover. Last I heard, they were dropping her off at the aquarium so she could say good-bye to her friends and some guy named Warren Leant."

I began to press out the last few wrinkles of the case. And I didn't like where they pointed. "She's at the aquarium? With Leant?"

He shrugged. "I guess."

"Ralph, have those agents stay with her."

"Why? Melice is dead. Terry's in a coma—"

"No. Trust me. Don't let them leave her alone with him."

"Why not?"

"A blind spot. Let's go."

He put the call through to the agents, I ducked into Lien-hua's room and told Tessa I'd be back in an hour or so, and then Ralph and I headed for the car.

107

Warren Leant met us at the door of the Sherrod Aquarium, and I politely requested that he lead us to the animal husbandry area.

"Is everything all right?"

"We'll see," I said.

A few moments later we entered the husbandry area, and he asked if we wouldn't mind to please hurry. "I have a board of directors meeting. A man was eaten by sharks here last night and it's a public relations nightmare. I'm sure you understand. We meet in half an hour."

"You might be late." I eyed the pool where Lien-hua had drowned, staring at the surface, straining toward freedom. "I'd like to look around for a minute. Ralph, can you wait with Mr. Leant?"

"Sure thing."

I whispered something to Ralph and then the two of them left together as I scanned the room. The criminalists had spent the night processing the site, and the only person they'd allowed back here was Cassandra, who I noticed was clearing out her office. On the ride to the aquarium Ralph had told me that the two field agents guarding her were still with her, but I didn't see them in the room.

Cassandra recognized me and set down the box she was carrying. "I need some time away," she explained. "Some space. This whole thing, it's too much for me."

I nodded. I understood.

"You OK?" she asked, eyeing the crutches.

"I will be. What about you?"

"I think so. Once this is all behind me."

"That may take a while," I said. "Because you made one mistake. Or maybe two."

Just a glint of bewilderment in her eyes. Just a glint. "What are you talking about?"

"You looked at the camera, Cassandra. None of the other women did."

Her right index finger became restless against her leg. "What camera?"

"Cassandra, please." I leaned unsteadily on my crutches. "From where you stood in the tank, it wasn't possible to see the camcorders. I know, I checked. All the other women stared toward freedom, but you stared at the back wall of the warehouse. You told me yesterday you didn't know what Melice was doing while you were in the tank. But you did know. You made it easier for him to make the video by staring at one camera and then the other. You knew where they were because you put them there."

"I have no idea what you're talking about." But her eyes betrayed her.

"I'd assumed Shade was one person instead of two. That's what threw me off, but now I get it. You, or maybe Terry, switched the chains. It was that simple. I counted the links. The other women had a shorter chain. You're nearly six feet tall, and the chain on your ankle was long enough for you to reach the surface, even when the tank was full. You put on a good show though, gasping for breath like that, but I'm guessing that after all your years of scuba diving and running triathlons, you can hold your breath pretty well too. Maybe two, three minutes? Plenty of time, even while we were there trying to break you out of the tank. So tell me, did you buy the warehouse, or was that Terry?"

"You're insane."

Cassandra looked past me toward the door. I thought maybe she was going to rush me. On crutches I knew I couldn't either run or defend myself.

Where are those two agents?

Before she could try anything, I went on. "I'm guessing the security at the base was too tight for you to get into Building B-14. That's why you and Terry couldn't steal the device yourselves. So, who found Austin? Did Terry? Or did you? Either way, you seduced Austin, gained his trust, his love, and the rest is history."

"Why would I let myself get kidnapped?" She began edging toward the staircase beside the acclimation pool.

I took two feeble steps toward her on my crutches.

"Answer me that," she said. "Why would I stand in that tank for twelve hours?"

I watched her carefully. "To get the one thing that matters most to you."

"And that is?"

"I have no idea, I'm not too into motives." And then, she bolted toward the stairwell beside the pool, but Ralph emerged from the mouth of the stairs where I'd whispered for him to have Warren Leant lead him. The two agents followed closely behind.

Cassandra made the mistake of trying to shove Ralph back down the stairs but he grabbed both of her arms, whipped her around, and had her on the floor and cuffed before she knew what hit her.

Project Ralph.

She struggled uselessly against him for a moment. Then, as he helped her to her feet, she leered at me, an unholy darkness descending across her face. "You still don't understand." Her voice, which had been relaxed and normal just a few moments earlier, now seared the air between us. "You have no idea what we have planned, Agent Bowers. No idea."

"You're right," I said, "I don't. I'm just an investigator, not a mind reader. Take her away, Ralph." I began to hobble toward the door. "My leg is really starting to hurt and I could use another cup of coffee."

108

Twilight

Tessa and I would be flying back to Denver tomorrow morning, so after the funeral we decided to visit the beach one last time to watch the sun set over the ocean.

With my crutches, I couldn't walk on the sand, so we found a paved path that led to a park bench beside the beach at Mission Bay. It seemed like there was so much to talk about, but that it was OK, too, if we didn't say anything at all.

Knowing how much Tessa hated dead bodies, I was surprised she'd decided to attend the funeral earlier in the afternoon. "You didn't have to go today, you know," I told her as we sat down.

"I was right there when it happened. I wanted to go." She toed at the sand. "So did you ever meet a living person named John Doe?"

"Not yet. Only dead ones."

A moment passed. "Jose Lopez," she said. "It's good to know his name."

I thought back to the funeral. I was glad the ME had been wrong; Jose did have a family. Fifteen transient men and seven women lined up with us to walk past the closed coffin. Some were crying. Some were quiet and reflective. Some were drunk. Some high. But all of them thanked us for coming and then either hugged us or shook our hands. I thought maybe they would ask us for money, especially since Ralph was wearing the new suit Tessa had helped him pick out, but none of them did.

I slipped my hand into my Windbreaker and felt the tooth I still carried with me. "Yes." I couldn't keep the sadness out of my voice, the thoughts of the case out of my head. "It is good to know his name."

She must have noticed that my thoughts were beginning to distract me again. "You OK?"

"Yeah. And I'm being a dad right now, really I am. But it's just that there's another part of me, the FBI part, that's still—"

"That's OK. I know you can't turn it off."

"I'm trying to, Tessa—"

"No-no-no-no," she said. "Not that part. Not the FBI part. The dad part. That's the part you can't turn off. I didn't understand before. But I do now. I think I finally get it."

Tessa doesn't always say the right thing, but when she does, she really nails it. I leaned over and kissed her forehead. "Thank you for saying that, Raven."

"I meant it."

"I know."

Silence then, as we gazed at the ocean stretching before us and watched the sun wander toward the horizon. Finally I said, "Tessa, remember when we were talking about me and Agent Jiang?"

"Mmm-hmm."

"And I said I'd let you know if we decided to move to anything that's a little more than nothing?"

"Mmm-hmm."

"Well, I think we decided."

"It's about time."

I stared at her. "But I wasn't sure you liked her."

"She's growing on me," she said. "And besides, she's good for you. A stabilizing influence." The sky began to turn grayish pink above us. "Sometimes," she added, "she even reminds me of Mom."

We watched the waves rush in and then ease back into the ocean. The steady, rippling heartbeat of the world, with all of its deadly currents and its soft ripples. The gentleness is as much a part of the ocean as the ferocity is.

The ocean is both terrible and calm.

Both at peace with itself and at war.

Eerie and beautiful.

And so is our world.

So are we all.

"Patrick?" Tessa said, interrupting my thoughts.

"Yes?"

"It's been almost exactly one year since Mom died."

"I know."

The sun rested hesitantly on the horizon, straddling the moment between day and night. "Sometimes it hurts when I think of her," Tessa whispered. "And sometimes it feels just right."

"It's the same for me."

A pause, as she turned to look at me. "Does it ever get easier?"

I watched a gull circle and dive, circle and dive toward the inky water. "I'm not sure," I said. "But it gets different."

A couple of soft moments passed; then Tessa looked away from me, toward the sky and the sea and the thin line between them. "Can I lean on you?" she asked quietly.

"Always." I put my arm around her shoulder, and she rested her head against my chest, and together we watched the sun disappear into the ocean.

So that it could rise again a moment later, on the far side of the sea.

EPILOGUE

Nineteen minutes later

The true Shade, the mastermind of everything, snapped another instant photo of Patrick Bowers sitting beside his stepdaughter and then smiled.

Yes, Terry was in a coma.

Yes, Cassandra was in custody.

Yes, the device had been destroyed, but still Shade smiled. After all, no one except the daughter from his first rather ill-fated marriage knew about him, so no one would come after him. And his daughter would never give him up; after all, she knew he would pay her bail and help her escape, just like he'd done with Melice.

His camera spit out the photograph. He snapped another.

Then Shade, the one who'd shot the bottle out of Melice's hand ... the one who'd identified Agent Bowers's voice on the phone ... the one who'd stood still and invisible as his daughter stepped out of the shadows beside him to make Melice think she was Shade ... the one who'd first introduced her to the compromised NSA agent, Terry Manoji ... the one who'd told Terry to shoot Bowers at the base of the neck ... the one who'd planned everything from the beginning, and so carefully coordinated the work of his two protégés, now he claimed a new enemy, set his sights on a new target: Special Agent Patrick Bowers.

Shade pulled the photo from the camera.

Click. Another picture.

He could have killed Bowers at any time. Yes, of course.

Even right now. But over the last four months, Terry had been very helpful filling him in on Bowers's past, and Shade believed he had a better punishment than death for Agent Bowers: fear.

Make him live in fear.

As the last photo printed, he scrawled a note, "I'm still here.—Shade." Then he opened the envelope, slipped the note and the photos inside, and sealed it shut.

Yes. Let Bowers live in fear. And Shade already knew the best way to do that. Terry had told him the secret last month.

Let Bowers face his past. Let him face the mirror image of himself—Richard Devin Basque.

Shade double-checked the Denver address and dropped the letter into the mailbox beside the Mission Bay parking lot. It wouldn't be difficult to get Basque declared "not guilty" at that fiasco of a trial in Chicago. Buy off a few jurors. Hardly a challenge at all. Then he'd deliver Agent Bowers to Basque and let him do what he did best.

"Bring it on," huh, Bowers?

All right. If you insist.

Then the ex–CIA assassin Sebastian Taylor smiled, lit a cigarette, and strolled through the cryptic moonlight to his car, thinking of fear.

The best punishment of all.

ACKNOWLEDGMENTS

Special thanks to Robert Bess, Lieutenant Andy Mills, Courtney Thompson, Sonya Haskins, Rhonda Bier, Sarah Bender, Trinity, Ariel, and Eden Huhn, Dr. Debbie LeCraw, Pam Johnson, George Hill, Lonnie Hull DuPont, Pamela Harty, Jennifer Leep, David Lehman, David Beeson, Shawn Scullin, Cat Hoort, Kristin Kornoelje, Michelle Cox, Al Gansky, Lucyah Della Valle, Janice, Frank, Roger, and the other staff at Ripley's Aquarium of the Smokies, and a big thanks to Dr. Todd Huhn, Chris Haskins, and Dr. John-Paul Abner for listening and for all of your helpful criticism and input. You three guys are idea machines.

And finally, to Liesl. Your patience and encouragement mean the world to me. This isn't my book. It's ours.

FBI agent Patrick Bowers has tracked down some
of the country's most dangerous killers.
Now he is about to become the latest victim.
Turn the page for a pulse-pounding sneak peek of

THE KNIGHT

Coming from Signet in September 2010

Thursday, May 15
Bearcroft Mine
The Rocky Mountains, 40 miles west of Denver
5:19 p.m.

The sad, ripe odor of death seeped from the entrance to the abandoned mine.

Some FBI agents get used to this smell, to this moment, and after a while it just becomes another part of the daily routine.

That's never happened with me.

My flashlight cut a narrow seam through the darkness but gave me enough light to see that the woman was still clothed, no sign of sexual assault. Ten sturdy candles surrounded her, their flames wisping and licking at the dusty air, giving the tunnel a ghostly, otherworldly feel.

She was about ten meters away and lay as if asleep, hands on her chest. And in her hands was the reason I'd been called in.

A slowly decomposing human heart.

No sign of the second victim.

And the candles flickered around her in the dark.

Part of my duties at the FBI's Denver field office includes working with the Denver Police Department on a joint task force that investigates the most violent criminal offenders in the Denver metroplex, helping to evaluate evidence and suggest investigative strategies. Since this crime appeared to be linked to another double homicide the day before in Littleton, Lieutenant Kurt Mason had asked for my help.

But some local law enforcement officers tend to be territorial, and from the moment I'd stepped off the task force helicopter, I'd seen how excited the four men from the crime scene unit were that I was here. It probably didn't help matters that Kurt wanted me to survey the scene with him before they processed the tunnel.

The mine was barely high enough for me to stand in, and narrow enough for me to touch both sides at once. Every five to ten meters, thick beams buttressed the walls and ceiling, supporting against cave-ins.

A rusted track that had been used by miners to roll ore carts through the mine ran along the ground and disappeared into the darkness somewhere beyond the woman's body.

As I took a few steps into the tunnel, I checked to see if my Nikes left an imprint but saw that the ground was too hard. So, it was unlikely we would have shoe impressions from the killer either.

With each step that I took, the temperature dropped, dipping into the low forties. The time of death was still unknown, but the cool air would have slowed decomposition and helped preserve the body. The woman might have been dead for two or three days already.

One of the candles winked out.

Why did you bring her here? Why today? Why this mine?

Whose heart is that in her hands?

The voice of one of the crime scene unit members cut through the dim silence. "Yeah, Special Agent Bowers is inside. He's taking his time."

"I should hope so." It was Lieutenant Mason, and I was glad he was here. He'd been on the phone since I arrived, and now I paused and waited for him to join me.

A beam of light swept past me as he turned on his flashlight, and a moment later, he was standing by my side.

"Thanks for coming in on this, Pat." He spoke in a hushed voice, a small way to honor the dead. "I know you're leaving to teach at the Academy next week. I'm hoping—"

"I'll consult from Quantico if I need to."

He gave me a small nod.

Forty-one, with stylish wire-rimmed glasses and swift intelligent eyes, Kurt looked more like an investment banker than a seasoned detective, but he was one of the best homicide investigators I'd ever met.

It'd been a hard year for him, though, and it showed on his face. Five months ago while he and his wife, Cheryl, were on a date, their fifteen-month-old daughter, Hannah, had drowned in the bathtub while the babysitter was in the living room texting one of her friends. Kurt and I had only known each other for a few months when his daughter died, but I'd recently lost my wife, and in a way the sense of shared tragedy had deepened our friendship.

Silently, we donned latex gloves. Began to walk toward the woman's body.

"Her name is Heather Fain." His voice sounded lonely and hollow in the tunnel. "I just got the word. Disappeared from her apartment in Aurora on Monday. No one's seen her boyfriend since then either—a guy named Chris Arlington. He was a person of interest in the case ... until ..." He let his voice trail off. He was staring at the heart.

I looked at Heather's body, still five meters away, and let her name roll through my mind.

Heather.

Heather Fain.

This wasn't just a corpse. These were the tragic remains of a young woman who'd had a boyfriend and dreams and a life in Aurora, Colorado. A young woman with passions and hopes and heartaches.

Until this week.

Grief stabbed at me.

Kurt's comment led me to think he might have reason to believe this was Chris Arlington's heart. "Do we know the identity of the second victim?" I asked. "Whether or not it's Chris?"

"Not yet." An edginess took over his voice. "And I know what you're thinking, Pat: don't assume, examine. Don't worry. I will."

"I know."

"We have to start somewhere."

I focused the beam of light on the heart. "Yes, we do."

Together, we approached the body.

Available Now
from
Steven James

THE PAWN

As an environmental criminologist, Patrick Bowers uses 21st-century geospatial technology to analyze the time and space in which a crime takes place. Using an array of factors, Bowers can pinpoint clues to solve the toughest of cases. His skills have made him one of the FBI's top agents—until now.

Called to the mountains of North Carolina to consult on a gruesome murder, Bowers finds himself in a deadly duel with a serial killer who seems to transcend Patrick's analytical powers. Forced to track the killer's horrific murders one by one, Bowers finds his techniques and instincts are put to the ultimate test...

"Riveting...a gripping plot."
—*Publishers Weekly*